THEY PLAYED FOR HIGH STAKES AND THEY PLAYED FOR KEEPS

The Grangers . . . lords and masters of a huge stretch of the Southwest, legendary for their vast wealth and ruthless lust to dominate all they touched . . . Tom Granger, who went east to escape the family empire, and returned to try to conquer it . . . Will Granger, aching to prove himself head of the family . . . Sue Granger, who used the family fortune and her own incredibly beautiful body to satisfy ever more shocking desires . . . all coming together in a struggle in which huge corporations and eminent politicians were mere pawns, and the prize was the ultimate in—

POWER

"An action-filled saga . . . the best fiction buy since *Centennial*!"
—*Chattanooga Times*

"Strong, engrossing, exciting, absorbing, masterful . . . a great novel!"
—*Nashville Banner*

Books by Richard Martin Stern

Power

Richard Martin Stern

BALLANTINE BOOKS • NEW YORK

Library of Congress Catalog Card Number: 74-82991

ISBN 0-345-25003-6-195

This edition published by arrangement with David McKay Company, Inc., New York.

Manufactured in the United States

First Ballantine Books Edition: May, 1976

Prologue

The crosshairs of a 4x scope followed the man as he walked. He was unaware, his concentration fixed on the 1:24,000 topographical map in his left hand and the opened lensatic compass in his right.

He wore an aluminum-frame backpack, tent roll above and sleeping-bag roll beneath the green nylon bag; his binoculars were secured to one shoulder strap. He was unarmed.

He had followed the fenceline, unpeeled cedar posts and four-strand barbed wire, through a ponderosa forest and now into an upland meadow; the fence continued up a rocky slope past an abandoned mineshaft to end at a sheer dropoff where not even mountain goats ventured.

In the meadow, at an altitude of something over eight thousand feet, aspens had turned to gold; here and there a scrub oak showed scarlet. The late-afternoon air was crisp, clear, and dry, a tonic. In the limitless bright sky a red-tailed hawk, the only witness, swung in slow circles, effortlessly riding the thermals that rose from the bare rocky slope.

The man in the meadow did not hear the shot that killed him; at three thousand feet per second the bullet far outdistanced the sound. And the echoes died unnoticed, except by the hawk, which, frightened by the sound, flew off down the valley.

The man fell face down, arms outstretched. The map and the compass came to rest just beyond his hands.

POWER

There was an early snow that night, and wind swept down the flanks of the great mountains to pile drifts against the fence in the meadow. By noon of the next day not even the green of the backpack bag showed; and keen though their eyesight was, vultures coasting overhead saw nothing but an anonymous and unidentifiable mound in the snow.

1

It was called El Rancho del Norte, and it sprawled over 775 square miles, 496,000 acres of mesa, high desert, plains, valleys, and mountains whose peaks, never entirely free of snow, rose high above the 11,000-foot timberline.

In what was then Territory, and for over sixty years now had been the sovereign State of New Mexico, one man, old Tully Granger, Granger the First as they sometimes referred to him, had put together the vast holding—some said by theft, or by chicanery, or by plain strength and brute force—and held it against all comers, Indian, Spanish, Anglo. The land endured, intact.

There were a number of entrances to the ranch, most of them protected by stout gates, all by cattle-guards. At the main entrance, which was the road from the village of Las Grutas, a gatehouse was occupied by José Valdes, his wife, and their brood of six, with a seventh well on the way. José, otherwise known as Joe was the third Valdes to preside over the gatehouse; the 30-30 that stood behind the door had been a gift to Joe's grandfather from Tully Granger well before statehood.

The main house, of stone, crenellated, turreted, bay-windowed, in all ways both massive and hideous, stood a mile inside the main gate on a slight rocky rise with a long view of the valley and of the mountains that looked down upon it. From old habit the land

3

around the house was kept clear of concealing vegetation, and there were no nearby buildings to block the field of fire. It had been a long time since the house had been a fortress, but memory remained.

The house was quiet now: the tendency was to walk on tiptoe. Matt Granger, Granger Second, Tully's son, aged eighty, was on his way out.

"Fighting a rearguard action every foot of the way," young Dr. Harry Walker said in the downstairs hall. "He told me if I didn't haul my ass out of his bedroom and leave him alone, he'd have me hung up by my thumbs." He smiled at Tish. "Those were his words, and I think he meant them, too. Your stepfather." He shook his head. A character, his expression said.

"I'll go see him," the girl said. "Sometimes he listens to me." She was a tall girl, slim and active, with calm eyes and reddish-brown hair worn short for convenience. She wore, as usual, faded jeans, a flannel shirt, and deerskin squaw boots. Crossing the hall, lightly climbing the stairs, her feet made no sound.

The old man was propped up in the carved bed. He was shrunken now, merely a husk, but the big hands on the coverlet and the wide shoulders against the pillows told what he once had been. He could smile faintly at the girl, showing teeth that were still his own. "The little pipsqueak sent you, did he?" The words were without rancor. "He wants to stick needles in me to keep me going, and he isn't going to. I'll go out my own way." The voice was not strong, but neither did it waver. And then, "What's funny?"

"You'll do it your way," the girl said. Her smile was sham; she was close to tears. "Haven't you always?"

The old man's face softened, "I'm a cantankerous old son of a bitch, honey," he said slowly. "I've been that way too long to change now." He paused. His voice turned gentle, "Even for you."

"I wouldn't ask." Words were difficult. She took a deep breath. "Tom phoned from Chicago. He has a charter plane waiting for him at Albuquerque."

The old man nodded faintly. Even with a charter

4

plane his grandson would not be in time, he thought; and found no reason for comment.

"Wayne Carter wanted to see you. I told him—"

"The truth, I hope, honey. Whatever it is, he can work it out with Tom. And you." One of the big hands moved in a faint gesture. "Give me a kiss and then beat it. I'm going to sleep."

Tish bent over the bed. The old man was unshaven and the white bristles were rough. He smelled, as always, of tobacco and spirits. She kissed him gently. "I'll stay."

"No, you won't." The voice was suddenly stronger. "It takes two to bring somebody into the world, but you leave it all by yourself. Beat it."

She crossed the room slowly. At the door she hesitated and looked back.

He was watching her and smiling with effort as he lifted one hand in a gesture of dismissal and farewell. It was spring: a ripening and a good time to die.

Tish walked out and closed the door behind her. As she walked back down the stairs she was crying.

They took off in the charter plane from Albuquerque, skirted the bulk of Sandía, and headed north by east, climbing.

"Rancho del Norte," the pilot said. "I've heard a lot about it, but I sure never been there." He was in his late forties, a trifle paunchy; speaking with a country-boy Texas accent. He glanced sideways at his passenger. "They'll let us land for sure? I don't want anybody shooting at me."

"They'll let us land." He was a big man, Tom Granger, as tall and as broad as his grandfather, in many ways a replica. He sat quietly now, watching the approaching mountains, thinking his own thoughts. You didn't know how much you missed the bigness of this country, he told himself, until you came back to it. Funny, in Spanish there wasn't even a word for it: home.

"That's Santa Fe over yonder," the pilot said. He pointed.

"I know."

"And over yonder Los Alamos, where what they call the Atomic Age got started."

Tom nodded. He was looking down at the river as it wound out of the mountains and into the mesa. It was partially obscured by a brownish haze.

"Our local smog," the pilot said. "We can't noways compete with LA and what I hear about big cities back east, but we do the best we can with what we have. That haze now has come two hundred miles down from those big coal-fired generator plants up to Four Corners." He glanced again at Tom. "Purty, ain't it?" He paused. "And you know the hell of it?" He paused again. "The electricity those generators produce don't come to us at all. The smog is all we get. The electricity goes to LA and Phoenix."

"I've heard."

"Even back east you heard? How about that?"

They were over mountains now, and to the north as far as they could see were more mountains, the backbone of the land; even now in late spring some still glistened with snow.

"I flew another fellow named Granger once," the pilot said. "Missed his commercial flight in Albuquerque, said the hell with waiting for another, hired me to fly him to Dallas same way I'd take a bus into town. Him and his wife, real purty lady, he called her Sweet Sue." He gave Tom another of his sideways glances. "Kin?"

"My brother."

"Well, now," the pilot said.

Bit by bit, Tom thought without resentment, the pilot was extracting information in the sly manner of the natural gossip. In a way it was amusing. There would be talk back in the Albuquerque hangar, even though there was nothing really to talk about. Grandson coming home because aged grandfather was dying —where was the news value in that? But the question was pointless because from childhood he had known the answer: from old Tully's time the ranch and the

Grangers were news, whatever they did, or didn't do.

"You know about that dead fellow they found up there?" the pilot said. "Two, three weeks ago it was? He'd been under the snow all winter."

"I hadn't heard," Tom said. And, automatically, "Who was he?"

"That's the hell of it," the pilot said. He was grinning. "They haven't done much of anything about him yet because they can't decide which county he was in when he was shot. County line runs right through the meadow where they found him."

The county line almost bisected the ranch; a fact that since statehood had always caused problems. Two sets of commissioners, two sheriffs, the inevitable tug-and-haul over jurisdiction, particularly back in the days when the mines on the range were still being worked; drunk miners in town, and cowhands, and, long ago, sheepmen too to mix into the equation; fences and water and God only knew what-all complicating factors —it was no wonder that Tom's grandfather had once threatened to secede from the state or set up his own county, whichever the pipsqueak governor down in Santa Fe preferred.

The tale was legend: "I'm easy to get along with," Matt Granger had told the governor in a voice that carried almost to the plaza. "Most times, that is. But, by God, if I have to, I'll shut up the ranch tighter than a bobcat's asshole and start shooting at any son of a bitch that sets foot on it from either county. You hear me?"

The whole town of Santa Fe had heard, Tom thought now, producing one of his rare smiles; the town had heard and had thought that, like Noel Coward's Alice, the Grangers were at it again.

He roused himself and pointed a little to the right of their course. "That bald peak," he said, "head straight for it. There's a meadow at its base. We'll land there." Home. He watched the sheer face of the mountain approach.

Once when he was a boy, he had climbed that sheer

rock face on a dare from his brother, Will. It had taken almost two days, and Tom could still remember that night spent huddled on a ledge no wider than the span of his hands, wondering if this was the way young Tom Granger was going to go out—a gloomy night-thought.

Came morning and he had stretched himself cautiously, stomped his feet to speed up circulation, tightened his belt another hole against his hunger and thirst, and started up again, one handhold, one foothold, one more heave and weight-shift. . . .

Old Matt Granger was waiting on top, just himself and two horses. "I ought to whale the shit out of you, boy," he said. For a wonder his voice was quiet. "You hear me?"

Tom nodded. His knees were weak, trembling, but he faced the old man with the sense of defiance that had always been between them.

"Then, goddamn it, say so."

"I hear you."

"You haven't got the brains God gave a chipmunk, but there's no point in me telling you all that again. You've heard it often enough. Just what in God's name got into you to do a fool thing like that, anyway?"

It had been Will, of course, with his sly smile that could always get a rise out of Tom. But all he said was, "I wanted to see if I could."

The old man raised his big fists and let them fall to his sides. "Get on your horse," he said. "If you can." He turned away.

Tom could get on the horse. Just. There was no strength left in his legs or his arms. He followed the old man down the back hump of the mountain in silence.

Long ago. Things remembered. Home.

Home? Think about that, he told himself. Because in the life he thought he had made for himself in the East, there were two things of importance: his job and the girl. And did they not spell home?

The girl's name was Grace, and she was Eastern-bred, city-oriented, at ease in her surroundings. She worked for a publishing house, and she knew interesting and presumably important people Tom had never heard of. They were invariably referred to by their first names. "Howard's new book came in today."

"Howard who?"

"Darling, you are marvelous!"

In the beginning Tom had not thought Grace's name suited her at all. She was tall and somewhat angular. Her movements lacked the smoothness smaller women displayed. But in time he came to see and understand the total coordination of mind and body that was her essence and to realize that grace and beauty alike were entirely a matter of perspective. To see her across a room, smiling as she moved toward him, became an experience to savor.

In her turn, Grace saw Tom as a modern-day Lochinvar out of the West, product of a civilization she had encountered only in fiction; large, strong, vaguely menacing, frightening in his directness. "I want to be wooed," she said once, "and you take me by storm. You didn't learn that in college"—she paused, smiling —"or in business school."

"There isn't time for wooing. I'm in a hurry."

"To get where?"

"Wherever I'm going."

Lying quiescent, watching him with that calm expression, smiling faintly, fondly, "Do you know where that is?" she said. And then, gently, "You can relax with me."

"Can I?" Why could he not? But he could lose himself in her for a time, and that was the next best thing to relaxation. And maybe, when he felt more at home in his surroundings, amidst the big-city bustle and haste, even relaxation would be possible.

"I hope so, darling."

Had he spoken his thoughts aloud?

Tim Jonas ran Jonas Construction Company and was his boss. And while Tim, himself a driver, understood a man's feelings that jobs were to be done, problems met head-on and obstacles brushed aside or crushed into the dirt, he nevertheless registered mild protest at Tom's intense devotion to his work.

"Boy," Tim would say, "it may sound strange, but I wish to hell you'd slow down."

"You're afraid I'll foul something up?"

"You know better than that." Pause. "In the three years you've come a long way." Another pause. "Running."

"You want this bridge built, don't you?"

"All right. It's your job. Do it how you will."

It was a bridge across a small nameless Jersey creek —no Verrazzano Narrows Bridge, this—but it was a beginning, Tom's own. He knew every beam, every truss, every rivet, every concrete support meticulously prepared and carefully poured. He knew to the fraction the rise or fall of the tides that affected the creek, and force and flow of the water itself. From long lonely periods of contemplation he was familiar with the local waterfowl and with the muskrat that made its home in the upstream reeds. He was accustomed to the harsh overhead cries of the gulls flying in from the harbor and the nearby shore, and the smell of salt sea air was always in his nostrils.

Once he had taken Grace out to the site, once only. She said, smiling, "This is my competition?"

"You were expecting another Washington Bridge?"

She should have known better, she told herself, than to tease this man about his work. "I was only joking. Don't be cross, please."

"I'm not cross."

"Just disappointed. I understand." Grace paused thoughtfully. A gull wheeled overhead, crying that someone had stolen his fish. She watched the gull idly. "What I don't understand," she said at last, "is why you are here at all." She looked at Tom and waited for reply.

"It's my job."

"That wasn't what I meant. Why are you even here in the East?"

"You mean I don't belong?"

Grace watched him steadily, in silence.

"The general idea," Tom said slowly, "is to make a life for myself, of my own. This"—his gesture took in the suddenly absurdly small structure spanning the tiny waterway—"is a beginning. There will be other, larger things, but for the present this is my job. To finish."

But there was the trouble, because he had not finished the job; he had instead walked out and left the bridge half done. It was, he thought, somehow symbolic, the first time he had ever walked out, even temporarily, on anything he had set his hand to; and the knowledge was not pleasant.

"One thing I'll say about you, boy," old Matt had said once. "When you start somewhere, you most generally arrive."

Well, this time he had quit the journey.

Oh, he had explained the reason, and Tim Jonas had understood. "It's a cliché," Tim had said, "but blood *is* thicker than water, and when there's a family need, you drop what you have in your hands and go." Pause. "And it isn't as if this job is that important."

"It is to me."

"I know that. And I appreciate it. But—"

"I'll be back."

"Sure you will."

"I mean it."

"I know you do, boy." Pause. "But sometimes things happen."

Grace had said, "I wonder if I'll ever see you again."

"Damn it, I'm not going to Mars. I'll be back."

"Tommy"—in all his life she was the only person who had ever called him that—"I'll only ask one thing." She paused, as Tim had, searching for the right words. "If you change your mind," she said slowly, "will you let me know?"

"I'm not going to change my mind."

She hesitated, and then smiled faintly. "All right."

11

Another pause. "Kiss me." The smile was shaky. "And ride off into the sunset."

Now, watching the sheer face of the mountain grow clear in detail, he thought of Grace and of Tim, and of himself, shirking responsibility.

"Place the size of this ranch," the pilot said, "has got to be a ballbreaker to run."

Tom's smile was grim. "It is," he said. "It sure as hell is."

2

Tish had a jeep parked in the meadow beneath the sheer face, and as the plane circled she tied a silk scarf to the jeep's antenna and stood back to let it fly in the wind.

"That," the pilot said, "is using the old head." Watching the fluttering scarf, he kept on around the meadow to land upwind, and taxied to a halt near the jeep.

Tom took out a pen and a loose check, filled the check out, handed it to the pilot, grabbed his bag from behind the seat and stepped out. "Thanks," he said, and walked to the jeep, the plane forgotten.

Tish was slowly untying the scarf. "Hi."

"Hi." Tom swung his bag into the rear seat. "Thanks for coming."

"It's a long walk." She stood uncertain, the scarf still in her hands. "You want to drive?"

"Not unless you want me to."

She turned away then without a word and got in

behind the wheel. The engine started with an almost angry snarl. Tom got in the off seat. They bumped away across the meadow.

For a time they drove in silence. Then, "He's gone," the girl said. "He went to sleep. I think he knew he wasn't going to wake up." She turned to watch Tom's face for reaction.

Tom nodded. "A good way to go."

"And you don't care, do you?" There was anger in the question. "You and he never got along."

"That's right. We never did."

"But you were the one he told me to send for." She turned again to face him. "Why?"

His rare smile was crooked. "Probably because I was easier to find than Will. He and Sue flit around too fast."

"They're in Gstaad. I sent them a cable."

Tom nodded.

"And I telephoned Seth Porter in Santa Fe. He's driving up."

"Good."

"Wayne Carter wanted to see Matt. Matt told me to have you see him."

"I don't even know who he is."

"He's a physicist," Tish said. "He's in charge of the atomic reactor they're building over in Long Valley."

"On ranch property?"

"That was Matt's decision. They leased the land." Tish paused. "With, I think, contingencies."

"What kind of contingencies?"

"I don't know." Sharper now. "I'm not a physicist. I'm not Matt. I'm not Seth Porter, who drew up the agreement. I'm—nobody." She turned to face him again. "Does that satisfy you?" Always, always he had had this power to whittle her down, demean her in her own eyes. "My mother was thirty years younger than Matt when they married. That made the whole situation—ridiculous, didn't it? I don't even know who my father was." She paused. "I've told you that before, haven't I? And all you said was, 'What difference does it make?' "

"Maybe I shouldn't have said that." Tom was looking up at the sheer face of the mountain above them. "Maybe there are a lot of things I shouldn't have said. Or done."

"But you aren't going to change, are you?"

Again that crooked smile. "Probably not."

"Matt said the same thing. About himself." The girl shook her head. "You Grangers."

Tom said easily, "Hard to get along with, I'll grant."

Again the silence as they bumped out of the meadow onto a dirt road. The scent of pines was strong. Faintly they heard the charter plane's engine revving up for takeoff; in a few moments it swept over them, trailing echoes in the trees, heading south. With a cargo of gossip, Tom thought. He said, "I understand they found a man. Dead. Shot." He watched the girl.

She nodded.

"Do they know who he was?"

"A man with a backpack, carrying a compass and a map." Her voice was expressionless. "Where he had no real right to be."

"I don't recall," Tom said, "that we shoot trespassers on sight."

The girl was silent.

"Or do we?"

More silence.

"The old man," Tom said, "has been ailing for how long?"

"Six months. Longer."

"Who's been running things?"

"A number of people."

"Clyde Burley?"

"Among others."

Tom nodded. He seemed to relax in his seat. "We'll start with him," he said.

Tish turned to look at him. "That means what?"

"I don't know yet."

"You'll have to break the ranch up for taxes." A statement, not a question; but it demanded an answer.

14

"I don't know that, either. Seth Porter will have ideas."

Her eyes were fixed on the road again. "But you don't care, do you?"

"I was born here and I grew up here," Tom said. "They sent me east to school, but every summer I was back."

"Before mother and I came. That's what you're saying, isn't it?" The girl paused. "But as soon as you finished college and business school you left and you haven't been back since. Why?"

"Because I made a new life, which I don't think I want to give up. You said it yourself. The old man and I never got along."

They were pulling up to the big house now. Tish said slowly, "I think he wanted you here."

"He could have asked."

Tish shook her head. Her smile was sad. "You know better. If you don't, you should." She set the hand brake and switched off the jeep's engine. As she stepped out, "I'll have your bag taken up to your rooms," she said, and then she hesitated. "I haven't said it yet, but someone has to." She paused. "Welcome back." She turned away and hurried up the steps.

He stood looking at the desk that had been his great-grandfather's and then his grandfather's. Once as a boy he had perched himself in the big chair, laid his hands flat on the desktop, and pretended that he was the man in control. When he heard old Matt's footsteps he had jumped down as quick as he could, and by the time the old man had opened the office door, the desk chair was back in its place and the boy was standing, innocently staring at the walls.

"Trying it for size, boy?" Matt had said, and smiled. "Maybe a little big for you right now." He had seemed amused.

Now, slowly, Tom walked around the desk, hesitated, and then pulled out the chair and sat down. Maybe still too big for me, he thought, but there is no other way than to try it for a little time anyway.

Somebody has to. He looked around the remembered room.

It was a large room, this office, as all rooms in the main house were larger than life-size; paneled in straight-grain ponderosa pine from trees felled on the ranch, sawed in the ranch's sawmill, stacked and dried on the building site back in Tully Granger's day. The wood was mellow with age, softly gleaming. There were trophies on the wall: a mounted grizzly head, massive and even in death defiant; a snarling cougar; an elk head, proud antlers broad as a man's easy stretch; a white-tailed deer head, twelve points; a bighorn side by side with a bearded mountain goat; a record rainbow trout and a smaller cutthroat known locally as a native. . . . All taken on ranch property.

There were pictures too, and as a boy Tom had studied them and almost memorized their identities and locations. There was young Teddy Roosevelt with his rifle and his bull elk, beaming at the camera through tiny round glasses; there the Russian Grand Duke with the unpronounceable name and the huge beard who had come ten thousand miles for his grizzly bear; two Secretaries of the Interior; a bourbon-drinking, dry-fly-fishing senator crony of Matt's; a stiffly posed shot of guests at one of the last barbecues held on the ranch; Barney, his grandfather's favorite quarter horse. . . .

There was a picture too of Tom's parents, the father in his lieutenant colonel's AAF uniform, wings and ribbons prominent. Tom thought he understood that this picture, of all those taken of Bill and Liz Granger, was the one his grandfather had chosen for the office wall because it alone caught the spirit of those few years when Bill Granger was actually doing something useful. Somewhere too, probably buried in a file, was a newspaper photograph of the *Andrea Doria* with the great hole torn in her side, final memory of the Bill Grangers.

There was a gun cabinet, shotguns, rifles, handguns scrupulously cared for, carefully kept under lock and key; in the heavy drawer beneath the glass doors ammunition was stored. Fly rods, reels, and boxes of tied files shared the cabinet with the firearms.

On the table against the wall next to the Tiffany lamp with the sculptured bronze buffalo base was the tantalus Tom remembered from his earliest days, its two decanters no doubt filled as always with the fine bourbon shipped to the ranch by the barrel direct from the distillery in the East.

As a ten-year-old Tom had mastered the intricacies of the tantalus lock and managed to get at one of the decanters. His first jolt of hundred-proof whiskey made him sick, and all Matt Granger did when he found out about it was laugh. "Serves you goddamn good and right, boy. Just remember puking next time you get too big for your britches or find yourself tempted to steal." And then he had added something Tom never forgot: "I don't say that honesty is always the best policy, but you'd sure as hell better look sharp before you decide it isn't."

Sitting at the desk, remembering, Tom looked at the far wall where the pieced-together 15′ series topographical maps showed the outlines of the ranch in black crayon, all seven hundred and seventy-five square miles of it. Accumulated honestly? Maybe, maybe not; you could get argument on both sides. There were still Spanish-speaking folks in Las Grutas, and elsewhere for that matter, who maintained that a part of the ranch was Spanish grant that could never have been transferred legally. Tijerina and his now quiescent Alianza came to mind.

Tom roused himself at the knock on the door, called, and waited to see who the first visitor might be. When the door opened, he said, "Hello, Clyde," in a carefully expressionless voice. "Come in. Sit down."

A big man with sandy hair and sun-bleached eyebrows who rolled as he walked as if his boots were too tight, he wore a flannel shirt and jeans hung low on his hips by a hand-tooled belt with a silver-and-turquoise buckle, keepers, and tip. Clyde Burley. He sat down and stretched out his legs. "Sorry Matt's gone," he said. "I just heard." He paused. "What now?"

"We'll have to see. Seth Porter's on his way up."

"And Will?"

"They're on their way too."

"But you're in the saddle?"

"Maybe."

Burley took his time, studying the hat in his hands, finally laying it on a nearby table. He looked then at Tom. "Your grand-daddy and I got along fine," he said at last.

Tom nodded.

"You and I—" Burley shook his head faintly.

Tom nodded again.

"Just wanted to get it out in the open," Burley said, "so's we know where we stand."

Tom nodded yet a third time. "Agreed."

"I got no contract," Burley said. "Matt wanted to give me one. I said no, if a man needs a piece of paper to hang onto his job, he'd damn well better quit anyway."

Tom studied the man. "Is that a question?"

"In a way."

Right up to you, Tom thought. "I don't want you to quit," he said, and paused. Somebody had to be here to run this place. "If and when I do, I'll tell you."

There was silence. Burley nodded, expressionless. "That's good enough." He started to rise.

Tom raised his hand. "Nothing's official until Seth Porter gets here, but I'd like a few answers first."

Burley sat down again, large, immobile as a rock. He waited.

"The dead man they found in the meadow," Tom said. "Up by the old mineshaft?" The only meadow he could think of that was bisected by the county line.

"That's the one. Jesús Valdes' riding fence found him. Saw the backpack in the snow."

"Who was he?"

"Nobody'd seen him before. No papers in his pocket. Compass, map, field glasses—" Burley shrugged. "Shot once. Rifle." He shrugged again. "Out there nobody to hear. They took him down to Las Grutas. Pepe Martinez"—the way he spoke the name, it sounded like a dirty word—"wants it to be that one of our people shot him just for going through a fence." Martinez was the District Attorney in Grutas County.

"What did Matt say?"

"He never knew. Didn't seem much point in telling him."

Maybe, maybe not. Tom let it go. "Tish mentioned an atomic reactor in Long Valley."

"Yeah." Burley's voice was carefully expressionless. "Fellow named Wayne Carter. Big words. Big ideas." At last expression showed: amusement. "He looks at birds through field glasses." The amusement disappeared. "Looks at Tish too."

It was Tom's turn to smile. "You object to that?"

Burley's shrug was perhaps a little too emphatic. "No skin off my ass."

Once again: maybe, maybe not. The last time Tom had seen Burley and Tish together they had seemed somewhat more than casual toward each other. No business of his, he told himself. "You and Carter get along?" he said.

This time the shrug was pure unconcern. "Enough. He stays in Long Valley, pretty well out of the way. He's got his own road for hauling in what he needs. His problems aren't with us."

"Who are they with?"

"Why not ask him?"

"I'm asking you."

Burley smiled faintly, without amusement. "Sheep die," he said, "and the first thing anybody thinks of these days is radioactivity." He paused. "Maybe so. I wouldn't know." He paused again. "A chicano kid in Las Grutas has what they say is leukemia. They never had any leukemia before that they know of. Maybe radioactivity again." A third pause. "Some fish float downstream, belly-up. Me, I think somebody used dynamite." He shook his head. "But what they're saying in Las Grutas is that there's radiation in the water, killing the fish." A final pause. "You asked."

"Matt knew about this?"

"Some." Burley hesitated. "He was tired. He didn't reach out for trouble any more. If it came at him, that was one thing. But this——" He shook his head.

Tom sat on at the desk after Burley had gone. From the walls the trophies and the pictures looked down on him. As they had looked down on Matt, and on old Tully too. That figure of speech of Burley's stuck in his mind: "He didn't reach out for trouble any more." Tom guessed that pretty well summed it up.

Because they *had* reached out for trouble, Tully and Matt, those two progenitors of his; they had reached out and grabbed whatever happened to be lying around and squeezed it with both hands until it hollered. The outlines of the ranch on the pieced-together maps was the proof.

These days you tended to think that tales of violence and strife in these parts were purely something dreamed up by Western-writers for TV series. The hell they were.

There *were* Apache raids.

The Lincoln County wars *did* happen.

Squatters did move in, and if they were strong enough, they stayed. But not on land old Tully Granger had taken for his.

Cattle did disappear. And so did the men responsible—when they were caught.

A gold shipment from one of the ranch mines was robbed en route to Santa Fe—as a kid Tom had heard the tale. "My daddy took two men," Matt told him, "one of them Joe Littlehorn, a Jicarilla Apache tracker. They were gone a week. Then they rode into Santa Fe, put the gold in the bank and came on home. What happened out there my daddy never told, and I never asked."

There had been an editorial in the Santa Fe newspaper once, Tom remembered, that referred to El Rancho del Norte as "an empire," and a "foreign country."

20

Well, in the sense of being almost completely self-contained and largely self-sustaining, it was an enclave, separate and distinct from the two counties that contained it, an inevitable source of envy and annoyance, constantly under accusation for this trouble or that.

Was water low in the stream that wound through Grutas County to the big river? Then somewhere on El Rancho del Norte they were diverting too much water for their own selfish purposes. It had to be.

Did Tito Gonzalez turn up missing one fine day? Then what else was more likely than that he had been caught taking a deer out of season on El Rancho del Norte once too often and the ranch people had seen to it that he never had another chance. (No matter that a letter from Tito Gonzalez eventually arrived in Las Grutas from Los Angeles: the story persisted.) And in all that country the ranch covered, even if Matt Granger had given permission to search, how could one man's body be found?

In one of his rare times of easy talk with Tom, old Matt had made the point: "We're the biggest man in the bar, boy, and whenever somebody's feeling his liquor or his oats and wants to make trouble, we're the natural target. They'd purely love to cut us down to their size. The only thing is"—the old man's smile was wicked—"in all this time they haven't figured out how to do it, none of them, not those little piss-ants in Las Grutas, not the other piss-ants down in Sante Fe. They say my daddy stole some of this land. I won't argue the point. Let them prove it, is all, and they've tried and they can't, and that purely gravels them."

There was another knock on the door. Tom lifted his voice. Tish walked in. She closed the door quietly. "You're the *patrón* now," she said.

"That isn't settled." Not even close, he thought.

"You know different." There was strength in her, a willingness to speak out. "Hadn't you better say hello to your people? They know you're back. They're waiting."

21

"The king is dead, long live the king?" Tom shook his head. "Nonsense."

"You know better than that, too." Tish turned away. Over her shoulder as she opened the door, "I'll go with you. You've probably forgotten names."

They were Pepe and José and Juan, Inocencio and Consuelo and Dolores, Lupita and Luisa and María Victoria. . . . They spoke a soft slurred Spanish with English words interspersed, and they smiled and nodded gravely and shook the hand of *el patrón* in welcome. It was good for a man to return to his own place; it was right.

Afterward, walking back to the office, "I called Wayne Carter," Tish said. "I told him you would see him tomorrow. He understands that you have too much to decide with Seth Porter first."

"I'm being managed," Tom said. In a way it was amusing.

"I'm trying to pay my way."

The amusement faded. "This is your home. You're part of the family."

"No." At the office door Tish stopped. "Mother was, because Matt married her. I just came along."

"Stepdaughter."

The girl's smile was without amusement. "No," she said again. "I'm no real part of it. Matt would have had to adopt me to make me part of the family. He didn't."

Tom tried to make it light. "Then maybe I will."

"If that's an offer," Tish said, "it is declined. I'll send Seth Porter in as soon as he gets here."

3

Seth Porter was well into his sixties; a man with white hair, a round face, and an easy, almost perpetual smile as if running the state's most prestigious law firm was the easiest thing in the world, something you did between fishing trips. "It's been a long time, Tom," he said. His handshake was firm, friendly.

Tom went to the tantalus and poured two drinks. "I don't think," he said as he raised his glass, "that I've ever even seen you with a briefcase."

Seth raised his own glass. For a moment he was solemn. "Good hunting, Matt," he said, "wherever you are." He took a long sip and nodded approvingly. "Briefcase," he said then. He shook his head. "Hell, there are papers in the car. They can wait." He sat down and in his mild way studied Tom. "What's important," he said, "is not the papers, but you—what you're fixing to do."

"I don't know yet." Automatically he walked around the desk and dropped into the big chair. "I've got a life in the East." Grace, he thought. And Tim.

"Engineer," Seth said, "with a business school degree." He nodded. "The East is where it's at, no doubt about it. We're just a backwater." The easy smile showed. "And some of us like it just that way."

"It's a good act," Tom said, "and when I was growing up, I believed it. The country boy role."

"It's more than an act." The older man was smiling still, but the words carried conviction. "I was born here. I grew up here. I went away to law school—and

23

I couldn't wait to get back." He paused. "Some don't feel the same way. They think getting away—New York, Chicago, San Francisco—is like getting out of jail." He shrugged.

Act, or a matter of conviction, Tom thought, it made no difference: there was no faintest crack in the façade. It had always been so. Seth Porter was that rarest of things: a man at peace with himself. Tom felt a sense of impatience that the same could not be said of him. "All right," he said, "what have we got? Those papers in the car say what?"

"Why," Seth said, "they put you in the catbird seat. You and Will share alike, but you're the man in charge." He paused. "If you'll take it, that is. The ranch, the paper, the radio station—though they may have to be split up."

"What will taxes do?"

"They'll take a bite, a big one, but we saw this coming, of course, and prepared for it as best we could. The cash position of the estate is sound. There are four, five directions you can go for additional cash. We can talk about details later."

"What about that atomic reactor?"

Seth sipped his whiskey. "That was Matt's idea. It's a lease that can be broken—for cause."

"If, for example," Tom said, "there are radiation leaks, radioactive pollution, that kind of thing?"

"Exactly."

Tom thought of what Burley had said about dead sheep, leukemia, fish floating belly-up. Those radioactive and deadly Central City mine tailings came to mind. "What was Matt's idea in leasing the land?"

Seth took his time. He said at last, "A variety of reasons. Matt purely hated that smog that's creeping down from those Four Corners coal-burning power plants, even if he can't see it from here. It'll get worse, he said, and it made him mad just to think about it. That was one reason. Another was that he knew some of the people at the lab who are sponsoring the project, and he liked Wayne Carter, and it does look as if they've come up with a reactor design that is efficient and safe, and with things the way thay are we need all the new sources of energy we can get." Seth paused. "They wanted an isolated location, Long Valley was ideal, and Matt went along." He paused again. "There is probably one other reason too. Under Matt and under Tully this place has always been ahead in all kinds of things—mining, cattle breeding, land conservation, reforestation, you name it." He smiled. "I think Matt wanted the ranch in on the ground floor in atomic-power generation too."

"The contingencies," Tom said, "they were your idea?"

"The nitpicking legal mind," Seth said. He was smiling again.

"You said protection from visitors 'and others,'" Tom said. "What others?"

"Well, now," Seth said, smiling again, "I wouldn't like to point a finger, but there are some folks who aren't exactly wild about the idea of efficient, safe, economical power generation from atomic fuel. Stands to reason, when you think on it."

"Oil people?" Tom said. "Coal operators?"

"A man with a lot of money invested," Seth said, "purely hates to see his business undercut." He paused. "Particularly when he's used to riding high and having things pretty much his own way. Buggy manufacturers didn't exactly cotton to the first automobiles. Some of them went out of their way to try to show that horseless carriages weren't safe." He paused again. "And I'm not sure they weren't right." He stood up. "You think on it, son. The whole thing. Sitting behind that desk just might give you more action than you bargained for. Old Tully gathered it together in the land. Matt held it together and added a few flourishes. Keeping it is going to present lots of problems." A third pause. "And as you said, you've got a life of your own in the East. So ponder on it."

Tom said, "You're not leaving?"

Seth was smiling again as he shook his head. "I don't get up here that often. Right now I have an idea a few fish might be hungry, and I just happen to have a rod and a few flies in the car, so with Granger permission. . . ."

"Help yourself," Tom said. He too was smiling. "We'll have your catch cooked for breakfast."

He sat alone again and stared unseeing at the far wall. Now for the first time he thought he could actually feel death in the house, the permanent absence of the decisiveness of the fierce old man in the upstairs bed; a sense, neither of loss nor yet of sorrow, but rather of responsibility impossible to avoid.

All problems came to this desk, and here they stopped. Seth Porter understood that and had made his understanding clear. "So ponder on it." Warning? Or goad? In effect as much of a dare as Will's that had sent Tom up the sheer rock face so long ago?

I'm old enough now, Tom told himself, to ignore that kind of nonsense. True or false? Know thyself. But who in hell ever really did?

There was another knock on the door. Annoyed with himself, he almost shouted, "Come in!" Tish stepped inside. "There is a woman at the gatehouse," she said. "José put her on the phone. Her name is Ethel Wilding and she wanted to see Matt. Now she wants to see you. She's driven all the way from Santa Fe." She saw the question in Tom's face and anticipated it. "I haven't any idea who she is or what she wants, but I don't think she's just sightseeing."

The buck stops here—that was the sign on Harry Truman's desk, wasn't it? And again that sense of unavoidable responsibility was strong. "Send her up," he said. "We'll see what she wants."

Ethel Wilding was in her late twenties, tall, rounded, assured. She wore a handsome tweed suit with a single silver-and-turquoise pin on the lapel and no other jewelry: carefully understated affluence. "Thank you for seeing me, Mr. Granger." She sat down. Her eyes were steady on Tom's face and her hands quiet in her lap. "I am a lawyer, Mr. Granger, and I am concerned about a number of things, the environment, ecology, and conservation among them." She paused, watching his reaction. "Do you find that amusing?"

In his present mood he found it solemn and pompous. A female with a message, he thought. "I'm for motherhood and against sin myself," he said. He paused. "Most times, that is. We breed and raise cattle here and send them off to be slaughtered. Does that offend you?"

"You are also allowing to be built on your property," Ethel Wilding said, "an experimental atomic reactor."

"So I have been told."

One Wilding eyebrow lifted in silent query.

"I arrived here," Tom said, "about an hour and a half ago." He smiled. "I haven't even decided yet if I am going to stay." He paused. "What exactly are you after?"

"Cooperation."

"The word covers a lot of territory, like environment, ecology, and conservation. They all mean different things to different people. You're against the reactor?"

"There are hazards."

"Sure there are, and they have to be weighed against possible good." His patience was wearing thin. "I assume that all precautions are being taken against radiation."

"There is a child from Las Grutas with leukemia."

"Are you representing him or his family?"

"Not directly."

"Are you representing sheepmen?"

"Not directly." Then, "I am not here to be catechized, Mr. Granger."

Tom leaned back in his chair. "I haven't found out yet just why you are here."

There was a short silence. "I've just come from Las Grutas, Mr. Granger." Her voice was expressionless. "And?"

"I identified a body in the local mortuary, the body

27

of a friend." Her eyes did not leave Tom's face. "He was found dead on your property."

"I heard."

"He had been shot."

Tom nodded. "Nobody seems to know who he was."

"His name was Walter Borden. He was a conservationist."

"Do you know what he was doing here?"

She hesitated. "No," she said. "But I intend to find out, Mr. Granger." She stood up suddenly. "With or without your—cooperation."

"Suit yourself."

She nodded. And then, glancing around at the trophy heads on the walls, and back again to Tom, "Do you Grangers enjoy killing animals?"

"A good question." Tom was smiling now. "A pleasure to meet you Miss Wilding." He paused. "Or is it Ms?"

Her car, a cream-colored Mercedes sports coupé, was making the wide turn toward the gate when Tom came out of the big house. He watched the car until it swung out of sight, and he wondered what Joe Valdes and his brood would make of it; probably they would see it as something from another world. Like the woman herself.

The jeep Tish had driven to meet the plane was still in the driveway. Tom got into it. Seth Porter would be fishing the main branch, he decided, and drove off to find out.

Seth was fishing the main branch, working a quiet pool beneath towering cottonwoods with the lovely little two-piece six-foot split-bamboo rod he had carried in his car as long as Tom could remember. Watching the man at his sport was pure pleasure and poetry in motion.

The pool was wide and against the far sheer bank was deep water where the big trout loved to loiter. Seth worked the rod in rhythmical strokes, the shining line curling and paying out, never still, never jerking, farther and farther across the pool without hesitation until at last the rod was poised, motionless, and the line sank and settled, oh, so gently, to the surface of the water. The tied fly at its end seemed almost to hover, a live insect displaying itself to whatever waited in the depths.

Tom waited for the flurry that would mean a strike. There was none. Unmolested, the colored fly drifted slowly with the current. "They saw you coming," Tom said. He watched Seth, unperturbed, reel in the line. "You don't care much if you catch them or not, do you?"

"All one." Seth laid the rod down carefully. He got out cigarettes. "Water's high. What's on your mind, son?"

"A lawyer named Ethel Wilding. You know her?"

Seth's smile was gentle. "We've tangled with her a few times. Bright girl with ideals." The smile spread. "Not like some idealists who think making a good living is a sure sign of decadence. She does fine." He paused. "Why?"

Tom told him of the woman's visit. He added, "Walter Borden. Does that mean anything to you?"

"I met him once. Geologist. From California, I recall. I don't think he worked much at his geology. Went off to Mexico, I heard."

"If he did," Tom said, "he went the wrong way. Ethel Wilding says his is the body in Las Grutas."

Seth took his time. At last he nodded and bent to pick up the rod. "In that case," he said, "I expect I'd better drive down and have a little chat with Pepe Martinez before he comes charging up here with a posse. Pepe's daddy was an impetuous fellow and a lot of it rubbed off on the boy."

"Pepe and I," Tom said, "are old friends. I broke his nose once." He paused. "Broke his knife too. He liked that even less."

4

There were only five passengers in the first-class section of the 727, O'Hare to Los Angeles via Albuquerque. The Will Grangers were comfortably arranged on the shaded starboard side of the cabin, far enough forward for a good view, far enough aft for a smooth ride. The Will Grangers were knowledgeable air travelers.

Sue had the window seat. Sue usually had first choice in any situation. She was of middle height, deeply tanned, small-waisted, full-bosomed, a blond girl in her middle twenties who had known from childhood that the world would always be good to her.

Will Granger preferred the aisle seat, where he could stretch his long legs. He was as tall as his brother, Tom, but of a less bulky, more elegant build. He too was well tanned. The spring skiing at Gstaad had been ideal: bright, clear, warm days with nights cold enough to restore the corn snow consistency. And skiing in shorts, you benefited from the direct sun and from the rays reflected from the snow.

"He was really rather a dear," Sue said. She was speaking of old Matt. She glanced at Will. "You don't agree?"

"He had a fondness for pretty girls." Will was smiling. "But there were other sides to him too." As there are to Tom, he thought, and did not say aloud. "Things always ran *his* way."

"You seem to have had what you wanted."

"Most of the time." Smiling still, his defense against the world. "I wanted to be an artist."

"You're kidding!" Her smile matched his own.

Will shook his head. "I'm afraid it's the truth. My mother thought it was a great idea. She saw me in terms of Rembrandt or at least Picasso—instant world fame." He was mocking himself, and yet the words themselves were true enough. "All those drawings I did. Birds, snakes, landscapes." He stopped and drew in a deep breath. "I think I was pretty much what they call a natural." He paused again and shook his head remembering. "In 1956 I was nine. That's when the bubble burst. My art career went down with the *Andrea Doria*. Matt took a dim view of artists."

"And your psyche has been scarred ever since." Sue's voice was light. Her smile was very broad. "Never mind, darling, we'll be artists at living." The smile disappeared. Sue said slowly, "I've never lost anyone. Did you miss her?"

"That's a funny question." Will paused for reflection. "And, you know, I don't know the answer. Matt thought I did. The ranch people thought I did. Death is very real to them. I'm not sure it was to me. She was just—gone, no longer there. I think Tom missed her more."

"I would have thought less."

Will's smile still held. "Don't let him fool you. He doesn't always show what he thinks." Or give warning of what he is going to do, he thought. And then: face it, he told himself, you have always been afraid of Tom. As you were of Matt. And growing up has changed nothing. If there had been any way out, he and Sue would not now be flying toward the ranch.

"Darling." Sue's attention rarely remained long on one subject. "What's going to happen now?" Somehow she gave the impression of a little girl asking for reassurance.

Well, I can't give it to her, Will thought. Aloud he said, "I don't know. I know what I hope will happen, but maybe it won't. Tom—"

"Aren't you equal? I mean as heirs?"

The smile turned inward now, mocking himself.

31

"Let's say," Will said, "that brother Tom is more equal than I am."

"Excuse me."

Will and Sue turned to look up at the big man in the aisle, one of the three other first-class passengers. He wore a muted plaid suit that sat on his heavy shoulders with the kind of fit only expensive tailoring could achieve. His smile was easy. "You're Will Granger, aren't you?"

Will nodded.

"Farley Wells." The big man held out his hand. "We met a few times in Houston. Petroleum Club, among other places." The smile altered subtly. "And the little lady, as I remember, is Sweet Sue." He paused almost imperceptibly. "A right appropriate name." He had Will's hand in his, and he shook it once with easy firmness. "May I buy you folks a drink?"

They sat together at the round table in the lounge at the rear of the compartment. "Going home?" Farley said. He nodded in answer to his own question. "I read in the paper about your granddaddy's death. I'm right sorry about that." He raised his glass. "Condolences."

Sue said, "You knew him, Mr. Wells?"

"Farley, please, ma'am. And, no, I never had the pleasure. But I knew *of* him, of course. One of the big ones, he and his daddy before him. Not many ranches like that left. Not many men left to put them together. Or hold them." Farley smiled suddenly. "I don't mean to sound Neanderthal, ma'am. Mostly I figure I'm straight Cro-Magnon. But I do purely admire a man who'll stand up on his hind legs and look the world right in the eye."

Will said mildly, "Spoken like a Texan." He smiled. "On the other hand, I'm not sure I disagree with you."

Farley pointed through the nearby window at the ground almost thirty thousand feet below. "Look down yonder. Brown, dry country, big as all outdoors. Did you ever stop to think how it must have looked to the Spanish when they got here? Coronado, say, head-

ing north to find those cities—1540, if I remember
rightly. Nobody really knew what was there, except
maybe the Indians, and Coronado didn't know whether
to believe them or not. Maybe he'd find water, for
instance, and maybe he wouldn't, and if he didn't, why,
that was the ballgame, but he went anyway—just
marched off to see what he could see and maybe
bring back a piece of it, if he got back at all." Farley
shook his head. He was smiling again. "They were
men, ma'am, men."

"One thing," Will said, smiling. "Old Matt would
have agreed with you."

Farley looked pleased. "I'm flattered." He tasted
his drink. "You folks being met at Albuquerque?
Because if you aren't, I'd be right pleased to carry you
as far as Santa Fe." He smiled quickly. "If the Hertz
people live up to their boasts, that is."

Sue looked at Will. Will said, "Thanks, but we
have a charter plane to fly us to the ranch."

"Oh, dear," Sue said. "Another of those little things
that flap their wings?"

It was the same charter plane Tom had flown in,
and the pilot made a point of mentioning it. The
same brownish haze traced the winding course of the
big river, but neither Will nor Sue noticed. The mountains stretched endlessly, their peaks gleaming in the
sun. "What I can't stand about this country," Sue said,
"is that it's so big! The Alps are civilized; they don't
sprawl all over creation."

Will smiled.

The pilot said, "The only times I ever seen them,
ma'am, they looked right unfriendly to me."

Sue opened her mouth and shut it again in silence.

Will said, "How was that?"

"Lookin' down from the chin turret of a B-17," the
pilot said. "All I could think of was what a hell of
a place those mountains would be to ditch in."

Will smiled again. "I take your point."

"Course," the pilot said, "like the lady says, these
mountains here do stretch to hell an' gone. Lose a

man easy. Like that fellow they found dead up on your ranch."

Sue said, "Oh, no. The Wild West?"

"I don't know about that, ma'am, but he was dead, shot, and he'd been under the snow all winter. They finally put a name to him: Walter Borden." The pilot looked at Will.

"I never heard of him," Will said. He started to point at the sheer rock face ahead.

"The meadow where we land, yeah," the pilot said. "I know the place. Landed there with your brother yesterday." He altered course.

Tish was waiting, with a station wagon this time, and, as before, a scarf tied to the antenna to show wind direction. "Will," she said in greeting. And "Sue." They did not shake hands. Together Tish and the pilot unloaded the luggage, stowed it in the rear of the station wagon while Will wrote out a check. Tish drove without asking, Will and Sue in the rear seat.

Will said, "Tom is here, I gather. The pilot is a chatty type."

"Tom is here." Tish's voice was expressionless. "So is Seth Porter."

Sue looked at Will in question.

"The legal eagle from Santa Fe," Will said. "He'll tell us how Matt wanted things arranged." And what was there in that to worry him? Never mind. His smile held steady. "Nice old boy, gives you the big smile and the country twang, talks a lot about fishing." He was watching Sue's expression. "And," Will went on, "was editor of the *Law Review* at Harvard and could have gone to Washington as law clerk to either of two Supreme Court justices, but came home instead."

Sue was smiling happily. "I didn't say a word, darling. Don't go defensive on me. This is your country, not mine."

The heavy station wagon bumped along in relative silence through the forest and the heavy scent of pines. Will said, "Has Tom taken over?"

"In a way." Tish's voice held nothing. "I don't think he's made up his mind yet whether to stay or go back east."

Then, Will thought, we'll just have to try to persuade him. He sat, smiling silently.

They crossed the main stream branch on the truss bridge. Well downstream Seth Porter was patiently working a quiet pool, and as the car swept into the trees on the far side of the bridge, Will saw the butt of Seth's rod lift quickly and the rod itself arch in strain. "He's got one," Will said, "and if I know the old boy, he won't lose it, either." Another man with bottomless self-confidence, he thought. Like Tom.

Tish, glancing in the driving mirror at Will's face, smiled faintly.

At the house they left Tish to cope with the luggage and went up the broad steps into the front hall. There was the carved office door. How often, Will thought, have I been summoned to stand in old Matt's presence and await his judgment? There was something of the same feeling of dread now as he knocked and opened the door.

Tom was in jeans and boots and a flannel shirt, the sleeves rolled up on his forearms. All he needed, Sue thought suddenly, was a big hat and a horse in order to ride comfortably into anyone's Western. A far cry from the sober dark suit he had worn at the wedding reception back in Larchmont. Will the real Tom Granger please stand up? As he came out from behind the desk she had to admit that he was impressive; and seeing the brothers together for the first time in almost three years, she was caught too by the resemblance between them.

They shook hands. "You made it," Tom said. He smiled down at Sue.

She rose on tiptoe. "You kissed me when I was a bride," she said, "and you welcomed me into the family."

Tom bent to kiss her briefly.

"We saw Seth Porter," Will said. "He had a fish on the line."

Tom walked back around the desk. "If it's the big one," he said, "he'll be happy. If it isn't, he'll throw it back. Sit down." He gestured at the tantalus. "Drink?" He watched Will shake his head. "The funeral's tomorrow," Tom said. "We wanted to be sure you'd be here."

Will said, "A holy man?"

"Father Enrique from Las Grutas." Tom produced his rare smile. "The padre is stretching things. Matt was no Catholic or anything else, but he and the padre were friends, cribbage-players, and whiskey-drinkers, and last year Matt gave the church a new front door." It was a side to the old man Tom had never seen before, and would never have seen if the priest had not driven up in his 1942 pickup as soon as he heard of the old man's death to offer his services in musical English and soft slurred Spanish, and explain his reasons.

"No hoedown," Tom said. "Just the family. You two, Tish, Seth Porter, our own people."

"And then?" This was Will. "You're staying here?"

"I don't know."

Sue said, "Is Tish part of the family?"

"She is." The two words held finality. "And she runs the household." Tom looked at his watch and stood up. "Ask her for anything you need. I've got to run down to Las Grutas." His smile was without amusement, directed at Will. "My old friend Pepe Martinez, now DA." The smile spread grimly. "Looking for some way to put the hooks to us." He walked to the door, the smile gone.

Will said, "If you don't come back, we'll send out the dogs."

"I'll come back," Tom said, and walked out.

The Past
1869

The village of Las Grutas was merely a collection of adobe huts, outhouses and stilted ramshackle granaries clustered around an adobe church when Tully Granger and four riders drove a herd of cattle into the area and settled down without so much as a by-your-leave. The War was finished and Texas wasn't big enough for Tully. He needed room to spread out.

The land was limitless and the big American—the term Anglo would come later—was so sure of himself that it occurred to no one to challenge his presence. Then too, five American rifles were a comfort to have around. Comanches did not venture this far from the Plains, but Apaches roamed where they would and took what they could get away with. It would be some years before their terror was finally stilled.

Tully and his four men built fences; the cattle came first, any kind of house could wait until approaching late-fall weather.

Two of the men rode back down to Santa Fe and returned with a wagon piled high with tools and supplies—axes, saws, splitting wedges, hammers, shovels . . . flour, salt, bacon, coffee, dried beans, a few jugs of bad whiskey. . . .

Tully poked around in the grottos for which the village was named, broke open rock samples, studied them, and kept his own counsel. Cattle were the first concern.

"It's piss-poor land for cattle," one of the men said

around the fire one night. "But there's the hell of a lot of it."

"And," Tully said, "there is water, and that's what counts."

Lack of water was the curse of this Southwest. Piñon, juniper, chamisa, grama grass, apache plume, and cactus could grow where man could not exist, and it was no accident that first the pueblos and then the settlements tended to huddle in the valley of the Rio Grande. Without its own small tributary, Santa Fe could not have survived.

But here in these great mountains water was no problem. The snows fed streams, summer thunderstorms brought more moisture; and marshy upland meadows called *ciénagas* gave proof that the land was not thirsty.

That first year Tully hired local people to build an adobe house twenty-four by twenty-four feet in floor area, with a packed adobe-and-dirt floor almost as hard as brick, *latías, vigas,* a corner adobe fireplace, and a sod roof. It sufficed as shelter against winter storms and snow deep as a tall man's waist. From it as a base they struggled out to tend the cattle.

The next year they built more fences, put up a windmill to keep a stock tank filled, and built a shed in which they set up the forge hauled in pieces by wagon from Santa Fe. They also, with the minor help of the villagers, fought off an Apache raid, and then under Tully's leadership did something that had never been heard of before: the five Americans followed the Apaches, surprised them at dawn in their dry camp, and with rifle fire gave them a taste of the terror they were accustomed to dealing out to others. It was six years before Las Grutas suffered another Apache raid.

Cattle came first, but it was the mineral wealth that provided the instant income. There was some gold and Tully found it; not enough to cause any kind of stampede, but enough to take down to Santa Fe to be shipped to the Denver mint.

There was silver, and it went the same route.

Not for years would Tully set up his own smelter

and in his own mines provide work for half the male population of a greatly expanded Las Grutas.

Cattle had to be driven down to Santa Fe and beyond, but in 1880 the Santa Fe railroad reached Lamy, seventeen miles from the capital, and from that time on the cattle operation was far more efficient and lucrative.

By then too the vast crenellated and turreted and hideous house was well under construction. The ranch was all but self-sufficient. It had its own smithy and sawmill, and corrals and breeder pens. It raised its own vegetables—corn, beans, tomatoes, chilis, onions, lettuce, squash; and its own fruit—apples and peaches. It bred its own hogs for slaughter, maintained its own small dairy herd, raised chickens and ducks for home consumption. It had its own problems, a continuing stream of them.

Ranch hands and miners drunk in Las Grutas on a Saturday night. "Jail them and let them sober up," Tully told the local sheriff, "and I'll pay their fines." Good men or even mediocre men were hard to come by, and the ranch was a lonely spot.

There was a rash of rustling, and the by now vastly extended fencelines could not be perpetually patrolled. But driven cattle left tracks, and there were no finer trackers in the world than the now friendly Jicarilla Apache, and there were plenty of Granger rifles and Granger men to take back what was theirs and inflict a lesson in the bargain—a lesson that would be remembered.

The Army objected. "You don't just string men up to the nearest cottonwood tree, Mr. Granger," a colonel pointed out.

Tully's reaction was unhesitating. "The hell I don't. When I catch them with my cattle, that is exactly what I do. If you want to charge me with murder, go right ahead. Do you think there is a jury in the whole Territory that would convict me?" He was a huge man, this Tully Granger, and impressive. "I held this ranch against Apaches. Do you think I'm going to take punishment from a flock of raggedy-assed cattle thieves?"

Denver was the boom town, long days of riding away before the railheads crept closer. Denver was also the financial capital of the mountain region, and the source of niceties and luxuries unobtainable in Santa Fe. Tully attended an auction at the demolishing of one of Denver's leading bawdy houses, and among other items, such as a tantalus and a Tiffany lamp with a cast-bronze buffalo base, he bought two enormous and ornate marble bathtubs that he had hauled at great expense down to the ranch.

Settlers flooded west, riding the transcontinental railroads. A few, but only a few, dropped off at Lamy, and of these only a handful ventured back into the mountains and challenged the ranch's domain. "Son," Tully told one of them, a young Eastern-educated lawyer filled with legal niceties, "I like your looks, and I think the Territory can use all of your kind it can get. But don't come up here telling me that I don't have a right to this land, because then what I'm going to have to do is kick your ass all the way back down to Santa Fe and maybe aboard a train bound for California. You are giving away too much weight."

The young lawyer thought about it, and agreed. The Granger reputation was not undeserved.

"Now," Tully said, "why don't you go back down to Santa Fe the easy way, settle down, and hang out a shingle? I need legal advice sometimes to cope with those piss-ants in the capital. Maybe you're the man for me. By the way, what's your name?"

"Porter, Mr. Granger, Oliver Porter."

"Well, you let me know if you decide to hang out your shingle."

Tully had few friends, and no intimates until young Oliver Porter set up law practice in Santa Fe, and in his quiet, firm manner began to stifle some of the wilder Granger impulses.

"I don't know why I put up with you," Tully said. "It's my money and if I want to put it in railroad stocks—"

"They aren't sound," Oliver said. He wore an almost perpetual smile, and his voice was easy. "Stick to what you know, cattle, mining"—the smile spread—"and stealing land." He paused. "We're making progress in obtaining some kind of title to what you have. One day that will come in handy."

"Goddamnit, the land was there. Nobody was using it. I took it over and made it useful. Can you deny it?"

Oliver shook his head, smiling still. "What I am trying to do is make sure that you can hold it legally, and pass it along." Another pause. "By the way, don't you think you ought to start a family?" Oliver was married and the father of a son. He enjoyed the family life.

"You lawyers," Tully said, "stick your noses into everything, don't you?" But the lonely ranch life no longer had its old appeal, and he had already been thinking that it would be nice to have a woman in the big house. "Next time I'm in Denver," he said. "I might look around."

Oliver smiled and said nothing.

Her name was Susan and she was raised on a ranch in the shadow of the Spanish Peaks, and then sent into Denver for female polishing. She knew some Spanish and she picked up more very quickly in the running of the big house. The women from the village who worked on the ranch worshiped her.

She was gregarious and she invited friends from Denver to come and stay a week, ten days, almost as long as they liked. To Tully's occasional grumbling, "You love it," Susan said. "You know you do. You've lived here alone too long, and you were getting to be like a bear with a sore paw. Now you can show off. How about a barbecue, a big one?"

Halves of beef pit-roasted over slow fires, caldrons of beans, chili, homemade bread, tomatoes, apple pies, beer, whiskey; entire families riding or driving miles to attend. The Territorial governor came up from Santa Fe. "Good politics," Oliver Porter said. "Personally I think he's an ass, but he can be useful, and if you're going to hold this place. . . ."

Hold it they did. Through the Panic of 1893, which wiped out bank after bank and sent the railroad into bankruptcy, El Rancho del Norte mined its mineral wealth, raised and shipped its cattle, entertained its increasingly distinguished guests. "That Duke," Tully told Susan, "whatever his name is, has a lot of fancy ways, but, by God, he's a man to ride with. That grizzly looked big as this house and mean as a rattlesnake, and the Duke just stood there, and said, 'If you please, Mr. Granger?' and then began shooting cool as you please. The bear was twenty feet away when he dropped. I was sweating."

Susan smiled sweetly. "No more grizzly-hunts for a time," she said, and she paused. "I want my son to have a father when he is born."

"I," Tully said, "will be goddamned."

"I think Matthew is a nice name," Susan said, "don't you?"

"We'll call him Matt."

That night Tully and the Grand Duke sat long in front of the roaring piñon fire, drinking whiskey and discussing the joys and problems of fatherhood. "You cannot tell them what you have learned," the Grand Duke said. "They must learn for themselves. You built this"—his gesture took in the entire ranch, and through his beard his teeth showed white—"and I find it incredible. In my country it could not happen. Your son—"

"He'll hold it together," Tully said.

"Suppose it is a girl, my friend?"

Tully drank his whiskey, wiped his lips and shook his head. "It won't be. A boy by the name of Matt, and they'll hear from him."

5

The village of Las Grutas now crawled along a rocky ridge that climbed into the nearby mountains. The Spanish *las grutas* means "the grottos" in English, and some of the caves not far out of town had undoubtedly been as they were for centuries; others were abandoned diggings, most of them, like gigantic ground squirrel holes, flaunting at their openings disintegrating piles of tailings.

Once the population of Las Grutas had been a boasted ten thousand, and weathered houses to accommodate most of that number still stood sagging, lining street after deserted street, remnants of shattered dreams.

The present population was closer to thirty-five hundred, although seven thousand were claimed, but Las Grutas was still the county seat and the center of Grutas County activity. There was some agriculture: alfalfa, pinto beans, squash, and an inferior variety of corn; some sheep-raising and some cattle-grazing for the most part on nearby Forest Service land. There was no industry.

A few houses boasted TV antennas, leggy affairs aimed hopefully in the direction of distant Albuquerque. There was a local radio station, Granger-owned, which sixteen hours a day broadcast Spanish-language programs, country music, news, and weather reports. In minor emergencies KRDN (Rancho del Norte) was happy to broadcast personal messages, whether the FCC liked it or not.

There was the weekly newspaper, *The Las Grutas Bugle,* also Granger-owned, which covered the area in a mixture of Spanish and English and dealt almost exclusively with local news.

There was a surprisingly good sporting goods store catering to fishermen, hikers, hunters, snowmobilers in winter, and, recently, cross-country skiers, all of whom presented the ranch with problems by straying into or deliberately entering ranch property, there to have their coronaries, accidental gunshot wounds, broken limbs, or snowmobile breakdowns. Not a few back-packers had had to be rescued from the higher peaks caught by weather that, as old Matt Granger had said, "Anybody with the brains God gave a titmouse could have seen coming and got ready for. When clouds build up and turn dirty-gray, for Christ's sake, what do they think's going to happen—a heat wave?"

There was the County courthouse, scene five years before of a shoot out between County officials and an aggrieved group of citizens protesting allegedly doctored land records. Pepe Martinez, County District Attorney, held forth in the County courthouse.

He was Tom's age, twenty-eight, with his eye on the Governor's chair in the Roundhouse down in Santa Fe. The ambition was well known. "And you may get there yet, Pepe," Tom said, sitting loose and easy in the DA's office, "but not by going out of your way to twist Granger tails." He had expected antagonism and was prepared to meet it at least halfway. So far antagonism had not yet surfaced. Strange.

Pepe's broken nose had been badly set; it was off-center and gave him a cross-eyed appearance that was now his trademark. "I'm talking about murder," he said mildly enough. "There is no—"

Tom raised one hand. "I'll take your word for it. I've talked with Jesús Valdes, who found the body, and with Clyde Burley, who went up and had a look and then called you. The man was shot. It could have been accidental, some damn-fool hunter, but where he was, out in an open meadow, the chances are nobody thought he looked like a deer." Tom paused. "So?"

"Shot on ranch property," Pepe said. "And you people have always—"

"What was he shot with?"

Pepe hesitated.

"You mean you don't know?"

"We know," Pepe said. "Near enough, that is. It was a heavy-caliber sporting rifle." His jaw muscles showed, but it was obvious he was trying to keep himself under control. Puzzling. "And what is funny about that?"

"Our people," Tom said, "just happen to go around carrying expensive heavy-caliber sporting rifles, do they? Use your head. If anybody carries anything, it's a saddle gun, a 30-30 carbine most likely, and then only if there's reason to think a lion or a bear is causing trouble." He paused. "You know the man's name. He was a geologist, and he had a large-scale topographical map and a compass. What was he after? There's your starting place."

"He could have been on the track of something. Gold, maybe. Uranium."

"Let's assume he was," Tom said. "Then why would any of the ranch people shoot him? If he found anything, we'd benefit. We own the mineral rights." He shook his head. "You're brighter than that, Pepe. Stop acting like one of those human piss-ants old Matt was always talking about." He stood up. "If and when you have anything sensible to talk to me about, I'll be available. Until then—*hasta luego*."

"Are you staying? Taking over from your grandfather?"

"I don't know yet."

Suddenly losing control, "You goddamn Anglos," Pepe said, "you think you own the earth."

"*Sin duda*," Tom said, "without doubt. But that is no reason," he went on in Spanish, "for you to assume that you have a divine right of some kind." He switched to English. "We don't shoot trespassers on sight, as you know. We don't eat our young, either. And there hasn't been a Black Mass celebrated in a long time. Scarcity of virgins." One of his rare attempts at levity. He walked out of the office and down the courthouse corridor, thinking as he went that public buildings everywhere seemed to have the same dead odor of inertia and petty intrigue. He was still keyed-up for a fight and so far none had been forthcoming.

Outside in the clear bright air he paused for a few moments to look at the mountains dominating the scene. He was not an introspective man, but he had often thought that against the permanence of those great snow-covered peaks, the transitory bickering and strife that went on among men here in the valley was really of about as much importance as a squabble among prairie dogs. Silently he revised what Pepe had said: We don't think we own the earth, he thought; we think we *are* the earth. He started for the ranch pickup feeling unaccountably better.

"Mr. Granger." The cream-colored Mercedes sports coupé paused beside him, purring. Ethel Wilding's arm rested on the door. Her eyes, expressionless, watched him. "Are you finally taking an interest in Walter Borden?"

Tom nodded shortly. "Because he was found on our land, and because Martinez seems determined to make something of it."

"I think you will find," Ethel said, "that a number of people in and around Las Grutas are prepared to lay the blame for anything that happens on Rancho del Norte."

"There's nothing new in that. They always have."

He watched the Mercedes roll away down the dusty street, and suddenly he turned away from the pickup and walked in the opposite direction toward the church, driven by he knew not what compulsion.

Father Enrique was in his cactus garden—cholla, hedgehog, claret cup, pincushion, prickly pear, a multitude of shapes and sizes, some plants already in brilliant flower.

"This small-little," the padre said in Spanish—*pequeñito* was the word—"is it not a marvel?" It was: a small pincushion cactus an inch and a half in diameter and two and a half inches high bearing on its top five flaming cerise flowers that together almost hid the body of the plant from view.

Tom found that he could smile down at the little cactus. "It puts on quite a show, probably to demonstrate its appreciation."

"No." The priest was definite. "It goes its own way in its own fashion. They all do. They have learned to fend for themselves. They need nothing from me." He had a shy gentle smile. "Perhaps that is why I enjoy them so much." The smile was gone. "You want to talk?"

"I think so."

"About Matt?"

Tom shook his head gently.

"Ah," the priest said. "I think I understand. We will go inside."

It was a small house with thick adobe walls. The floor of the main room was brick, polished, and worn by generations of footsteps. At this elevation, seventy-five hundred feet, even on this bright day a small fire burned in the corner fireplace, two piñon logs standing on end in the local fashion, giving off their pleasant pungent odor, flooding the room with welcome warmth. Tom and the padre sat in heavy wood-frame chairs on stretched cowhide seats. The padre smiled gently and waited.

"I've been away," Tom said. "You know that. Maybe I've been away too long and I've forgotten how it was." He was thinking of Pepe Martinez, who had been so much less belligerent than he had expected; of Ethel Wilding, a peripatetic Cassandra, crying trouble; even of Tish's attitude, and Clyde Burley's, although the feeling had been stronger this morning here in the town. "Maybe I'm seeing things."

"What kind of things?"

Tom spread his hands. His smile was almost bitter, mocking himself. "I don't know. But I'm not usually —tuned to subtleties."

"Fear," the priest said slowly, "almost has an odor. Dogs can smell it. Somehow I think we recognize it too, without knowing it."

Tom scowled. "Fear," he said. And then, "The reactor?"

"Partly that, but only partly." The priest paused. "The rest is you, the ranch, change. What is going to happen now that Matt is gone." His gentle smile reappeared. "We knew him. We knew that with him any change would be minor. The ranch would be there, with jobs, more money in town." He shook his head. "Instead, there is young Carlita with leukemia. And there are dead sheep, dead fish, now a dead man. And Matt is gone. And who knows what you will do with the land? Maybe you will shut down the ranch, or make it into Forest Service land, and what can the town get from that? Maybe a few grazing privileges, that is all. Maybe—it has been said—there will be other reactor plants built on the land, more leukemia, more dead sheep, dead fish." Again the slow, shy, sad smile. "To generate electricity, is it not? But we have all the electricity we need." He gestured toward the fireplace. "And we have wood for heat." He paused. "We have welfare checks and food stamps, and as long as the ranch is there with jobs and money to spend in Las Grutas, we will endure as we always have." He paused again. "But what if all is changed? What then?"

Tom walked slowly back to the pickup, got in and just sat, his hands resting lightly on the steering wheel, his eyes in distant focus on the mountains. What then? the priest had asked. Well, what indeed?

The fact of the matter was, of course, that the town needed the ranch far more than the ranch needed the town, and that kind of imbalance inevitably produced difficulties, resentment, eventually bitterness. You supported dependents at your peril: the statement was axiomatic. But probably Matt, and Tully before him, had not even looked at it in that way.

They had taken wild land and tamed it; caused it to produce mineral wealth, to support cattle, to prosper and become secure against all kinds of attack, and if in the doing they had also just happened to adopt a dying village and keep it alive almost by largesse, where was the continuing obligation? How many do-gooders could dance on the head of a pin?

Tom got out of the pickup again and walked up the street in the bright warm sun to the office of the *Las Grutas Bugle*. For a wonder the office was open, Kelly Garcia apparently taking a breather between newsgathering and ad-peddling. "Well, well, well, well," Kelly said. "Will you look who's here! How are you, tiger?"

Tom sat down. Now that he was here, he wondered exactly what he hoped to discover. It was, he thought, a day for off-balance behavior.

Kelly said, "Gathering local lore? Seeing how it looks from ground level—or below? The worm's-eye view?"

"More or less," Tom said.

Kelly was the older man by twenty years, a failed city newspaperman, uncompetitive, comfortable in this isolated world. He leaned back in his chair now and put his feet up on the desk. "Well, the lead story is the dead man Walter Borden, the mysterious walker. I even had a call from the *L A Times*. His family had been wondering what happened to him." He shrugged. "All I could tell them was that he got himself dead. Pepe Martinez—"

"I've talked with him," Tom said, and left it there, subject ended.

"Okay," Kelly said. "Little girl with leukemia. You've heard about that?"

"And about dead sheep and dead fish." Tom paused. "Any proof that the reactor is to blame?"

"You don't need proof. All you need is rumor."

True enough; it had always been so. "What about the girl?"

"Hospitals are expensive. And leukemia doesn't cure real good."

And what would Matt have done? No matter. Matt was gone, for good. "Run a story in the paper," Tom said. "Have it put out over the air. Ask for donations—"

"*Amigo.*" Kelly's voice had lost its lightness; it was

tinged now with scorn. "You forget where you are. It would be a miracle if we raised the price of a short beer."

"I understand that," Tom said sharply. "The point is that once you've made your plea, nobody has to know where the money comes from. I'll see that there's enough to get her to Albuquerque or Denver and at least find out where she stands."

Kelly's eyes were shrewd. "Mind telling me why?"

"Maybe I'm not sure." Tom paused. "What else is happening?"

Kelly smiled suddenly. "You know about a bill introduced into the state legislature at this session?"

Tom shook his head.

"A state plan," Kelly said, "to raise funds to buy El Rancho del Norte." His smile spread as he watched Tom's face. "How do you like that?"

Tom took his time. He said at last, "I wasn't aware anybody had said the ranch was for sale."

"Maybe somebody thinks different."

"Maybe." Tom stood up. "I wonder why." He paused. "You know who introduced the bill? Who's behind it?"

"Sam Waldo introduced it." Kelly paused. "The general thinking is that Sam couldn't pour piss out of a boot if the instructions were printed on the sole." He paused again. "I don't know who's behind him."

"Then find out," Tom said. "And call me." Sometimes hunches were ridiculous, but sometimes a faint warning bell began to toll and a man did well not to ignore it. He walked to the pickup again.

6

Wayne Carter arrived at the ranch house in a gray four-wheel-drive pickup. Tish met him and walked with him up the broad steps. "Tom isn't here," she told him, "but he called from the village and he's on his way."

She was not sure how the two men would get along, and she wished that the uncertainty did not worry her. Tom was, well, Tom. Wayne, on the other hand, was quiet, slightly professorial, with a sense of humor he kept for the most part under wraps. She liked him and wished him no discomfort. "Let's wait for him in the office," she said.

Wayne had been in the office before, but never with time to look around in leisure. He walked now from picture to picture, trophy to trophy, hands behind his back in the museum goer's posture; a middle-sized man in his early thirties, solid and fit, dressed in chino trousers, six-inch laced boots, a plain cotton flannel shirt and an old tweed jacket with chamois elbow patches. He turned at last to smile at Tish. "Fascinating," he said. "A family ledger." He pointed at the picture of Bill and Liz Granger. "Who are they?"

Tish told him. And she added with a sense of surprise that she had never noticed the similarity before, "They must have been a lot like Will and Sue, scurrying around the world, doing whatever the rich do to amuse themselves. I never knew them."

Wayne sat down in one of the leather club chairs and studied the girl. "But Tom isn't like that?"

51

Tish could smile as she shook her head. "Tully, then Matt, then a skipped generation—and Tom."

"You like him?"

Tish sat down and slowly stretched her legs. She studied the toes of her squaw boots. "I don't know," she said. "Sometimes—" She stopped, and smiled apologetically. "I've leaned on him." She paused. "I was fourteen and there was a hand here on the ranch, an Anglo, who gave me a bad time. I could have gone to Matt, but I didn't want to do that. And I didn't know how to cope by myself." She paused again. "Then Tom came home on vacation from school in the East. He saw what was going on and told the hand to quit bothering me." A third pause, remembering. "It didn't take, so Tom called the man out of the bunkhouse one evening, and in front of all the other hands he beat him until he couldn't stand and then told him to get off the ranch or he would kill him." She shook her head, remembering her own shock, and guilty sense of relief. "Tom," she said, "was just sixteen, not even full-grown."

Carter said slowly, "I see what you mean." His glance swept the room again. "Granger consistency." He smiled at Tish. "And I would guess that when Matt heard about it, he said that Tom had done right, but that a next time he had better clear it with Matt first?"

It was exactly what Matt had said, but how could this man have understood? "They never got along," Tish said.

"No." Wayne's tone was judicious. "I shouldn't think they would."

Somehow the subject was uncomfortable. "How's the bird-watching?" Tish said. Happier topic.

"Only what I happen to see. I've been—busy."

Tish hesitated. "Is there trouble at the reactor?"

"We have a few problems." Wayne stood up as the door opened and Tom walked in. He waited while Tish made the introduction. They shook hands briefly. "I was just about to ask Tish," Wayne said, "if she would care to take a picnic one day and wander in the woods. Matt gave me permission. Does it still stand?"

"Hunter?" Tom said.

"Only with binoculars or camera."

Tom nodded. "Then help yourself," he said, and walked around the desk to sit down. To Tish, "How about having a couple of beers sent in?" He smiled at her. Dismissal. "Sit down," he said then to Wayne Carter. "Apparently you have things to talk to me about, and I have a couple of things on my mind." He smiled again. "You go first." He leaned back in his chair to study the man and listen.

He had encountered physicists and mathematicians before, and you never knew, he told himself, what one would be like because they came all shapes and sizes and, contrary to conventional thinking, they were very unstereotyped in their thinking. For every absent-minded, unwordly Einstein, there were a hundred who were very much up-to-date in the world outside their discipline, and quite capable of coping with civilization's daily problems. He was inclined to think that Wayne Carter was one of the hundred.

"Obviously," Carter said, "you know about the reactor."

There was a knock at the door and a maid came in smiling with the beer. Tom spoke to her in rapid quiet Spanish as she set the tray on his desk. He handed Carter a bottle and a glass stein, took his own and began to pour carefully. Without looking up, "You wanted a place, and Matt liked the idea." He set down the empty bottle, took a long pull of the beer, and sighed. For the moment, Pepe Martinez, the dead man in the meadow, the priest with his worries, and Kelly Garcia could be forgotten. "But they attached conditions," he said.

Carter sat forward in his chair, ignoring his poured beer. "Nobody pretends, Mr. Granger," he said, "that any kind of atomic reactor is foolproof for the following reasons: A, there is always a chance, only a chance, mind you, of a runaway reaction and a meltdown. B, there is always the problem of heat dispersal. And C, there is the problem of radioactive-waste disposal." He paused. "With appropriate design, construction, and normal care in operation, the chances of a runaway reaction are practically nil. And the percentage of purity of the fissionable material used in a reactor is quite low, so the chance of an atomic explosion that most people fear simply does not exist."

The man had to have faith in what he was doing, Tom thought, and found no fault in that. An engineer had to have faith too that when the bridge he had designed was built, it would stand. No difference. "Go on," he said.

"Heat dispersal," Carter said, "can be handled in any of a number of ways, and I can assure you, as I assured Matt, that the local environment will not be harmed. It will even be benefited. I'm an environmentalist myself, Mr. Granger, and I subscribe very strongly to the thesis that if we don't stop looting this planet of ours, we are headed for certain catastrophe."

A trifle pedantic, but clear, Tom thought. He nodded and had another long swallow of his beer.

"Disposal of radioactive waste," Carter said, "can be a stickler. You don't care about the minutiae, so I'll just say that some of the materials have a half-life measured in thousands of years, so we'd better be careful where we put them and intend to leave them. We are exploring some of the abandoned mines near Long Valley. One of them, an abandoned lead mine, seems close to ideal."

Tom set his stein down on the desk. "Leukemia, dead sheep, and dead fish," he said. "I've been hearing little else." He watched Carter carefully.

Carter took it calmly enough. "There are also complaints about radio reception," he said. "And some say the water tastes funny." He spoke without emotion. "Last week there was a thunderstorm, and word got around that the thunderhead was actually a mushroom cloud, precipitating radioactive material." He paused. "Not true, of course, but that is what you would ex-

54

pect me to say, so it doesn't carry much weight, I'm afraid."

Tom took his time. He said at last, "I'm an engineer, not a physicist or a physician, but my guess would be that if there were enough radiation to kill sheep and fish and cause leukemia, you, right on the spot, would already be a pretty sick fellow."

Carter's smile turned bitter. "I'd be dead, or close to it, and so would everybody else on the project." He paused, and now his voice matched the bitterness of the smile. "The fact of the matter is that all we have done so far is basic construction. There is no radioactive material on the site, and there hasn't been. We're far from ready for it. That's what makes me so damn mad. All these rumors and nothing—absolutely nothing—behind them."

You didn't need proof, Kelly Garcia had said; mere rumor was more than enough. Too true. Tom finished his beer and set the empty stein down gently. "Did you and Matt talk about this?"

Carter shook his head. "Maybe we should have," he said. "I don't know. But your grandfather was an old man, and I hesitated to pile trouble on him. Sooner or later the rumors will stop."

Tom was thinking of what Seth Porter had said. "Maybe," he said, "and maybe they'll get worse. Who's starting them?"

It was evident that Carter had not even considered the question. A small frown of puzzlement appeared and was quickly gone. He smiled again. "Rumors don't have to be started deliberately," he said. "Everything that has to do with atomic physics is mysterious to most people and probably dangerous as well. They think of Hiroshima and Nagasaki and the H-bomb tests. They—" He stopped to study Tom's face carefully. "You don't believe that? But every reactor built in this country has been surrounded by rumor."

"I believe that." Tom paused. "And some of it may even have been innocent." He paused again. "How do the oil and gas and coal people feel about atomic reactors generating power?"

Carter was smiling again. "Some are against it, of course. Some oil companies are looking into atomic power generation on their own, but there are others who like it just the way it is, depletion allowance and all." He dismissed the possibility of chicanery with a gesture. "Those people don't start rumors, Mr. Granger. They have other, more powerful weapons. Almost unlimited funds, for one."

Tom was amused. "They wouldn't stoop to rumor, you mean?" He shook his head in mock wonder. "You take a more charitable view of humanity than I do." He paused. "You had something else in mind?"

Carter now was clearly uneasy. "A gun," he said. "A rifle. It turned up on the site one morning last week. Nobody knew anything about it. I thought if one of your ranch people had lost it—" He hesitated. "But that doesn't make much sense, does it?"

Tom sat quiet and kept his voice unconcerned. "What kind of rifle?"

"Like that." Carter was pointing at the gun case. "The one on the right with the telescopic sight. I don't know much about guns, but it looks expensive—"

"It is." Tom was thinking of Pepe Martinez's description of the weapon that had killed Walter Borden as a heavy-caliber sporting rifle. Well, that description fitted the rifle in the gun case, and, presumably, the rifle Carter spoke of as well. "What do you mean," he said, "it turned up one morning?"

"It was leaning against a wall," Carter said, "as if someone had put it there and gone off, forgetting about it." He paused. "But that was last week, and nobody has come to claim it, and it doesn't look like the kind of possession anyone would forget indefinitely."

"And you don't like it."

"There are a lot of things I don't like," Carter said. "We had a fire some time ago. It could have been accidental: spontaneous combustion isn't out of the question."

"But you don't think it was." Tom's voice was expressionless. "And yet," he said, "you think rumors about poisoned water and mushroom clouds are innocent ignorance."

There was in this man the same bluntness there had been in old Matt, Carter thought, and to him as to Matt what the effect might be on another was a matter of no concern. "I deal in tangibles," Carter said, and was annoyed with himself for being pushed back on the defensive so easily.

Tom stood up, walked over to the gun case, unlocked it, and took out the rifle Carter had pointed out. Automatically he worked the bolt and verified that the weapon was unloaded. Wordlessly, he handed it to Carter.

Carter turned the rifle over and over in his hands. It was obvious that he was not used to firearms. "It looks a lot like the other," he said, and looked up at Tom in question. "I'm no expert."

"How about weight?"

Carter hefted the rifle. He nodded. "About the same."

"That," Tom said, "is a three-fifty magnum. It's a lot more rifle than most men like. Heavy-caliber sporting rifle is an apt description. If I were you"—he paused to consider the implications and then set them aside—"I'd take the rifle you have into Las Grutas and turn it over to Pepe Martinez, the DA. He'll ask you a lot of questions. I suggest that you answer them." He took the rifle from Carter's hands, replaced it in the cabinet, and locked the door again. The key went on top of the cabinet where only a tall man could reach. "One thing," he added, turning, "and you might bear it in mind. Pepe doesn't like Anglos." He walked back to his chair and sat down. "So your work progresses," he said, "and there are rumors, and some people are afraid—"

"Needlessly." Carter's voice retained its stubborn bitterness.

"That," Tom said, "is beside the point. If they think there is danger, they are afraid."

"I can't help that."

Less worldly than he had thought, Tom told himself. The man did not have complete tunnel vision, but he was steeped in his project and what happened outside it tended to seem unimportant. "All right," he said, "those are the facts. Now what?"

"That," Carter said, "is at least partly up to you. With Matt gone, what happens here? Will the ranch be broken up? Sold? Our lease——"

"I can't tell you what is going to happen yet," Tom said. "But consider your lease secure—as long as there aren't too many accidents, dangerous accidents." He paused. "Or trouble because of your presence. We've existed with these mountain villages for a long time, and we won't jeopardize our position now. If we have to break the lease for cause, we will."

Carter said slowly, "Without a regret."

Tom nodded. "Without a regret."

"The land-baron view."

Tom nodded again. "We've been called worse than that." He stood up and walked to the door. With his hand on the knob, "About Tish," he said gently. "She is part of the family."

Carter waited but Tom said no more. He got out of his chair. "And you," he said, "are head of the family now that Matt is gone, is that it?" He paused. "I'm being warned off?"

"Just warned," Tom said. "I want to see her happy, not hurt. Bear that in mind too." He opened the door. "I'd like to know how your talk with Martinez comes out. And I'd like to know if any more fires start or any other accidents happen." Through the open doorway he saw Tish waiting in the big hall. "Take care on your picnics," he said to Carter.

"I don't worry about animals. I've yet to find one——"

"Then think about men," Tom said. "They aren't

always harmless." That warning bell was tolling softly. "And take care of Tish."

"That I will do." Carter walked out of the office.

Tom watched him go. I'm getting in deeper and deeper, he thought, and found no easy way out.

The phone call was from Grace, and the connection was bad. "I miss you." Her voice was faint and distant. "And it's raining and the whole world is gray."

Tom's eyes were on the gun cabinet, and his thoughts dwelt on a dead man in a meadow, an atomic reactor where radioactive material had yet to be positioned, and that warning bell in his mind. "It's nice here," he said, and instantly realized how inane the remark sounded, but could find no words to remedy it. Grace's voice sounded indistinctly. "I didn t hear you," Tom said.

"I said, 'I wuv you.' " This time overloud.

"Oh."

"And I want to be weighed!" A pause. "And I don't care if this line is being monitored, either!"

And what did a man say to that? "I'm sorry," Tom said.

"I thought you might be." A final pause. Then, quietly, "Good-bye, Tommy." The line went dead.

He called back, but there was no answer.

7

There was the new Inn, where he could have stayed, of course, but Farley Wells had known Santa Fe for a long time and he preferred the old La Fonda Hotel, with its thick walls, its quiet upper rooms, and its galleries that looked out over the town.

There was a message for him at the desk. His face was thoughtful as he carried it upstairs. In his rooms he tipped the bellhop, closed the door carefully, took off his jacket, loosened his tie, and went slowly to the telephone. The number he called was in Houston, the private unlisted line, of course, and to the voice which answered he said merely, "Farley here, J.R."

It was a quiet voice, rarely inflected, never raised, a voice that expected and always received full attention. "I just got back, Farley. I have your report."

"Yes, sir."

"I wanted to make sure that we understood one another."

No comment required. Farley waited.

"Our position"—it was the royal plural—"is somewhat anomalous. Or let us say flexible. We own uranium deposits, so obviously we are not against atomic reactors per se. And we would not like to be placed in the position of openly impeding progress."

"I understand, sir."

"On the other hand, in that state we also own high-sulphur-content coal deposits. And with the need for energy as great as it is now, this is the time for those coal deposits to be mined and used."

"Yes, sir." Elementary, Farley thought; but it was one of the old boy's many strengths that he liked things spelled out, misunderstandings avoided, orders received loud and clear. Then if you stubbed your toe, there were no acceptable excuses.

"So," J.R. said, "I approve your ideas, but I want no adverse publicity, and above all no trouble."

"Yes, sir."

"With that understanding, Farley, you have a free hand."

Farley hung up and walked slowly to stand at the windows looking out at the two asymmetrical towers of the cathedral. They were truncated, even blunt, and the impression they gave was that of strength rather than beauty. Far better, Farley thought, than soaring Gothic towers of stone lace. When you got right down to it, there was no substitute for strength. Or power.

The old man on the telephone was living, breathing proof of that. A word from him and drilling began in a new field, production was increased or decreased, a ten-million-dollar contract was signed or rejected, an overseas representative scrambled out of bed in the middle of the night and hurried to a meeting he had not even known was contemplated. . . .

Or he, Farley Wells, was given carte blanche, and he had damn well better not fail. All right, that was how it was.

There was one thing to remember, however: J.R. was also a great believer in what Farley thought of as overkill; not infrequently he sent two representatives to work separately and in ignorance of each other at different lines of attack to reach the same objective. It was something to bear in mind.

The telephone rang and Farley went to answer it. "Sam Waldo here, Mr. Wells," the voice said. "I'm in the lobby."

"Come up." Farley's voice was cordial. "I brought along some sipping whiskey I'd like your opinion on." As he hung up, he made a wry face, quickly wiped away. In his opinion Sam Waldo was a slob, and Farley Wells took no pleasure in his company.

State Legislator Sam Waldo was short and fat and loud. He wore a brown-and-gold striped suit, the jacket too short and too tight, the trousers too long so that they gathered in lumpy folds on the insteps of his cowboy boots. He wore a Fort Worth Stetson, which he took off and laid carefully on a table before he shook Farley's hand. "I'm mighty glad to see you," he said. "It's real fine that you're here." He accepted a shot glass of whiskey and sniffed it appreciatively. When he smiled his cheeks resembled small shiny apples and his small eyes almost disappeared. "This liquor's been keeping real fine company," he said. *"Salud."*

Farley sat down. He had turned back the cuffs of his sleeves, baring thick hairy wrists above large well-manicured hands. He made few gestures as he spoke. "How are things going, Sam?"

"Real fine, Mr. Wells, real fine. Here's the bill I've sponsored." Sam took out folded Xerox letter-sized sheets bearing official stamps, cabalistic numbers, and a quantity of signatures, most of them illegible. He started to hand it to Farley.

"I'll take your word for it, Sam," Farley said. "If you say it's right, then I know it's right." He watched the flush of pleasure in the fat cheeks. "Will it pass?"

"It'll get a do-pass in committee, that's for sure. And I can get it through the House. There're enough good old boys who owe me favors."

"The Senate? The governor?"

Sam sipped his whiskey, his little finger well extended. He set the shot glass down with delicacy, and leaned forward confidentially. "I'll tell you how it is, Mr. Wells," he said. "I'd like to say yes, I would for sure. It'd be real fine if I could tell you it was going to be like shooting fish in a rain barrel." He paused. "But I'm just not sure, I'm purely not." He appeared to be awaiting judgment.

Nothing showed in Farley's face and his voice held no edge. "How much, Sam?"

"Well, now, Mr. Wells, it isn't. . . ."

Farley's voice was gentle this time "How much, Sam?"

Sam hesitated.

You could almost hear the wheels in his head, Farley thought; they moved ponderously and with indecision. The man probably played poker with cronies every week—and lost every big pot. Farley waited patiently for the weighing process to end, avarice balancing trepidation on the problem of what the market would bear.

Sam licked his lips. "Well," he said at last, "maybe—" He paused and swallowed. "Would five thousand more be too much?"

"A lot of money, Sam."

"I know it is, Mr. Wells, a lot of money."

"But," Farley said, "you probably have a right smart number of directions for it to go."

"I sure do. You wouldn't believe. . . ."

"And so," Farley said as if he had heard nothing, "under the circumstances I think we'll push another five thousand into the pot. Wait here." He walked into the bedroom. He was gone only a little time, returned with a thick bundle of bills, and handed them to Sam. Then he sat down again. "Count them, Sam."

Sam's smile was embarrassed. "Why, I wouldn't think of. . . ."

"Count them." It was a command.

Farley sipped his whiskey while he waited. And when the fat fingers were through the bundle of bills, and Sam was smiling and nodding satisfaction, "We expect results, Sam," Farley said.

"You'll sure get them, Mr. Wells."

"We'll be mighty disappointed if we don't." Farley paused. "Keep that in mind." He made one of his rare hand gestures. The gold watch on his wrist flashed. "We don't mind spending money. But we like for it to buy something."

Sam sat silent and uncomfortable.

"I'm sure you'll do your best," Farley said. "Just make sure your best is good enough." He stood up. Interview ended.

POWER

At the door, rancher's Stetson held tight in both hands, money already tucked away, "One thing, Mr. Wells," Sam said. "I can't go beyond the legislature and the governor. You see how that is."

Farley was silent, waiting.

"What I mean is," Sam said, "even if we get the bill through, and signed. . . ."

"When, Sam, not if."

"That was what I meant. It sure was." Sam hesitated. "But that doesn't actually buy the ranch, Mr. Wells. I mean, all it does is appropriate the money to buy, if the Grangers will sell, you see what I mean? And maybe they won't."

"Maybe."

Sam hesitated. He took a deep breath. "I pushed this, Mr. Wells. I been telling everybody we ought to buy the ranch, keep it for the state, for recreational area."

"A mighty fine idea."

"You suggested it, Mr. Wells."

"I don't rightly remember that, Sam," Farley said. "I seem to remember it was your idea, and like I said, a mighty fine one it is. You'll have the conservationists behind you, and everybody who likes to fish and hunt or just walk in the mountains. You'll be a mighty big man."

Sam took another deep breath. "I'll look awful foolish too, Mr. Wells, if after I scramble and scratch and finally get the bill passed and signed—then the Grangers tell us to go to hell, they're not selling." He paused. "How about that?"

Nothing changed in Farley's face or voice. "Let me worry about that, Sam," he said, and opened the door. "Thanks for coming up."

When Sam Waldo had waddled off down the corridor, toes turned out, fat bottom waggling importantly, Farley closed the door and went to stand again at the windows facing the cathedral.

Beyond the fraternal-twin towers the Sangre de Cristo mountains looked huge against the sky; Lake Peak still showing a sizable patch of snow beneath its summit.

It was big country—the point had been made many times—and it wore its sometimes violent history with ease and even comfort.

Successive waves of Indians had disputed the territory and its hunting rights; the Conquistadores had invaded from Mexico, carrying the banner of Spain; Mexico itself had governed the territory until the Anglos swept in to take what they chose and thought they could hold. Strife was the norm.

Big country, big stakes; Farley's own estimate of the value of El Rancho del Norte was thirty million, give or take a couple. And if the state would pick up the tab, so much the better, but one way or another the ranch was going to be—neutralized.

The telephone rang again, and Farley went to answer it. It was a woman's voice this time: "You don't know me, Mr. Wells. My name is Ethel Wilding. I am an attorney here in Santa Fe, and I have an interest in an area that seems to concern you as well. May we talk?"

"What area is that, ma'am?"

"Las Grutas, El Rancho del Norte, and the Grangers."

Nothing showed in Farley's face while he thought it over. He said at last, "Would you care to come up, ma'am?" He smiled. "I'm harmless."

"That I very much doubt, Mr. Wells, but I'll be pleased to come up."

When he opened the door to her knock, Farley's first thought was that she was a stunner; a bloodline filly with the kind of confirmation a man loved to see. And the way she looked at him, sizing him up in her calm, self-possessed way, it was plain that what was in that high-held head matched all the rest of her for quality. "Sit down, ma'am. If you'd care for a drink, I have some whiskey I'm proud of."

Ethel Wilding sat down. "No drink, thank you." And then, without change of expression, "I really don't think you are the simple country boy you try to make out, Mr. Wells."

"Well, now, ma'am." Smart as a whip, Farley

thought. He was beginning to enjoy himself. "Just what can I do for you?"

"Do you know a man named Walter Borden, Mr. Wells?"

Farley pondered the question. Slowly he shook his head. "Far as I can think, ma'am, I do not. Should I?"

"He is dead. He was shot sometime last fall on the Granger ranch. He lay under the snow all winter. They found him this spring." She spoke the words as if by rote, without emphasis. "He was a friend of mine."

"I'm sorry to hear it, ma'am." Pause. "What was he doing on the ranch? Or is that a question I shouldn't ask?"

"He was a geologist."

Farley waited, but she said no more. "Is that an answer?" he said.

She took her time, self-possession intact. Then, "Would you mind telling me what your interest is in El Rancho del Norte, Mr. Wells?"

Farley's eyebrows rose. "You take me by surprise, ma'am. I have never even seen the ranch." Not quite true: he had flown over it and studied certain parts of it through binoculars and on maps, and he knew the ranch very well indeed.

"Please, Mr. Wells." Her voice was sharper now. "Nothing in this town is ever a complete secret. Sam Waldo is a self-important fool. Casting his vote against Daylight Time and liberalized abortion laws is about the most he can manage by himself. When he sponsors an innovative bill, such as the one authorizing the State to buy El Rancho del Norte, it is obvious that someone has done the thinking for him."

"And you suspect me?" Farley allowed amused incredulity to show.

She had her impatience under control, but her voice altered subtly. "I told you I was not impressed by the simple country boy front, Mr. Wells, the barefoot oil attorney from Harvard Law School."

Farley stood up and walked to the windows. His back to the room, "Why would a geologist get himself shot, ma'am?" he asked. "Do you have a theory on that too?" He turned to watch her reaction.

She took her time. She said at last, "I could make a dozen guesses, Mr. Wells, but none of them would have any value. Walt was a conservationist. . . ."

"Big word, ma'am. Like a good political speech, it covers everything, and touches nothing."

Tom Granger had said the same. In a subtle way, Tom Granger and this man were much alike, Ethel thought, both large, strong, direct, caring little what others thought; dangerous men to provoke. "What do you know of geothermal energy, Mr. Wells?"

Farley sat down. He smiled. "I've heard of it. I took a course in geology once." He had taken his college degree in geology, and then gone to law school.

"In Yellowstone," Ethel said, "the geysers demonstrate how close to the surface there is heat, energy that could be used."

Farley nodded. He said nothing.

"Over behind Los Alamos there is the crater of an extinct volcano, a huge one, and how much heat still lies beneath it, probably not too deep, nobody knows."

Another nod, mere acknowledgment.

"Here and there in this country there are hot springs. *Ojo caliente* is the local name."

"You've done your homework."

It was as if he had not spoken.

"In some places in the world," Ethel said, "underground heat, steam, has been tapped, brought to the surface, and used to drive generators for electrical power." She paused. "No smoke in the atmosphere. No possible radiation." She paused again. "You smile. Why?"

"You'd have made a fine Bible-banger, ma'am. A real rip-snorter. I do admire to see conviction at work."

"I don't enjoy being laughed at, Mr. Wells."

Farley inclined his head in a faint nod. "Admiration, not amusement. But if I offend, I apologize." He stood up again and looked at his watch. "Your tastes don't seem to run to pure whiskey, ma'am, and I can appreciate that. Each to his own." His voice was friendly. "There is a fine, quiet bar downstairs where I'm sure they'll provide whatever you do like. Will you join me in a drink?"

The man was maddening, Ethel thought. Somehow she had expected either cooperation or a blunt suggestion that she mind her own business. But as with Tom Granger, she had gotten exactly nothing but veiled male amusement. I have been playing in the minor leagues too long, she thought, dealing with little men like Sam Waldo. Maybe it is time I remembered how the good ones behave. "I'd be delighted," she said.

The bar was quiet and dimly lit. Farley led her to a small corner table, and seated her carefully.

"Let me guess." Farley hesitated as he sat down. "A martini? On the rocks? With a twist?"

Ethel smiled. "Your sophistication is showing. You are exactly right."

Farley ordered and leaned back in his chair. "What brings you to these parts, ma'am?"

"Ethel." She smiled at his nod of acknowledgment. Then, "A man I knew in Los Angeles talked a great deal about New Mexico, Santa Fe in particular. I came and I liked what I saw, so I stayed."

The drinks arrived. Farley raised his glass and studied it thoughtfully. He set the glass down. "Would that man's name be Walter Borden?"

Ethel nodded.

Farley thought about it again. "He disappeared. You looked for him. He turned up dead on the big ranch, shot." He paused. "I am sorry. I mean that."

"Thank you."

"Maybe you'd rather not talk about it."

Ethel hesitated.

"Or," Farley said, "maybe you'd like to talk about it. Sometimes when you bring things out into the sunlight they change color."

"A philosopher, Mr. Wells?"

"Farley, ma'am, please. And I'm strictly an amateur."

Ethel considered her drink in silence. "Walt and I," she said at last, "went to college together. UCLA.

POWER

We used to body surf down near Playa del Rey. Then some people built a jetty, and that changed the currents near shore and our beach was eroded until it was too steep for body surfing." She watched Farley steadily. "A little thing," she said, "but to us it was important."

"I can understand," Farley said.

"Do you know Owens Valley?" Ethel said.

Farley shook his head.

"It's in the Sierra Nevada, and I've seen pictures of it when it was a lovely little upland valley, green and lush and peaceful." Ethel paused. "But Los Angeles wanted water, and they had used up what had been beneath the city, so they built an aqueduct to Owens Valley." She paused again. "They sucked it dry. It is desert now." A third pause. "You called me a Bible-banger. Maybe I am. But I resent what selfish people do without even thinking of the effect they may have on others."

"And your friend Walter Borden felt the same?"

"Even more so. He didn't have to work. He could have done whatever he pleased without worrying about money. But he went into geology, and ecology, and tilted at windmills like Don Quixote, and really changed very little if anything. But he kept trying, and laughing at himself." Pause. "He called himself a sabre-tooth mouse." She was silent.

"Until somebody shot him," Farley said.

Ethel studied him quietly. She nodded. "Exactly," she said.

"And you blame the Grangers?"

Ethel shook her head. "I am a lawyer. I look at the evidence. Beyond the fact that he was found on the ranch, there is nothing to indicate that the ranch people had anything to do with it. There is no motive that I can see." Pause. "And what may have been the gun that killed him has been turned in to the Las Grutas DA by a nuclear scientist who is building a power plant on the ranch property—and that makes very little sense either."

"But," Farley said, "you do have ideas."

She was silent for a little time studying her drink,

turning the glass around and around in her slim fingers. She looked up at last. "I have lived here long enough," she said slowly, "to know that violence sometimes happens for no discernible cause, or what appears to be no discernible cause. A knifing on Saturday night. A traveling couple sleeping beside their car off the highway—shot dead. A girl from a commune caught and raped by five men." She shook her head. "There is no pattern. These things just—happen."

Farley watched her quietly.

"We associate violence with big cities," Ethel said. "And it is true—New York, Washington, even Albuquerque, leading the nation in crime rate. But the smaller places have their tensions too. Particularly here. Chicano, Anglo, Indian—those feuds have never been settled." She shook her head again, angrily this time. "I'm not really digressing. Walt could have been shot as a result of somebody's fury rising out of pure frustration, somebody lashing out at a lone Anglo maybe he had never even seen before."

"But," Farley said, "you don't believe it."

"I told you," Ethel said, "I look at the evidence. Or try. That rifle the physicist turned in. If it is the gun that killed Walt, then the senseless rage theory doesn't stand up. An expensive rifle like that doesn't fit the picture of a poor frustrated man striking back at the world that has held him down."

Beauty and brains, Farley thought; a rare combination. Much woman. "You think well."

"For a woman?" There was anger, plain to see.

Farley smiled. "I don't think of myself as a male chauvinist pig." His drawl was exaggerated. "I truly don't. It's been my experience, counselor, that for a woman to compete she has to be better than a man at the same job. It isn't fair, but fair doesn't have much to do with the way things are arranged." He paused. "Drink up." He smiled again at her faint frown. "Then," he said, "we'll go on to dinner and you can tell me more of what you think."

"Why?" She bristled still, but some of the resentment had faded.

"Because I'm interested, ma'am. Both in what you say, and in you." He paused. The smile spread. "As a woman. Now don't tell me you resent that, because I wouldn't believe it."

8

It was a brief ceremony, sparsely attended. Clinging to the old customs, Father Enrique spoke the words in Latin, while Tom, Will, Sue, Tish, Seth Porter, Clyde Burley, and the ranch people stood silently around the grave. The women among the ranch people wept.

It was both an end and a beginning, Tom thought, and it had all happened before. Over there was Tully's grave, and beside it that of Susan, his wife. Beyond the gaping hole into which they were now lowering what was left of the fierce old man named Matt were the headstones of his two wives, Martha, Tom's own grandmother, and Helen, Tish's mother. Each represented a quantum jump from familiarity to instant change. And who knew what would happen next?

They began filling in the grave, and that was that; end of chapter. Tom stood for a few moments in silence, conscious of the great mountains looking down, changeless. Then he thanked the padre and walked slowly with Tish and Seth Porter back to the house. Will and Sue followed as the ranch people drifted away.

Inside the house Tom hesitated. They all watched him as he considered the propriety of conducting a business discussion with the old man's grave not yet filled in; and found himself thinking how Matt would snort in derision if he were here to see the hesitation. "Boy, you do what has to be done. There is no point in putting it off." How often had that been said? Tom opened the office door. "Come on in," he said. "All four of you."

Tish shook her head. "I'm not part of the family."

"You are if I say so." Tom urged her through the doorway, and went around to take the chair behind the desk where he waited until Will closed the door. "Seth will explain the situation," Tom said.

Seth wore his easy smile. "There is very little to explain. With the exception of a number of relatively small bequests, Tom and Will inherit everything. Tom is named executor along with the Santa Fe bank and myself. In effect that puts Tom in charge." He paused. "If he wants to be, that is."

Will stirred in his chair. He wore his defensive smile. "Well?"

Tom looked around the room.

Seth, smiling still, sat placid, imperturbable.

Tish was looking at the floor. No mention of her in the will, Tom thought, and what did that mean? That Matt had assumed she would be taken care of? So be it.

He looked at Sue. She was watching him with a strange, intent expression as at a play when the curtain has just risen.

Will's smile had faded a little, but his eyes had not left Tom's face.

Tom thought of the priest speaking of the village, of Kelly Garcia and his comments, of Wayne Carter and rumors that flowed. He said at last, "For a time, anyway."

Will's smile was pure relief. "Nothing to it," he said. "Find a buyer and split the loot."

"Maybe," Tom said.

There was a short silence. Will said, "That means what?"

"Maybe we don't want to unload."

"Maybe you don't," Will said, "but I do. A feudal

estate in the mountains has no appeal for me. The place is an anachronism." He was holding himself under tight control. It was difficult. He wanted to look at Sue, and dared not. "We want to live our life," he said to Tom.

"You can. Just as you have."

"And you'd stay here?"

"About that I don't know. I haven't decided yet."

Will said, "Look. Let's be reasonable. I want out."

Tom sat silent, unmoving. They all watched him.

"All right," Will said in a changed voice, "tell me why."

Tom nodded. "I'll give you several reasons. The village. The people on the ranch. The power plant that's building." And, he thought, that visceral feeling that had been with him ever since he looked at the mountains and felt that he was home, but he doubted if Will would understand this.

Will surprised him. "And I suppose," he said, "there is some kind of place loyalty involved too. The only family homestead. The ancestral home. That kind of nonsense."

Tom nodded slowly. "Some of that too." How deep it went, he did not know, or what effect it might have on any decision, but in honesty it had to be considered.

Will took a deep breath and let it out slowly. When you came up against Tom in one of his stubborn moods, the name of the game was sheer frustration. It had always been so. As too with Matt. But all he could do was try. "I don't think we owe the village a thing," he said. "We've kept it alive. Maybe it's time it was allowed a decent death. There's no future for those people back here in the mountains. You know it, and I know it."

Tom was silent.

"The ranch people," Will said. "The faithful retainers." He shook his head. "The regime has changed. They couldn't expect it to go on the same way forever." He paused. "And what's this about a power plant? What do we owe them?"

"You want money," Tom said.

"Exactly right. My share." Despite himself, Will's voice was rising. "And if you think. . . ."

"Don't threaten me," Tom said. "You know better than that." His voice was quiet, even mild. "I'll make up my mind and I'll do what I think is best. And if that makes me a petty tyrant—" He shrugged. "Why, so be it." Why was it, he thought, that always he had had to dominate this brother of his, put him down? Why could he never find the words to accomplish the same end without inflicting pain? "I'm afraid that's how it is," he said. It was as close as he could come to apology.

Will looked at Seth Porter. "Suppose I sue for my share?"

"Why," Seth said, loose and easy, "you could try, son. There's nothing we lawyerfolk like better than a little litigation." His smile was avuncular. "But I wouldn't advise it, I surely wouldn't. I think you'd be wasting your time. And money."

Will looked again at Tom. "I've waited and waited," he said. "I lived out my purgatory as a kid here on this godforsaken ranch. You loved it. I hated it. Now you want to keep it up, play emperor the way Tully did, and Matt." He shook his head. "I said it. I want out." He paused. "And I'll find a way."

Nothing changed in Tom's face. "Have you had your say?"

Will nodded shortly.

"So I'll stay on for a while at least," Tom said. "And I'll do what I think best." He looked around at them all. "Any further questions?"

When Will and Sue had walked out and closed the door, Tom looked at Seth Porter. "Comments?" he said.

Seth was smiling still. "As a horseback opinion," he said, "I'd say that they'll be coming at you from all sides, son." He paused. "The way they always have at anybody sitting behind that desk."

Tom thought of what old Matt had said about the Grangers being the biggest men in the bar, target for anyone who craved trouble. "Kelly Garcia," he said, "says there is a bill in the legislature authorizing the state to buy the ranch. Do you know about that?"

"Sam Waldo's bill," Seth said, as if that explained all.

"Did he think it up?"

Seth's smile reappeared. "He says he did. But I'm not sure I'd believe Sam if he told me the time of day. More likely somebody thought up the idea and fed it to Sam in little pieces he could understand, possibly well-buttered little pieces. Sam has an appetite."

It matched Kelly Garcia's estimate, Tom thought. "What could be behind it?"

"Any number of thoughts, some innocent, some not."

Tish said suddenly, "You don't want me any more, do you?" She got up from her chair, and stood for a few moments, looking at Tom in silence. She said at last, "I'm glad you're staying for a little while, anyway." She was close to tears. "It isn't going to last, is it?" And then, quickly, "I know it isn't." She hurried to the door and went out. The door closed softly.

"In my experience," Seth said, "problems come in batches. Maybe litters is a better word. Like hound puppies."

Tom was staring at the closed door. Grace's phone call still rankled. I don't understand womanese, he thought. "She says," he said, "that Matt never adopted her." No question, but it demanded an answer. He looked at Seth.

"I suggested it to him," Seth said. "Once. You didn't make suggestions to Matt more than once. He said he'd think about it. Probably it slipped his mind." He was silent for a little time. "What could be behind Sam Waldo's bill," he said presently, dismissing Tish, "is an honest effort to put the state in a position to bid on the property if you decide to put it up for sale; so keep it as recreational area and out of the hands of developers. That could be it."

"But you don't think so."

"If it were my idea," Seth said, "and that was what I honestly wanted, Sam Waldo is the last man who would come to mind as sponsor. He carries weight. He knows where a lot of skeletons are hidden. He does favors and makes friends in his redneck way, and a lot of people are obligated to him. But when he pushes something, there is almost always something in it for Sam Waldo, and I don't see honest conservationists contributing to Sam's private pension fund just to get him as a front man."

"Then what is your guess?"

"Guess is what it is, son. I've got one of our bright young boys nosing around, but until he comes up with the scent I'm purely shooting from the hip at shadows." He paused. He said finally, "I'd say that it's *against* something rather than *for* it. It isn't usual to try to get the state to buy property; most times it's the other way around: an attempt to get the state or the government to turn something loose—mineral rights, timber rights, water rights, or just plain land for development."

Tom said slowly, thoughtfully, "The only thing we're doing that we haven't been doing all along is building that reactor over in Long Valley." He looked steadily at Seth.

"My thoughts had been running the same way, son." Seth stood up, walked slowly around the room and came to stand in front of the gun case. "Quite an arsenal," he said and turned to face Tom again. "A new kind of reactor," he said. "Breeder-type. Experimental. As I understand it, it generates fuel instead of just using it up." He walked back to his chair and sat down. "Pretty wild thinking," he said.

Tom sat quiet in his chair. "I'm listening."

Seth took his time. "Suppose," he said at last, "this new breeder reactor is successful, real successful, just what the doctor ordered to produce power until we finally get around to taking our energy from the sun, which is what the bright boys like Wayne Carter say we're going to have to come to eventually."

Tom thought about it. "Say it's successful. What then? One power plant."

Seth said slowly, "What about a gaggle of them, a whole atomic TVA up in these mountains, generating power for the entire Southwest? Sounds like science fiction? But the things they're doing today up on the Hill at Los Alamos sounded like science fiction only a few years back. That meson facility for cancer research, for example." He paused. "But power generation isn't the end of it, if you listen to young Wayne Carter." He got out of his chair again and walked slowly back and forth as if before a jury box. "His ideas are pretty hard to resist. That's part of what sold Matt."

"I'm listening."

Seth took his time. Then he sat down again. "In a reactor," he said, "you've got heat to get rid of."

One of Carter's three points of potential trouble. Tom nodded.

"Suppose you pipe that heat into the ground?" Seth said. "A network of buried heated waterpipes? What happens?"

Tom was beginning to see it now, a possibility he had not even considered before. "You raise the ground temperature," he said.

"Exactly." Seth was smiling as at a bright young pupil. "And when snow falls, it melts, and instead of ten-foot drifts, you have moist growing land, with plenty of sunlight like we get all winter." He paused. "And you've turned Long Valley and maybe adjacent areas too into year-round agricultural land instead of land that's only good to graze one cow to every so many acres because the summer growing season is too short. Ponder on it, son."

Tom did. It opened all manner of vistas. Waste reactor heat that had to be disposed of somehow, why not benefit from it?

"Some places," Seth said, "where they need electric power *and* more fresh water and have ample salt water handy—Israel comes to mind—they can use the excess heat for desalinization. Here the agricultural possibility comes up instead." He paused. Smiling no longer, "But what chance would there be for the AEC or anybody else to set up a number of atomic generators *and* develop fertile ground on land the state had bought and devoted to recreation?" He paused again. "I'm a suspicious fellow by nature, son. I'm guessing that Sam Waldo's bill is a pressure move—and I'm guessing that the pressure has just begun."

In a way, Tish guessed, she was somehow kin to the wild creatures who roamed the mountains, because her instinct when she was hurt or troubled or frightened, as now, was to seek solitude rather than solace.

One of the ranch jeeps was handy. She drove it away from the big house, deeper into the immensity of the ranch.

For a time the dirt road led through piñon and juniper in near symbiosis, chamisa, sparse grama grass, cholla, and occasional clumps of prickly pear in chartreuse bloom. Then, climbing, the road entered the ponderosa forest, and suddenly the scent of the big pines was all around her.

She pulled the jeep off the road, switched off the engine, and got out. In the shelter of the trees there was an almost cathedral hush. She began to walk. On the carpet of needles her squaw boots made almost no sound.

A Steller's jay scolded her. A nuthatch, trudging head-first down a nearby tree, paused to study her and decided that she was harmless. A mountain chickadee swung upside down from a small branch and talked in his squeaky voice.

She came to a small stream and paused to admire a clump of tiny pinkish violets. Further on Indian paintbrush caught her eye.

She was alone in familiarity, strangely soothed.

But it would not last. There was the recurrent, devastating thought. She had lived the larger part of her life in these mountains and meadows, mesas and valleys, and she wanted no other. Now she blamed herself that she had failed to understand that the vast ranch actually was, as Will had said, an anachronism, as out of tune with reality as the feudal states she had once loved to read about, a dream world about to awaken.

As long as Matt had lived—even in old age unfearing, unconquerable, keeping her world intact—she had seen no reason to question her own place in the scheme of things. Only once had Matt urged her to leave.

"Honey," he had said, "this is the hell of a place for a young female. And I don't think Santa Fe's much better. You know Denver. Go on up there. Take an apartment, get a job, meet some people your own age. What is it they say? Live it up a little."

"I like it here."

"And I like nothing better than having you here. You bring light into a dark house. But, goddamnit, I may be a selfish old man, but I'm not so selfish that I'll spoil your life just to make mine happy. I'm not that much of a bastard. How do you want to go. Fly? Drive? And when? How about tomorrow?"

And so she had gone to Denver, because when Matt made up his mind something moved. And from the beginning she had hated it.

There was nothing wrong with Denver. When she had been at college at nearby Boulder, Denver had been fun, the entire area had been fun. There were shows to see and music to hear; good food, skiing, walking, picnicking, camping, tennis, swimming—all the benefits of a good-sized city combined with the country she loved. Then where was the difference now?

The difference, face it, was being on her own, no longer in a sense protected by the fact of college; competitive, as some would say, although she had always disliked the jargon of the psychology lab.

Living in the city, she was lonely and homesick for her solitude, her long quiet walks and glimpses of life even more shy and retiring than herself: the flitting shadow in the forest that could be a deer, a scuttling badger, a marten scarcely seen, otters at play, a single soaring eagle, a mother bear with her cubs. . . .

She met people her own age in Denver, bright, brushed-up, interesting people, but their interests were not hers. They had projects, schemes, ideas about business and commerce, investments, speculations, knowledge about the stock market and land values and whether the Olympics were actually going to come to Denver. They were a bustling part of a bustling scene:

with it, involved, above all, busy. They were not for her.

Oh, she could fit in when she chose. And at times, for brief periods, she could even enjoy herself. But always there was the nostalgia for the peace and, yes, the protection of the vast ranch. And after six months she had gone back.

"I tried, Matt. There's something lacking in me."

"There's not a goddamn thing lacking in you, honey. If I were fifty years younger, I'd show you, I sure as hell would."

"Please, Matt, let me stay here."

They were in the big office. The old man got out of his chair and took a turn around the room. Then he sat down again. "Honey," he said, his voice unnaturally gentle, "you can stay here until Hell freezes over. You know that. This is your home, and if this is where you want to be, then this is where you stay. It's just that I purely hate to see anyone as good as you go to waste." He reached for the tantalus, opened it, and poured himself a jigger of whiskey. He sipped appreciatively. "Well, hell," he said at last, smiling now, "it'll work out, honey. Some day a young buck will ride in and take one look at you and that'll be it. The son of a bitch won't be good enough for you. There's only one man who is, and he's fifty years too old. But this new one, whoever he is. . . ." The old man stopped. "Now what in the world did I say to make you cry?"

The trouble was, of course, that she was Tish Wilson, sometimes erroneously called Tish Granger; and only she herself knew what an insufficient being she was and had always been: insecure, constantly wary, knowing full well that in any kind of crisis she would be found wanting right out in front of God and everybody. Maybe that was why she preferred the shelter of the forest to the unprotected plain. And how silly could you be?

She had never discussed any of this with anyone. She had been twelve years old when her mother died, and there had been only Matt, Tom, and Will, small comfort, left surrounding her. Oh, there were the ranch women, Consuelo, Dolores, Lupita, Luisa, Maria Victoria, and they were dears, but their world was the world of the village of Las Grutas not of the ranch office or of Santa Fe, Denver, San Francisco, Omaha, New York, places the Grangers knew and where they were known. And the children of the ranch people viewed her, as they viewed all Grangers, with a kind of unshakable awe, a barrier through which one could not pass.

When she was little, she had invented a sister, a twin, and at night alone in bed she had made up stories in which the two of them faced problems, even dangers, and together emerged triumphant. Together: there was the heart and core of the matter. And together was only in make-believe. In reality she was and always had been alone.

She came to a large fallen tree and hoisted herself up to sit on its rough bark. The trick was to blend into the landscape, by total immobility to remove yourself as a threat to any creature, however small or shy. She breathed slowly, silently, and waited.

A Canada jay came first, camp-robber, whiskey-jack, call him what you would, he wore his jaunty gray costume with arrogance. He landed almost at Tish's feet and studied her with an impish eye. "No food?" he seemed to be saying. "But people always have something?"

Tish made no move, no sound. The jay hesitated and then flew off, screaming *Foul!*

Movement stirred in her peripheral vision. Tish turned her head with infinite slowness. A small woods mouse stood on his hind legs, studying her, and as she watched he raised both forepaws and daintily cleaned his whiskers, his dark eyes never stirring from her presence. Satisfied at last, he dropped to all fours and went on about his business, digging here, poking there, suddenly disappearing as if by legerdemain.

There was a snuffling sound and a black and white

skunk trundled on, a small beast without fear. Tish watched him almost with envy.

How long she sat on the fallen tree she had no idea. She saw three deer and a single elk, a bobcat silent as the night, two more mice, and a red fox.

When she let herself down to the ground again and stretched as high and as wide as she could to eliminate the stiffness, she felt strangely purged, cleansed, refreshed. She walked back to the jeep. Maybe things *would* remain the same, with Tom instead of the old man sitting behind the big desk holding her world together. Maybe.

Nonsense.

She could have wept.

9

The northwestern half of the ranch lay in Jicarilla County, the northernmost and most mountainous county in the state. Here the great peaks reached almost to the sky, and on their upper slopes lay the areas of Alpine tundra, where tiny hardy plants defied wind and temperature extremes—dwarf blue forget-me-nots, greenish-to-crimson sorrel, white pussytoes, yellow meadow cinquefoil clinging to rock and what soil there was in this backbone of the land.

"Country fit only for picas, marmots, and mountain goats," old Matt had often said, "but, by God, you look up there and you see what the man meant when he said, 'I lift up mine eyes unto the hills,' or whatever it was." You tended to forget that when he chose, old Matt could quote the Bible or Shakespeare by the yard. There were depths.

POWER

Dos Piedras, the county seat, lay in an upland valley long since denuded of timber for building material and firewood. Buck-and-rail fences straggled across open ground, but there were few cattle and only an occasional field under cultivation. For as long as Tom could remember it had been so.

"We endure," his friend Tito Abeyta had told him once. "What the hell else can we do? It's an Anglo world, your world, and we don't fit in it. There's no way out."

"You got out," Tom had said.

"I got to college, if that's what you mean, because I was big and strong and good at knocking people down on a football field." He patted his right knee. "But after this, no longer good enough for the pros, so here I am, back again."

"You could have stayed away. Albuquerque, Santa Fe, even Denver."

"You miss the point. Out there I don't fit except on a football field. I'm a part-chicano, part-Indian freak. Back here I'm the one-eyed man in the land of the blind, King Tito among his own."

Tito wore the Sheriff's star now, a .357 magnum on his hip, and a battered and sweatstained hat pushed back on his black hair. "You came back too," he said. "To stay?"

Always the same question, Tom thought, and wondered if he would ever find the answer. "For a while," he said.

"It always figured," Tito said, "that you'd take over after Matt. You're the same kind of son of a bitch." The words were without insult. Pause. "What can I do for you?"

And there, of course, was the stickler. Because I don't know what I'm after, Tom thought, and found the position ridiculous. "What's the feeling in Jicarilla County?" he said.

"About what? Watergate? Most of my *primos* never heard of it." Tito was grinning. "You can do better than that, boy. How do we feel about what?" He paused and the amusement disappeared. "About Rancho del Norte? You? That atomic power plant? A dead man in a meadow? Is that it?" It was. He knew it. He leaned back in his chair and scowled at the ceiling. Then he looked again at Tom. "Uptight? Why? You don't scare worth a damn, or you never did."

Tom took his time. "I like to see what I'm up against," he said at last. "And this time I can't find it." He was silent for a few moments. Then, "A couple of things that don't add up." He told Tito about the rifle that had been found at the generator site. "That, for one," he said.

Tito got out of his chair and prowled the office, a big man, tall, solid, moving easily despite the weak knee. He plumped down in the desk chair again. "Did Pepe Martinez, that prick, tell you about their burglary? No? Last fall it was. A pro job. No chicano punks that time. They just about wiped out Wendall's."

The sporting goods store in Las Grutas; rifles, shotguns, fishing tackle, skis, snowshoes, camping gear. . . . "So," Tom said, and waited.

"And you've had your own problems on the ranch," Tito said. "No skin off my ass because it all happened in Las Grutas County near as we can tell."

Tom said quietly, "What kind of problem?"

"Rustling. Good old-fashioned rustling. With big semi cattle trucks that can be two hundred miles away by daylight. Beef prices what they are." Tito shrugged. "Clyde Burley hasn't mentioned it to you?"

Tom shook his head in silence.

"Well," Tito said, "it's not the kind of thing a man likes to boast about." He shook his head. "What I don't like is the feel of it. It's big-city professional stuff, and what we're used to here is a knifing every now and again, or somebody gets out his deer rifle because somebody else is making passes at his wife, or Saturday-night drunks, that kind of thing. Not professional heists like the Wendall's job. Not twenty-thousand-dollar semitrailer vans making a planned hit-and-run. What it amounts to," he said, and his smile was not happy, "is that you goddamn Anglos are bringing the efficient ass-end of your culture back into our mountains, and we don't like it." He paused. "You asked me what I thought, felt." He spread his hands.

Tom was silent, thoughtful. He said at last, "I don't much blame you."

"Look," Tito said and leaned forward, hands spread in emphatic gesture, "there's more. It's different, but in a way it's all part of the same thing. Hippies, Yippies, flower children, call them whatever the hell you want. They set up a commune. They work. I'll give them that. But what they don't see, or just plain don't give a shit about, is that the life-style they're so proud of, free and easy, live it up, love everybody and do your thing, that kind of living is just plain insult to—okay, my people. We believe in the Church, in the family, in hard work, and in women who run the home, raise the kids, cook the meals—and behave themselves." He paused. "Do I sound like a Christer?"

A big hard man filled with smoldering anger, Tom thought; a man exposed to two cultures, not entirely at home in either; a man bewildered. "Go on," he said.

"A pickup truck comes into town," Tito said. "There're two, three guys with beards and long hair, black hats, and dark glasses, trying to look like God only knows what. But there are a couple of women too, and they're barefoot and wearing the tightest, shortest cut-off blue jeans you ever saw, wearing bandanas, for Christ's sake, nothing more, tied more or less over their tits, and they wiggle and waggle when they walk. Beautiful people. And you know what?"

I could guess, Tom thought, but I won't. "Tell me."

"The pickup truck gets stopped someplace out in the hills. The guys with the black hats and beards find out they aren't supermen after all. And the chicks get raped, gangbanged. And I have to round up the randy macho punks who did it, and they look at me and say, 'What the fuck, they asked for it, didn't they?' "

The priest had said almost the same thing, Tom

thought, using different words and different examples. They're fighting a rearguard action against encroachment—and losing. What was there to say?

"In the East, the Middle West," Tito said, "it's different. Or out on the Coast, where they come in from Asia. People come to this country and want to learn the language, the culture, they want to fit in, that's why they came. But we're different, Indian, chicano: we were *here,* and you people ran all over us, and we don't want to fit into your culture and we'd rather speak our own language and worship our own gods, or God." He paused. "The only thing is, we can't do either because we live in your world." He paused again. "But we don't have to like it." A third pause. "Does that answer your question?"

Tom drove slowly back to the nearest ranch entrance and rattled in over the cattleguard. He passed a meadow where a dozen head of cattle grazed. Angus and Charolais mix, a relatively new hybrid breed, old Matt's doing. Tom had lived long enough in cities to know how city people thought about farmers and ranchers: they saw them as conservative to a fault, resisting any change. The hell they were, and there was proof.

Down on the King Ranch they had developed the Santa Gertrudis breed of cattle, big, hardy, more meat to the pound of animal. Look at the breed of turkeys developed in Beltsville; time was when turkeys were all legs and wings and you had to buy an eighteen-pound bird to get any eating at all. Now those plump, succulent little eight- and nine-pounders were the delight of many a housewife.

No, in the ranching or farming business if you wanted to be successful, you experimented; you tried new things and took chances that would curl the hair of a city-dweller working at a steady job.

And so, really, it was all a matter of viewpoint— just as it was with Tito Abeyta, Pepe Martinez, Father Enrique, yes, and Will too. Different people looked at the same facts from different angles.

And what did all that fancy thinking prove? Exactly nothing. Friend, he told himself, philosophy is not for you.

Clyde Burley now; there was something he could get his teeth into.

Burley was in his office, which was a combination tack room, lounge, and closed-circuit-TV-center. He listened quietly while Tom told what Tito Abeyta had said of rustling. He nodded. "We lost altogether about fifty head. Good stock."

"Fifteen, twenty thousand dollars' worth of beef," Tom said.

Burley nodded in silence.

"Any ideas?"

Burley shook his head. "But if you want to blame me—"

"Get the chip off your shoulder." Tom turned and walked away. Outside, I'm still looking for a fight, he thought, and wondered why.

"Because you don't want to be out here in the first place, luv. Simple as that." Sue's voice behind him.

Had he spoken aloud? Turning, he made himself smile. "Does it show?"

"You get used to the fleshpots, so I'm told," Sue said, "and the healthy outdoor life loses some of its charm." She was smiling as she tucked her arm through Tom's. "Take me for a walk."

"Where's Will?"

"Sulking." Smiling still. "Better yet, take me for a drive. Show me some of this feudal domain. I think you could use a little relaxation."

Tom hesitated. Slowly he nodded. Why not? Why the hell not? "Let's go," he said.

They left the ranch over a rail cattleguard. The road climbed in wide swinging curves, following the contours of the great mountain. They passed an abandoned mine, crossed a dry ravine, and Tom stopped to shift down into four-wheel drive and low transmission. "Hang on," he said, and turned off the road onto a dirt track. They began to climb more steeply.

They were above timberline now, and the high clear

air was chill. A single bird floated effortlessly on wide wings, white head and tail plain against the sky. "Bald eagle," Tom said. "Mature. It takes three years for them to look like that. If they live that long."

There was something in his tone, Sue thought, and pressed the question: "Why wouldn't they live?"

"You give some men a gun and there's no telling what they'll shoot."

Sue thought of the trophy heads on the office wall. "Do you hunt?"

"I used to."

"No longer?"

"Nothing noble. I lost my taste for it."

They bumped along in silence for a time, following scarcely visible tracks in the dirt and bare rock. Ahead as far as they could see more mountains rose in tumbled mass, and Sue thought again of the intimacy of the Alps as compared to this vastness. Involuntarily she shivered.

"Cold?" Tom said. He slowed the jeep, stopped. "We'll go back down."

"No." He was sweet, this big man; considerate. "I want to go on wherever you want to go." She was frightened, somehow—more than she cared to show. "I enjoy it."

Tom smiled and put the jeep in gear. They bumped off more slowly than before.

Sue said, "Are you still looking for a fight?"

"Are you baiting me?" He knew little of this girl, his brother's wife. He knew little of women, he thought, period.

Sue had watched Tom put her husband down almost without effort. It was a scene she would not forget. "That's part of the game," she said. Automatic coquetry. "We can't compete on even terms so we pick our tactics." She paused, and a smile appeared. "And our times and places." She was not sure exactly what she had in mind, but it was an exciting game to play, and she could not resist.

POWER

They topped a last steep rise and Tom braked the jeep to a halt. Northward the mountains stretched endlessly. To the south the land flattened to mesas and then rose sharply again into the bulk of Sandia. On the horizon to the southwest a single peak rose plain in the sun. "Mount Taylor," Tom said. "It's a hundred and twenty-five miles away." He pointed to the ribbon of brownish haze that ran curving in the middle foreground. He was thinking of the charter pilot. "And that is our smog," he said, "coming from coal-fired power plants two hundred miles away."

"Fascinating." Sue's voice and smile mocked him. "Not the mountain or the smog," she said. "You. Your enthusiasm. Why are men always looking at distant things?"

"Instead of at you?"

Her smile now was secret. "Since you mention it— yes. Am I worth looking at?"

"You are."

"But I don't think you ever noticed before."

"Wrong. At the wedding I took one look and wondered how in the world Will had managed to catch you."

"That's nice." Sue paused. "Maybe I wanted him to catch me."

"I hope so."

"But maybe," she said slowly, "if I'd seen you first, it would have been different."

"That is nonsense, and you know it." His tone was sharp.

Sue shook her head gently. "You're the original. He's the not very good carbon copy. It doesn't take long to see that."

"What I ought to do," Tom said, "is put you over my knee and paddle your bottom."

She had a feeling of exhilaration, of flirting with danger. "If that's your idea of fun, I'll go along." Her smile spread. "My bare bottom, of course. I'm told it's rather shapely."

Tom turned in the seat, caught her shoulders in his hands and shook her. She offered no resistance. "You're

89

my brother's wife," he said. His voice was low-pitched, angry. "We'll both remember that. Is that clear?"

Sue was smiling, the female triumphant. She took her time. "We'll see," she said at last. "We'll just have to see."

10

Will Granger drove into Las Grutas, where Kelly Garcia waited in the newspaper office. "Long time," Kelly said, "no see." He stood up, shook hands briefly and sat down again to wait in silence.

"Nothing special on my mind," Will said, a statement only partially true: what was on his mind was special, but he did not know how to go about resolving it. "How're things?"

"As usual," Kelly smiled, and continued to wait.

"You've been here how long?" Will said. "Five years?"

"Closer to ten."

"And if anybody knows what's going on," Will said, "you do."

"What kind of goings on?"

Will fidgeted in his chair. He disliked what amounted to demeaning himself before this newspaper bum, but there was no other choice. "Is the ranch for sale?"

Kelly's eyebrows rose. In his mind he walked carefully around the question examining it for booby-traps, and found none. Still. "What does Tom say?" he said.

Will held his temper in check. "Tom," he said, "wouldn't tell me a thing, even if I asked him. He's the *patrón,* and he loves it." He paused. "Is it for sale?"

Kelly studied on the matter. He had no desire to say anything Tom Granger would disapprove of. On the other hand, Sam Waldo's legislative bill was open knowledge. "There's some," he said, "who apparently think it is. Or will be." He explained about the bill.

"Sam Waldo," Will said, and committed the name to memory.

Kelly hesitated. Then, "If you want to talk to somebody," he said, "don't make it Sam Waldo." Kelly had been busy on the telephone to Santa Fe. "There's a dude up from Houston, name of Wells, Farley Wells, and the word is that he knows more about that bill than Sam does—even though Sam drew it up and presented it. . . ."

Except for guests, people in the ranchhouse breakfasted early. It had always been so. Seth Porter was there on this morning, already thinking about the streams; Tish by habit; Tom.

Over bacon and eggs, "I'd like a guide," Tom said. He looked at Tish. "Are you available?"

"You know every inch of the whole ranch."

"But I want to see exactly where that body was found." Tom paused. "And I want to see where fence was cut and cattle driven through to rustling trucks." He saw the change in Tish's eyes. "And I want to see that reactor site." He paused again. "And anything else that's new since I was here last, including a commune in Jicarilla County—you know it?"

Seth Porter watching, listening, smiled his placid smile and thought his own thoughts.

"Of course," Tish said. "You're the *jefe.*" She pushed back her chair and stood up. "I'll see to house chores and be right with you." She was gone.

Seth Porter drank his coffee. His face was expressionless.

"All right," Tom said, "whatever it is, say it."

"Nothing on my mind, son, except what kind of fly

I'm going to try in that big pool. I purely resent having a trout that large laughing at me."

Tom took his time. "You had a phone call last night."

Seth smiled. "Son, don't tell me this whole house is bugged." He had another sip of coffee. "Incomplete information," he said, "so there was no real point in telling you about it. But Sam Waldo has a kind of sponsor, an oil lawyer from Texas name of Farley Wells, and he's in Santa Fe." Seth paused. "As a matter of fact, Wells was squiring Ethel Wilding around last evening. Dinner and some after-dinner listening to piano music over in the Palace." He finished his coffee, set the cup down, and wiped his lips with his napkin. "But like I said, information that doesn't mean much of anything. Yet."

Tom thought about it. "Your idea of pressure still holds?"

"Son, if it's pressure," Seth said, "then this is just the start. I know of Farley Wells, and he's not a boy they send out on a man's errand." He pushed back his chair and stood up smiling. *"Permiso?"* he said.

Tom smiled up at the placid face. "Good fishing."

He sat on over a cup of coffee laced with fresh ranch cream. It had not occurred to him before, but it was probably Tish's doing that his old silver napkin ring with the grizzly bear standing on it had been taken out of heaven only knew which cupboard, polished until it gleamed, and then with white napkin neatly rolled placed at the head of the great table—and he had automatically seated himself where it was. He looked around the room smiling.

The table would seat twenty without crowding. The ceiling of the room was beamed with great timbers cut and sawed here on the ranch, rack-dried and finished out by imported adzemen. The floors were of brick, polished by four generations of boots and patient scrubbing. The heavy wrought-iron wall sconces, originally holding oil lamps, had long since been electrified, but their past-century appearance was intact.

Things well built and carefully, even lovingly tended

endured, he thought, and for the first time understood some of old Matt's fierce possessiveness and pride in this empire that had come to him.

He finished his coffee, carefully folded and rolled his napkin and tucked it into the grizzly bear ring. Funny, he didn't even remember where that ring had come from; it had always been at his place at the table and he had accepted it without question.

On impulse he pulled out the napkin and studied the inside of the ring. There it was, faint as could be: Matt. His grandfather's childhood ring, given to him— why? There were, he decided, a great many things he was seeing for the first time; and failing to understand.

Sue walked in, Will behind her. Sue was in jodhpurs and a short-sleeved cream-colored silk shirt. Will wore loafers and odd trousers and carried a light jacket. They said their good mornings.

There was strain between himself and Will, of course, Tom thought, but it had not erupted into any kind of open antagonism, and he wanted to keep it that way. "It doesn't look as if you two are going in the same direction," he said. His tone was friendly.

"Lover," Sue said, "is driving to Santa Fe on a mysterious errand. I'm not all that fond of Santa Fe, so I'm going riding." She paused. "If there is a flat saddle in the tack room." She smiled. "And if you would like to ride with me—"

"Sorry." Once alone with her was enough. "Clyde will have a hand ride with you."

Tish came in, soundless on squaw-booted feet.

Sue said immediately, "I'll have fruit juice, tea, and toast." For a moment the words hung in the air, deliberate put-down.

Tom said, "Consuelo's coming. She'll take care of you. Ready, Tish?" He smiled at them all.

Will said, "Anything you want in Santa Fe?" His voice was careful.

Tom thought about it. Slowly he shook his head. There was something strained in Will's manner, something sly and a trifle furtive. But it could wait. "I'll be going down myself in a day or two," he said. "Just stay out of trouble." He held the door for Tish, followed her into the great hall and out to the waiting jeep. There, "You drive," Tom said. "I'll be back in a moment." He trotted into the house.

When he returned, he carried a 30-30 carbine, which he set upside down in the rack across the rear window. Tish watched him in silence as he tossed a belt cartridge holder with twelve cartridges into the open glove compartment and then stepped into the seat. "Don't ask me why," he said, "because I don't know." He was smiling in half-apology.

Tish's face was expressionless as she put the jeep into gear and drove off.

There were those, Will knew, who raved about the grandeur and the beauty of this drive to Santa Fe, and he would have to admit that from a purely scenic point of view, it was spectacular. But he was unable to disassociate mountains from memories, and for him the beauty was forever spoiled.

He and Tom were brothers. They looked very much alike. They had shared the same experiences of ranch life and Eastern schools, and by Behaviorist dogma, as Will understood it, they ought to have been very similar specimens. But they did not even play in the same league, and never had.

Will had grown up in Tom's shadow, admiring and despising, in a sense of loving and hating, and never understanding his older brother.

Tom could and would shield Will from Matt's wrath, but Will doubted that it was out of affection, rather, he thought, it was out of a perverse desire to defy the old man as a matter of principle. Still it was handy to know that his brother would shoulder the blame for almost anything he chose to do. On the other hand, Tom had neither compunction nor hesitation about settling matters between themselves.

Tish growing up was a temptation. Tom intervened. "Leave her alone," he told Will. "I won't tell you again." The temptation remained, but it was overshadowed by fear, and Will thereafter kept his physical distance.

Will needed people. Tom did not. Tom cherished his solitude. As a boy he had disappeared for days on end with sheath knife, blanket roll, fry pan, salt, and fishing rod; and when he returned, grimy and in the later boyhood years whiskery as well, usually wet through from the latest thunderstorm, there was yet a quality of peace in his eyes and a smiling calmness in his manner that spoke louder than words of some kind of communion Will did not even begin to comprehend.

Old Matt understood, although all he ever said was, "Good fishing, boy?"

"Yes, sir. Good enough."

Maybe, but not always. Times Will remembered when after one of those expeditions Tom could not put away enough food at dinner, and although no word was spoken about it, it was understood that he had been on starvation rations for days. And loving it. There was the incomprehensible part.

There were books in the library of the big house, and in these Will could take refuge. He could have drawn or painted too, if he had liked, but he found himself unable to bear old Matt's obvious scorn. Reading, however, was something else again. In later years Will was to realize that Matt himself, although he rarely paraded his knowledge, was something of an authority on American history in general and Southwestern history in particular, and the mail brought in from Las Grutas frequently contained letters from Austin, Albuquerque, Tucson, or Berkeley on the stationery of the Universities of Texas or New Mexico, Arizona or California, a running correspondence maintained with professional historians. But Matt was more interested in making history than in writing about it.

There were other books than histories. There were the classic novels, ranging from Dickens and Trollope through Kipling and Stevenson and into Hemingway and Faulkner, Dos Passos and Steinbeck, and these Will devoured, imagining himself in the leading roles, and could for a time shut out what to him was the impossible humdrum of ranch life.

Again, not Tom. Tom read—even, Will had to admit, for pleasure—but he also fitted into the ranch life as a foot fitted into an old boot, and where Will wished that the Eastern school term would not end, Tom could not wait to get back to these thrice-damned mountains and into jeans and boots and on the back of a horse, even if it meant nothing more interesting than riding fence.

How did you figure a man like that? A brother?

Will topped the rise at Tano Road, and the city was spread secretly beneath him, parts of it hidden behind hills or in arroyos, its low buildings hugging the earth, seeming to blend into the vegetation. On the horizon the bulk of Sandía pushed against the sky; closer, the Ortiz mountains rose in jagged array, blues and purples mingled.

He drove into town, parked in the municipal lot, and walked the two blocks to La Fonda. He saw no one he recognized. On the house phone, "Will Granger here. If you have a few minutes, I'd like to talk to you."

There was no hesitation, not the faintest pause while the coin of recognition dropped. "Delighted," Farley Wells said. "Come up. We can talk here."

Riding up in the ancient elevator, Will wondered exactly what he was going to say and, as far as that went, what it was he actually had in mind. Sooner or later, confrontation with Tom? Well, if that was what had to be, so be it, but Will would rather have someone else leading the charge. Maybe Farley Wells. Comforting thought.

Farley Wells was in shirtsleeves, the cuffs turned back on his thick wrists. He shook hands in a strangely gentle manner, as if he knew his strength and understood the necessity of keeping it under control. "Good to see you again," he said. And when they were seated, "And how is the little lady?"

"Sue is fine." Sue would always be fine. "What I

came for—" Will began and wondered how to continue. He was used to making his wants known and having his whims catered to, but it occurred to him that he was now engaged in a very different kind of negotiation, one that required finesse he was suddenly unsure that he possessed. "The ranch," he said, and hesitated. "I understand there is a bill in the legislature, authorizing the state to buy the ranch."

Nothing changed in Farley's face, but his eyes turned expressionless, the eyes of a gambler in a high-stakes game. "So I have heard," he said.

"A man named Waldo," Will said. "Sam Waldo, I believe."

Farley nodded in silence.

"And I have also heard," Will said, "that you know more about the bill than he does."

The room was suddenly still. Farley said gently, "Now I wonder where in the world you heard that."

"From a newspaperman." Had he said something wrong? The tension in the room was palpable. Why?

"Newspapermen get funny ideas," Farley said. He paused and studied Will carefully. His voice was still gentle. "You don't like the idea of the bill. Is that it?"

Here at least Will felt on safe ground. "I think it's great. I'm all in favor of it."

There was a long pause. Farley said at last, "Do you mind telling me why?"

"Why," Will said, "I want the damn ranch sold. To somebody, and I don't care who, the state, the atomic people, anybody." His tone said that his reason ought to be perfectly clear.

A trace of a smile appeared and lifted the corners of Farley's mouth. He stood up. "I've never believed," he said, "that the time of day had anything to do with whether a man took a drink or not. And I have some bourbon I'm right proud of. Maybe you'd care to sample it?"

The tension was gone from the room, friendliness replacing menace. The sense of relief Will felt was strong. "I'd be delighted," he said.

POWER

The road they had taken from the ranchhouse rose steeply in a wide swinging curve. At the top, "Stop here a moment," Tom said, and stepped out of the jeep to look down at the scattered ranch buildings. Tish shut off the engine and came to stand beside him.

The buildings represented no single kind of architecture, nor were they placed in any pattern of symmetry. As the ranch had grown and new sheltered space was required, new buildings had been put up, however and wherever it was handy. It was as simple as that.

There was the isolated main house, a mass of stone. There the enormous wooden barn, neatly painted, with its hay storage, its milking stalls, its separated stalls, each covered by closed-circuit TV where the blooded cows were brought to calve; Clyde Burley's office and breeding files were there; the now neglected breeding pens were adjacent. Over yonder was the smithy where Tom had spent countless hours turning the blower crank at the forge, watching the coals turn red and then white, watching the economical moves of the farrier as he heated, shaped, cooled, and then fitted horseshoes to the ranch's riding stock.

"Look familiar?" Tish said.

As the palm of his hand, Tom thought; although if he had been asked to draw even a schematic of the building layout, he doubted if he would have had it right.

"I still have the knife you made me," Tish said. From a worn Nicholson file, heated, hammered, heated again, the ringing blows of the blacksmith's hammer filling the smithy and draining the strength from Tom's young arm. Then the grinding, sparks flying in a shower, the foot treadle ceaselessly pumping, the stone turning, the water dripping slowly from the suspended tin can. "It was a birthday present, do you remember?"

Old Matt had shaken his head and taken Tom aside. "Boy," he had said, his voice for once strangely gentle, "that isn't exactly the gift for a girl."

Tom shook his head stubbornly. "She needed a knife.

She didn't have one. She can dig plants with it. She's always doing that."

And Matt had thought about it and slowly nodded. "You may have something at that," he said, and chuckled. "It's big enough to dig up a cottonwood tree."

"I remember," Tom said now, his eyes still on the buildings below, his mind watching the years unfold.

There was the corral, where, painfully, he had mastered the art of sitting a bucking horse, thereby demonstrating human mastery. Over there were banding and gelding corrals. There was the adobe stable, old Juan Domingo's pride, and there the wooden bunkhouse where he had stood in the evening and called out—what was his name?—Marley, the Anglo hand who had been pestering Tish.

Near the main house was the vegetable garden, row upon row of neatly tended plants, protected by wire fence from marauding rabbits. "No flower gardens," Tom said. He glanced at Tish. "When your mother was alive—"

"Yes," Tish said, and that was all.

The windmill still stood, but it was no longer used. In that cinderblock building off by itself diesel generators now provided electricity for lights, pumps, barn equipment. At considerable, but no impossible cost, power lines could have been run into the ranch from Las Grutas, but Matt preferred his independence. The telephone was something else: in this modern world communication was essential.

There were clusters of small adobe houses where some of the ranch families lived. And died, Tom thought, to be carried to the village for solemn burial. Small children played near the houses; the sounds of their play reached clearly above the faint throb of the diesel generators. Here and there was movement, a man on horseback, a ranch pickup raising a plume of dust, two colts in the far pasture, kicking up their heels and racing in wide circles. . . .

A living, breathing functioning organism, the ranch, Tom thought, and turned away. "Let's go," he said.

"I think the meadow first, where they found Borden."
Back to the present.

Tish parked the jeep in the shade of a ponderosa,
and led the way along the fenceline into the upland
meadow. "It was a wet winter," she said to Tom,
"more snow than usual. This is the result." She pointed
to a colony of blue iris, waved her hand at scattered
buttercups, and at orange Indian paintbrush, startling
against the green of the meadow grass.

"Not the kind of place where you'd expect violence,"
Tom said, and found the statement ridiculous because
violence like gold was where you found it, anywhere.
"Can you locate the dead man?"

Tish could. "I came here with Clyde."

"Why?"

"To see if I could recognize him. Somebody had
to." She paused. "He was lying here, face down, his
arms—stretched out. The map and the compass were
still there." She paused again. "He had been shot from
behind."

Automatically Tom turned to face the edge of the
ponderosa forest. "Two hundred yards," he said, esti-
mating the distance. "Shooting fish in a rain barrel."

"Clyde said just about the same thing."

Tom was still studying the trees. "Did you look for
a cartridge case? Or the slug?"

"There was none. Clyde had the woods combed."
Tish hesitated. "And after a winter of wind and snow,
no tracks in the pine needles."

Tom had turned back. He studied the fenceline as
it climbed to the rocky dropoff and ended. "Where was
he going? There's only that abandoned mine, and
there's nothing there. I've been in it." As a kid—
another adventure to arouse old Matt's ire so long ago.

"Goddamnit, boy," Matt had said, "abandoned
mines aren't for kids to blunder around in. You get
lost in there—"

"I didn't."

"When I talk, you listen. That mine goes down a
long way."

"Yes, sir."

"How far did you go?"

"Until it began to get too hot."

The old man had nodded. "They had the same trouble with underground heat in the Comstock, only it was rich enough to keep on digging. This one wasn't. Now you listen to me, boy. You stay the hell out of that mine. You hear?"

They were hearing clearly over in Las Grutas, Tom had thought, and probably in Dos Piedras as well. "Yes, sir," he had said, and that was all.

Now, looking up the slope to the mine entrance, "Compass and map," he said, "but what in the world was he after?" He paused. "More important, what was there about what he was after to cause somebody to gun him down?"

Tish shivered. She turned away. "Look," she said quickly.

A flock of wild turkeys came trotting out of the trees, saw the girl and the man, and altered course immediately. A few of the smaller birds took flight. The big tom in the van merely speeded up his pace. Like magic they disappeared on the far hillside.

Tom, watching, found that he was smiling. "Ben Franklin," he said, "wanted them to be our national bird instead of the bald eagle, which he said was only a fish thief." He looked down at Tish. "Did you know that?"

She shook her head slowly. She too was smiling. "But I like it."

One more quick look around the meadow. It told him nothing. "Let's go," Tom said. "Where was the rustling?"

As the crow flew it was not far, and the same fence was involved. But by jeep track, avoiding the thick ponderosa growth, it was a mile or more. Here the surfaced county road ran by pastureland, and only the four-strand barbed-wire fence blocked entry.

"No trick at all," Tom said. "Cut one section of fence and open it up. Drive the beef through, up ramps into the trucks—and away you go." He paused, remembering what Tito Leyba had said. "Two hundred miles away by dawn." He was looking at Tish. "You look skeptical."

"Fifty head," Tish said. "You don't find that many together very often, and to round them up at night, in those trees—" She shook her head.

"It happened," Tom said.

"Yes. But how?"

Tom turned to stare at the meadow and at the trees beyond. He said slowly, "Maybe you have a point."

"Unless," Tish said, "somebody came before dark, on horseback, say, and rounded up the fifty head and held them in the trees until the trucks came."

Tom nodded slowly. "And then what? When the trucks were loaded, what did your rider do? Turn his horse loose and go off in a truck?"

"Or stayed." Tish's voice was quiet. "If he was local, he would stay, wouldn't he?"

Tom studied the girl's face. "Did you tell this to Clyde?"

"No."

"Why not?"

"It's just a guess."

"Maybe a good guess." Tom's voice was angry. "Maybe too goddamn good. Somebody on the ranch—"

"You don't know that!"

Tom took his time. "No," he said, "I don't know it. But I'll damn well find out." He paused. "When was this, do you know?"

"I can look up the date." Tish hesitated. "It was only two days before the first big snow, and by the time Clyde and the hands really got into studying what had happened, the snow came along and hid everything."

There were times, Tom thought, when even the weather seemed to conspire against you. Another thought: "Was this the only time they hit us?"

"I think so."

"Any other ranches been hit?"

"Not around here that I've heard of."

Why not? There was no immediate answer except

old Matt's, "We're the biggest man in the bar, boy. When somebody wants to show what a hell of a fellow he is, we're the one he comes after."

Maybe that applied, and maybe not. And maybe, Tom thought, nobody else in the area has been hit simply because we have the best beef. "All right. Let's go."

Tish got into the jeep and started the engine. Sitting quietly, both hands on the wheel, "The commune?" she said.

"Have you been there?"

"Once, and I hated it."

"Why?"

Tish hesitated. "They make me uncomfortable." Her smile was turned inward, mocking herself. "I'm the outsider. They're playing some kind of make-believe game, and I don't understand it. The girls go around either in granny dresses or minishorts. The guys with their beads and dark glasses, always the dark glasses, and I can't see what they're thinking, but I think I know anyway."

"Tito Abeyta said there'd been some rapes."

"And some beatings." Tish shivered again.

"Have we had any trouble with them?"

Tish shook her head. "Clyde drove over when they first settled. He told them who he was and where the ranch boundaries were and said that if they wanted to go on ranch property, they'd have to have permission because we didn't want any accidents."

It sounded like Clyde Burley, Tom thought; and remembered the man's statement that old Matt no longer reached out for trouble. Obviously, Clyde Burley was doing it for him. "No point in my going there, then," he said. "Let's just drive around. I don't have the feel of the place yet." He paused. "Then the reactor site."

They bounced back onto ranch property over yet another cattleguard and reentered the ponderosa forest. "Back east—" Tish began, and stopped.

Tom smiled at her. "What about back east? You've been there."

"I've never lived there."

"Like living anywhere." Tom paused. Grace, he thought. And Tim. The job. "Well, not really. It—Stop the car!" He had the door open and was out and running before the car had come to a halt.

A chicano boy of perhaps eighteen was stumbling through the trees. He held one hand pressed to his cheek and blood oozed through his fingers. He saw Tom, stopped, looked around wildly, and then stood still, waiting, his eyes sullen.

Tom slowed to a halt. "What's happened?"

"Nothing."

"That's a pretty large nothing."

The boy was silent, unyielding.

"Where're you going?"

"So, okay," the boy said, "I'm on your fucking ranch. You—"

"I asked where you were going," Tom said. "I know where you are." He paused. "Dos Piedras?" He watched the boy's slow reluctant nod. "We'll take you," Tom said. "Somebody'd better look at your face."

"It's nothing. I told you."

Tom ignored it. "What's your name?"

"Abeyta. Luis Abeyta." The boy's head came up. "Mean anything to you?"

Tom smiled. "You're one of Tito's *primos*, cousins?"

The boy hesitated. "You know Tito?"

"We're old friends." Tom took the boy's arm. "Come on. We'll take you into Dos Piedras."

The boy sat in the back seat, hand still pressed to his cheek. Tish drove out to the country road and started to turn right. The boy said, "The other way." His voice was hard, angry.

Tom turned in his seat and looked straight into the muzzle of the 30-30, which the boy held by the small of the stock, the forefinger of his free hand resting on the trigger. The hammer was cocked. "Like I said," Luis said, "the other way. *Izquierda,* turn left."

Tom said quietly, "Why?"

"Because I fucking well say so."

Tish said in a voice that was not quite steady, "That's toward the commune."

"So." Tom's voice was still quiet. "That's what happened, is it, Luis?"

"Four of them." The boy's voice was a snarl. "They jumped me. One of the chicks—" He shook his head in anger. The rifle muzzle did not waver. "Waving those big tits at me. I followed her, and they were waiting. Now I'm going to show the sonsa bitches. Let's go!"

"There's no shell in the chamber," Tom said.

The boy's eyes dropped automatically to the rifle in his hand.

Tom's hand moved with astonishing speed, caught the barrel of the rifle and pushed it up. In the enclosed car the sound of the shot was deafening and a hole appeared in the roof. Tom wrenched the rifle out of the boy's hand and carried it up to the front seat. He let out a long breath and looked at Tish. "Dos Piedras," he said.

Tito Abeyta was in his office, hat pushed back on his dark head. He looked at Luis and then at Tom.

"I didn't bang him up," Tom said. "Apparently he went snuffling after one of the commune girls and she set him up for a beating." He paused. "And Luis was going back to start a civil war—with my rifle."

Tito leaned back in his chair scowling. "Goddamn young stud." He was looking straight at Luis. *"Con cojones? Muy macho, no? Mucho hombre?* Shit! What I ought to do is show you what a real beating is." He stood up suddenly and Luis ducked. "But what I'm going to do," Tito said, "is go out and tell those goddamn hippies that if they don't behave themselves, I'm coming at them for real." He paused. "And that goes for you young chicano punks too, *comprende?"*

There was silence.

"I asked you a question," Tito said. His voice was quiet.

"I heard." Luis's voice was scarcely audible.

"That isn't the point. Did you understand? If there's

any trouble around here, I'm going to start it—and finish it. Is that clear? Now, goddamnit, answer me."

Luis hesitated, machismo struggling with fear of the big man. Fear won. "Okay," Luis said in that scarcely audible voice. "Okay."

Tito looked at Tom. "You want to go with me and meet your neighbors?"

The thought had been in Tom's mind. "I think it might be a good idea," he said. "Tish can wait here for us."

11

They had come from the points of the compass—from Burlingame and Brookline, from Madison and Mobile, from Seattle and Shaker Heights—to meet in this small commune, not by arrangement but by drifting chance; some with wide-eyed hope for what might be, some merely with deep anger at what was and a conviction that any change in what was popularly known as life-style had to be for the better. And there were some who were simply taking the easy irresponsible way; and after a time these would tire of this phase of their existence, as they had tired of all others, and would move on to something new.

The shifting population was currently nine men, eleven women, and four small children. In age the adults ranged from Joe's twenty-nine to Cindy's fifteen-claiming-to-be-eighteen; none of the young children was over three.

" 'Take me to your leader,' is that it, man?" This was Joe, in a black hat with a red feather perched on wild dark hair, a full beard, dark glasses, jeans, and sandals, naked and tanned to the waist. "Man, we don't have a leader. This is a free society." Joe had a master's degree in sociology. "If it's a bust—" He left the sentence hanging as he faced Tito and Tom, resentment plain.

"No bust," Tito said. His voice was quiet. "Just a warning. There's a chicano kid—" He told Luis's story briefly.

"That one," Joe said. "Yeah. Look, man." He spread his hands. "We don't want any trouble."

"You almost had more of it than you'd have been able to handle," Tom said. "The kid was coming back here with a thirty-thirty."

Beyond the collection of VW buses, pickups, and aged school buses that stood in a bare dirt enclosure, the four small children played in front of an adobe structure from which a thin smoke column rose. A young woman stepped out of the doorway, glanced at the visitors, and then stared at them boldly. She wore sandals and a skirt that trailed the ground.

"What are we supposed to do?" Joe said. "Tell me that. We're, like, living in a hostile world, Israel surrounded by Arabs. We own this place—"

"You bought it?" Tom said.

"We bought it, man. You can look it up in the crummy county records."

Tom looked at Tito. Tito nodded. "They bought it."

"It isn't much." Joe was studying Tom. "At a guess, you're from the big ranch? Just slumming?"

"If that's the way you want to look at it."

"What other way is there?"

Tom's voice was cold. "Maybe a neighborly call. To see whether it was worthwhile taking the gun away from the kid." He paused. "I'm not sure it was. You're on a collision course, the world's against both of you, and maybe you're bucking for martyrdom. If you are"—he paused again—"there isn't much I can do to stop you. Maybe Tito can."

Joe said suddenly, "The shit you learn in books.

About how man is a thinking animal and he *can* get along with his fellows if he'll give it the good try." He shook his head. "Crap." He gestured at the parked buses and trucks, at the adobe building and the children playing in the bare dirt.

The woman in the long skirt had been joined by another, this one in tight, scant cutoffs, the briefest of halter tops partially covering her. Both watched the three men with open curiosity.

"What have we got, man," Joe said, "to get a bunch of chicano kids all uptight? Nothing here they want. We don't bother them. Why can't they leave us alone?" He glared up at Tom. "You've got that great big goddamn ranch. You own half the earth. Why don't they lay it on you?" He paused. "Or do they? I heard about some cattle rustling." He paused. "And other things."

Tito said gently, "What other things?"

"Things, man. Like, who gets shot for walking on ranch property? Like, how does a pile of lumber over at that reactor catch fire?"

The man had neatly turned the conversation around, Tom thought. He watched Tito for reaction.

"We'll take care of those things," Tito said. His voice remained gentle. "That still leaves you. And your women, which is what you've got that gets the chicano kids all uptight."

"Man." Joe shook his head. "Man, we're living in the twentieth century. You don't keep chicks under lock and key. They're people!"

"The only trouble with that," Tom said, and surprised himself by the saying, "is that it isn't the twentieth century in these parts, and God knows if it ever will be." Not in the villages, he thought, and not on the ranch itself, as far as that went: the ranch was, as Will had pointed out, a feudal anachronism.

Joe was looking at Tom with a strange new expression. "You just think that one up?"

"You," Tom said, "had better think it over."

Driving back to Dos Piedras, Tito large and silent

beside him in the jeep, "What did we accomplish?" Tom said.

Tito shook his head. "You don't accomplish anything very often, amigo. Most times what you do is remind somebody you're still there, and maybe, just maybe, he remembers when he's tempted to do something foolish."

He sees deeper than I had thought, Tom told himself.

"You get to the quarterback after he's already let the ball go," Tito said. "You could miss him, but you don't. Instead you give him a good shot, as good as you can, just so he'll remember you're around. Then maybe on another play he'll hesitate or hurry his throw because he's got you in the back of his mind like death and taxes."

It was a philosophy of determination, perseverence, implacability, Tom thought. Tito was the hunter patiently following his game, secure in his bone-bred knowledge that in the end it would be the beast, and not the man, who would falter or panic. "You're trying to run them out?" he said.

"What makes you think that?"

"You'd like us all to go, wouldn't you?"

Tito flashed white teeth in a large smile. "Yes, and no. We're infected with your goddamn Anglo diseases, and there isn't any cure, so we just have to live with them."

Deliberately failing to understand, "Diseases?"

"We crave the things you've taught us to want, the nice shiny things like cars and TV sets and washing machines and the rest of that crap." Tito laughed shortly, without amusement. "Until the Spaniards came, nobody on this continent had ever even seen a horse. But by the time you Anglos from the East started moving west, the whole plains Indian culture was based on the horse. You put a plains Indian on foot and he was a dead Indian. That's how deep your diseases go."

Tom was silent.

"Sure we'd like you to get the hell out," Tito said. "We'd like back the land El Rancho del Norte has. But, and there's the point, that land was there for a long time before your great-granddaddy began buying it and stealing it and kicking people the hell off it; and then he fenced it, and ran cattle on it, and opened up mines, and changed watercourses, and planted crops and built buildings—when nobody before him had ever done a goddamn thing with that land except hunt deer and elk and maybe fish a little.

"So," Tito went on, "a lot of us admire him, and Matt, but we resent the hell out of them too." He was watching Tom's face in profile. "And," Tito said, "if that makes me sound like a half-assed social anthropologist or even a shrink, why, blame your goddamn Anglo education. At college I had to study something besides organized mayhem on a football field."

Tom was following his own thoughts. "How do they live? How did they buy the land?" Speaking again, of course, of the commune.

"If you mean," Tito said slowly, "are they maybe rustlers, or did they have something to do with the Wendall's burglary, the answer is no. Some of them get monthly checks from home. Don't ask me why. One of them, I think the one we were talking to, has a bank account I'd like to have." Tito paused. "Why do they live like that?" He shook his head again. "The books I was supposed to read didn't go that far."

Tom remembered what Tish had said—that the commune people were playing some kind of make-believe game and she was the outsider. Maybe it was as simple as that. And maybe not.

Tish was waiting in Tito's office when they drove back into Dos Piedras. She came out to the jeep, tall and slim in her faded jeans and flannel shirt; her squaw boots moved soundlessly on the packed dirt.

Tito had swung himself out of the car and was standing, fingering the hole in the jeep's roof. He bent down to speak through the open window. "You were lucky, amigo."

Tom merely nodded.

"That size hole in you or the lady here—" Tito left the sentence unfinished. He straightened and held open

110

the door for Tish to slide in. Then he closed the door gently. Bending again, "Take care. I've noticed that people who ride around with guns sometimes end up having to use them."

"A half-assed social anthropologist, a shrink, *and* a philosopher," Tom said. He was smiling.

Tito nodded and smiled back, showing the white teeth. *"Vayan con Dios,"* he said, and slapped the side of the jeep with his hand in a farewell gesture as he stepped away.

Tom drove for a time in silence. He was thinking of the commune people, of the local people, and of the Anglos like himself who were also an integral part of the scene. Taken together, they formed, he decided, an explosive mixture, and precisely what might come of that was anybody's guess.

Around the world during these past twenty-odd years colony after colony had revolted and thrown out their European masters. And what was this part of the country in essence but a colony, susceptible to the same strains of envy and hatred?

Tish said suddenly, "I didn't know you and Tito Leyba were such good friends."

Were they really? Tom thought about it. "I'm not sure," he said.

It was Tish's turn to smile. "And," she said, "I don't remember you as being unsure about much of anything."

"Maybe," Tom said slowly, "I'm seeing a lot of things differently." Why the faint feeling of annoyance? "And don't ask me why, because I don't know the answer."

The Long Valley road was blocked by a gate over the cattleguard. On either side of the road cyclone fence stretched into the trees, its top guarded by three strands of barbed wire. A uniformed guard came out of the gatehouse as the jeep drew up. "You have passes?" Polite, but firm.

"Call Wayne Carter," Tom said. "Tell him Tom Granger is here. With his sister."

Tish waited until the guard was back inside the gate-house. "I'm not your sister." Her voice was low-pitched, angry.

"All right." Tom was smiling. "What do you want to be? Your mother married my grandfather, so that puts you in my parents' generation. What do I call you—Aunt Tish?"

Still in that low vibrant voice, "Oh, damn you, Tom!" Tish drew a deep, unsteady breath. "You can be such a bastard at times! And at other times—" She caught her lower lip between her teeth, and sat silent.

"I don't pretend to understand females," Tom said.

"That's nothing but a pose. The whole trouble is you see more than enough and you always have."

"You underestimate yourself."

"Matt kept saying that, and it isn't true. There's nothing worse than being told that you're better or smarter or prettier than you know you are. Can't you see that?"

"Maybe," Tom said, "it's about time you started believing your critics." His voice was gentle. He seemed about to say more, but the guard came out of the gatehouse, swung wide the gate, and gestured them through; and the words were not spoken. They entered the reactor site on a blacktopped road that curved through the trees.

The trees ended and the Long Valley vista opened to view: grassy meadow, stream, steep glaciated sides, and at the far end the majestic mountains plain against the sky.

"I always thought," Tish said, "that this would be an ideal place for a house. Instead—" She was silent.

"Instead," Tom said, "progress." He bore down hard on the word, thinking of the priest in Las Grutas saying that they needed no more electricity, that what they already had was ample for their simple needs. "Think," Tom said, "of all the electric can-openers and electric carving knives and portable electric hair-driers this valley will supply power for."

"I am thinking of it," Tish said, "and I want to cry."

Wayne Carter was waiting in the doorway of a construction trailer. Behind the trailer a long, low windowless building of unpainted concrete, terminating in a great dome and clashing with the natural beauty of the landscape. Men in hardhats swarmed in the area amidst the inevitable disorderly mess of a construction site: piles of lumber, tanks of fuel, idle backhoes and loaders and self-propelled cranes, bundles of reinforcing steel, piles of cement covered against possible rain, stacks of sheet metal and tanks of oxygen for the welders. . . .

"It is not very pretty, is it?" Wayne Carter said. "Maybe one day there will be some provision for beautification in the budget." He shrugged. "Come in. I can offer coffee."

There were drawings spread on a large drafting table, along with a desktop computer and Wayne's hardhat. A blackboard stood against the wall. Wayne gestured toward the drawings. "There's more to see on paper than in actuality. As I told you, we're not very far along." He made a small deprecatory gesture for Tish's benefit. "I don't know how much of this will interest you."

Tish hesitated. "Is it secret?"

"Not at all." Wayne was smiling. "Scientists have far fewer secrets than the people they work for." He paused. "And I don't know how much you already know about reactors."

"Assume," Tom said, "that we don't know a thing."

Wayne leaned a hip against the drafting table. He took his time. "Some," he said at last, "can explain complicated subjects better than others. I'm not sure how good I am, but I'll try." He was silent for a time. Then, "I guess the first thing to understand is that the purpose of a generator reactor is to produce heat. That heat is used to change water into steam to drive turbines that actually generate the electricity." He spread his hands. "Same principle as the fossil-fuel generators—oil or gas or coal. Consider the reactor as a furnace."

Tom was watching Tish. He saw her small frown of concentration. He saw too the interest in her eyes, not only in what the man was saying, but in the man himself as well.

"The fossil fuels," Wayne was saying in his slightly pedantic way, "produce heat by combustion. We produce heat by fission. We do this by bombarding atoms of fissionable material with elementary neutral particles called neutrons. When a neutron moving at enormous speed strikes the nucleus of an atom of fissionable material, the atom breaks into various pieces and in so doing releases more free neutrons that in turn collide with other atoms, breaking them up, and so on. This is the chain reaction that produces the heat we want. It is the same reaction that produced the atomic bomb, but by controlling it we keep it within usable bounds."

"Controlling it how?" This was Tom, asking the question for Tish's benefit.

Wayne nodded acknowledgment. "By using materials that will absorb neutrons, graphite, for example, so only a few neutrons are allowed to go around smashing atoms. We can speed up the reaction or slow it down by pushing graphite rods into the midst of the fissionable material or withdrawing them and letting the neutrons bounce around more freely."

Tish nodded slowly. Both men watched her. She smiled suddenly. "I'm with you so far, but what is fissionable material?"

Wayne smiled faintly. "That is the heart of the matter. There are only four materials available in any quantity that are capable of sustaining the fission process. Two of them are uranium. They are the same chemical element, but they have different atomic weights—we call them isotopes: uranium-233, and uranium-235. The other two are plutonium, also isotopes: plutonium-239, and plutonium-241." Wayne paused. "All four are rare, hence expensive, and as a matter of fact, only one of them, uranium-235, exists in any quantity in nature. If we want any of the other three, we have to produce it artificially." He paused again. "But there are ways of getting around at least some of the rarity, hence expense, and that is what we intend to do here."

The man just might be very good, Tom thought as he had thought back in the office at the ranch, and found a measure of resentment rising in his mind. Ridiculous, but there it was. "Explain that," he said.

Wayne nodded. "I'll use one example. You'll remember that uranium-233 is one of the four materials capable of sustaining the fission process: that chain reaction which produces the heat we want. It has to be artificially produced, and the way that is done is by adding a neutron to yet another material, thorium-232, which then, through steps you don't care about, is converted into uranium-233."

Tish looked puzzled. Tom hid his smile.

"It isn't all that complicated," Wayne said. "We do it in the following way. We artificially produce enough uranium-233 to cause and sustain our chain reaction. And in the reactor we also put some more thorium-232, which we call a fertile material, placed where it can absorb some of those free neutrons that are flying around, and by absorbing them can eventually be converted into uranium-233—the same fissionable material that is running the chain reaction. So we produce more fuel than we use, which seems to be a contradiction in logic, but is not." Pause. "For obvious reasons, that kind of reactor is called a breeder reactor, which is what we are building here."

It was, Tom thought, a clear and concise explanation; and his opinion of Wayne Carter rose another notch. He thought, too, of what Seth Porter had told him of Wayne's ideas of turning Long Valley into a year-round agricultural showplace, and it occurred to him that there was something of the visionary along with the obvious scientist in Wayne Carter's makeup; in Tom's judgment a not very usual combination.

"If you'd care to look around," Wayne said.

Tom shook his head. "I just wanted to see the general layout." He hesitated. "Any more—accidents?"

"Not since the fence went up."

"Fences can be cut."

Wayne said slowly, "We know."

Tish, watching, listening, found herself puzzled by what appeared to be sudden tension between the two men. It was as if each was issuing a warning of some kind, incomprehensible to her female mind and for which she could find no cause.

Sounds of work reached them jointly. Tom said, "You took the rifle to Pepe Martinez?"

"That same day." Wayne paused. "He didn't seem to want to believe my story of how I came by it."

"Pepe wouldn't." On that, at least, they agreed. "We'll go along," Tom said. "Thanks for the explanation."

"Any time."

"How about dates?" Tom said. "Completion? Actual operation?"

"We have a schedule. We're holding to it pretty well." Wayne's tone indicated that schedules were difficult to adhere to exactly. "Months of construction still ahead. We won't be in actual operation until well into the late fall of next year."

Ample time, Tom thought, for anything to happen. That bill in the state legislature, for example, could be long passed and well imbedded in public consciousness before the reactor was even close to beginning its operation. He wondered if he should tell Wayne about the bill and the possibility Seth Porter had foreseen; and decided against it. "Good luck," he said. "Let us know if anything else happens."

Driving back to the ranch with Tish, very conscious of the hole in the jeep's roof, remembering with vividness the heedless rage that had showed so clearly in Luis Abeyta's face and manner, feeling again that presentiment of trouble from he knew not which possible source, "How would you like to spend a few days in Santa Fe?" he said.

"Tell me why." Tish's voice was expressionless.

"To do a little poking around for me. See what a man named Sam Waldo is up to. And another man named Farley Wells. Find out what you can from the State Police about cattle rustling." Tom glanced at her face. "Well?"

"Why me?"

Spoken aloud, Tom thought, the words were going to have a strange sound. And yet their import was true. "Because I can trust you," he said.

Tish hesitated. Then, "Is it that?" she said slowly. "Or is it that you want me tucked away in a safe place—just in case?" She looked up at the hole in the roof and shivered faintly.

Tom was smiling. "So you feel it too," he said. "I was beginning to wonder if I was the only one."

12

Sue was luxuriating in the large ornate marble bathtub in their suite when Will came in, just returned from Santa Fe. He perched on the bath stool to admire the sight. "The story is," he said, "that Tully bought two of those tubs at auction when a plush Denver whorehouse was torn down."

"And I fit the picture?" Sue was smiling, enjoying herself. She was quite aware of her body's splendor, and she was equally aware of its effect on this husband of hers when she chose to flaunt herself. "Is that what you're saying, sweetie?" She sat up and began slowly to soap her shoulders and breasts. "What would I bring for hire?"

"Plenty."

"And it's all yours for free." The smile spread. She lifted her breasts with both cupped hands. "Lucky, aren't you?"

"Smart."

Sue lay back in the tub. In the now soapy water only the rounded outlines of her body showed as if through a translucent curtain. She arched herself and watched her nipples appear above the water. She smiled up at Will. "Don't start pawing the ground, sweetie. All in good time. What did you do in Santa Fe?"

It was a game they played of tease and tantalize, and not for the world would either have broken the rules. In their lives time was never a factor, and all pleasures, great or small, were to be savored to the full—because how else could the long slow days and nights be filled?

"I saw a guy," Will said.

"How fascinating." Sue sat up again and leaned far forward. "Do you want to soap my back?"

Will took off his jacket and knelt beside the tub.

Sue's back was smooth, silky, deeply tanned, showing not even a trace of bikini halter. When Sue sunned prone, she undid the halter; and if when she turned over and sat up those magnificent breasts were briefly exposed to casual view while she fastened the narrow strap, who was harmed thereby? There was too little beauty in the world.

Will's hands moved slowly, sensuously, spreading lather on the tanned skin. "As a matter of fact," he said, "I saw two guys." He paused, grinning. "One of them was female."

"Oh?" Automatic response.

"Jealous?" Will ran his hand down Sue's ribs to her waist, back again; and slid it forward to cup one firm breast and fondle it gently. "Well?"

"Who was she, sweetie?"

"A lawyer."

"You're kidding." Sue moved his hand away from the breast. "I told you: all in good time." Her tone was without annoyance. "Why?" she said.

"She's also a stunning female, and she's coming up here." Will dried his hands and went to perch again on the bath stool.

Slowly Sue sank back into the water and lay quiescent for a few moments, her face and eyes thoughtful. There were times, as now, when she exhibited an unexpected shrewdness. "Again," she said, "why?"

"The man is coming too." Will was obviously pleased with himself. "Incidentally, he's the man we had a drink with on the plane." The coincidence had not occurred to him until this moment, and, briefly, he wondered if he was being maneuvered. Nonsense. "Maybe it wasn't entirely by accident," he said slowly, "that we were on the same flight." No matter.

"Sweetie." Sue's voice held a faint edge. "You haven't told me yet why they are coming, either one."

"Because I invited them."

"To stay?"

Will grinned. "It's as much my ranch as it is *el patrón's,* right? If I want houseguests, who's to say no?"

Sue was silent, unmoving. Her eyes were steady on Will's face.

"It's called unanimity of purpose," Will said. "You and I want the ranch sold, *verdad?*" He paused. "Farley Wells wants the ranch sold." He paused again. "The lawyer female wants to be on the scene and is not above doing a little persuading in *el patrón's* direction." He spread his hands and his grin was very confident. "So we join forces right here on the ground. Doesn't that make sense?"

In many ways, Sue thought, he was a small boy with a small boy's love for intrigue. On the other hand, he was the man she had chosen, and so far she had had no reason to regret having chosen him. And, as he said, there was a unanimity of purpose, so maybe for once he had intrigued effectively. And he was sweet. She began to smile, and her body stirred gently, sending small ripples against the sides of the vast ornate tub. "You were soaping my back," she said.

"I finished."

The slow smile spread. "Now how about soaping my front?" Sue arched herself, and the nipples reappeared above the water. "I told you: all in good time."

119

She paused. "I think this is a good time." She paused again. "Don't you?" A third pause. "And I think this tub is plenty big enough for two."

Ethel Wilding drove. Farley Wells sat relaxed in his bucket seat and watched the wooded landscape flow past. "Folks back east," he said, "haven't even much idea what this part of the world is like."

"Do they care?"

Gently, "There's a cynical streak in you, honey. Root it out. The world isn't all that bad."

"It depends whether you look at it from above or below."

Farley was smiling. "Well, now, I'd say you eat pretty high on the hog. This automobile—"

"I didn't always." Ethel glanced sideways. "Maybe you did."

"Honey"—Farley's smile spread—"I was born on a quarter-section of West Texas dust that kept blowing away. I can still taste it."

Ethel relaxed a trifle. "And how did you get out?"

"I walked. No, I hitchhiked. I was pretty big for my age, and nobody thought much about a kid on the road. I was headed for the oilfields. I was going to strike it rich."

Ethel's rare smile lighted her face. "And did you?"

"In a roundabout way. I went to work for a wild-catter." Farley too was smiling. "The well blew in and suddenly he was rich. It didn't last. With him, it never would, and he knew it. He always had to drill one more hole, and they were usually dry." He paused, unsmiling now. "He got drunk one night and got into more of a fight than he could handle. I helped him out and helped him home, and like a grateful drunk he gave me a fistful of cash and told me to get the hell out before I caught the disease too." Another pause. "And he told me something else, and that was what stuck. 'Kid,' he said, 'you don't make the big money with your hands no matter how lucky you are. You make it with your head.'" Farley's sudden smile was deprecatory. "Pure corn, isn't it? But it was the right time and the right place, and it sounded to me like the wisdom of the ages, and from that point on it was all I could think about." The deprecatory smile reappeared. "End of story."

"I like it."

"How about you?"

Ethel shrugged. "I worked my way through college and law school."

"How?"

"Modeling." She turned to glance at his face. "Mostly in the nude. The pay was better. Does that shock you?"

His smile was fullblown now, no longer deprecatory. "Honey, I don't say I'm shockproof, but I don't shock easy, and I don't see anything there to be shocked about. You want something enough, you find a way to get it."

In many respects, Ethel thought, she and this man were alike: both self-made, both determined, both without what fainter-hearted people would probably call scruples—whatever they were. In a way she had been fond of Walter Borden, and she had admired his efforts toward and shared his views on conservation, but the man had lacked the iron Ethel found in herself and now in Farley Wells. It was strange that her thoughts should be running in these directions.

Farley said, "You've met the brother." He paused. "What's he like?"

A great deal like you, she thought. Aloud. "He's a big one. I'd say he is tough."

"Not like Will?"

Now where had this phrase come from, so apt in the present context? "The shadow," Ethel said, "and the substance." She turned again to glance at Farley's face.

It was in repose, all emotion concealed. He was looking straight ahead, and as Ethel watched, he smiled faintly, and then turned the smile on her. "Honey," he said, "before this is over we may have some fun." The smile spread. "The stakes are big, and I never did care for penny ante." He paused. "Now let's talk more about you."

"Why?"

"Because, as I said the other night, I'm interested." He paused again. "In a mighty attractive woman. Have you ever married?"

"No."

"Why?" Farley raised one hand to forestall response. "Because you've never found a man to match you." He nodded, and the smile reappeared. "Does Tom Granger come close?"

That is none of your business, Ethel thought, and immediately reversed herself. "He could."

"Is that why you're coming along on this visit?"

Again her first reaction was resistance, swiftly stifled. "I don't think so."

"But you're not sure." Farley nodded. "Enough prying." He paused. "You haven't met Sweet Sue, have you? She is stunning, sexy, and spoiled. It is a dangerous combination."

Ethel had no comment. The trees rushed past and the two-lane road rose winding, deserted, the only sounds the whisper of the engine and the faint humming of the tires. Ethel braked swiftly, automatically, at a sudden sign of movement. A deer crossed the road ahead of them and disappeared into the trees on the far side in three great bounds.

"Good eye," Farley said. "And sound reflexes." His tone was approving. His relaxation had not faltered. "They do mess up a car when you hit them at speed."

"What about the deer?" Ethel's tone was sharp, resentful.

"Easy, honey."

"Or don't they count?"

"We were getting along just fine." Farley's tone was still easy. "Let's not spoil it."

She was a high-strung and high-spirited filly, Farley thought, and probably the way to train her was by slow gentling rather than by the usual range method of slapping on a saddle, climbing aboard, and by sheer strength and determination demonstrating who was in charge.

On the other hand, it was his experience that most females liked to be shown a certain amount of muscle just to make sure that the man they had encountered was at all worth fooling with. "That's a fair-sized chip you carry around on your shoulder," he said. "Just daring somebody to knock it off?"

Ethel's voice was tart. "As you said, we were getting along just fine. Let's not spoil it."

13

Will had described Ethel Wilding as a stunning female, Sue remembered; and as usual, when Will's judgments were concerned with skiing performance, sports cars, sailing yachts, or women, he was quite correct.

The Wilding female, unlike Sue herself, was of the long-limbed, high-breasted, narrow-but-well-rounded variety, all parts in harmonious proportion. Perhaps a trace of Sapphic tendency? Women with such figures sometimes leaned in that direction. It would, Sue thought, be fun to find out. In Sue's world of leisure bisexuality among females carried no particular stigma. A woman's body with all its intricate equipment was designed for pleasure, wasn't it? Then why limit its potentialities to sometimes less than totally satisfactory male attentions?

"Hi," Sue said. "Welcome to the family homestead."

Tom, Tish, and Will appeared in the doorway and together came down the broad steps. "Miss Wilding," Tom said. His voice was grave. "Welcome."

"Are we?" And then, quickly, "I apologize for that, Mr. Granger. It was pure female nastiness."

She and he struck sparks, Tom thought, and wondered why. Not that it mattered. He walked around the car to shake hands with Farley Wells. "You are welcome too," he said.

"Why that is right kindly of you."

Ethel listening, reflected that the drawl was turned on and off at will; merely one more convolution in Farley's complicated personality. Will the real Farley Wells please stand up? Ridiculous thought.

"We'll have your car put under cover," Tom said. "I think we're in for some weather. And someone will bring in your things." He nodded to Tish to attend to it, and led the way back up the steps into the great hall.

Sue said to Ethel, "I'll show you your rooms. You'll want to freshen up." Was there in Ethel's answering smile some kind of deep secret understanding and response? Stop imagining things, Sue told herself; you've only just laid eyes on the woman. And yet sometimes that was how these things happened: instant familiarity that was almost intimacy. "You'll have the suite next to ours," she said, and could not help adding: "With a marble bathtub that has to be seen to be believed. It apparently came from a Denver whorehouse."

Ethel smiled. Farley's assessment of Sue Granger was accurate: spoiled, stunning, and sexy; one of those vest-pocket Venuses totally devoted to herself, undoubtedly a handful for Will and with an eye open for any attractive man or perhaps even another woman. Herself, for example? There were vibrations in the air. Ethel would wait and see.

Tom, Will, and Farley Wells were in the downstairs office. "This," Farley said, "is sipping whiskey." He savored its aroma and rolled a small taste around on his tongue. "I've always said you could tell a lot about a man from the whiskey he drinks."

Tom, amused, said, "Teetotalers?"

"I stay as far away from them as I can. I don't trust them."

Tom smiled again. They were, he thought, sizing each other up, not in the casual manner of new acquaintances, but, rather, as men already marked for adversary roles, a very different thing indeed. Strange, but there it was. "You and Will," he said, "just happened to meet on the plane and then again in Santa Fe?"

Will stirred in his chair, but neither man paid him heed.

"Well, now," Farley said, " 'just happened' isn't something that's easy to believe, is it? The fact of the matter is that if I hadn't run into your brother, I'd have come right up here to see you anyhow. Now that's plain talk, isn't it?"

Seth Porter had said that Farley Wells was not a boy they sent on a man's errand, Tom remembered; and decided that as usual Seth was right. This was a man who would be open and frank most of the time, evasive only at need, leaving deviousness for its own sake to other, lesser men. "Obviously," Tom said, "about the ranch and what's going to be done with it, no?"

Farley had another sip of his whiskey. "Well, now," he said, "there aren't many large holdings like this one left intact, and when it begins to appear that maybe there will be some changes, a lot of folks start sniffing the wind." He paused. "For a lot of different reasons." His tone was mild and friendly. "You can see how that would be."

Will watched the two men with fascination. There was between them an almost palpable antagonism, the line drawn, the dare already issued, and yet no voices were sharpened, no hackles visibly raised, and to someone just coming into the room all would have seemed sweetness and light. At times like this his own voice tended to be uncontrollably and embarrassingly shrill. He wondered if the difference was that he felt things more deeply than some, and told himself that that was not it at all. These two men, apparently without effort, managed to control themselves, and he could not. It was as simple as that.

"You tell me," Tom said.

Farley set his glass down and leaned back in his chair. "Up Montana way," he said, "and over in the Four Corners area not too far from here, there's coal, lots of it. That's energy that's needed now and will be needed a lot more in only a little time."

"You think we have coal here?"

"Maybe. But there are other things too. When gold was pegged at thirty-five dollars an ounce a lot of mines were shut down because they didn't pay. With gold now at a hundred and seventy-odd dollars an ounce, things are a little different. Silver is up too, and lead and copper, and you used to mine all of them."

True enough. Tom found himself thinking of the abandoned mine near the meadow where Borden was shot dead.

"But," Farley said, "I'm not telling you anything you don't already know better than I do."

The man was smart, and likable, Tom thought, and from Seth Porter's assessment, not to be trusted an inch. "There is also," he said slowly, "atomic energy." He watched for reaction.

Farley sat forward and had another sip of his whiskey. He leaned back again. "Some folks," he said, "think that's where our future energy supply lies. For ten, fifteen years fission reactors. Then maybe fusion reactors." He smiled and shook his head gently. "Fusion reactors, putting a bridle and a saddle on the hydrogen bomb, setting up right here on earth to work for us the same process that goes on in the sun." He paused. "It makes you think, doesn't it?"

Tom was silent, watching, waiting.

"Fossil fuels," Farley said, "coal, oil, gas—those we know how to handle. Maybe they're dirty, but they can be cleaned up. It's expensive, but it can be done. But when you go messing around with the atom—" He shook his head gently again. "Oh, I know it's being done, reactors at work and so far no big troubles." He paused for emphasis. "So far." He paused again. "But one meltdown, one reaction that gets out of hand, and there is hell to pay and no pitch hot, radioactive wastes and byproducts in underground water flowing God only knows where, lethal materials with half-lives measured in tens of thousands of years—"

"I've heard the warnings," Tom said.

"Why, now, of course you have." Farley was smiling again. "And I do start sounding like an old-time evangelist, don't I, a real Bible-banger? I'm sorry about that." He had another small taste of his whiskey and leaned back again. His gesture took in the trophies on the walls, the pictures, the gun cabinet. "A lot of history in this room," he said. "You can almost feel it looking down on you." He pointed, smiling still. "Young Teddy Roosevelt, isn't that one? Friend of old Tully's?"

The man was very good, Tom thought; never pushing too hard, shifting ground with ease, handling himself like a boxer with a good left hand. "They hunted together," he said.

"And I'll bet they talked a lot too," Farley said. "About this big broad country and whether it would ever fill up and settle down and lose its get-up-and-go; or whether a man out here would always be able to call his land, and his soul, his own, make his own decisions, take his own chances, and not have to kowtow to some pipsqueak from government, whether he came from Washington or Austin or Santa Fe."

"Or," Tom said, "a man named Waldo with a bill in the legislature?"

The office was still. Will sat motionless, watching both men, almost holding his breath. But the tension was quickly gone.

"You know Sam?" Farley said easily.

Tom shook his head.

"A fat-assed self-important little redneck pipsqueak with now probably the only good idea he ever did come up with." Farley gestured again at the Roosevelt picture. "Teddy would have approved. Country like this kept just the way it is, wild and wonderful, where a man can take a deep breath and not smell big-city stinks; land for timber and for cattle, for fishing and hunting and just plain walking, not cut up into little pieces fit only to support a jackrabbit and maybe two horny toads let alone a family moving out here from the East, thinking they've bought a piece of Heaven because a New York newspaper ad said so."

"And," Tom said, "not a place for an atomic TVA project, either. Isn't that really what you're saying?"

Again the office was still, and again Will, sitting silent, was astonished at the way the two men handled confrontation.

Farley's voice was unchanged, still easy, friendly. "I've always liked a man who said what was on his mind." He sat forward, picked up his whiskey glass, and sniffed at it appreciatively. His eyes did not leave Tom's face. "Maybe," he said in the same friendly conversational tone, "maybe one day you and I will have to go around and around laughing and scratching like two tomcats in a gunny sack. I kind of hope not." He paused. "But if that's how it comes out, why it will be a real pleasure."

Tom lifted his own glass. He too was smiling. "Fair enough," he said. "We'll see how it works out."

Tish rode a fine red mare named Sam. Clyde Burley was up on a big buckskin gelding with quarter-horse speed and the catlike nimbleness of a cutting horse. They rode at a walk side by side through the ponderosa forest, the horses' hooves making scant sound on the pine-needle floor.

"Tom wants me to go down to Santa Fe," Tish said. She glanced at Clyde to watch his reaction. She had known him for a long time, and she thought she knew him well. She was aware that his interest in her went beyond mere friendliness, and she was flattered and a trifle uneasy that it should be so. She was not without experience with men, most of it dating back to college and the Denver period, but in the presence of those like Clyde, who took more than a

casual interest in her, she always felt insecure and uncertain, totally unlike some women—Will's wife, Sue,
came to mind—who seemed from the cradle to know
how to behave with the opposite sex. "He wants me
to look into some things," she said. She hesitated.
"Cattle rustling among them." Again she glanced at
Clyde's face.

"I don't blame him."

"Are you blaming yourself?"

"Partly." They rode for a time in silence. "Man's
in charge," Clyde said, "then whatever happens goes
right back to him. Man dead in that meadow. Cattle
rustled." He swung his head to stare down at Tish.
"That hole in the jeep roof, what caused that?"

Tish told him.

His reaction surprised her.

"Poor goddamn chicano kid," Clyde said. "We've
put them down and stomped all over them, and then
we wonder why sometimes they go loco." He paused.
"Wouldn't you?"

Probably, Tish thought. Or possibly. "I don't know,"
she said.

"I sure as hell would," Clyde said. He turned in
the saddle to face Tish squarely. "Tom," he said. "He
thinks I had something to do with the rustling?"

"I don't think so." On the other hand, she thought,
there was the theory she had given Tom that someone local was involved. "How," she said, "did they
round up fifty head of cattle at night?"

Clyde was facing forward again, loose and natural
in the saddle. "If it was me," he said, "I'd round
them up in daylight and hold them, easy enough,
until the trucks came after dark."

So he had seen it too, Tish thought. She took the next
step. "A stranger would run the risk of being seen,
wouldn't he?"

"A lot of country. Room to hide." Clyde was scowling now. "If you're saying it could have been one
of the hands, why, yes, it sure as hell could. The only
thing is"—he shook his head angrily—"I don't want
to believe it."

Again they rode in silence for a time. Tish said at last, "Do you think I should go to Santa Fe?"

"Why ask me? I'm just hired help."

"Don't be like that."

He could smile. "If the boss wants you to go to Santa Fe, you go."

True enough. Somehow the words put matters in proper perspective. "I'm hired help too," Tish said. She touched her heels to Sam's belly and the mare lifted immediately to a trot and then a gallop. Behind, Tish heard the quickening sounds of the buckskin's hooves and, strangely, she could have laughed aloud from sheer ebullience. Catch me, she thought; I want to be caught. By someone.

Ethel Wilding had changed from town clothes to tailored safari pants, desert boots, and a plaid shirt with the sleeves rolled up on her tan arms. She wore no brassiere and her breasts stirred gently as she walked. She met Tom at the foot of the broad staircase. "It is a castle," she said, and smiled. "It is straight out of the Middle Ages, updated, of course, with electricity and central heating, but the spirit remains."

Tom too could smile. "Something like that."

"And you are the *patrón*."

"Temporarily. I have other responsibilities." How was Tim's bridge coming along? How was Grace? I must phone her, he thought.

Ethel studied the man with open interest. "And yet," she said, "I would have thought that the role would appeal to you, and you would settle into it easily, and permanently."

Will's view too, Tom thought, not that it mattered. Or did it? It had not even occurred to him that there might be a conspiracy afoot, which was probably ingenuous of him. There was no doubt about Farley Wells's feelings, but until this moment, Ethel Wilding had seemed mere window dressing, decorative but relatively unimportant, companionship for Wells. "We'll see," he said. And then, on a different note, "You're a guest, Miss Wilding——"

"Ethel, please."

Tom made a small nod of acknowledgment. "First names are easier." Pause. "There are horses, if you care to ride. There is no formal swimming pool, but there are places, Will can show you, where the stream will serve. I warn you, the water is cold."

"I like to walk."

Again that small nod of acknowledgment. "Wherever you like."

"Will you walk with me?"

There was challenge in the question, Tom thought. More of Will's strategy, knowing full well how he, Tom, would respond?

"Of course," Ethel said, "if you are busy with *patrón* matters——" She left the sentence unfinished.

Tom hesitated. Then, "Come along," he said, and led the way to the door. He wondered if somehow Will was watching, and laughing.

In the sun it was bright and warm. Overhead the sky was limitless, but over nearby mountains clouds were gathering, white turning to dirty gray as the shadows and forms changed from the internal forces that were building.

"That," Ethel said, "is the weather you meant?"

"We'll have a little time before it comes down to us."

"I'm not afraid of getting wet."

They angled down to the stream and took a path that followed the water's curving course. The path was wide enough for two, and they walked side by side at a steady pace.

The girl walked well, Tom thought, swinging her legs from the hips without unnecessary motion, planting her feet straight, arms swinging naturally, head high, shoulders back. The movement of her breasts did not escape him; as, he supposed, it was intended it would not.

"You grew up here," Ethel said. It was not a question, and there was assurance in her tone. "I envy you."

"It was a good life. During the school years I couldn't wait for summer to get back."

"And yet you left."

Tom walked in silence for a time. Great cottonwood trees lined the stream, and their uppermost leaves were beginning to stir. Storm coming, he thought. Prudence suggested that they turn back. The hell with it. The girl had asked for it. He walked on steadily. "I left," he said finally in agreement. "Old Matt and I—" He shook his head. "Both stiff-necked. I asked him once if he and Tully, his father, ever got along. 'We kept our distance,' was what he said, and I understood what he meant." Tom looked at the girl. "And so I left. Does that explain it?"

Ethel took her time. "You resent me," she said at last. "Tell me why."

Why, indeed? An attractive, intelligent, worldly female. Why should she raise his hackles as she did? "How long have you known Will?" Tom said.

Ethel smiled. "I met him yesterday. With Farley. You are wondering why the sudden invitation to come here?"

"It is as much his ranch as mine."

"But there is a difference." Ethel waited until he was looking at her for explanation. "You love it," she said then, "and he hates it. He wants to sell it—"

"And I don't?" Tom hesitated. "Maybe," he said. "I don't know yet."

High overhead the cottonwood leaves were rustling, stronger, stronger; and the sunlight that filtered down through the trees had lost its sharp definition. Time to turn back. Again, the hell with it. Tom said suddenly, "And what is your role?"

Ethel closed her eyes briefly. "I'm not sure."

"Your first interest was your dead man." Pause. "And environment, ecology."

"You make them sound like dirty words."

A sudden gust of wind set branches to rattling above them. "We're going to get wet," Tom said.

"I told you I wasn't afraid. I'm not water soluble."

"I'm trying to figure out just what you are."

"A woman."

"That's obvious." Pause. "For the record," Tom said, "a very attractive woman."

"Thank you, sir." There was mockery in her tone. "But you are unimpressed."

"Am I?" Tom stopped walking, turned, and caught her shoulders in his big hands. "I'm as susceptible as the next man." He slid one arm around her and lifted her chin with the other hand. She made no struggle. "Is this what you're after?" He bent to kiss her.

Her lips were firm, then softening; her body pliant against his. It was a long kiss, suddenly deep and breathless.

High in the mountains thunder muttered. Overhead the trees began to thrash. And then the first heavy raindrops splattered down through the leaves, suddenly cold on heads and shoulders.

Tom released her. She was smiling, somehow triumphant. "Now we go back," Tom said. "You've accomplished what you intended."

"Is that the way you see it?"

"How else?"

The rain was falling heavily now, and wind whipped the branches of the cottonwoods. Thunder muttered again, closer this time.

"You," Ethel said slowly, "wouldn't believe me if I told you."

They turned then and began to walk quickly back along the streamside path.

Thunder crashed now, muttering no longer, and the cottonwoods bent and sprang with the force of the wind. Beneath the trees there was some protection from the driving rain, and solid footing on the path, but Tom would have it otherwise. He caught the girl's hand, and half-leading, half-dragging urged her into the open, angling up the steep hillside where only piñon and juniper grew, and the full force of the storm beat upon them. Ethel tried to resist, but he was too strong for her.

Lightning flashed and the whiplash crack of the thunder was immediate, crashing all around them. The ground itself seemed to heave, and the cold driving rain was torment. A huge tumbleweed came bounding past, wind-driven, defying gravity in great soaring leaps. And then, beneath the sounds of the wind and the thunder, there was a new sound, low-pitched, ominous, and Tom paused in their scrambling to look back at the stream.

Through the cottonwood trees suddenly they could see it: a solid wall of water, brownish-white, crashing down the water-course, filling it, rising high above its banks, tearing at the footpath and the hillside above.

It passed beneath them with a roar and crashed out into the broader valley, where the land flattened and the water could spread and dissipate its force; and as they watched the cottonwood trees seemed to rise slowly from the flood and shake themselves, and what was left of the footpath emerged once more, boulder-strewn now where there had been no boulders, covered with branches and roots and small trees torn loose in the few moments of fury.

They turned away then and hurried on.

Will and Sue were in the great hall when Tom and Ethel burst in, dripping. "There used to be a saying," Will said, "about people who didn't have the sense to come in out of the rain." He was smiling to strip the words of their sting.

"I've heard it," Tom said. Strangely enough he felt looser, easier than at any time since he had stepped out of the charter plane in the meadow. "My fault," he said easily. "I saw it coming."

Ethel was shaking her head in wonder. "But you couldn't have seen that—torrent coming?"

"Flash flood," Tom said. "In the mountains they happen, and you stay out of narrow places."

Sue said nothing. She was staring thoughtfully at

Ethel's breasts, plainly visible beneath the soaked thin fabric of her blouse. Not as large as some she had known, Sue thought, her own included. But adequate, more than adequate: enticing.

14

Kelly Garcia, editor of the *Las Grutas Bugle,* spoke rapid, idiomatic local Spanish as well as accentless English. He was not sure which he preferred. The Anglo world of Kansas City and Albuquerque newspapers had treated him with little more than contempt and here in Las Grutas he was an important fellow. On the other hand he still retained a yearning for the big time, maybe even New York or Washington—an impossible dream.

But he was not a bad newspaperman, and he could recognize a story when he found one. As now, the morning after the new incident. And his pulse quickened as he began to gather his facts.

First from Pepe Martinez, Grutas County District Attorney: "How many head rustled this time?" Kelly asked.

"Who can tell?" Pepe was scornful. "On a ranch that size, can you count how many cattle you have left today and subtract that number from yesterday's inventory and get an exact tally?" The broken badly set nose was lifted in arrogance.

"All right," Kelly said, "when did it happen, and how do they even know?"

Pepe counted points on his fingers. "The fence was cut some time last night. Cattle tracks lead to the highway. There are oil drippings where apparently the trucks waited."

"How do you know there was more than one truck?"

Reluctantly Pepe nodded acknowledgment of the validity of the question. "There's a man named Archuleta in the hospital in Santa Fe. The State Police found him and got him out of his pickup. He was in the trees, conscious, with two broken legs. Two cattle trucks swinging wide around a curve and going like bats out of hell ran him off the road less than a mile from the cut fence. It was well after dark." Pepe shrugged. "It's too much coincidence to think they weren't the trucks loaded with Rancho del Norte cattle."

Kelly was taking notes. "Any leads at all?"

"Ask the State Police. Ask Jesus Christ Tom Granger."

Kelly understood the obvious annoyance. "Makes you look bad, no?—things like this happening in your home county?"

"They could happen anywhere."

Kelly let it go. "Archuleta," he said, "didn't manage to pick up a license number, did he?" He sighed at Pepe's headshake of denial. "Too much to hope for," Kelly said, and tucked away his folded copy paper and pencil. "I'll see what they say out at the ranch."

Tom was in the big office, angry, but under control.

Kelly said, "The wire services will want a story on this." He thought of adding "amigo," and decided against it. In just these few days the old easy relationship between himself and Tom had apparently altered. Something to do with sitting behind that big desk, no doubt. "You have objections?"

"No." Tom paused. "Just don't make us look any sillier than we are."

Kelly thought he understood what was behind those words, too. El Rancho del Norte was huge and powerful and wealthy—and unable to defend itself against as elemental a danger as cattle rustling. "It's okay, then, if I talk to Clyde Burley and some of his people?"

"Help yourself."

When Kelly was gone, Tom sat on alone, staring at the far wall.

Tish, summoned, knocked and came in, and after carefully closing the door, sat down in a chair against the wall. She said nothing. Old Matt had treated her like this on occasion too, and rather than resenting it, she felt flattered.

"Even if I don't say anything to you," old Matt had told her once, "I know you're there, honey, and that's what counts. Times when you have to make decisions, it's a lonely world, and just knowing you've got someone you can trust standing by is worth more than you can know."

Was it the same now with Tom? Tish didn't know, but she hoped so. There was a likeness between grandfather and grandson that was above and beyond mere physical resemblance. She waited quietly.

Tom said at last, "Santa Fe it is." He paused. "If you will."

"Of course I will." If the boss says go, you go. But it was more than that, far more; too complicated to understand, merely to accept.

"State Police," Tom said. "Marty Romero, if he's still there."

"He is."

"I'll give him a call." Tom raised his hand to tick off points on his fingers. "As much dope as they have on rustling anywhere in the state. Method of operation. Possible or even probable destination for the stolen beef. That kind of thing. Marty can help."

Tish nodded.

"That fellow Archuleta in the hospital," Tom said. "Have one of Seth Porter's bright young men go with you to see Archuleta. Get everything from him you can. Point out that we're on the same side. If we catch up with the people behind the trucks, we'll see that Archuleta gets some kind of recompense for what happened to him."

Tish smiled and nodded again.

"Ask Marty too," Tom said, "if the state attorney

general has any thoughts. Sometimes they used to work together, sometimes not. Marty will know."

Tish said, "You spoke of Sam Waldo."

"I haven't forgotten him. I want whatever Seth can have his people find out about that bill. Farley Wells—" Tom paused. "What do you think of him?"

"I'm no judge."

"I've told you before, stop underestimating yourself."

Tish hesitated. She said at last, "I think he's a great deal like you. He works harder at being friendly, but I think he can be a real bastard too."

Tom was grinning. "A fair summation." The grin disappeared. "And I want a geologist with mining experience. Again, see Seth for advice. We have old records here, test data, compiled profiles. I want someone who can study them and then go out and see for himself." He leaned back in his chair, and stared again at the far wall.

Had he touched all bases? He thought that for the present he had. Information first, action later. He looked again at Tish. "Stay at La Fonda," he said. "I want to be able to reach you."

Tish nodded again. She stood up. "On my way."

Tom waited until she was at the door. "One more thing," he said, and paused for emphasis. "Take care of yourself, you hear?"

Tish was smiling.

"I mean it," Tom said. "I don't want anything to happen to you."

Warm thought. Tish's smile spread. "And you take care of yourself too," she said. She hesitated. "You're the only one who can hold it all together." She turned then and walked out quickly.

Tom sat on, motionless. Could he hold it all together? He was not sure he could, and he was still not sure he even wanted to. The ranch *was* an anachronism; the fact was beyond dispute. And if he did choose to try to hold it together, he was selling himself into slavery, automatically tying himself to the land as old Matt had been and Tully before him. Was that what he wanted?

A property the size and complexity of El Rancho del Norte took on a character of its own, demanding attention, even devotion from those who would master it. And so far he, Tom, had only scratched the surface of the job of running the ranch, a condition that would have to be altered drastically if he intended to stay.

Then too, there was Will's feeling about selling the ranch. And how much weight should be given to that? By Matt's decision he and Will shared equally. How much right, then, did he, Tom, have to do as he liked without Will's approval? Face it, he told himself almost angrily, you're hair-splitting; when it comes right down to it, you'll do what you like anyway. And what was that? Go back to the other life, perhaps? He had left here once, hadn't he?

He pushed back his chair and stood up. The important thing right now was last night's rustling, and although he doubted that he could do anything that had not already been done, the urge to do *something* was irresistible. Out in the hall he called for Consuelo and told her to pass the word to have a horse saddled for him. The jeep was all very well, but where he was going was horseback country.

The horse a young chicano boy led up was a big sorrel gelding Matt had ridden often. And Matt's working saddle and handwoven saddle blanket were on his back. Subtleties at work? Tom took the reins. To the boy he said in Spanish, "What is your name?"

The boy scraped the dirt with the toe of his boot. "Chico Valdes."

"Your father is José?" The gatekeeper.

"Sí, patrón."

Tom nodded. "Thank you, Chico."

"De nada, patrón." The boy had not looked up. Now he stood watching as Tom swung into the saddle and moved the gelding off at an easy running walk. Then abruptly the boy turned and ran back down toward the stables as a young colt might run on a sudden whim.

Tom rode angling into the trees on the flank of

the great mountain. How long had it been since he had been on a horse? Two years? Three? It felt good, easy, natural. He could not remember learning to ride any more than he could remember learning to walk. Or fish. Or shoot a rifle. Strange—he had never thought of it that way before.

Matt's saddle fitted him to a T, and that was strange too, because the saddle had been made to measure for his grandfather by that fabled Denver saddlemaker—what was his name?—long since dead.

There was nothing at all strange about it, Tom told himself; it was merely that he and old Matt were the same size. But how often could you put on another man's clothes and feel comfortable? And a made-to-measure saddle was no different, particularly a saddle that with fifty or sixty years of riding had to have conformed at least a little, as clothing did, to its wearer.

He was annoyed with himself as he rode on, letting the gelding pick his own path and pace, around the flank of the mountain, and down an open slope to flatland. There he lifted the gelding to an easy trot that could cover mile after mile without strain.

The land was dropping subtly, out of the ponderosa pines into piñon and juniper growing in near symbiosis. Here and there a cholla cactus seemed to writhe like a soul in torment.

They passed cattle grazing singly or in small groups, and Tom was reminded of Tish's point that it would take a man on horseback to round up fifty head and hold them for the trucks. He thought too of her suggestion that the man on horseback might very well be local, attracting little attention even if he were seen during daylight hours. It made sense.

The ranch had now been hit twice by the truck rustlers. Or, Tom wondered, was he jumping too quickly to the conclusion that in each instance the men in the trucks had been the same?

Sitting loose and easy in the saddle, legs almost straight, pelvis moving rhythmically with the gelding's steady trot, relaxed by the old familiarity of motion, he thought about it and decided that two different sets of trucks, two different sets of men were too much of a coincidence; logic dictated that both strikes were by the same people. And what did that suggest?

Nothing, he told himself. Further venture into speculation would be a mere exercise in futility.

Movement caught his eye, and he turned in the saddle to watch two deer bound away as if on gigantic springs, their white rumps flashing. They reached the barbed-wire fence, cleared it without effort, and disappeared into the trees beyond. What was it he remembered Matt's telling him had been the slogan of a fence manufacturer so long ago? Yes, there it was: Deer high, bull strong, and hog tight. That about covered the possibilities, he thought, and found himself smiling.

The gelding's ears pricked forward suddenly, and a stiffness came into his slowed gait.

"Easy, boy," Tom said and bent to pat the smooth neck. "What is it?"

And then he saw, moving through trees with clumsy swiftness: a black bear, disturbed in his berry-eating, wanting no part of man on horseback.

Tom patted the gelding's neck again. "It's all right," he said. "He's more afraid of us than we are of him." Nevertheless, he thought, we give him a wide berth. Even a black bear, frightened or startled, was a dangerous beast. And a grizzly, now—Tom shook his head at that thought.

In all his life on the ranch he had only seen two grizzly bears. One had been distant, but unmistakable, moving without haste up a talus slope. But the other had been a mere hundred yards away, suddenly clear and plain on a mountain path, upwind. The great beast had stared, puzzled, for the moment indecisive, and Tom had stood frozen, scarcely daring to breathe.

He had a rifle, a 30-30, and not for the world would he have tried to use it. Oh, with one shot, two, or even three he might have wounded the grizzly mortally, but he would not have lived to know about it. Even with a heavy-caliber rifle, as he had heard Matt say often enough, you shot at a grizzly only when you were above him, well above him; or no matter how much lead you put into him, he would get to you.

A grizzly could outrun a horse, kill a steer with a single blow of his paw, flip over without apparent effort to uncover a pika or a marmot a rock two men together could not lift. And his temper was short. *Ursus horribilis* was his scientific name, and he lived up to every syllable of it.

There on that mountain path Tom had stood and waited and the world had seemed very still. The bear had sniffed the air, but, upwind, he could catch no scent. Ponderously he had heaved himself up to his full height for a better look; and to Tom he had seemed big as the main ranchhouse, where he suddenly wished he were.

Then the bear had dropped to all fours again, and with a final glance turned away and ambled down the mountainside.

That night at dinner old Matt had listened and then passed judgment: "For once, goddamnit, boy, you showed sense." He shook his head. "Grizzly," he said. "There aren't many left. If he's just passing through, we leave him alone."

And Tom said, "And if he isn't?"

"If he starts taking cattle," Matt said, "then we go after him. But not with a 30-30."

Will said, "Were you scared?" Was there mockery in the question, or merely curiosity?

Tom chose to find mockery. "Pissless," he said, and that was all.

"You'd have been more of a damn fool than I ever thought you were," Matt said, "if you hadn't been." End of conversation.

Now, remembering, Tom reined the gelding away from the black bear's direction and lefted him again to a gentle trot.

The ground began to rise. Ahead of the mountain slope trunks of aspens showed pale amongst the evergreens, and their leaves shimmered in almost undetectable breeze. In autumn their leaves would turn to gold, blotches of vivid color against the green of the pines. Not like New England, Tom thought, but in its own way quite as lovely. Chauvinism stirring? He smiled at the thought, and on impulse lifted the gelding to a gallop.

He came at last to the scene of last night's rustling. The same spot as the other time, he thought; a winter separating the two crimes. Was weather all that had prevented further depredations? Food for thought. Now that good weather had returned, were they in for a rash of thefts? He sat quiet on old Matt's saddle and thought about it while his eyes automatically swept the area, noting the trampled ground where the cattle had been held, the quantity of droppings that argued a considerable period of confinement.

Night patrols as defense against further raids? It would be impossible to patrol the entire vast perimeter of the ranch. On the other hand, his own knowledge, and Clyde Burley's, and careful study of the topographical maps could narrow the areas of vulnerability to a numbered few. Immediate access to good surfaced roads was the primary consideration; cattle trucks were not four-wheel-drive vehicles to take into rough country.

Cooperation from the State Police was of course another direction to turn. In this mountain country topography dictated where the few roads could be built, and while nightly roadblocks would obviously not be practicable, roads leading from the places he and Clyde Burley would pick out could be kept under some kind of scrutiny. He would call Tish in Santa Fe and ask her to talk with Marty Romero about the possibility.

Sitting motionless, thinking about it all, his eyes caught a glint from something—a piece of metal?— in the trampled earth, and he bent to look more closely. Something buzzed suddenly above him like an angry hornet, and simultaneously the explosion of a shot echoed in the trees.

Tom stayed where he was, bent low over the gelding's withers, his weight shifted suddenly forward, his heels banging hard against the gelding's side. They took off at a dead run, across the open ground, into the far trees, away from the direction of the shot.

If there was another shot, he did not hear it, and nothing touched him. Into the trees, and safety, he reined the gelding down and turned to look back. No one followed. He thought about trying to work his way back on foot to see if he could catch a glimpse of the shooter—and decided against it. Lucky once, he told himself; don't crowd it. At a steady trot they headed back toward the main ranchhouse.

15

Farley Wells borrowed one of the ranch cars and, alone, drove to the Long Valley atomic site. To the guard at the gate, "Tell Doctor Carter, please, that Tom Granger sent me," he said. Not wholly true, but close enough.

What Tom had actually said was, "You might as well meet him. And he might as well meet you."

"Well, now," Farley had said easily enough, "aren't you jumping at conclusions, maybe?" And then, quickly, with that candor that was part of his stock in trade, "You're probably right, at that, feeling the way I do about atomic power."

The guard was back shortly to open the gate, and Farley drove through. Where the trees ended and the Long Valley vista opened to view, he stopped the car for a long admiring look.

He was flatland born and bred, and to him these

mountains had an almost mystical quality. T
diastrophism they were born, through erosion th
but always over the ages they renewed the
by further contortions of the earth's crust; a
process was repeated without end.

What he was looking at appeared immuta
was not. It was merely that man's short lif
could not encompass more than a tiny fraction o
constant process of change, and since man tends
measure all things against himself, subjectively be
lieving only what he sees, the mountains had always
been and would always be as they now appeared.
Even when you knew better.

He roused himself at last, reluctantly put the car
in gear and drove on.

He was very much interested in meeting Wayne Carter, and he had no preconceived notion of what kind
of man he would turn out to be. The stereotypical
concept of an atomic physicist—pipe-smoking, unworldly, absent-minded—was, Farley knew, as ridiculous as the concept that all Chinese looked alike, or that
all oil men wore big hats. He doubted that Wayne
Carter would be as good at Farley Wells' business as
he, Farley, was; few men were; but beyond that he
would not allow himself to think.

He parked the car near the construction trailer and
got out to stand for a few moments studying the bulk
of the reactor building and the bustle of construction
activity. Somewhere inside the building he could
hear the insane chatter of rivet guns, and through an
open doorway he could see two welders at work, with
their masks down looking for all the world like lunar
astronauts.

The basic construction was pretty well finished, he
told himself, but the actual fitting out of the reactor
complex itself would be a long process, so there was
still ample time. He turned to see Wayne Carter in
the doorway of the construction trailer. "I'm a guest
at the big ranch," Farley said easily, and lest there
be any misunderstanding at the start, he added, "My
business is gas and oil."

ayne nodded. "Come in."

arley had been in construction trailers without
nber. Like offices and libraries, he thought, they
ded to reflect the character of their owners. This
e was neat, orderly, and in its sparse way com-
rtable. He was impressed. "I've heard tell," Farley
aid, "that what you're doing here is in the nature
of a pilot project."

"In a sense," Wayne said, "all breeder reactors
are pilot projects. There is a great deal we don't
know about them yet."

"Sort of like running before you learn to walk, isn't
it, Doctor?"

"You could look at it that way."

"The only thing is," Farley said, "if you fall down,
everybody gets skinned up." He smiled suddenly. "Strike
that, Doctor. I'm sure you try not to stumble."

"We take precautions," Wayne said, "just as you
do when you're drilling a well or laying a pipeline"
—he paused—"or unloading a supertanker." He
paused again. "What can I do for you, Mr. Wells?"

It was a question to which Farley had no real answer. He had come merely to size the man up, and
now that he had there was no real point in staying
longer. On the other hand, it was his experience that
very little knowledge of any kind went to waste: like
odd things stored in the attic, you never knew when
it might turn out to be useful. And, of course, verify-
ing knowledge already obtained was rarely a waste of
time. "As I understand it," Farley said, "what you are
setting up here is a molten-salt breeder reactor."

Wayne's eyebrows rose slightly. He nodded.

"Fluorine salts of uranium, thorium, lithium, and
beryllium, if I remember correctly," Farley said.
"Uranium-233 is the fissionable material. Thorium-232
is fertile and will breed."

Wayne was smiling now. "You've done your homework. Are you a scientist, Mr. Wells?"

"Purely a layman." A little of the drawl appeared.
"But when things interest me, I try to find out about
them."

Wayne leaned his hip against the drafting table. Idly, automatically he picked up a pencil and turned it slowly in his fingers. Then he put it down again with an air of decision. "You are against atomic reactors, is that it?" he said.

Farley smiled gently. "Well, now, let's just say I think they have their dangers." He paused. "I don't always go along with Ralph Nader or the all-out environmentalists, but in this case I find myself thinking right along with them."

"Is that all it is?" Wayne paused. "Or are you against reactors on principle because they threaten fossil-fuel monopoly?"

J.R. had stated their position clearly. "That would be pretty shortsighted, wouldn't it, Doctor?" Farley said. "We're already in a bind for energy, and that isn't something that will automatically cure itself." He shook his head. "Some folks think we won't ever whip our energy probelm until we start using sunshine to develop power."

"I happen to be one of them," Wayne said. "But in the meantime breeder reactors like this one are going to have to carry some of the load. We have oil enough to last perhaps fifty years. We have coal to last on the order of ten times that. But with coal we could end up fouling our atmosphere beyond recovery. At least fission reactors don't do that."

"A true believer, Doctor." Farley was smiling again. "I do like to see a man with faith in what he does." He paused. "Even if I don't agree with him."

Wayne was silent for a little time. He said at last, "I get the impression that I am being warned."

"Now whatever gave you that idea, Doctor?"

"Somehow I don't see you taking the trouble to come here out of simple curiosity." Wayne paused. "Men of your caliber don't do things without reason."

"I am flattered."

"Tom Granger told me that rumors don't start by themselves. I didn't believe him. Now I'm beginning to wonder."

"Rumors get started in a variety of ways."

Wayne nodded. "And for a variety of purposes, and not only in political campaigns." He was slow to anger, but his temper was rising now. "You said it would be pretty shortsighted to object to reactors because they threaten fossil-fuel monopoly."

"I did indeed, Doctor."

Wayne shook his head. "Logic has nothing to do with it." He paused. "Once when I was a kid I watched two scorpions on the bottom of a horse trough. They were drowning, but they were still trying to fight each other. We're fouling the only planet we have, and if we aren't careful we'll make it uninhabitable. We're running out of energy we have to have for survival. But instead of trying to work together, too many people are grinding their own axes, storing up wealth and power they may never get to enjoy." He paused again. "I think you are in that category, Mr. Wells."

Farley's face had lost none of its easy friendliness. "Like I said, Doctor"—he spoke the words with slow emphasis—"a true believer. They are rare."

Farley drove slowly back toward the gate. Where he had paused before, he stopped the car and got out to look once more at the Long Valley vista. Geology-trained, he marked the steep glaciated sides of the valley, the cirque at the valley's end from which the ice flow had descended. He breathed deep of the clear thin air. It was like a tonic.

He liked Wayne Carter, and there was, of course, a great deal in what he had had to say. But the true believers, the zealots, rarely win out in a pragmatic world, and a man is less than practical if he fails to keep his eye on his own interests rather than on broad generalities, however convincing they might seem.

In Farley's opinion a good share of the world's woes arose, and had always arisen, from motives that were beyond reproach but failed to stand the test of practicability. "Love thy neighbor" somehow became ritualized and formalized and dogmatized into the slaughter of the Crusades and the horrors of the Inquisition.

No, Wayne Carter was undoubtedly a highly capable man, but as long as he kept his eyes on distant horizons, he ran the risk of stubbing his toe and falling on his face. It was, Farley decided, a pity.

He got into the car again and drove on to the gate. Through it, he hesitated briefly and then turned left instead of right, toward the village of Dos Piedras rather than toward the ranch. After all, he thought, a man had every right to see an old friend, didn't he?

Tito Abeyta was in his office when Farley walked in. He had a spur on the desk in front of him, and a loose rowel lying beside it. He looked up, saw Farley, did a slow take and then pushed back his chair and stood up. "I will be goddamned," he said. He held out his hand. "How are you, Mr. Wells? And what are you doing here in the boondocks? You're only the second one I've seen from Houston since I came back."

Farley sat down. He was smiling. "We miss you, Tito. Both on the field and, I hear tell, in the locker room as well." He wondered who the other man from Houston had been, and what he was doing here, but those questions could wait. "How's the knee?"

"It works." Tito sat down, automatically adjusting the .357 magnum and its holster. "No complaints. I had six years." His gesture took in the office and the entire village. "Now I have this." He paused. "A little different from Houston." He smiled without amusement. "But I call it home. How is Houston?"

"Houston," Farley said, "is fine. We'd like to win more ballgames, but—" He shrugged. "I'm staying at the big ranch, Tito."

"With Tom Granger?" Tito smiled again. Then, answering the unspoken question, "I've known him since we were kids. Summers he and I used to hell around together. A hardnosed son of a bitch when you get right down to it."

"I'm Will Granger's guest."

Tito leaned back in his chair and stared thoughtfully at the far wall. "I wouldn't have thought," he said slowly, "that you and Will would have much in common, Mr. Wells." He looked at Farley. "Do you know him well?"

Farley shook his head. All information was welcome, he thought, grist for his mill. He waited.

"He's a funny one," Tito said, "and you wonder that a bloodline that produced old Tully and Matt and Tom could come up with him. His father never amounted to much either, but he was a flyer and by all accounts a good one during the big war. Will has never done anything." He paused. "Maybe living out here he never had a chance. Maybe." He paused again. "Or maybe he sees things I don't see." He smiled suddenly. "I was a defensive lineman and they aren't supposed to think, are they, Mr. Wells?" And then, "You interested in the big ranch?"

"I find it interesting," Farley smiled faintly. "Straight out of the Old West. Rustling and everything."

"I heard." Tito's voice was expressionless. "Grutas County, not mine."

Farley said slowly, "And the atomic reactor? Is that in your county?"

Tito shook his head.

"I was hoping," Farley said, "that it might be." He was silent for a little time. Then, "Let's say that I'm interested in Doctor Carter's project, and I would be happy to be kept up to date on its progress." He paused. "Or its problems." Another pause. "Of course I'd be willing to pay for somebody's time and trouble to keep me informed. And I think you know that I'm not exactly thought of as a tight-fisted man."

"A lot of people are interested in that reactor," Tito said.

Farley's eyebrows rose gently in question.

"Those of us who live around here," Tito said. "We don't exactly love the idea of atomic reaction going on in our backyard. People who live in Hiroshima would know the feeling. So would those poor bastards who built their houses out of Central City uranium-mine tailings."

Farley nodded. "Anyone else?"

"There is sure as hell somebody. Before they put up that fence they were having lots of problems." Tito shook his head. "But, like I said, it's outside my jurisdiction." He hesitated. "Still, I expect I could manage to keep up on things."

"As a favor to me," Farley said. "I will appreciate it." Then, "You said I was the second one from Houston to drop by. Who would the other be?"

Was there change in Tito's face? Hard to tell. "Joe Harlow," he said. "Remember him, Mr. Wells? He's been off in Saudi Arabia, he told me, doing chores for the old man. Happy to be back, he said."

Chores for J.R., Farley thought, and tucked the information away. "What was he doing up here?"

"Hunting. They come to these mountains from all over."

Long after Farley had driven away, Tito sat on at his desk. Twice he opened the drawer and looked at the three one-hundred-dollar bills Farley had left with him. Half a month's salary. Just for listening to local gossip and passing along its essence? Tito thought not. He had an idea there would be more to it than that. It would be interesting to see what it might be.

16

Tish enjoyed Santa Fe. Sometimes in winter she came to stay in town and ski the nearby basin—although she preferred the steeper Taos slopes or the great open mountains of Colorado. Summers she sometimes came for the opera. She knew a number of people, and she felt quite at home on the narrow potholed streets.

Visiting hours were fixed and strictly enforced at St. Vincent's Hospital, but Seth Porter was on the Board of Trustees, and, as he explained over the telephone, a talk with José Archuleta without the visiting presence of his many relatives might very well cast some light on the recent crimes in Grutas County. Permission for off-visiting-hours interview granted.

"I'll send Jimmy Thomas with you," Seth told Tish. "He's young, but he's bright, and he speaks Spanish."

Jimmy Thomas was red-headed and bubbly, a product of Stanford Law School, where he had edited the *Law Review*. He was in love with Santa Fe. Together they walked from Seth Porter's office down Palace Avenue to the hospital. The day was clear and bright, cool even in the warm sun.

"It's probably old hat to you," Jimmy said, "but I can't get over the clear air, no smog, mountains all around close enough to reach out and touch. Do you know that in thirty minutes from the office I can be on any one of half a dozen trout streams?" He paused "Well, maybe that's an exaggeration, but you see what I mean. And in winter seventeen miles up to the ski basin. Less than that to pack into the wilderness."

Tish was smiling.

"I said something funny?"

"No." Tish's smile turned gentle. "I like your enthusiasm."

Jimmy blushed. "How about that?"

Archuleta was in a ward of six beds. Both of his legs were in traction, and from time to time he moved his upper body, using arms and shoulders with great caution, still hoping that somehow he might find a comfortable position. There was sweat on his forehead as he talked.

"It was dark—you know? I seen lights through the trees, tha's all, an' here they come, two big son a beetches, they take up the whole goddamn road—" His smile of apology to Tish was a grimace. He shifted himself gently in the bed. "Me, I go into the trees you know? What else is to do? Big goddamn cattle trucks, going too fast." He spread his hands. "Tha's all. Benny Baca, he find me. He state cop."

Jimmy said gently, "We're trying to find the trucks, Mr. Archuleta. And when we do the people involved with them are going to answer for a number of things. Your accident among them."

Archuleta said, "Hospital cost money. Doctor cost money. I can't work. My truck, she wrecked." He rolled his head on the pillow.

"All of that," Jimmy said, "we'll take into consideration if you can help us find the trucks." He paused. "For example," he said, "did you notice what color they were? I know it was dark, but—"

"No color. Just dirty. Dust an' mud an' cowshit, you know?"

Jimmy contained a smile. He nodded. "You could see cattle inside?"

"Like I tell Benny Baca, full of cattle, both of them, son a beetches down from Colorado."

Jimmy said slowly, "Why do you say they were from Colorado, Mr. Archuleta?"

"License plate."

Jimmy's eyebrows rose in surprise. "You could read them?"

Archuleta waggled his head in negative impatience. "It was dark, you know? An' I was busy. But they had plates."

Jimmy nodded. "Presumably. But how do you know they were Colorado?"

Tish said, "I think I understand. They had license plates on the front, is that it, Mr. Archuleta?"

"Tha's right."

"New Mexico cars and trucks," Tish said to Jimmy, "have plates only on the rear. So Colorado is the best bet, isn't that what you meant, Mr. Archuleta?"

"Tha's right."

There was more, but none of it was germane, merely pitiful. It was Tish who said at last, "I think we'd better let you rest, Mr. Archuleta." She stood up. "Thank you very much. You've been most helpful."

"De nada." One hand lifted helplessly. "If you find the sons a beetches—" The sentence was left unfinished.

"We'll see that you get everything that's coming to you, Mr. Archuleta," Jimmy said. "That is a promise."

Outside again in the bright day, "I hate going to hospitals," Tish said. "They make me feel guilty because I'm healthy while people like that poor man hurt."

Jimmy was thinking of something else. "It was clever of you to catch that license bit," he said. "I missed it." There was admiration in his voice. He hesitated. "Are you going to be in Santa Fe for a day or two?"

"At least."

"Then," Jimmy said, "maybe I could see you again. Unofficially, I mean." He was grinning broadly. "Like maybe dinner?"

It was strange how easily she could relax. "That would be very nice," Tish said.

She walked slowly, thoughtfully, down Palace Avenue, turned across Cathedral Plaza, and walked on to La Fonda. The old lobby was dim and cool, the tiled floor smooth underfoot. It had been a fairy palace when she was much younger, a place of dreams seen only on occasional visits down from the ranch with her mother and sometimes old Matt as well. The hotel was older now, a bit shabbier, and by comparison with other hotels she had known far smaller than she had thought it then, but she loved it still.

She stopped at the desk for her key. There was a message in her box to call Lieutenant Romero of the State Police, and she went up to her room to make the call.

"Tom called me from the ranch," the lieutenant said. "He asked me to tell you everything we know, which is very damn little, but if you want to come out here, I'll do my best."

"Right away," Tish said. It was a measure of the esteem in which the ranch was held, she thought, that there was no trace of resentment in the lieutenant's voice. She hung up feeling a little excited and by association important.

It was the new State Police complex out on the Albuquerque highway, low, massive, unstuccoed, glaringly gray against the brown landscape and the jagged Ortiz mountains. She was shown immediately to the lieutenant's office.

She had met him once or twice. He was middle-sized and wiry with dark hair and dark angry eyes, a mixture it was said of Anglo, Apache, and Spanish, college-educated, utterly unlike poor José Archuleta lying with both legs in traction in the hospital bed. It was also said that Marty Romero might very well have been head of the State Police had it not been for his penchant for speaking his mind to everybody, including the governor.

He was polite now, and unhurried. "How is Tom?"

"Angry."

"I don't blame him for that."

"And," Tish said, "not sure that he isn't going to throw in the towel and walk away from the whole— mess." Saying it, she could have wept.

"I don't remember Tom ever throwing in the towel," the lieutenant said. "Or Matt. And from what I've heard, if you leaned hard on old Tully, all you got was a broken back." He walked around to sit behind his desk. He laid his hands on the desktop. "We had a rash of cattle rustling last fall when beef was scarce and high priced in the markets."

"We had that one strike," Tish said.

"But only that one." The lieutenant paused. "South and east, ranches a tenth the size of Rancho del Norte were hit half a dozen times. The same in Colorado, Wyoming, Montana, Nebraska. And your hit came just before the big snow, long after the other action had petered out." He paused again. "I don't know what I'm implying, if anything, but when you find something that stands outside of a pattern, you wonder about it."

Tish said, "Wonder how?" And then, answering her

own question, "Ours might have been local, not organized, is that what you're thinking?" Face it, she told herself, you suggested the possibility yourself.

"Could be." The lieutenant's voice was expressionless.

"But this one wasn't." Tish said. "The trucks were down from Colorado." She explained what Archuleta had said.

Marty Romero listened quietly. "My men missed that. They shouldn't have." His voice did not change, but it was clear that someone was going to wish he had not missed that little bit of information. "Did you get anything else?"

Tish shook her head. Nothing but a dinner invitation, she thought, and stifled a giggle.

"Tom went out to see for himself," Marty Romero said. "Somebody shot at him—"

"Oh, no!"

"They missed." Marty saw the relief in Tish's face. He tucked it away in his tracker's mind, as he tucked away all signs. "So," he said, "it would seem that not everybody connected with the hit went off in the Colorado trucks, no?"

Right back to my first guess, Tish thought, and wished it were not so. "Somebody local to round up the cattle and hold them," she said. "But Tom wasn't there until today, and it all happened last night, so why would anyone still be there?"

Marty Romero nodded. "Maybe somebody came back. Maybe he had left something. Tom said there was something on the ground, something metallic, he thought, but he didn't have time to see what it was." He smiled without amusement. "And he didn't stay around to find out, which was smart of him."

Tish was silent for a little time. She said at last, "You said there was a rash of rustling last fall. Has it picked up again this spring?"

"Not to the same extent." He sat immobile, this Anglo-Apache-Spanish lieutenant, patient as rock. "Like I said, beef was scarce last year and prices were high. They've tapered off a little now. Yours is only the second strike in the whole state this year."

Tish thought about it. "What was the other one? Where?"

She thought well, this Anglo chick, Marty decided, and tucked that conclusion away too. "Way east and south," he said, "so we can be pretty sure no Colorado trucks were involved."

"So," Tish said thoughtfully, "the pattern is broken again."

"It may mean something," Marty said, "or it may mean nothing." He shrugged. *"¿Quién sabe?"*

Tish stood up. "Thank you."

The lieutenant rose too. "Anything else," he said, "and I'll get back to you." He watched her walk out, tall and slim, mountain bred, he thought; in an odd way not unlike himself because he sensed in her too a feeling of not belonging strong almost as his own. Misfits together, he thought, and smiled wryly at the conceit. On the other hand, each in his own way, and at his own business, thoroughly competent. Strange.

Jimmy Thomas sat in Seth Porter's office. The old man tried to give you the country-boy act, he thought, while he was actually about as bucolic as Widener Library. There were times when he resented the performance, which was, he told himself, just because he was young and maybe a little too big for his britches. If he ever turned out to be half the success Seth Porter was, he'd be luckier than he ever expected to be—and he'd damn well better remember it. "Yes, sir," he said, "that's the word: Sam Waldo is passing out a few hundred here and a few hundred there. Not something that is easily proved, of course."

Seth showed his patient smile. "We're not after legal proof, son. Nailing Sam Waldo's hide to the barn door doesn't interest us. It wouldn't even look pretty. Have you talked with the conservationists, Sierra Club and the others?"

"Yes, sir. They're high on the Waldo bill. They never expected it from him, but they're all for it. All that real estate kept in wilderness." Jimmy shook his head in wonder. "And there's another thing," he said, "the conservation people aren't in favor of that atomic reactor project, either. And I'd have thought they would be. It's either that or fossil-fuel generating plants like those up at Four Corners, sending their smoke all the way down here."

Seth was smiling still, but the smile was a trifle strained. There were times, like now, when he felt like an elder statesman or a teacher of youth, two roles he did not relish. But someone, damn it, had to explain the obvious to the brighter young-uns or they never would get things straight. He stifled a sigh. "A thing to learn, son," he said, "is that no matter what the books say, man isn't a logical animal. Most times he thinks with his stomach, or he carries his logic only partway." He paused to watch for effect.

"I'm not sure I know what you mean, sir," Jimmy said.

"What I mean, son, is that those Four Corners plants are there at least partly because the conservationists wouldn't hold still for hydroelectric power plants in the Grand Canyon. Would spoil the natural beauty of one of nature's wonders, they said—and maybe they were right, at that. But they *had* to have more power in places like Phoenix and Los Angeles, so the utility people said, 'How about coal-fired plants up in the Four Corners area, where there's lots of coal and lots of open space?' And the conservationists said okay. Now they aren't sure it was such a good bargain after all."

A tendency in himself he had to fight, Jimmy knew, was that of seeing one side of a question, finding it without flaw and deciding that was it. Because always, always there was somebody with a contrary view, and all too often he had supporting arguments that sounded just as good as yours. The trick was to look carefully at both sides, find the strengths and the weaknesses of both arguments and plan your strategy accordingly. There was nothing new in this concept. It was merely that some truths had a way of taking a long time to get through to you. "I didn't know that, sir," he said.

"I'm not too happy about atomic power plants, either," Seth said. "On the other hand, what are the alternatives? Fossil-fuel plants, which tend to be dirty and which will run out of fuel anyway in not too many years, nobody knows exactly how many, but we'd better be ready for it whenever. Or there is geothermal power, which is already in use some places and which is being looked into right here as well. But it isn't something that will happen tomorrow. Then there is solar energy, and some think that's the only eventual solution. But research takes money, and until recently Washington wasn't interested: there weren't any votes or much prestige in playing with solar panels out in the desert. They don't even go *bang* for the TV cameras."

He had done it again, Jimmy thought; and was tempted to stand up and try to kick himself. "I hadn't thought of it that way, sir."

"It's all very well," Seth said, "to say that we don't need electric can-openers or electric hair driers or all that air-conditioning that uses so much power. And I don't doubt for a moment that we waste almost as much energy as we use. We eat too much too, but how do you go about putting a whole nation on a diet? People won't even stop smoking when you can prove that they're killing themselves." He paused.

"No," he said, "the fact is that we have to have new sources of energy, and we'll just have to do the best we can to keep pollution or risk to a minimum because in order to get energy, we have to have either pollution or risk as matters stand now, and I'd rather take the risk of that reactor than the stink of more coal-fired plants and the strip-mining that feeds them."

"I guess I see your point, sir," Jimmy said.

"Back to Sam Waldo," Seth said. "What's your head count on his bill in committee?"

He didn't want an actual head count, Jimmy thought, unless the results were in doubt. And they were not. "It will get a do-pass," he said.

159

"And on the floor?"

"In the House it will go through without trouble." Jimmy paused. "In the Senate it may be closer, but I think there'll be enough horse-trading and enough debt-paying and enough just plain bribery to get it through. Sam Waldo——" He shook his head.

"Don't ever bet a man at his own game," Seth said, smiling, "and this is Sam's game, and he's just as good at it as the man in the carnival with the pea and the three shells." Seth paused. "And just as crooked." He paused again. "Now what about the governor? Which way will George go? Veto? Or will he sign?"

"There'll be a lot of pressure on him to sign," Jimmy said. "A couple of people I've talked to, newspaper people and others, think this is the kind of story that might get nationwide attention. Everybody talking about the need to protect wilderness land before it's all gone, and one state, and a poor one at that, actually doing something about it. Hunters, fishermen, conservationists from all over the country may be interested, not to mention local pressure."

"It's local pressure I'm thinking of," Seth said. "George counts votes, and votes don't come from out of state. Could the House and Senate override a veto?"

Jimmy thought about it. "It would be a close thing. I think very close."

Seth nodded. "And George doesn't like close things. Most politicians don't. They like to win big. Everybody likes a winner." He smiled again. "Just the way things are."

Jimmy said, "What about the Grangers, sir? The bill doesn't provide for condemnation of the land; it merely appropriates money to buy it, assuming it is for sale."

"The Grangers," Seth said, "are of two minds." He smiled suddenly. "Two equal minds, but at the moment one is more equal than the other. It is a situation that could change."

The telephone on Seth's desk buzzed discreetly. He picked it up, frowning faintly at the interruption. "Yes?"

"I am sorry to bother you, Mr. Porter," the operator said, "but Miss Tish Wilson is calling. She sounds upset."

"Put her on." Then, "Tish, what's happening, honey?"

"Somebody shot at Tom." The more she had thought about it, the more it had upset her. "Lieutenant Romero told me. They missed, but what if they try again? And —why? What does it mean?"

"I don't know, honey, but I'll see if I can find out. I'll call you back." Seth hung up and sat for a moment in silence, unsmiling now. "I knew Tully," he said. "I knew Matt. I know Tom. And Will." He shook his head, looking across the desk now at Jimmy. "They're a violent breed. They had to be to take what they did, and hold it. And if there is one thing that is true in this land we live in, it is that violence begets violence."

Jimmy not understanding, shook his head.

"Somebody shot at Tom Granger," Seth said. His face was grave. "Somebody could be trying to change the equality I mentioned."

17

Tom had been in no hurry to tell anyone on the ranch about the shooting episode. He was not necessarily secretive by nature, but neither was it his habit to talk before seeing reason for it and examining possible reasons against. He had ridden straight back to the ranch, turned the gelding over to a stablehand, and gone into Clyde Burley's office.

Clyde was there, large and solid and angry, scowling at papers spread on his desk. He looked up when Tom came in. Then he leaned back in his chair. "Okay," he said, "say it. Another fifty-sixty head gone, Angus-Charolais mix, good stock. My fault."

Tom sat down. He could still hear the snarl of that bullet and the sound of the shot that followed. He imagined he would be able to hear them for some time to come. If he had not bent down in the saddle to look at whatever it was on the ground. . . . "I'm not blaming you," he said. He felt even a sense of relief that it could not, obviously, have been Clyde Burley who fired the shot. Unless, of course, Clyde had been driving a car, in which case he could have been back here long before Tom arrived. But there had been no car in sight. Nevertheless. "You looked over the place?" he said.

"First thing this morning. Just after dawn. Soon as I heard." Clyde shook his head. "Maybe one of those Apache trackers they talk about could have made some sense, but I couldn't, and I don't know any Apache trackers, anyway."

"I do," Tom said. "Just one." Marty Romero. He tucked the idea away. "Have you been back since?" He kept his voice uninflected.

"I've been sitting right here on my ass, trying to figure out just how you patrol a perimeter the size of this ranch without night helicopter flights and radar like we had in the Army."

"It's an idea," Tom said. "Keep thinking." Scratch Clyde as a possible bushwhacker, he thought. "And give some thought too," he added, "to the map. There are only so many places where roads good enough for big cattle trucks skirt our fenceline." He paused. "When you've picked out the spots that seem likely, we'll go over them together and see what we can figure out." He paused again. "Okay?"

Clyde nodded shortly. "You're the boss."

"I'm aware of it." Very much aware.

He walked back up the hill to the main house. First things first, he thought, and shut himself in the

162

POWER

big office to call Marty Romero in Santa Fe and ask for his cooperation with Tish. That done, he kept Marty on the line with the other matter:

"Somebody had a shot at me." He told the story. Then, "What are the chances of your coming up? We could use a tracker." He paused. "Even if he is lieutenant of the State Police." He hoped it sounded light.

"Trucks don't leave tracks, amigo."

"Men do. And horses. And among other things, I'd like to know who shot at me. I don't like it."

There was a short silence. Then, "We'll see," Marty Romero said.

Tom hung up and sat at the big desk. Then he rang for Consuelo to bring him a beer, and when she returned with it, "Shut the door," Tom said. "Sit down, Connie."

Consuelo perched uncomfortably on the front six inches of a chair. She smoothed her skirts and waited patiently.

Tom poured his beer and drank deep while he thought how to go about it. Head on, he decided; there was no other way. I am *el patrón;* the thought presented itself unbidden. "After the Señorita Tish left," he said, "and after I rode off—" He hesitated.

"*¿Sí, señor?*"

"Did any of the others leave the ranch? Don Will, Señor Wells, Señorita Wilding, Señora Granger?"

"Only the Señor Wells. Don Will gave orders that an automobile was to be provided. The señor wished to visit Valle Largo."

Long Valley, Tom thought, the atomic site. It was the opposite direction from the spot of the cattle rustling. "The others are still here?"

"*Sí, señor.*"

"Have the goodness to ask Don Will to come in."

He drank his beer while he waited. And then, new thought, he got up from his chair and went to study the contents of the gun cabinet. No rifles missing. Nor had he thought there would be. He doubted that anyone seeing him ride off could have known exactly

163

where he was going; in any event ambush seemed unlikely. Still—

"Going hunting?" Will's voice from the doorway. He was smiling. "I was told *el patrón* required my presence."

"Close the door," Tom said. "Sit down. You want a beer?"

"In a little while a Bloody Mary. In the meantime nothing." Will sat down and stretched his legs, smiling still. "I understand we've been rustled again?" His tone said that he could not have cared less.

"Your money as well as mine."

Will shook his head. "I won't think of it as money until I have it in my hand. Until then it's just beef on the hoof, no more interesting to me than it ever was."

"Just a matter of curiosity," Tom said, "what is of interest to you?" They were worlds apart, he thought, scarcely speaking the same language. Had they ever been otherwise? And whose fault was that? His?

"That's easy." Will's smile was relaxed. "Going where I want when I want and doing what I want." The smile altered. "You aren't going to give a lecture on *noblesse oblige,* I hope?" He watched Tom's headshake. "Good. Old Matt used to try to tell me that I ought to become a useful member of society." The smile returned to its full flavor. "It went something like this: 'Goddamnit, boy, when are you going to get your ass moving and do something to make you worth the powder to blow you to Hell with?'"

Tom could hear the old man, disappointed in his own son, trying to rouse his grandson into some kind of useful activity and almost blowing a fuse in the process. His tirades with Tom had been of a different nature, two personalities perpetually clashing. He said as offhandedly as he could, "Somebody tried to kill me this morning." He watched Will's smile freeze and then disappear.

"If you're serious," Will said, "and I assume you

are, are you pointing a finger at me? Because I haven't seen you all morning until now." He paused.

"Rifle shot." And again he could hear the snarl of the bullet passing by where his head had been only a moment before. It was anger now that he felt, deep, solid, strong.

Will was unsmiling now. "Only one shot?"

"I didn't stay to see if there would be more."

Will was silent, thoughtful. "What price a hunter wanting to take a deer off-season, firing at something that moves? It happens."

It did happen indeed, Tom thought; in deer season when the woods were thick with flatland dudes carrying high-powered rifles, even ranch property, technically off-bounds to hunters, could be dangerous terrain. But he thought the possibility did not apply this morning. "I doubt it," he said.

Will nodded as if he had expected no different. "Then," he said, "I have exhausted my theories." But he made no move to rise from his chair. "I was planning to have a talk with you anyway," he said. "Now is as good a time as any." His eyebrows rose in question.

"Fire away," Tom said, and settled into his chair to listen. I know what it is going to be, he told himself, but let's see how he presents it.

Will took his time. "There is a bill down in Santa Fe," he said, "to appropriate state funds to buy El Rancho del Norte. You know about that?"

Tom merely nodded.

Will sighed. "I might have known you would." He paused. "So whát does it mean to you?"

"I don't know yet."

"Sooner or later you're going to have to make up your mind."

"Sooner or later I will." Why did he resent Will's asking about what he had a perfect right to ask about? Answer me that, he demanded silently.

"In the meantime," Will said, "Sue and I—dangle. Is that how you like it?"

"You're not hurting for money. You can go wherever you like, whenever, and do what you want, just as you always have."

"And what if you decide to put a tether on us?"

"I won't."

"How do I know that?"

"Because I'm telling you. I haven't seen the figures yet. After taxes things are going to be a little tighter than they were—"

"There it goes."

"But not so tight that you'll feel a pinch any more than I will. Matt always gave you whatever you asked."

"It was his to dole out as he wanted. What you're controlling is half mine. I want it. All of it."

"So you said."

"And I'm going to get it."

"You said that too. But the point is that I'm not going to break up this ranch, or sell it just to make you happy. Maybe selling will make sense. Maybe I don't want to stay here, tied to the land the way Matt was."

"You love it." Will's temper was wearing thin, and his voice was rising.

"Don't work yourself up," Tom said. "It won't do any good and you know it." His own temper was short. "Go have your Bloody Mary. I've got work to do."

He sat on motionless after Will had left the office. They were on a collision course, Tom thought, and what might come out of it was anybody's guess. What had been said between them up to now was mere preliminary; sooner or later there would be a blowup. So be it.

He finished the beer and set bottle and mug aside. He had spoken only simple truth when he had said that he had work to do. So far he had only looked over ranch records, plans, unanswered correspondence. Old Matt had let things slide these last few months. And, Tom told himself, Tish was right: I ought to have been here, but I didn't come for the same reason he wouldn't ask me: pride. He decided that he was beginning to look at himself with different eyes and not liking very much what he saw.

Will mixed two Bloody Marys with the kind of expert care he gave to things that really mattered. First the Worcestershire and salt in the bottom of each glass, with a dash of Tabasco and a little lemon juice. He stirred carefully. Then he added vodka, ice, and tomato juice, stirred well, sniffed the mixture, added a stalk of celery as garnish, and carried the two drinks out to the terrace, where Sue waited in the sun on a chaise lounge. Will felt better, eased, no longer quite so uptight about his talk with Tom.

He raised his glass. "Cheers." He sampled the drink. He had to admit that the home-squeezed and frozen tomato juice did have a very special taste. There was something to be said for living on a self-sufficient ranch, but not really very much.

Sue said idly, "What did Tom have in mind?"

Will's voice was quiet. "He wanted to tell me that someone with a rifle tried to kill him this morning." Out here now, sitting in the sunshine, it sounded incredible. Oh, Will told himself, such things did happen, of course, but to people you didn't know, scruffy people, violent people. He looked carefully at Sue to see how she was taking it.

Sue sipped her drink slowly. Strangely enough, she did not seem perturbed. "Nothing that happens here in the Wild West would surprise me," she said. She paused. "Could it have been an accident?"

"Tom says no."

"How could he tell?"

"I don't know, but he seems sure." He wanted to drop the subject; just talking about it made him uncomfortable. He raised his glass and studied it in the sunlight. "If I do say it," he said, "this is a superb Bloody Mary."

"You can always turn to bartending, darling"— Sue paused—"when we run out of money." She smiled up from the chaise.

"We aren't going to run out of money." Damn it,

Will thought, it was what came from having to come back to this thrice-damned place. Everything looked different, sounded different. He and Sue had never quarreled over money. Why should she raise the subject now? "Tom gave me his word," he said.

"That was nice." She smiled again. She paused, and the smile disappeared. "It was different," she said, "when your grandfather was still alive. It seemed—right that you, we got money from him." She paused again. "Do you see what I mean, darling? But half of it is yours now, and you can't get it. We're on a—tether."

It was precisely what he had said himself to Tom. Why should it annoy him to hear it now? Again he had the feeling that it was the place that was to blame, and how could you fight mere surroundings? "Damn it—" he began, and then was silent.

She sipped her drink. She said quietly, "It *is* a good Bloody Mary, darling"

With heavy irony, "Thanks."

They were silent in the sunlight for a time. Sue said at last, "Where's Ethel?"

"I wouldn't know. I'm not as interested in her as you are."

So he had noticed? What difference? "Darling, don't be stuffy."

"There are times when these little lesbian affairs of yours—"

"The word is bisexual." Sue was completely at ease. "And you used to take a different view."

"Maybe I've changed."

Her answer surprised him. "Yes, you have, and I don't know why." Her tone was quiet, thoughtful. She was looking, not at Will, but at the distant mountains. "It's different here. You're different here." She looked at Will then, unsmiling. "You may not feel it, but I do. When I rode yesterday—" She shook her head. "It isn't real! You ride for miles and you don't see anybody or anything except maybe a cow or two or a deer—"

"Not even a Sheraton Hotel or an Elizabeth Arden

salon," Will said. "Tough." How ridiculous could he be, he asked himself, being defensive about a place he detested?

"Let's not quarrel, darling." Sue's voice was quiet again. "What did Tom say that upset you?"

Was he that transparent? He supposed he was, and the realization did nothing to restore equanimity. "I told him about the bill down in Santa Fe to buy this goddamn place. He knew about it already."

"Of course."

Will glared at her. "That means what?"

"Your brother isn't stupid, darling. And neither is that bucolic lawyer. And why do you suppose Tom sent Tish to Santa Fe?"

Will thought about it. "All right. So he knew. I asked him what it meant to him and he said he didn't know yet." He paused. "That's all."

"No." Sue shook her bright head gently. "Then you told him you wanted your share and you were going to get it." She paused. "Didn't you?"

"What if I did?"

"Darling." Sue's tone was patient. "Your brother won't be pushed. Even I can see that. The more you try to push him, the more he sets his chin and digs in his heels."

True, of course, but that made it no more palatable. "So just what am I supposed to do?" Will said. "Take his edicts like a little gentleman?"

Sue was silent for a time, her eyes fixed on the distant mountains. At last she rolled her head to look at her husband. "Darling, do we need the money? I mean really need it. Isn't just knowing it's there enough?"

"No."

"Tell me why."

Will drank deep. He remained silent.

"Do we owe money, darling? Is that it?" Sue paused. The silence this time was eloquent. "How much?"

"Enough."

Sue looked again at those distant mountains. She said slowly, "Have you told Tom?"

"No. Do you think it would do any good? Basically he's like old Matt, a Christer. You're supposed to earn your way in this world, but since I don't do that, the least I can do is keep my nose clean, stay away from gamblers and loan sharks, and be a good little citizen."

Sue's eyes were still on the mountains. "I see." Her tone was quiet, somehow decisive.

Will studied her. "That means what?"

"Darling," Sue said slowly, "he isn't about to sell the ranch, at least not in a hurry and maybe not at all." She turned her head to look at Will. "Correct?"

"You know it is."

"And," Sue said, "you are not about to go to him with your problem." She paused. "I assume it is a problem?"

"It is, and I'm not." It was not a very heroic role he was playing, Will told himself. Well, screw it. He wasn't cast in the heroic mold. He had never thought of himself as being like old Matt or Tom, larger than life-size. He looked suddenly at Sue. "What did you say?" His voice was sharp.

"I was just asking, darling." Her voice was quiet, totally calm. "Someone tried to kill Tom this morning, you said. What if he had succeeded?"

Yes, what? Think that one over, friend. Or in your sneaky little subconscious have you already? Will had a long finishing pull at his drink. He set the empty glass down. "Then," he said, his voice quiet now, "we'd get the bundle." He stared at Sue. "Just what are you thinking?"

"Why, nothing at all, darling. I was just—wondering." She looked up as Ethel Wilding walked toward them. "Hi," Sue said. "I wondered where you were." She sat up and swung her legs from the chaise, got to her feet. "Come for a walk with me. Lover here is in a grumpy mood. I want someone to laugh with."

18

After Sue and Ethel had walked off together, Will sat alone in the sun with his thoughts. Nothing that had happened here in the Wild West would surprise Sue, she had said. And precisely what had that meant? Merely that she was taking quite calmly the fact that someone had shot at Tom? Or was it more than that?

There were times when Will was sure he knew Sue inside and out. There were other times, like now, when he seemed to catch echoes from depths within her he had not even begun to plumb.

He turned in his chair to watch the two women walking together in the direction of the stream. Sue's departure had been deliberate, and Will had the notion that its purpose had been precisely this: to leave him to digest their conversation and from it draw conclusions Sue herself had already reached and accepted.

Sue was spoiled; there was no question of that. And Sue's thoughts were first and foremost upon herself. Well, as far as that went, so were his upon himself, weren't they? So they made a good pair, right? But maybe it wasn't right; maybe—new thought—it was all wrong.

He had never thought about it before; he detested people who were always searching their souls and finding *reasons*. But maybe this once there was something to think about. He and Sue, too much alike, acting on each other, compounding their—weaknesses? As some couples you were always reading about compounded their strengths? What then?

He turned to look again at the two women. They had reached the path that followed the stream, and were almost out of sight in the trees. As Will watched, Sue slipped her arm around Ethel's waist. The last he saw Ethel had made no attempt to draw away.

Will picked up his glass and walked slowly, thoughtfully back into the big house. He mixed himself another Bloody Mary with the same careful attention to detail and went back out into the sunlight.

There was no way of telling how far Sue's attentions to Ethel would go. There never was. There were times when Sue seemed merely to be amusing herself with another woman through the kind of innocent intimacies schoolgirls indulged in, secret smiles and hand-holding, walking arm-in-arm. Then there were other times, like that afternoon in Cannes when he had walked in to find Sue and that cute young maid naked together on the bed. No mere innocent hand-holding then.

"Don't be stuffy, darling," Sue had said just now.

Well, Will supposed she had a point, because that warm afternoon in the Cannes hotel room he had ended up being anything but stuffy with Sue and the cute young maid. He had often wondered whether Sue had planned it that way, and he was inclined to think she had. He was quite aware that when she chose, Sue could maneuver him almost at will. Was that what she was doing now?

Oh, not as that other time in a sexual way. Ethel Wilding was not a young French maid. No, if Sue was trying to maneuver him this time, it was with a far different purpose in mind. Face it, he told himself angrily; stop pussyfooting around. What your wife has dangled in front of your nose is the fact that you, and she, would be far better off if your brother were dead. The Cain and Abel bit. Am I my brother's keeper?

He drank deep, and did not even taste the drink. One attempt on Tom's life already by an unknown rifleman for reasons also unknown. And he, Will, demonstrably innocent, all morning Sue's company in plain view of the ranch people. What did that add up to?

Sue had seen it of course far sooner than he. Oh, not for the world would she have come right out and showed him the opportunity the unknown rifleman had provided. Sue's way was rarely direct. No, all she had done was ask innocently what if the rifleman had succeeded, and by asking had opened a door in his mind on dark and dangerous thoughts.

Had she even known that they were not new thoughts, that as long as he could remember he had resented living in his brother's shadow and had tried at least on one occasion to remove it? Had he ever told her that it was he, Will, who was responsible for Tom's climbing the face of the mountain that overhung the meadow where the charter plane had landed? He could not remember telling her, but neither was he sure that he had not. And if he had, had she guessed that he had hoped, even prayed that Tom would not come back alive? And been bitterly disappointed when Tom had ridden safely back to the ranch the next day, following a furious Matt?

For days Will had lived in fear that Tom would guess the real motive behind the dare. But he had not. There was an arrogance in Tom that kept him from comprehending that his brother or anyone else might actually wish him harm. And that, of course, made it all the more maddening.

Will was surprised to find that he had finished his second drink. He thought about it and decided against having another. He prided himself that he was not a lush as were so many whom he and Sue met in their wanderings. Nor was he interested in drugs. And his sexual deviations were limited to an occasional slap and tickle if it came his way, or a rare episode such as that bit of troilism with his own wife. When it came right down to it, as he had told himself in not infrequent fits of mild depression, he did not even have the virtue of a real vice, which made him a colorless character indeed. All he could manage to do was spend money. Which brought him right back to the main point of the morning: he would be far better off if big brother Tom were dead.

Farley Wells drove back to the ranch from Dos Piedras in a thoughtful mood. Tito Abeyta was going to be useful; there was no doubt about that. The big man was no stereotypical ex-professional athlete, brawny and stupid. He was smart, maybe too smart for his own good. It was Farley's opinion that the smarter a member of an underprivileged minority was, the more difficult it was for him to adjust to things as they were.

But what Tito had told him about trouble at the reactor before the fence was put up was disquieting to Farley because he did not understand it, and he had never subscribed to the what-you-don't-know-won't-hurt-you school of thought. It was precisely the things you didn't know and could not prepare for that frequently went off like a land mind underfoot. Was Joe Harlow involved? But J.R. had said that he wanted no trouble. Farley thought about it.

He knew something of the northern villages of New Mexico with their centuries-old traditions and prejudices, and he could quite comprehend that the atomic reactor would be resented locally. But he could not see the locals mounting any kind of organized offensive such as Tito had seemed to indicate had plagued the Long Valley project. Resistance to Anglo encroachment was traditionally sporadic and sometimes violent, but almost never a planned campaign. He wondered if Tom Granger had ideas on the subject.

Tom was in the big office and he called "Come in" to Farley's knock. He nodded to his visitor and leaned back in his chair.

"I hope I'm not intruding," Farley said.

"You are a guest, Mr. Wells. Sit down. What can I do for you?"

Farley closed the door and took one of the leather

visitor's chairs. "I met Doctor Carter." He paused. "A very able man, I should say." There was no trace of the drawl. "And I had a little visit with an old friend from Houston, Tito Abeyta." All open and aboveboard.

Tom's eyebrows rose, and then lowered as he nodded. "I see. The football."

"I have an—interest in the club." Farley was watching Tom closely. "Did I—say something?"

Long Valley was the opposite direction from the rustling site, Tom thought, but the road to Dos Piedras went right past. He could not see Farley as a bushwhacker. Still. "I'm a little jumpy this morning," he said. "Somebody took a shot at me."

"Here?" It was Farley's turn to show surprise.

Tom shook his head. "Out in the hills."

Farley was silent, thoughtful. "Any idea why?"

"Ideas," Tom said, "but that's all." He made a gesture dismissing the subject. "It shouldn't concern you."

Farley thought about it further. "Does El Rancho del Norte have a history of local trouble?" he said. "Could that explain it?"

It could, of course, and Tom had already thought about it. Kelly Garcia would be the man to look into the possibility. Kelly's local contacts were innumerable, and Kelly's ears were sharp. In the meantime, speculation was futile. He said as much.

Farley accepted it without comment. "I understand," he said, "that there have been—problems at the atomic site."

Tom studied the man. "So I've heard." His voice was expressionless. "And rumors," he added. "You've heard about them?"

Farley had not. He was interested.

"Dead sheep," Tom said, "dead fish, a little girl in Las Grutas with leukemia." He must remember to ask Kelly if the story about the girl had been put out and donations solicited. "A thunderhead that some thought looked like a mushroom cloud. Water tasting funny." The more he thought about it, the angrier he became.

"And there hasn't been any radioactive material any-where near the site—and won't be for some time."

Farley nodded slowly. "It didn't look as if they were very far along."

"There is also," Tom said, "the matter of that bill in Santa Fe, authorizing the state to buy the ranch." He found no reaction in Farley's face. He would have been surprised if he had. The man probably played a superb game of poker too. "Add it all up," Tom said, "and it seems pretty clear that somebody doesn't want a breeder reactor in these mountains." He sat quietly, waiting.

Farley smiled easily. "I imagine quite a few folks don't." He paused. "Although I don't really see the connection between some rumors and a bill in the state legislature, now, do you?"

"Maybe. Maybe not."

"Tito," Farley said, "is not just ignorant mountain folks, and he doesn't like the reactor idea."

True enough. Tom said nothing.

"He told me about the commune," Farley said. He paused. "Most ways, I consider myself a tolerant man. Live and let live." He shook his head. "But the young folks who play the tune-in, turn-on, drop-out kind of parlor games purely gravel me." He paused again. "I have a nephew. He's twenty-four now. He was a Phi Beta Kappa his junior year at the university. Two years ago, just before graduation, he quit school. It wasn't relevant, he said."

Tom thought he could guess the rest, but he said nothing.

"For six months," Farley said, "his mother and his daddy had no idea where the boy was. And then one day he came home, or, rather, someone brought him home." A third pause. Farley's face was angry. "For the last year and a half," he said, "he's been in an institution, one of those places where they try to straighten folks out so they can at least live in the world again." He shook his head. "Maybe he'll make it, and maybe he won't, but the chances are against."

"I've seen the commune," Tom said. "Does Tito

think there are drugs involved?" It was something he had not considered. Would it explain any of the things that had happened? Certainly not the cattle rustling. Possibly the rifle shot. Food for thought.

"He didn't say." Farley's voice was noncommittal again. "But there is where your rumors might come from."

Tom nodded slowly. "I hadn't thought of that."

"Folks on the back-to-nature kick don't like a lot of things some of the rest of us are used to. Maybe I don't like some of them myself." Farley's voice was quiet. "I don't like to see bulldozers moving in and knocking down every growing thing so a new trailer park can be set up. I don't like smog over Los Angeles or New York or, for that matter, Houston. I don't like rivers or lakes that stink from pollution."

Tom was smiling now. "And you don't like atomic reactors."

Farley seemed to relax. "True enough."

"Because with oil and gas prices what they are now, atomic power is very much competitive?" Tom shook his head. "You people have had your day of riding high."

"Maybe. I wouldn't wager on it."

"What else wouldn't you wager on?"

Farley smiled. "Why, as to that—" The smile spread. "No comment."

"You play them close to your vest."

"I've always found that was the best way."

The antagonism between them was almost out in the open now, Tom thought, and maybe that was all for the best. "You wouldn't have had anything to do with the rumors about the reactor, would you?" he said.

"No." Farley took his time. "And you can believe that."

"Or the problems Carter had?"

"Same answer."

"Sam Waldo is your only approach—so far?"

Farley said slowly, "You're doing a right smart amount of guessing."

Tom nodded. "About a lot of things."

177

Farley sat quietly, thinking. He said at last, "I've answered some of your questions. How about a little quid pro quo?" His voice was uninflected. "Are you going to try to keep the ranch as it is?"

"Maybe."

"I kind of think maybe means yes."

Tom shook his head. "It means what it says."

"Your brother—"

Tom's smile was wicked. "My brother is and has always been a spoiled brat. He is married to a spoiled female. Neither of them has ever done a useful thing in their lives. I'll make the decisions here on what I think is best, regardless of them or, for that matter, the legislature in Santa Fe." The smile spread recklessly. "My grandfather told the governor once, and I quote: 'If I have to, I'll shut the ranch up tighter than a bobcat's asshole and I'll shoot any son of a bitch who sets foot on ranch property.' " Tom paused. "I'm beginning to know how he felt." He paused again. "I'm beginning to find out a lot about him that I never saw before."

"That kind of thinking is a little out of date."

"Maybe." Tom sat up straight. "But that's how it is."

19

Lieutenant Marty Romero drove his own pickup truck on the road from Santa Fe to El Rancho del Norte. He drove without haste, enjoying the day, which was bright and clear, and the views of mountains, meadows, and streams, which were spectacular. He saw deer, elk, antelope, pheasants, and a lone black bear, and he smiled at them all, feeling a kind of kinship with whatever life inhabited his land.

A rifle with telescopic sight rested in the rack across the rear window of the cab. A shovel and coiled tow cable bounced on the truck bed. The four mud-and-snow tires hummed a steady tone on the surfaced road.

Marty had no illusions about his motives for the trip. Tom Granger had asked him to come, but that was only part of it. The main part was a desire to see for himself the odd and potentially volatile mixture of mountain villages, commune, atomic reactor, and big ranch lying in these two northern counties. Add the rustling and the dead man lying beneath the snow all winter, and now someone taking a shot at Tom Granger. Marty had a feeling in his bones that something was about to erupt.

Before leaving Santa Fe he had called Tish at La Fonda, told her of Tom's request, and assured her that one of his colleagues would keep her informed if there was anything new on the rustling. She had surprised him by her shrewdness.

"It isn't just—Tom, is it?" she had said. "I mean, it's everything, isn't it?"

And Marty had said, "What do you mean by that?" Automatic evasion.

"I can't explain it, but—everything changed when Matt died. Not really, of course, but it seemed that way. It was as if while he was alive everything held together. When he died it all came—unstuck." She paused. "I guess that's silly. I mean, it's just my feeling."

It was maybe closer to fact than she knew, Marty thought, but all he said was, "I'll nose around a bit. Maybe coming in from outside I'll see some things the people already there have missed."

"Please," Tish said, "a—message. Tell Tom to take care of himself. If someone is shooting at him—" She left the sentence unfinished.

"Will do," Marty said.

He did not drive straight to the ranch. Instead he

stopped off in Las Grutas and went in to see Pepe Martinez. Some county officials were jealous of their jurisdictions, and although diplomacy was not Marty's long suit, there were times when he agreed that a soothing word here and there could be useful. He explained about Archuleta's testimony that the rustling trucks came from out of state. "That puts it more or less in our lap," he said.

Pepe scowled and rubbed the broken nose. He could find no flaw in the reasoning. "Okay," he said as if Marty had been asking for permission.

Marty came out of the courthouse and started for his truck. Then, on impulse, he turned away and walked the length of the main street to the church and parish house. Father Enrique was in his cactus garden. "A little talk, Padre?" Marty said. He knew the priest and liked him although he had no part of any religion.

They sat in front of the piñon fire in the sparsely furnished room where Tom and the priest had sat. "I'm not sure exactly what I'm after, Padre," Marty said. "What I have is a feeling, little more than that." A feeling—as when hunting he suddenly knew with certainty that the elk he had been tracking was browsing in the meadow just around the next turn in the trail.

The priest smiled. "Sometimes feelings are the surest guides. They come from the voices inside." He studied Marty. "What kind of feelings are these?"

"Bad." He paused. "Violence," he said.

"Tom Granger sensed fear."

"His own?"

The priest smiled again and shook his head. "In the village."

Marty thought about it. "And what do you sense, Padre? You know your people."

Father Enrique was silent for a long time, staring into the flames as if searching for the answer there. He said at last, "I think the one word is anxiety." He turned to look at Marty.

"Over the reactor?"

"That partly." The priest paused. "But also the

ranch. The young Grangers. Rustling. Burglary on a large scale right here in the village. The dead man in the meadow." He paused again. "All of these to simple people are frightening because they are unknowns. If Juan gets drunk on Saturday night and he and José have an argument that ends in a fight, even a fight with knives, that is something that is understood." He smiled gently. "Not condoned, but understood." The smile disappeared. "But if great cattle trucks appear out of nowhere in the night and José Archuleta has to be taken to the hospital in Santa Fe—" He shook his head. "What could happen next? And to whom?"

Marty walked back to his pickup and got inside. He sat for a little time, staring at the mountains, the clear blue sky where a single red-tailed hawk circled effortlessly on flat wings. He was probably hearing voices, he told himself, and smiled at the concept of an Anglo-Indian-Spanish Joan of Arc. Dealing with feelings and vague fears, a man could end up walking in small circles talking to himself. What he needed were a few facts. He roused himself, started the engine, and drove bumping out of town toward the big ranch.

Joe Valdes came out of the gatehouse, took Marty's name, and went back inside to telephone. Sitting, waiting, Marty would have been willing to bet that a 30-30 leaned against the wall behind the gatehouse door. You drive on this property, he thought, and you drive back seventy to eighty years. There was rustling then too, and men found dead, shot; so nothing really had changed. He watched Valdes come back out, open the gate, and swing it wide. Marty put the pickup in gear and drove through.

Tom was waiting in front of the big house. They shook hands. "Thanks for coming," Tom said.

"De nada." Marty paused. "You're looking good, amigo, big and mean." He showed white teeth in a quick smile. "I have a message from your stepsister. You are to watch out for yourself."

"I had already decided that." Tom gestured at the pickup. "Care to take a ride?"

Facts were what he needed, Marty thought. "Let's go."

They parked off the blacktop road. "The trucks were apparently loaded right there," Tom said, pointing. "There was where the fence was cut. I was on my horse there when the shot was fired." It was all he needed to say, he thought; just hold out the piece of clothing for the bloodhound to sniff and he will do the rest. He got out of the pickup to watch.

Marty wasted little time on the blacktop. He went through the barbed-wire fence as a boxer enters a ring in one easy stooping movement. Then, motionless, he began to study the ground.

It was not black magic, Tom thought, but it smacked of it when you watched a real tracker at work. It was, rather, what some had described as genius: an infinite capacity for detail. Time had no meaning; haste was unknown. Bit by minute bit, most of them invisible unless pointed out to the ordinary eye, the picture was assembled, adjusted, brought into final focus, memorized for all time. There was about the process a kind of inexorability that was unnerving, even frightening to watch because inevitably you found yourself thinking of the hunted, the rabbit watching the fox, the deer hearing the baying of the hounds, and the word that came to mind was despair.

Marty had moved slowly, carefully. Now he hunkered down for a closer look at the ground. Tom leaned against the pickup's fender and waited.

He smiled thinking of Tish's message. Little mother of all mankind. And animalkind. How many waifs and strays and injured creatures had she brought to the big house and protected as if they were her own?

"Good God, girl," old Matt had said once, "I like beasts as well as the next man, but a skunk in your bedroom?"

"He's hurt, and he'll behave himself, you'll see."

And, Tom thought now, I'm damned if he didn't. Tish had even given him a name: Arpège. Memories long tucked away, but not forgotten. After a long time he roused himself at the sound of Marty's voice. "Yes?"

"If you can get through the fence without hanging your ass on the barbed wire," Marty said, "I think I can tell you a few things."

The ground looked to Tom exactly as it had looked this morning, but now it was about to reveal its story. He could not shake that feeling of awe.

"Your horse, incidentally," Marty said, "has a loose shoe on the off fore. You're lucky he didn't throw it when you took off." He paused and pointed. "One other horse here. Tracks and partial tracks there and there and there. He gathered the cattle and held them. Easy enough." He paused again. "Then he got off his horse over here. Now why would he do that? He tied the horse to that branch and he walked over here, just about where you were when the shot came and you took off." Marty was watching Tom's face. "What does that suggest?"

Tom shook his head.

"Think about it," Marty said. "Suppose you've got tracks of his horse made at two different times? One set while he was rounding up and holding the cattle, and the other set maybe this morning when he came back? And that second time he got off his horse. He's a big man, incidentally, big as you are."

Clyde Burley came immediately to mind. And Farley Wells.

"In this ground, pine needles and all," Marty said, "the tracks aren't good, but he is big, you can tell by his stride." He paused. "Why would he get off his horse that second time he was here? You said you saw something on the ground. Would he be looking for it? Because he had lost it in the dark the first time he was here? How about that?"

When it was explained, it made sense, Tom thought. Slowly he nodded. "There was no horse here when that shot was fired."

Marty nodded. "Obviously, or you would have seen it. So he was just coming back and he saw you before you saw him." He made a small gesture indicating that the next step was obvious. "So we'll backtrack a little and see where he came from. Unless——" He smiled. "Things were simpler some time ago. You got on your horse then, and you rode wherever you were going. Now you saddle up and lead your horse into a trailer and drive until you're almost there. So we'll probably lose his tracks at the road a little way on. But at least we'll find out a few things."

Tom could not see the horse tracks even when Marty pointed them out to him. "Blind as a bat," Marty said, smiling. "The tracks go both ways."

"I just don't have X-ray eyes."

They had walked seventy-five yards. Marty stopped and pointed down. "You can see that, can't you? This is where he was when he fired at you. His horse shied a little. See the tracks? Look back. A clear field of fire. You weren't looking, or you might have seen him. But he saw you, amigo, and he had a clean shot and if you hadn't bent down, it might have been a different story. Let's go on, but I think I know what we'll find."

They did. The tracks Tom could not see led through a fresh cut in the fence to the road. "Trailer here," Marty said, "and off he went. It could have been in either direction." He paused. "I've got some pliers in the truck. We can fix this fence."

They drove back toward the ranchhouse in silence. Tom said at last, "Why can't you tell me the color of his hair?" So close and yet still so far; it was maddening. He turned in the seat. "Will you know his tracks if you see them?"

"His horse's tracks, not his. Those pine needles, amigo—" Marty shook his head. Then, "Why can't you remember what you saw on the ground? That's the trouble with you Anglos: you look at things but you don't see them." He paused and the white teeth showed. "One of the troubles."

Marty would have remembered what he had seen, Tom thought; it would have been as permanent in his mind as a photograph, instantly available for examination. "Okay," he said, "lay it on. It was something metallic. Round, I think, but I'm not even sure of that.

I bent down to look closer and he fired and then I was thinking of other things."

"Smart, maybe," Marty said, "but not heroic."

Back at the big house, "You're staying," Tom said.

"For a day or two." Again the white teeth. "Put me in the servants' wing." From behind the seat Marty took a worn pair of saddlebags and the rifle from the window rack. He walked with Tom up the broad steps.

Tom called for Consuelo. "Connie will show you to your room," he said. "When you're ready, come down to the office."

Again he sat behind the big desk and stared at the trophy-laden wall for inspiration. As Matt had, he thought, and probably old Tully before him. He had the fleeting notion that they might be watching, and waiting to see how he performed. Funny, at this moment it seemed that he fitted the big chair as comfortably and as completely as he had fitted Matt's old saddle this morning.

The door opened and he turned to look. It was Will. "Marty Romero," Will said. "What's he doing here?"

"I asked him to come." Tom paused. "Just as you asked Wells and the Wilding woman."

"Why?"

"Did I ask your reasons?" And then, cut it out, he told himself; there's no need to go all defensive. "It ought to be obvious why I asked him," he said. "Cattle rustling is still a crime." He paused. "But why are you uptight about it?" He smiled suddenly. "Planning a caper of your own?" Picture Will being so bold.

"I don't like fuzz, particularly half-breed—"

"Hold it right there." Tom's voice was sharp. He controlled himself with effort. He said slowly, "Whatever gave you the idea that you're a goddamn bit better than anybody? Because you aren't and you never were. Matt had it right when he said you weren't worth the powder to blow you to Hell. This is as much your place as it is mine, but, by God, if you start throwing your weight around like any snotty-nosed redneck Anglo peckerhead I'll kick your ass all the way down to Albuquerque and aboard an airplane heading east." He paused. "Is that clear?"

The room was still. Will's face was white. He hesitated, seemed about to say something, changed his mind and turned away.

"And the next time," Tom said, "knock!"

The door slammed. It had been slammed before, Tom thought, many times, and it hadn't broken yet. Suddenly he found himself smiling. By God, he thought, I'm even beginning to sound like Matt.

He was still smiling when Marty knocked and came in, closed the door behind him. "I see cream on your whiskers, amigo. *¿Qué pasa?*"

"I don't think I could explain." Simple truth. "Sit down. Whiskey?" He stretched out a long arm for the tantalus, poured two shots, handed one to Marty.

Marty held the glass and looked slowly around the room. "I've never been in here before," he said, and smiled at Tom. "Matt never asked me in, and you don't just walk into another man's kiva." He crossed the room to stand in front of the gun cabinet. "Quite an arsenal." He walked back to one of the visitor's chairs. "I've never been in the office of one of those big board chairmen in the East, either, but I imagine it has this same kind of feel." He smiled suddenly. "Power, amigo, the power to say yes or no, make the decisions that make things happen." He paused. "What are you going to do?"

"I wish people would stop asking that."

"They won't until you make up your mind." Marty paused. "Your stepsister said you wanted a geologist. I gave her a couple of names." He paused again. "Quite a girl."

"She doesn't think so."

Marty nodded. "I saw that." He sipped the whiskey and nodded approvingly. "Well," he said. "we've seen the tracks. Any ideas?" He paused. "The trucks, incidentally, probably were down from Colorado." He told Tom what Tish had told him. "My people missed that. I kicked a couple of asses."

Tom thought about it. "The man on horseback," he said, "was, is obviously local."

"*Claro.*"

"It could be one of our own people."

"Any particular one?"

"Yes, goddamn it, it could be only one: Clyde Burley. He's big enough to fit my tracks, and he's the only one who might have connections in Colorado. The rest of the ranch people are local."

Marty nodded. "And have never been fifty miles away from Dos Piedras or Las Grutas in their lives." He nodded. "We'll check it out." He studied his whiskey for a little time in silence. Then he looked up. "Something maybe you haven't thought of, amigo." He paused for emphasis. "Somebody shot at you. We think maybe we know why: because you were seeing something on the ground he didn't want you to see." He paused again. "You didn't see it and you didn't see him, either, but maybe he doesn't know that. *¿Comprendes?*" His voice was quite calm. "So maybe he'll have another try, no?" He nodded toward the gun cabinet. "It might be an idea if you went heeled, at least for a little while." He raised one hand to forestall comment. "I know. I know." Showing the white teeth in a broad smile. "Cops don't like private citizens walking around with guns to protect themselves, but right from the beginning this damn place has been a law to itself, and a lot of things that have happened up here would curl a good cop's hair. I'm not a good cop." He paused. "There are times, most times, when I don't know what the hell I am. The Anglo, the Indian, and the Spanish all put in different directions." He drank deep. "Good whiskey, amigo." Pause. Sigh. "It would be."

You knew someone, man and boy, for twenty years, Tom thought, and one day, as now, a curtain lifted just a little and you saw that you hadn't known him at all. He would have said that Marty Romero of all men had most completely come to terms with himself. Now this; and the anger he had felt toward Will's expressed bigotry returned in full force. He thought of nothing to say.

"That room they gave me," Marty said, "is a little larger and grander than La Fonda's bridal suite."

"You'll just have to put up with it." They smiled at each other.

Marty stood up. "There's some daylight left," he said. "I want to move around a little. I'll talk to some of your people, okay?"

"Help yourself."

"And I may go have a look at that commune and the reactor site and I'd better pay my respects to Jicarilla County—Tito Abeyta."

Tom nodded again. "We follow the old customs. Dinner at six." He smiled suddenly. "It drives my brother and his wife wild. They think nobody eats before nine."

Marty was at the door. "There have been times, amigo, when I thought I was lucky to eat at all. Time doesn't matter." He flipped his hand in a farewell gesture. "Keep looking over your shoulder," he said, "and keep something to shoot with where you can reach it. See you." He was gone.

20

Jimmy Thomas was prompt: his phone call from the lobby of La Fonda came at precisely seven o'clock. "I'll be right down," Tish said, and was. Together they walked out to Jimmy's little red sports car.

Jimmy held the door for her, and then came around to slide in beneath the wheel. "I hope you like Spanish food."

"I do." Tish was smiling.

"Chimayo?"

"One of my favorites."

Jimmy started the engine. It erupted with a snarl. "Then away we go," he said and pulled out from the curb.

North and then west at the Scottish Rite cathedral and north again on the long slant up to the highway, the tires humming eagerly on the blacktop. "I was afraid you'd say no," Jimmy said.

"Whatever gave you that idea?"

"I'm a very junior junior in the firm. And you're—"

"I'm hired help at the ranch."

Jimmy turned to glance at her face. It was expressionless. "That isn't the way I heard it."

"Then you heard wrong." Still facing straight ahead. "Does that disappoint you?"

"Good Lord, no." He found that he was smiling. "It makes it better." He swung the little car onto the highway and began to accelerate. "Look." The moon was rising behind the mountains. "It's full tonight, I think."

Tish was smiling. "It's lovely."

They topped the rise and began the long swoop into the valley. There was light enough to see the wind-carved formations in the soft rock, looking for all the world as if they had been constructed by man. To their left the open opera building was silhouetted against the sky, black-seeming against the flaming orange and turquoise of the sunset. "It's popular these days," Jimmy said, "to think that Maxfield Parrish's colors were improbable. That's because the Eastern art critics have never been out here to see a sunset. I think that when Parrish died, he came out here and he's sitting up there now with his paint pots, doing the job."

Tish liked the concept. She sat smiling, relaxed in her seat.

"Do you ski?" Jimmy said suddenly.

"Yes."

"How about the opera?"

"I come down for it every summer." I did, she thought, but how will it be now? She put the question aside. "You too?"

"It and the skiing are two of the reasons I'm here." Jimmy glanced at her profile. "Don't tell me you fish too?"

Tish smiled. "My stepfather gave me my first rod when I was nine." And Tom, then eleven, cut the hook out of my shoulder, and we never told Matt or Mother how clumsy I'd been.

"Fishing," Jimmy said, "is the third reason I'm here." And it's beginning to look, he thought, as if now maybe I have a fourth.

"There's good fishing on the ranch," Tish said.

"So the old gentleman says."

Tish surprised herself by saying, "I could ask Tom to invite you up for a weekend." Whence came this sudden boldness? But he was sweet, easy to be with. "I mean," she said, "if you'd like that."

Jimmy opened his mouth and closed it again carefully. All he said was, "I'd like that very much."

Past Camel Rock and the castle formations of the Tesuque pueblo land, the moonlight casting strange shadows in the rocks. At the bridge they took the Nambe turn, left church, school, and houses behind, and were suddenly alone in the night, their headlights marking the road ahead, the endless fencing, the sculptured rocks casting shadows, and always the piñon and juniper and scattered cholla. A jackrabbit came into their lights, hesitated briefly and then laid his ears back and put his belly to the ground as he raced to safety.

"Hurry!" Tish said. "Oh, hurry!" And as the rabbit disappeared, "Oh, good!"

Jimmy smiled at the road. "My thoughts exactly," he said. He had not been at all sure what a date with this female would be like. There was about her a quality of reserve stemming from he knew not what source, and that quality could have made communication almost impossible. Instead, talk was easy and loose and natural, and Jimmy could have whistled for sheer ebullience and joy. "Santa Fe," he said, "is not exactly bursting with young unattached female types."

"Nor young unattached male types," Tish said. She was smiling again, thinking of old Matt urging her, no, ordering her to Denver where eligible young men were more numerous. Well, it had done no good, and after all this time, here now in Santa Fe had she at last met someone who mattered? Ridiculous, she told herself, you have just begun to know him. But the feeling persisted.

Jimmy said, "Damn fool. If he wants to pass, let him."

Tish turned in her seat. Headlights were just behind them, close, too close. She faced forward again, and closed her eyes briefly.

"Nobody else on the road," Jimmy said, "and he wants to play games." He glanced at Tish. "Shall I pull over and——"

"No, don't, please!" There was urgency in her tone. This was not the friendly confines of the ranch. This was open, lonely country where anything could happen whether you believed it or not.

"Damn it," Jimmy said, "if he wants——"

"No, please!" Tish took a deep breath. "Can you—run away from them?" There was more than one person in the car behind; she would have bet on it. There were probably three or four, young, male, macho, possibly drunk. . . . "Please," she said again.

Jimmy tromped hard on the accelerator and the little car almost jumped out from beneath them. The headlights dropped back, and then came on again. "Hang on," Jimmy said. "There are curves ahead."

They went into the curves, reaching for more speed. The tires screamed and the little car swayed but clung tenaciously to the road. The engine howled. Behind them the headlights fell back, farther, farther, and then failed to show at all around a final curve.

The road dropped into the village of Santuario, and Jimmy slowed. When he made the turn into the restaurant drive, no lights followed.

He parked the car, switched off lights and engine, and sat motionless for a little time.

"I'm—sorry," Tish said. "I was probably frightened for nothing."

"Wrong." In the darkness Jimmy's voice was solemn. "It could have been just fun and games." He paused thoughtfully. "But it could have been something else too, and I ought to have thought of that right at the beginning." He shook his head. "Night, a lonely back country road, a pretty girl—" He left the sentence unfinished, snapped open his door, stepped out and walked around to hold the door for Tish. "I think we deserve at least one Margarita and probably two. Or even three." He was smiling. "Okay?"

Tish swung her legs out of the car. When she stood up, she was smiling. "Okay."

When they came out of the restaurant, the moon was high, casting deep shadows in the nearby hills and lighting bare ground as if with snow. Jimmy held the door for Tish, walked around, and got into his own seat, and then, reluctant even to start the return drive that would end the evening, just sat, his hands resting lightly on the wheel.

"It was a lovely dinner." Tish's voice was quiet in the darkness.

"I don't remember what we talked about," Jimmy said.

Tish was smiling now. "Neither do I."

Jimmy was silent for a time. Then, "You'll be going back to the ranch?"

"I don't know when. It—depends."

"On what?"

"Tom. What he wants."

Jimmy said slowly, "Granger the Third, is that it?"

"That's not fair, Jimmy."

He half turned in his seat. "Tell me why."

"You make it sound as if Tom were a king, or something." She paused. "And in a way," she said, "to all those people on the ranch and those who live around the ranch and depend on it, I guess he is. Because he has to be. Don't you see that?"

"The buck stops here, you mean? That kind of thing?"

"Don't be bitter."

He had retained the capacity to laugh at himself. "Not bitter," he said, "so much as jealous. He can order you around and I can't. That's what bugs me."

It was better now, easier. "And what orders," Tish said, "would you give me if you could?"

"I'd think of something."

"That isn't very flattering." Bolder than she had ever been. Strange, but that ease remained.

"You mean I ought to have something already in mind? Okay. How about this for a start?" His arm around her shoulders, he drew her to him, and with his free hand lifted her chin. She was unresisting.

It was a long kiss, tentative at first but gaining increasing urgency. They broke at last and sat quiet, their breathing a trifle unsteady.

Tish smiled in the darkness. "Was that an order?"

"A sample. They come in batches."

Another kiss, deeper, more urgent than the first. Jimmy's free hand went to her breast, held it, moved it gently, and when the kiss was ended remained in place. Tish covered it with her own hand and for a time they sat quietly in companionable silence.

"I think we'd better go back now, Jimmy."

"Yes." He made no move. "A sports car isn't very comfortable." Pause. "The hell of it is," he said, "I don't have any place to take you. I have two wild roommates, lawyers both, and——"

"It doesn't matter."

"It does. I ought to have a splendid pad to show you."

"With etchings?" She was still smiling as she gently removed his hand from her breast.

"Etchings, Indian pottery, anything to lure you

there." His hand, resting lightly on her thigh, held hers. He squeezed it gently. "The question is, would you come?"

"Probably."

"Or would I need the king's permission?" Then, quickly, "Strike that. Counsel apologizes."

"I'm over twenty-one, Jimmy. My personal decisions are my own."

"I sit rebuked."

Tish disengaged her hand from his. "We'd better go now."

"Are you angry?"

"No."

"Sure?"

"Yes."

"Prove it."

A third kiss, longer than the others, deeper, more urgent. They broke at last and sat back in their separate seats.

Jimmy said, "Goddamnit."

"I know. I'm—sorry."

"Will I see you tomorrow?"

"Maybe. Probably. I—hope so."

"Unless you hear from—the boss."

"Yes." Pause. "He trusts me, Jimmy."

"I don't blame him for that. But I wish he'd get himself another emissary." Jimmy sat up straight then, sighed, pushed the key into the ignition, and started up the engine. "What if I stormed the bastion?"

Tish giggled. "I'd let down my long shining hair so you could climb to my apartment."

"I'd hold you to it." He backed the little car around, and they sped down the drive in the bright moonlight.

Outside La Fonda one more long kiss. "I'll walk you into the lobby," Jimmy said.

Tish had her door open. She swung her legs out. "No need. Thanks for a lovely evening."

"Just the beginning."

Tish was standing now. She bent to look into the little car. "I know," she said. "Good night, Jimmy."

She was gone across the sidewalk, into the entrance corridor, walking quickly.

She picked up her key at the lobby. There was a message telling her to call Mr. Granger at El Rancho del Norte. Tears were not far away as she climbed the stairs to her room.

She did not intend to make the call that night, and when the phone rang in her room as she was getting ready for bed, she was tempted not to answer it. But habit was strong, and the ringing phone imperious. She picked it up with reluctance.

"Hi." It was Jimmy. "Just wanted to wish you good night."

"Thank you." She was smiling now, looking at her reflection in the dressing mirror. "If this were television, your timing would be perfect."

He laughed softly. "Like that, is it?"

"Like that." She paused. "Altogether."

Another soft laugh. "Sorry I'm not there."

So am I, Tish thought. Aloud she said, "Good night, Jimmy. Thank you again for a lovely evening." She hung up, put on her night gown, and climbed into bed. Surprisingly, she slept easily and well.

She called Tom before the coffee shop opened in the morning. "I'm seeing Seth Porter later this morning," she said, hoping to forestall recall. "He'll give me the latest on Sam Waldo and his bill."

"Good." Pause. "You were out last night."

Was there accusation in the statement? Tish faced it squarely. "Chimayo for a long dinner. One of Seth Porter's young men." She hesitated. "Was there something you wanted?"

"Just to talk to you. To see that everything was all right."

Tish thought of the car behind them last night on that lonely road. She closed her eyes briefly at the memory, and then found herself wondering how Tom would have reacted. "Everything is fine." She hesitated again. "How about you?"

"Marty Romero's here and nobody has taken another shot at me." There was a smile in the voice.

"That's all. Let me know what Seth says." Pause. "And take care." Another pause. "Farley Wells is coming back to Santa Fe today. I have an idea he'll look you up."

Tish thought about it. "And?"

"Take care."

Tish nodded silently. She had a glimpse of her reflection in the dressing mirror, and that reminded her of Jimmy's call last night. Or, rather, she thought, emphasized the memory because it had not really been out of her mind. "Tom."

"Right here."

"I think I may be in love, Tom."

The silence grew, stretched. Tom's voice said at last merely, "Take care." And that was all.

21

The geologist's name was Pete Barkley. He was in his forties, quiet, soft-spoken, thoughtful. "Times," he said, "it pays to study maps and reports. Other times I like to go see for myself. This place has been a kind of hobby of mine for a long time."

Tom's eyebrows rose briefly. "Oh?"

Pete Barkley smiled gently. "No lost treasure or anything like that. No lost goldmines. Just good solid mineral deposits your great-grandfather and your grandfather mined—"

"Until they petered out."

"Well, maybe. Until the economics went haywire, anyway. But economics changed."

Farley Wells had said the same. Tom nodded, and said nothing.

"Your grandfather had me out here two, three times."

"I didn't know that." Tom thought about it. "Looking into what?"

"Uranium for one. Geothermal possibilities for another."

The abandoned mine above the meadow came instantly to mind. Heat had stopped work in that shaft, back when heat was thought of as only a nuisance rather than a potential benefit. "And?" Tom said.

"You've got some hot springs. Little ones. *Ojos calientes*. And," Barkley said, "you've got a mineshaft that gets hotter than the hinges not too far down."

"I know about that one."

Barkley took his time. "Your grandfather thought all you had to do was pump water down a hole and it comes up steam. There's more to it than that."

Tom leaned back in his chair. "I'm listening."

"Just pump water down a hole," Barkley said, "and sooner or later you cool the rock around the hole and then you don't get any more steam. So what you do is what they call hydro-fracturing. You know about that?"

"Only vaguely."

"Well," Barkley said, "you hook a bunch of big diesel engines in series and you turn them all on full throttle at once and blast water down your hole for maybe five, ten seconds at a time, many times. You fracture the hot rock at the bottom of the hole, break it up so cold water pumped down goes into a million cracks and crevices to be heated instead of just one. Then you may be in business with a continuing supply of steam to drive your turbines to generate electricity. The advantage of geothermal steam generators, of course, is no pollution of the kind the fossil fuels put out and no radioactive wastes like what the atomic reactors have to cope with."

Tom's mind was back to the meadow near the hot

mine. "A fellow named Borden," he said, "was found dead near that mine."

"I read about it." Barkley paused. "He came to see me once. He'd heard I'd been out here. He was interested in the geothermal possibilities." He paused. "But a man doesn't get himself dead just because he's thinking about heat."

True enough. Or was it? Something to ponder. "Look around," Tom said. "What I want is a general report. Then we can narrow things down and see just what we have." He smiled suddenly. "My ancestors put this thing together, and they took quite a bit out of it." He paused. "But maybe all they did was skim off the cream." He paused again. "And, as you say, economics change. Let's see where we stand today."

Through his window Tito Abeyta watched the pickup truck roll up the potholed street and stop outside his door. Marty Romero got out, and Tito scowled and wondered what in hell he wanted up here in Jicarilla County.

He had known Marty for a long time, and was not sure whether he liked him or not, but was inclined to think not. There was about Marty an implacability that was not pleasant to think about. Tito himself was well used to violence and perfectly willing to resort to it at any time. But what was in Marty Romero was more than a willingness to violence, it was a willingness to go through violence and beyond to achieve whatever he thought necessary. Slow roasting over open fires came to mind.

From the open doorway, "Hi," Marty said and walked in, moving, Tito had always thought, like one of those undersized running backs who were rarely where you thought they were going to be and were all spring steel and sharp angles if you did manage to lay hands on one.

"Hi," Tito said and leaned back in his chair. "What brings you to these parts?" He paused. "The rustling was in Pepe's county, not mine."

Marty sat down. "But since I'm here, I pay my respects." He showed the white teeth. "Besides," he said, "the trucks came from Colorado, which means they came through Jicarilla County, no?"

Tito sat up. "What makes you think they came from Colorado?" He listened while Marty told him about José Archuleta in the hospital. Tito scowled. "Maybe," he said, "and maybe not. It was dark, wasn't it? And if he was going off into the trees——" He spread his big hands.

"We'll see." And there in the calm confidence of the two words was that sense of implacability showing. The man would track the two trucks through Hell and out the other side if necessary.

"I wish you luck," Tito said. "You want me to ask around up toward the state line? Did anybody getting up to piss in the night see a couple of cattle trucks heading north?"

Marty smiled. "That might help." The smile disappeared. "And somebody took a shot at Tom Granger yesterday. Did you hear about that?"

"Where?"

"Where the cattle were rounded up and held and loaded into the trucks. Somebody on horseback."

"Why?"

"Anybody's guess."

Tito studied Marty's face. A waste of time. "What's yours?"

Marty shrugged and smiled and shook his head. "I'm reserving it." His tone changed. "How're things? Benny Baca behaving himself?" Benny Baca was the State cop in the area.

"We get along," Tito said. He lifted his big shoulders, let them fall. "Things are quiet. We keep them that way."

Nothing changed in Marty's face. "Does your commune cause any trouble? Over Mora way they have problems from time to time."

Shop talk, not really important but sometimes useful; how another man handled a problem that could pop up in your territory, something to think about or just tuck away; give and take.

Marty's voice changed again. He was looking with near amusement at the .357 magnum on Tito's hip. "You're still attached to that thing?"

Tito smiled. "I even fire it off now and then. It impresses people."

Marty stood up. "Mind if I look in on your commune?"

Tito got up too, large and solid. "Help yourself." He smiled. "Just don't let those tightassed chicks with the big tits take your eye off the ball."

"Thanks for the warning," Marty said. They shook hands. Marty went out to the pickup truck and got in behind the wheel.

Tito was still standing, watching, as the pickup rolled away and took a turn out of sight. He went back to his chair. Now just what in hell was that all about? he asked himself. The little bastard was telling me something, but I don't know what. He decided that he did not like Marty Romero. And he decided too that even if Marty knew he wasn't liked it wouldn't bother him a bit. Not one fucking bit. Or distract him. There was that implacability again. Tito had a sudden feeling as of scampering mouse feet running up and down his spine. Somebody is walking on my grave, he told himself, and smiled grimly at the concept.

There were two VW buses, one battered pickup, and a superannuated school bus parked near the adobe building of the commune when Marty drove up. He got out of his own truck and looked around.

There was a neat vegetable garden, fence-enclosed against rabbits: rows of squash, lettuce, corn, and onion sets; stakes for tomato plants and pole beans. Marty eyed it with approval.

There was no corral that he could see, and no stable. No horses? Probably not. These were city people for the most part, mechanized from childhood. Still.

"Looking for something?" A female voice behind him.

Marty turned to look at her. She was young, how young he could only guess, but he doubted that she was eighteen. He wondered if one of those pitiful bulletins describing runaway children applied to her. Probably. In her skintight cutoff jeans, and the bandana that did little to cover her breasts, she presented herself with a boldness that argued comfortable background and the kind of built-in arrogance that would take her her own way at a whim.

"Have you had a good look?" The girl was smiling. Then the smile faded. "What are you, some kind of fuzz? I can smell it."

Marty showed the white teeth in a broad, easy smile. "That's a pretty sharp nose," he said, and he added almost offhand, "particularly for such a young chick."

"I'm eighteen. And it's none of your goddamn business anyway."

Marty shook his head slowly. "It could be, *chica,* if we decided to look into it and found you were, say, fifteen or sixteen instead." His voice was still easy. "So don't push it."

He turned away, ignoring the girl, as Joe walked up, black hat, black beard, dark glasses, jeans, and sandals, the full costume in place. "Something you want, man?"

"As I started to tell the *chica,* just looking around."

"He's fuzz," the girl said. Her voice had lost some of its belligerence.

"I can tell," Joe said. "What are you after, fuzz?"

"Do you have any horses?"

"No horses. We're not the horsy set."

"Do you have a rifle?"

There was hesitation this time.

Marty smiled. "Never mind. Most people do. There's no law against it, only against using it the wrong way."

Joe said slowly, "Like what?"

"Like trying to kill somebody."

"When?"

"Yesterday. Not far from here."

"Man, man—" Joe lifted his hands and let them fall. "This Wild West is out of sight! You people believe your own TV image!"

Marty was smiling again. "Could be."

"And you think we had something to do with it? Far out, man!"

The smile still held. "No," Marty said, "since I've seen you, I don't think you had anything to do with it, but the chance was there. Even jailbait here could pull a trigger."

Joe said quietly. "What's with the jailbait crack?"

"You can't guess?"

"Look," Joe said in the same quiet voice, "we don't bother anybody. Cindy says she's eighteen. What am I supposed to do—examine her teeth to see if she's telling the truth? There are a lot of stupid laws—" He stopped and sighed. "I know, I know. They are laws, so we're supposed to genuflect before them."

"You expect other people to," Marty said. He was smiling no longer. "You live under the protection of those stupid laws. They're all that keep you from being massacred." He paused. "The difference is that you figure you're above them, that you can do what you like while everybody else has to toe the line." The smile this time was bitter. "Right now I'm interested in cattle rustling and attempted murder. I'm not going to waste my time checking *chica* out. But somebody may want to. And somebody may want to shake you down for drugs too."

Joe's smile was weary. "Why us, fuzz? Answer me that? Why is it always us?"

The big black hat, the ferocious beard, the dark glasses—"Because you're asking for it. And in your own infantile way you love it when it happens because it means that somebody is paying attention to you, which is the whole purpose of your masquerade. You and Marie Antoinette, only she played at being a milkmaid." Marty turned away and walked to his pickup. As he drove off, Joe and Cindy were still standing watching him. It was, he thought, a pity, a waste;

they could have been useful members of society. And who was to blame? Answer me that, you smart cop.

He had one more destination in order to touch all bases: the reactor site. He knew about it, had been at some pains to inquire about it, and had done some library research on reactors in general and breeder reactors in particular because he had no patience with the kind of cop who walked in and started asking questions about matters he knew absolutely nothing about.

He had not known about the fence and the guarded gate, and he whistled softly when he saw them. A lot of money involved; but then, the cost of the project itself ran well into the millions, and against that the price of a half-mile of cyclone fence wasn't much. A matter of perspective—as most things were.

He thought he recognized the guard, but he gave no sign when he gave his name, waited for the gate to be opened, and drove on through. Then the man's name came smoothly to mind: Pete Baca, one of Benny Baca's *primos*, cousins? So? It was at the moment without importance.

He slowed the truck as the Long Valley vista opened to view. Lovely wild country being despoiled; helpless thought. He drove on, parked by the construction trailer, and got out to look at the reactor building.

Men in hardhats moved purposefully about, giving the impression of ants around an anthill. Or, Marty thought, more aptly, of slaves laboring at the construction of the great pyramids. Because there was a kind of religious overtone to this mass of concrete and steel, a feeling that here you were face to face, not as in conventional power plants with combustion, fire, which man had been familiar with since Prometheus; but rather with a form of energy that could not be seen or heard or felt, totally mysterious, existing in tangible form only in complicated equations written on somebody's blackboard.

"Lieutenant—Romero, is it?" Wayne Carter's voice from the trailer door. "Come in. What can I do for you, Lieutenant?"

People received cops, Marty had long ago decided,

usually in one of several predictable ways: with resentment, as at the commune; with eagerness to cooperate, which frequently meant some kind of guilty conscience; or with open fear, which could mean anything. It was rare that he was received, as now, with only mild curiosity. "Tell me about your fence," he said and sat down to listen.

"We put it up for the usual reasons," Wayne said in his dry way. His voice told nothing.

"Protection." Marty's voice told nothing either. "That argues a need. Has it protected, Doctor?"

"More or less."

"I'm interested in the less. You've had thefts?"

"No."

"Vandalism?"

"I suppose you could call it that." Wayne paused. "A window broken here, an obscenity sprayed on a wall there—" He shrugged. "The kind of thing that happens at every construction site."

"In cities," Marty said, "not out in the mountains. Mountain people think differently." He was silent for a long time, thinking about it. "It isn't meant to stop you or even slow you down, is it?"

"I wouldn't know, Lieutenant."

"I think," Marty said slowly, "that it's just intended to annoy you. The question is: Why?"

"Is that the reason for your visit, Lieutenant? To ask that question?"

Marty smiled. "No, Doctor. I'm not sure I even know the reason. I'm trying to find a—pattern."

Wayne Carter's face showed mild interest. "What kind of pattern?"

"I don't know that, either." Marty paused. "Let's see if I can explain." He took his time. "You have a big ranch and two villages that have lived together a long time, a stable situation. Then you add a hippie commune and a nuclear reactor, and things begin to happen. Suddenly rustling comes back. There is a planned burglary, big-city type. A stranger turns up shot, dead. Vandalism at the reactor site. More rustling and yesterday an apparent attempted murder on ranch property."

Wayne Carter was frowning now.

Marty said, "Add rumors about radioactivity—"

"Where there isn't any radioactive material," Carter said.

"Okay. Then stir in a bill down in Santa Fe to buy the ranch when the ranch isn't even for sale." Marty cocked his head and smiled. "A lot of strange things to explain, wouldn't you say?"

Wayne said, "And you expect to tie all that together?"

"Maybe, maybe not. But when a lot of things out of the ordinary start happening, there is usually some basic cause. The priest down in the village calls it 'anxiety.' That's pretty much like 'sin'—a little too broad for me. I tend to think that things happen because people want them to happen. I want to know which people, and why."

"That's out of my line, Lieutenant."

"Maybe, maybe not, but you can't help being part of it." Marty gestured toward the open doorway, the organized bustle around the concrete structure. "I've heard some pretty wild things about what you're doing here, and what might come out of it. A generator network and a power grid, climate change—" Marty shook his head. "That's pretty far out, Doctor. Me, I always get a little uneasy when the Rain Dance ends in a cloudburst."

A faint smile lifted Wayne's lips and brought tiny laughter crinkles to the corners of his eyes. "You mean because there might be something to it after all?"

"Exactly. Everybody forgets the times the Rain Dance doesn't bring anything. But when it does live up to its billing, your scalp begins to prickle and you want to look all directions at once to see what might be coming at you."

Wayne's smile had disappeared. "You are talking about the little girl with leukemia?" He was prepared to deal with that nonsense.

"I'm talking *beyond* the little girl with leukemia,

Doctor." Marty's voice was quiet, solemn. "Are the rumors just malicious mischief? They could be. Or are they part of a plan?"

"To do what, Lieutenant?"

"Get you out of here, stop your project from ever getting off the ground." Marty paused. "Even if it means taking over the ranch." He paused again. "And the first step in a plan like that, a power play, might very well be to persuade the people around here that they're a lot better off without atomic power on their doorstep, no matter how much pie in the sky they might hear about." He paused. "Think about it, Doctor, and if you come up with any ideas, let me know."

He drove back to the ranch, thinking that he probably had not accomplished a thing. On the other hand, sometimes when you were hunting, your mere presence stirred up game; and he had let himself be seen in a number of quarters. Sometimes too, of course, what you stirred up was not game, but something entirely different, like, say, a mother bear with cubs busting out of a berry patch, just looking for trouble. Well, that was the chance you took when you went hunting in the first place.

Sue Granger in a scanty bikini was artfully arranged on one of the chaise lounges in the sun. She smiled. "Sit down, Lieutenant, and tell me what you've been doing. I'm dying to know how detectives work."

Marty sat down nearby. He was, he supposed, no more susceptible than the next man, but it was hard to keep his eyes on Sue's face and away from the generous curves of her body. Tito Abeyta had warned of the chicks at the commune. They were nothing compared to this one, who probably from puberty had spent the greater part of her time and most of her thought to finding ways to make herself alluring. And she had succeeded in spectacular fashion. "You just keep looking until you find something," Marty said. And he added, "You hope."

Sue shifted her position a trifle. The movement displayed one full breast almost to the nipple. She seemed unaware. "Did somebody really try to shoot Tom?"

"He says so, and he usually doesn't bother to lie."

" 'Doesn't bother.' " Sue was smiling again. "That's an odd way to put it."

"Most people," Marty said, "lie because they feel they have to. Tom doesn't usually get himself in that position." He paused. "At least he didn't used to." The bottom part of the bikini, whatever you called it, was so scant that Marty wondered if Sue shaved her pubic hair. He had heard of such things. He wondered what the ranch women thought. They didn't even shave their legs or underarms. One more example of the vast differences between these mountain village people and the outside world. Were at least some of the causes he had spoken of to Wayne Carter hidden in that cultural gradient?

"Are you still looking, Lieutenant?" Sue said. "Or have you found something?"

"Still looking." Damn the woman anyway. She was deliberately flaunting herself, amused at his discomfiture. "I've just come from the reactor site."

Sue wrinkled her nose. "I don't pretend to understand those things. And I don't like them. They frighten me."

The inevitable reaction, Marty thought: ignorance breeding fear, which in turn could breed angry action. He had a lot of ideas, he told himself, and they added up to nothing. He got out of his chair.

"Leaving, Lieutenant?"

"I want to talk to Tom."

"Duty." She was smiling. "If you must. But before you go——" She paused and sat up. Her hands went behind her back. "There's sun lotion there on the table. Do my back, please." Her hands came into view holding the ends of the halter. She turned over to lie face down. In the process both breasts were fleetingly exposed.

Marty picked up the sun lotion. He looked down at the almost naked body, the smooth, tanned skin, the seductive curve of waist and dimpled hips, the tapered legs. He stood uncertain, and behind him

Ethel Wilding said, laughter plain in her voice, "A little out of your line, Lieutenant? Would you like me to take over?"

Marty turned. Ethel too wore a bikini, as scant as Sue's. She smiled as she held out her hand. Marty put the lotion in it and fled ignominiously.

At the doorway of the big house he stopped and turned to look back. Ethel was rubbing the sun lotion into the smooth skin of Sue's back with slow, gentle, almost sensuous motions of her flat hand. Her concentration was complete. She did not even glance in Marty's direction. The incident, Marty thought, was over, forgotten as if it had never happened. Only he had been affected; the two women were untouched. Arrogant Anglo bitches was the phrase that came instantly to mind. Arrogant Anglos, period—male and female both. He wondered how many others felt the same.

One of the ranch cars drove up and stopped by the steps in a shower of gravel. Will got out. He glanced at the two women on the terrace, seemed about to call out something, and changed his mind. He came up the steps two at a time. To Marty, "Caught anybody yet?"

Here at least, Marty thought, was something he could deal with: an Anglo male in a foul mood. He smiled. "Don't be impatient."

"Sometimes I wonder," Will said, "just what we pay you people for."

Marty's smile spread. "Don't tell me you pay taxes, Will! On what earned income?"

"Damn you—" Will watched Marty's smile and the words just stopped. He started through the doorway.

"There's a question cops ask themselves in almost every detective story," Marty said. "Do you know what that question is?"

Will stopped and turned. He said nothing.

"*'Cui bono?'*" Marty said. "Who benefits?" He watched surprise come into Will's face. The man had never had to learn to hide his feelings. "If Tom were shot, killed," Marty said, "how would you be affected?"

He smiled again. "Aside from being grief-stricken, I mean?"

Will opened his mouth and closed it again carefully. "You have a dirty mind."

Marty nodded. "It's part of my business," he said and walked past Will into the big hall to knock on the office door. At the sound of Tom's voice he went inside and closed the door.

Tom had a pile of paperwork on the desk in front of him. His smile was wry. "Insemination records," he said. "Once upon a time you had range bulls and cows and they bred whenever they felt like it. Then you decided that some bulls were pretty special, so you kept them in pens and charged a fee for them to cover anybody's special cow. You don't even give them that much freedom any more. It's all done by artificial insemination, at least with blooded cattle. Do you know that we've got enough of Grand Champion Boxeur's sperm in the deep freeze to last for one hundred years? If it will still be potent in a hundred years.'"

"You and I, amigo," Marty said, "will not be around to see." Suddenly he felt better. At least there were some Anglos you could talk to without immediately feeling defensive. "And probably a good thing too." He was smiling. "As for artificial insemination, all I can say is that I'm glad I'm not a bull."

Tom leaned back in his chair. His smile now was filled with amusement. "Anyone in particular in mind, Marty?"

Marty sat down. He hesitated. Then, "Your sister-in-law in that bikini." He paused. "And her friend." His voice became singsong. "I am not used to thees thing, amigo. I am simple Anglo-Indian-Chicano boy——"

Tom laughed softly. "And the paleface women get to you?" He nodded. "They get to me sometimes too, and that's just the way they like it, the bitches." His voice was without rancor. "But I can't honestly say I wish it were any different." His tone altered. "Anything new?"

"I have walked through the woods with loud footsteps," Marty said. "Anybody who is interested knows I am here." He shrugged. "Whether I have done any good or not, I can't say."

Tom said slowly, with concern, "But you're not going back to Santa Fe?"

"Not yet, amigo. I have a feeling that this is where the action is."

Tom smiled, relieved. "And you can always ogle the pretty girls."

22

Kelly Garcia's knowledge of these two northern counties was encyclopedic and intimate. From villages to minor clusters of huts to tiny farms, which by local standards represented moderate prosperity, he knew and was known. He was well acquainted with the local Forest Service people too, and from them from time to time he had gathered bits and pieces of information that, squirrellike, he stored away against possible need. With State Game and Fish field men it was the same. You never knew what information might come in handy.

Right now his problem was not lack of information but excess. Too many facts and shrewd guesses crowded themselves through his mind, jostling elbows, as it were, and tangling one another's footsteps in a milling mass of confusion.

The trick, of course, was to sort it all out logically, because there had to be some logic involved. But the problem was to find square one, the starting point, and this he had so far failed to do.

Which came first: motive, or opportunity? chicken or egg? And how did you recognize the governing motive even when you saw it? In Kelly's experience greed, jealousy, and hate ranked high in the list of motives that tend to produce crimes, particularly crimes of violence. For the moment, scratch jealousy. On second thought, leave it in; there were other kinds of jealousy than that springing from male-female causes, which was what you tended to think of first.

He drove his dusty superannuated VW beetle at a moderate pace, never shifting into top gear. It was probable, he had often thought, that through long familiarity the little car could probably have found its way back to Las Grutas all by itself; certainly it seemed to need no guidance now while Kelly labored with his thoughts.

Like Marty Romero, Kelly had been struck by the concatenation of strange events, all of which suddenly followed the appearance of the reactor project and the commune in this isolated area. Unlike Marty, he had an uneasy feeling that there were forces at work, awesome in their power, against which a country newspaperman ventured at his peril. But the lure of a story was irresistible.

From the wire service people in Santa Fe he had picked up a fair amount of background on Farley Wells. "He's visible," the wire service man had said. "By all accounts a nice guy, but the word is too that it's a lot easier to go along with him than it is to drag your feet when he asks a favor. He is J.R. Benson's man, and that says it all."

As far as Kelly was concerned, it did indeed say it all. He had never met or even seen J.R. Benson, and as far as he knew the old man's picture had never appeared in a newspaper. But like H.L. Hunt and Howard Hughes, J.R. was no myth, and every now and again something happened to demonstrate that fact. Was competition causing trouble? Then either break the competition with a price war, or buy it up and fire the management. Stories abounded, but hard facts to support them in court never seemed to turn up.

The impression Kelly carried in his mind was of a mean old man sitting at the center of an enormous network of power, snapping his fingers and causing fortunes to disappear, men to despair, new enterprises to spring into life, and more money to roll into already bulging coffers. It was the kind of impression that gave Kelly the shivers.

It was a far cry from the shadowy old man in Houston to cattle rustling here in these remote mountains, Kelly was prepared to admit, and he had no evidence that there was even the slightest connection. But Farley Wells *had* come to the ranch, and by so doing, he *had* in a vague way brought J.R. Benson here as well, because men like Farley Wells did not go places and do things without purpose. But rustling? Ridiculous.

The VW, apparently of its own volition, came around a bend in the road, in obedience to Kelly's lifted foot, slowed and then stopped precisely where Marty Romero's pickup had halted. Kelly gazed at the barbed-wire fence that had been cut for the cattle to be driven into the trucks. The temptation to visit the site was irresistible. He switched off the engine, got out of the little car and like Marty ducked through the fence strands.

He had not yet heard of the shooting attempt on Tom Granger's life, but if he had no doors would suddenly have opened, no signs would have appeared in the sky. The knowledge would have been merely one more fact to fit into the jumble that was already in Kelly's mind.

He stared at the ground. It told him nothing, and he wondered why he had even bothered to look. He started to turn away and saw the man watching at a distance of no more than fifteen feet. Behind the man a horse stood patiently, its reins wrapped around a small branch.

"I thought I'd find you here," the man said. His voice was easy enough.

"Just trying to figure a few things out," Kelly said. "And getting nowhere," he added. He did not yet even feel uneasiness.

"You ask a lot of questions."

"It's my business."

"Sometimes your business causes trouble." Still easy, relaxed. "They call it character assassination. You've heard of it?"

Kelly was uneasy now, but not yet frightened. He had heard remarks like that before. What newspaperman had not? "I've heard," he said. "But usually the assassinated character turns out to be something less than lily-white. There was a vice president once upon a time, as I recall it, who protested too much."

The man's voice lost some of its easy quality. "That wasn't what we were talking about," he said. He gestured. "You were poking around here. Why?"

"I told you. Trying to figure a few things out." Kelly paused. "And getting zilch."

"But you had some reason for coming here in the first place. That has to be." The man's voice was quiet now. "And that makes it bad. Too bad."

"Look," Kelly said, "why shouldn't I come here? Why—?" He stopped and stared unbelieving at the gun pointed at his chest. "Now look," he said again, more in resentful protest than in panic, although panic was already tugging at the fringes of his mind.

"Too bad," the man said again.

Panic took over. "Sweet Jesus!" Kelly said. "Look! I don't know anything! Not a thing!" But now of course he did know a bit, entirely too much; suddenly he had his starting place and the computer-stored facts in his mind were beginning to slide smoothly into place. He tried to ignore them. "I just came here! I don't know why! Dear God! You can't—!"

The shot echoed briefly in the trees, and after that there was no sound. The man waited until he was satisfied. Then he walked without haste to his horse, undid the reins and swung easily aboard. He rode off at an easy running walk.

It was Benny Baca, the State Policeman, who saw Kelly's VW the next day and recognized it. As he stopped his patrol car and got out to see what might have prompted Kelly to stop in this remote spot, four turkey buzzards flew heavily out of the trees. Benny Baca went through the fence to have a look.

His normally swarthy face was pale when he came back to the patrol car and got on the radio to make his report. "Oh, yes," he added at the end, "Lieutenant Romero's at the big ranch. Plug him in too. I'll wait here." He hung up the microphone and walked across the road. There behind a clump of chamisa he vomited.

Tom Granger rode in the pckup with Marty Romero. Tom's face was set, angry, and his thoughts were a high fierce chant. "Kelly Garcia," he said. "A chicano with somewhere in his ancestry a touch of Irish, I suppose. He couldn't make it on the outside, and he knew it, and he was never going to shake even this mountain world. But, goddamnit, he didn't have to die like this—for no reason."

"You said he was poking around, no?" Marty said. "Then maybe he found out a little too much." He paused again and glanced at Tom. "Which could mean that somebody plays rough when he thinks he's being crowded." A third pause. "It could also mean that he still thinks you're crowding him."

"If I knew who he was, I would."

"*Claro*. But since you don't, you'd better look all ways at once whenever you walk out of the ranch house."

There was an ambulance that doubled as a morgue wagon and a Grutas County sheriff's car parked with Benny Baca's patrol car. Marty got out of the pickup. "Stay here, amigo. There's nothing you can do, and I don't want your big feet walking around on the scene." He ducked between the barbed-wire strands and disappeared into the trees.

It was impossible to sit still. Tom got out of the truck and began to walk slowly back and forth: ten, twelve paces and return; aimless pacing, mere physical release.

What Marty had said about Kelly's maybe knowing too much made sense. Kelly knew his way around these mountains and villages as few did. Mountain people forever suspicious of strangers would talk to Kelly Garcia as to one of their own.

Where, then, might he have gone and what might he have asked? Foolish question because the answer would be forever hidden. Except, of course, to the one man who, as Marty had guessed, might have felt that he was being crowded. What was the phrase he, Tom, had once read? Anxiety of helplessness. Sheer frustration. Rage was the natural result.

How long he paced aimlessly, he did not know. Marty Romero came back out of the trees and ducked again through the fence. His face was bleak. "I would say our same big man, amigo. Again, his tracks in the pine needles are unclear. But it was the same horse, tied to the same branch." He shrugged.

Tom said, "Kelly—" He did not know how to phrase the question.

"Maybe he knew what hit him," Marty said, "but not for long. One shot." He touched his chest. "It went clear through him and off into the trees somewhere. We'll look, but I don't think we'll find the slug."

"A rifle again," Tom said. "From a distance?"

"From fifteen feet, and he was shot from the front so he saw the man and probably recognized him, but he can't very well tell us who it was."

What was that old idea that a dead man's eyes retained a picture of the last thing he saw? Myth, of course. Still.

Apparently Marty was thinking the same thing because he shook his head and said, "Not after the

vultures have been around, amigo. And the skunks."
He opened the pickup door. "Coming?"

Tom got into the truck. "Where?"

"To find out where Clyde Burley was." Marty's
voice was cold. "And that big dude from Texas."

"He went back to Santa Fe."

"Maybe he stayed there, and maybe he didn't. We'll
find out." Marty hesitated. He glanced at Tom's face.
"And just on a wild hunch, amigo, I'll want to know
where your brother was all day yesterday too."

Tom thought about it. "Not Will," he said.

"If you mean," Marty said, and showed the white
teeth in a quick smile, "that Will wouldn't shoot a
man in the front, I agree. Unlikely. Still." He shrugged.

"You never did like him."

"That is true." The smile was gone. "Very early I
told him that if he didn't stop snuffling around after a
little *chicana* daughter of a friend of mine in Santa Fe,
I would cut off his *cojones* and stuff them down his
throat." Marty paused. "He believed me."

I don't blame him, Tom thought. Aloud he said,
"You could have told me."

Marty nodded. "I could. But a thing like that a
man prefers to handle himself." He paused. "Wouldn't
you?"

Clyde Burley was not in his office. Tom and Marty
came out and started for the pickup and here came
Clyde, riding up on the big buckskin. He swung down
and dropped the reins. The buckskin stood as if
rooted. Clyde looked from face to face. "Trouble?"

It was Marty's play, Tom thought, and he waited
in silence.

Marty said, "You ride this horse much?"

"He's my top horse. Why?" There was resentment
in the question.

Marty merely nodded and walked a few steps to
the horse's rear, stood quiet studying the tracks in
the dirt. Then he came back. "Yesterday afternoon,"
he said, "where were you?"

"What is this?"

"I asked a question."

"I heard." Antagonism plain. "So?"

"I think you'd better answer it," Tom said.

Clyde hesitated, defiance plain. Then he shrugged. "You're the boss." And to Marty. "I spent the afternoon with Emilio, trying to save a cow and the calf she was trying to drop. The cow is one of Boxeur's get, and she always has trouble." He looked at Tom. "We managed. Mother and child are doing well." Again to Marty: "Satisfied?"

"Probably."

"Now," Clyde said, "what's it all about?"

Tom told him. Clyde whistled softly. "Same place," Tom said, "and probably the same man who took a shot at me." He had not thought of it in precisely this way before, and the concept was suddenly appalling. I could have been the one lying in the trees for the buzzards and the skunks to desecrate, he thought, and restrained a shudder with effort. He looked at Marty, and waited.

"I want to call Santa Fe," Marty said. "We'll have a few questions asked down there."

Santa Fe in the person of a State Police sergeant listened respectfully. "Will do," the sergeant said. And then, "Kelly Garcia. Goddamn. Who would do a thing like that?"

"That," Marty said, "is what we're going to find out. You can call me here." He hung up and got out of his chair to prowl the big office. At the gun cabinet he stopped. Over his shoulder, "One of your guns is missing, amigo." He turned to look at Tom. "Sporting rifle, bolt action, looked to be the thirty-aught-six." Photographic memory. He paused. "Will?"

"Maybe." Tom hesitated. "No, probably. He knows where the key is, and none of the ranch people would touch the cabinet." He was scowling. "But there are all sorts of reasons why he might have taken it. Damn it—"

"*Claro.*" Marty's voice was quiet, calm. "Some people like to shoot at tin cans or jackrabbits." Pause.

"Though usually not with thirty-aught-sixes." Another pause. "Is he a good shot?"

Tom made himself relax. "Okay. He's a good shot. Or was. But what you're thinking doesn't take a good shot. Not to hit a man from fifteen feet."

"Or," Marty said, "miss another man from seventy-five yards. True." He walked back to his chair and sat down. "Anything you're not telling me, amigo?"

The man was implacable, Tom thought, and friendship meant nothing. "Like what?"

"I don't know."

"Nothing," Tom said. And then, "Clyde's horse was not the one?"

"Not the one. If the boot tracks were only a little plainer—" Marty shrugged. "We'll find him." There was finality in the tone.

"Before he kills someone else?"

Marty smiled without amusement. "That, amigo, is the question."

Tom sat on at the desk after Marty had gone. The East seemed very far away, and in time remote. I am getting in deeper and deeper here, he thought, and where do I owe my primary allegiance? To this ranch I once turned my back on? Or to the place where I started my own career, and to the people like Tim who depended on me? And what about Grace? There had been no further word from her since that abortive and unpleasant phone call. And I haven't done anything about that, either, he told himself. Well, that at least could be remedied. He reached for the telephone.

Grace was at her apartment, and her voice was cool. "Is it still nice out there?"

"I've had problems."

"They're endemic. They crop up here too."

"Do you want to come out? I'll meet you in Albuquerque."

There was hesitation. "Tempt me."

"You said something about being weighed."

"I didn't think you would remember that." Grace paused. "Let me think about it, Tommy."

Damn it, distance was more than a dimension; it was a barrier. "Up to you," Tom said.

23

Seth Porter sat in the governor's office in the new state capitol known locally as the Roundhouse. They were longtime friends; Seth the older by twenty-five years and still retaining much of the authority of their younger days.

"My people tell me," Seth said, "that Waldo's bill will pass easily in the House, and probably squeak through in the Senate. What will you do then, George?"

The governor was a big man, ranch-bred, more at home on a horse than behind the polished desk. He stretched his legs and contemplated the toes of his boots. His strengths were a blend of shrewdness, political sagacity, and a feel for the popular sentiment. He was also reasonably honest and didn't like to be pushed. But he enjoyed being governor, and treated the position with caution. "Well, now, I'd have to ponder a bit on that." His voice had a Western twang.

"Sam Waldo doesn't usually do things out of the goodness of his heart," Seth said.

The governor smiled.

"In fact," Seth went on, "if ever I were foolish enough to sit in a poker game with him, I might expect to find five aces in the deck." He paused. "At least."

The governor smiled again. He was not basically a

silent man, but he had long ago found that listening did have its purposes.

"Of course," Seth said, "Sam's personality has nothing to do with the merits of the bill. I grant that. But the fact that it is Sam's bill makes it suspect right from the start. Sam doesn't fish. I don't think he hunts. And he's too fat for backpacking."

"And so," the governor said, "why is he interested in a wilderness area?" The governor thought about it. "What do you think he really wants?"

"To stop that atomic reactor, and the possibilities that may come from it." Seth paused. "You've heard about them?"

The governor nodded and was silent, thoughtful.

"I think we need to try everything we can," Seth said, "and I'd just as soon not see any more coal-fired generators unless we have to have them." He paused. "But there is a lot of low-grade coal up in the strip-mining country that somebody would like to see used, somebody who has enough money to buy Sam Waldo and half the legislature and never even feel the cost, and will maybe put pressure on you to go along."

"I don't buy easy, Seth." The tone was quiet. When you say that, smile.

"I know you don't. But I haven't lived as long as I have without knowing that pressure can be applied in other ways than money."

The governor's faint nod was acknowledgment. In office you learned things never before dreamed of. Trust old Seth Porter to understand that.

"If that reactor works the way Carter and the lab people think it's going to, George, and those far-out possibilities do open up, and a power grid can be established right here in the state, supplying a good share of the Southwest with its electrical energy—" Seth paused, smiling. "The state could pick itself right up by its bootstraps and get out of the poor-neighbor class, and wouldn't that be fine for whoever sits in that chair?"

The governor was silent.

Seth heaved himself to his feet. "I've taken enough of your time, George."

"Always glad to talk with you." The governor was standing too.

"Ponder on it," Seth said.

The governor nodded.

"And when somebody comes around to do a little arm-twisting in favor of Sam's bill—"

"Nobody has come yet, Seth."

"Somebody will. I'll bet my bottom dollar on that."

They shook hands. The governor walked with Seth to the door, opened it and held it wide. "Thanks for coming in." His voice and his face were thoughtful.

Jimmy Thomas, summoned, lowered himself politely into a chair in Seth's big office. As far as he knew his conscience was clear but it was always hard to shake the sniggly feeling that you weren't called to the principal's office merely for innocent merriment. He sat quiet and waited.

"Have a good time the other night, son?" The old gentleman was smiling and his tone was mild.

So that was the direction. "Yes, sir. A very good time. She, I mean Tish is—something special." Jimmy hesitated. "You don't have any objections, do you, sir?"

Seth was still smiling. "It probably wouldn't do any good if I did." Subject dismissed. He leaned back in his chair. "I've been talking with the governor. I don't know which way he'll go if the Waldo bill comes to his desk. And I don't think he knows, either. I hung a carrot in front of his nose, but somebody else may have a big stick. You can never be sure how these things will come out."

Jimmy said, "But will the Grangers sell even if the Waldo bill does pass?" He had the immediate feeling that he had asked the wrong question.

Seth took his time. He said at last, "You haven't thought it through, have you, son? Your mind maybe on other matters?"

Jimmy sat silent, rebuked and still puzzled. He waited.

"Assume," Seth said, "that what we're dealing with is pressure to get rid of that atomic reactor and prevent any others from being built. A pure power play to wipe out possible competition."

"Yes, sir. But—"

Seth raised his hand and there was silence. "With that assumption," Seth said, "then think of Sam Waldo's bill as enabling legislation—that is, legislation expressing the view of the legislature that would be desirable if El Rancho del Norte were purchased by the state and set aside for recreational purposes, and authorizing the purchase."

Jimmy was beginning to see it now, as he ought to have done before. Too much Tish in his thoughts?

"If the Grangers are willing to sell," Seth said, "well and good. The appropriation is there and there is nothing to stand in the way." He paused. "But if they aren't willing to sell, then what could be the next step?"

Inwardly, Jimmy squirmed. "I see it now, sir. I just hadn't thought enough about it." He paused. "The state could exercise its right of eminent domain, have the property condemned, and buy it at a fair market price, whether the Grangers liked it or not."

Seth nodded. "Exactly. That is what could happen, and given enough pressure that is probably what would happen."

"It doesn't seem fair."

Seth's smile was wicked. "Fair doesn't very often have much to do with anything. The state highway department decides to build a new road. Houses are in the way. The state is sovereign, it exercises its right of eminent domain, the houses and the property they are on are condemned and bought by the state, and the road goes through."

"Yes, sir."

"On the face of it," Seth said, "this bill of Sam Waldo's is presented as benefiting a great number of people, hunters, fishermen, campers, backpackers, scenery and wilderness enthusiasts, conservationists, anybody who likes to get out into the wild." He paused. "The Grangers," he said, "are billed as selfish cattle and land barons, which of course they are." He paused again. "But what isn't mentioned is that Sam Waldo didn't have the wit to think this up all by himself, that somebody thought it up for him, that the people who will benefit most are a very small and wealthy group with fossil-fuel interests, and that the public as a whole will foot the bill for higher fossil-fuel costs if the atomic reactor project is done away with."

Jimmy thought about it. He could find no flaw in the old gentleman's reasoning.

"My feelings," Seth said, "happen to be on the side of the Grangers, cattle and land barons though they may be. Old Tully tamed the land and enriched it. Matt carried on. I don't know what Tom will do, but if he wants to hang on, I think he ought to have the right."

In Jimmy's mind the concept of *King* Tom Granger was inescapable. Did he have the *droit de seigneur* as well? Fleeting, unpleasant thought. Damn it, Tish was never far from his mind. "I guess I feel the same way, sir."

Seth was smiling again. "You sound less than sure about it."

"No, sir. It's just—" He stopped, unsure exactly what he wanted to say.

"It isn't black-and-white," Seth said. "Atomic generators are frightening things. Have you been to the science museum at Los Alamos?"

"No, sir."

"I recommend it. You'll find food for thought there. Take an especially good look at the model demonstrating a chain reaction. Kids love it." Seth showed his quick smile. "I'm not sure I do. There is a glass cover over a table filled with holes. In each hole there is a Ping-Pong ball, just sitting there. Then they roll one more Ping-Pong ball on the table and it falls into one of the holes, it doesn't matter which one.

What happens is that the weight of two balls in one hole sets off a spring, and both balls come flying out. Then you have two balls rolling around and each of them falls in a hole and four balls come flying out, and so on. In less time than it takes to tell it, the glass cover is filled with flying Ping-Pong balls and the picture I get is total chaos, and I can't help wondering how in the world a chain reaction similar to that can ever be controlled." He waved one hand in a mild gesture. "Oh, I know that it can be, or at least so far in atomic reactors it has been. As far as I know, a perfect record so far. Still." Seth was silent.

"I had a physics course in high school," Jimmy said. "We didn't get very far into the details." He smiled. "At least, I didn't."

Seth nodded. "Few people do. In anything. We leave it to those who say they know, and some do and some are liars, but it all sounds convincing." He sat up straight. "Do you know Farley Wells?"

"No, sir." Jimmy hesitated. "He took Tish to dinner last night." The bastard, he thought.

Seth was smiling again. "So I heard. Why don't you talk to her and see what he had in mind?" He paused and the smile spread. "Unless you find that an onerous chore?"

"I'll—manage," Jimmy said.

Again Sam Waldo sat in Farley Wells's hotel room, sipping some of that fine whiskey. Farley concealed his distaste for the man as he watched him, pinky elegantly extended, forehead crinkled in what Sam assumed to be a connoisseur's sampling expression, waving the shot glass to and fro beneath his nose before each sip. A pompous and not very bright ass, Farley thought, and the only man he had ever known who could strut sitting down. You used what tools came to hand to do any job.

"The bill is moving, Sam?"

"It surely is, Mr. Wells, it surely is." Sam was obviously pleased with himself. "In the House it's a shoo-in. And in the Senate—" Sam paused and winked. "I know where a few bodies are buried. All I need to do is walk around carrying a shovel and looking like I'm going to dig them up, and we'll have all the votes we need."

It was a revolting operation, Farley thought; but he was a good soldier and good soldiers carried out commands. "That's fine, Sam."

"I haven't talked to the governor," Sam said. He set the empty shot glass down with care as if to emphasize his words. His expression was no longer quite so gleeful. "You never can tell about him. He's independent as a hog on ice, and sometimes he's mean as a bobcat as well. And old Seth Porter's been at him—"

"Oh?" Farley paused. "Do you know that?"

Sam smiled again. "There isn't much goes on in the Roundhouse I don't know, Mr. Wells, there purely isn't. One of the girls in the governor's office—" He winked again. Slowly the smile faded. "Old Seth is lawyer for the Grangers. Does that mean they've decided not to sell?"

"I don't know, Sam."

"Because like I said, that would make me out an awful fool, now, wouldn't it? After all this trouble and arm-twisting?"

"Let me worry about that," Farley said. "Have another shot."

Again the extended pinky and the business beneath the nose. Sam sighed after the first sip. Then he hesitated. "One thing I don't understand, Mr. Wells, I purely don't." Pause. "Why do you want the state to have all that property, anyway?"

"I don't, Sam. You do. For recreational purposes." Farley's voice was calm. He paused, and decided that no flattery could be too gross. "I wouldn't be surprised," he said, "if they named it Waldo Park. You'd like that, wouldn't you, Sam?"

"Well, now," Sam said, and sipped again at his whiskey.

When Sam was gone, waddling importantly down the corridor, Farley closed the door and went to stand at the window, staring out at the cathedral and the great mountains beyond. Waldo, he thought, made the room somehow soiled, and the air dirty. The cathedral bells rang and a flight of pigeons took flight, wheeling and circling. When the bells were again silent, they returned one by one to their cornices.

People were like that too, Farley thought. They panicked and then, when the immediate crisis was past, they forgot the cause and returned to normal activity. All that flap about the energy crisis, for example; soul-searching and the looking under rugs for villains, the breast-beating and the solemn resolutions to sacrifice, phony as hangover vows on New Year's Day. Then with only a little easing of the situation, things pretty well returned to normal and the wailing was forgotten. But in the meantime, controls had been relaxed.

Now, as J.R. had seen, was the time to push for the use of all that lovely low-grade coal—at a profit, of course. And that was what he was here for, wasn't it?

He took a turn away from the windows and put his thoughts back on what Sam Waldo had said. So canny old Seth Porter had been at the governor, had he?

Farley had never met Seth, but even in Houston they spoke of him almost with reverence as a stereotypical country lawyer who, when occasion warranted, had been perfectly capable of skinning brushed-up Wall Street legal-types alive and nailing their hides to the barn door. Western-bred, Farley had great respect for his neighbors and peers, and a measure of contempt for the frequently demonstrated insularity of the Eastern megalopolis.

Farley walked to the phone, sat down, and looked up the number of Seth's law firm. The best defense was frequently attack, particularly surprise attack. A confrontation might be just the thing to catch old Seth Porter off-balance. He put through the call, gave his name to the law firm operator, and waited quietly.

It was only a moment. Seth Porter's voice came on the line, polite, even cordial. "Mr. Wells. Delighted to hear from you. I've been expecting your call. Shall we get together for a little talk?"

So much for surprise attack.

24

Up in the Four Corners area, where Utah, Arizona, Colorado, and New Mexico meet, the huge coal-fired generators poured into the air as much pollution as the entire city of Los Angeles, and dispatched their generated electricity south and west to the great metropolitan areas.

More power plants were planned, some were already under construction. More airborne pollution would follow the winds down the Rio Grande as far as Albuquerque, two hundred and fifty miles away. But, as Napoleon is alleged to have said, you did not make an omelette without breaking eggs. The air-conditioned Southwest demanded more and more electricity, didn't it?

In research facilities and engineering departments across the nation alternate sources of energy were being carefully studied for practicability:

Atomic reactors of new and different kinds, refined breeder reactors, even reactors containing in enormous magnetic fields the awesome power of the fusion process, which is the basis of the hydrogen bomb;

Solar heat collectors, already practical but far too

expensive, were undergoing refinement after refinement in an effort to find a design that could be mass-produced at reasonable cost;

Geothermal explorations were under way and plans were already in existence for the generator plants the earth-contained heat would power;

There were those who studied the ocean tides as man had from his beginnings, watching the forty-foot rise and fall of the sea at the Bay of Fundy and Lynmouth, and calculating how that enormous energy source could be harnessed to drive generator plants;

New windmill designs were already on drafting boards;

Fuel-cell design was under close scrutiny, and further experiments with the fuel-cell principle itself merely awaited funds;

Low-temperature physics had already shown the way to superconductivity, and designs for underground transmission lines supercooled by liquid helium were beyond preliminary investigation;

Storage of electrical energy was the thorny problem, and there were investigations into the feasibility of water movement as a possible solution, as well as into variations on that old standby the flywheel;

The search went on and would continue, but so far too little, and already very late.

25

The body of Kelly Garcia had been taken to Las Grutas, where Dr. Harry Walker doubling as medical examiner performed his examination and made official what had been evident from the start: Kelly had died of a gunshot wound.

The area in the trees had been searched, but no bullet had been found, and the killer had not been generous enough to leave a cartridge case for examination. The make and caliber of the weapon used was anybody's guess.

Marty Romero sat in Pepe Martinez's office. "Like the other one," Marty said, "it's your baby, of course. Your jurisdiction." He paused. "But if you like, we'll cooperate and give you any help we can."

Pepe scowled and rubbed the broken nose. He disliked State Police interference. On the other hand, the State Police had facilities that were far beyond the reach of poor Grutas County. "Okay," he said.

"You'll get the credit, of course," Marty said. "What credit there is," he added.

That made cooperation more palatable. Pepe nodded sagely. "Any ideas?"

Always he was fascinated by patterns, with their recurrent or aberrant themes. "It happened where the rustling took place," Marty said. "And it's where somebody took a shot at Tom Granger only the day before. Then Kelly Garcia. The three could tie together."

Pepe had not known about the attempt on Tom. He said as much. He added, "Goddamn pity they didn't get him, the arrogant Anglo bastard."

Marty hid his smile. He was familiar with the tale of Pepe's broken nose, and he could appreciate the enmity that was its legacy. "At a guess," he said, ignoring Pepe's remark, "Kelly could have been getting too close to somebody. Tom tells me he was nosing around."

"He came here and talked to me," Pepe said. "He probably talked to a lot of people. He was an old woman for gossip."

Marty wondered if Pepe liked anybody, not that it mattered. "Our man rides a horse," he said.

Pepe snorted. "Half the county fancy themselves *vaqueros*."

True enough, but hardly helpful. Marty stood up. "I'll be around. You have any ideas, call me at the ranch."

Pepe nodded glumly. His smile was bitter. "The great El Rancho del Norte. Do you know in my whole life I've never even been on the son of a bitch? I tried two, three times as a kid, and always somebody ran my ass off in a hurry."

Enmity deep and solid, Marty thought; something to keep in mind. How many others felt the same? He walked out to his pickup, and then, as before, changed his mind and walked down the street to the parish house.

Father Enrique was pulling trespassing grass from his cactus garden. "You might think," he said, and then shook and sucked his forefinger, "that the plants would know I am trying to help them." His voice was tinged with sadness. "But the cholla, yes, and the prickly pear as well defend their territory even against me." He squeezed the forefinger and a tiny drop of blood appeared. "It is all right," he said to the cholla. "You are forgiven." He stood up. "You wish to talk about the terrible thing that happened to Kelly Garcia?" He nodded and led the way into the house.

"We have a madman loose, Padre," Marty said when they were seated. "He must be found."

"And how can I help?"

"You hear much."

The priest shook his head. "What I hear in the confessional—"

"Other than that," Marty said. "People talk to you as they do not talk to others."

"True." The priest was nodding now. "I will listen."

"And ask."

The priest's face was puzzled.

"Who did Kelly Garcia talk to?" Marty said. "He saw Pepe Martinez and Tom Granger. Who else? And what questions did he ask? The mountains have eyes, Padre, and ears. The wind has a voice." My god, I'm even sounding mystical, he thought.

But the priest was unsmiling. "I will try," he said.

230

Will carried a rifle when he left the car and went up the steps to the big house. At the office door he hesitated, and then knocked as he had been told before he opened the door and went in. The office was empty, and he felt a little foolish about knocking after all.

The key was on top of the gun cabinet in its usual place. Will unlocked the cabinet and was about to replace the rifle when Tom's voice stopped him.

"Did you fire it?" Tom said from the doorway. "If you did, it gets cleaned before it goes back." He walked into the office to stand beside the desk, big and solid and close to anger. "What were you doing with it, anyway?"

"I don't particularly like your tone." Will paused. "If you want to know, I was sighting it in."

"Where?"

"In the blind bend of the big arroyo. Where we always did."

Tom made himself relax. He nodded wearily. "Tell Connie. She'll have someone clean it for you." And then, puzzled now. "Sighting it in? What for? Going hunting?"

"I might."

"There's nothing in season."

"I might find something."

Tom shrugged and went around the desk to sit down. "Suit yourself." He stretched out a long arm and poured a drink from the tantalus. Then he looked up at his brother. "Want one?"

Will shook his head in silence. He wanted to leave and yet would not because leaving might smack of flight. Instead, "You're uptight. Why?"

"Kelly Garcia." He told Will what had happened, and could see no reaction other than near incredulity. Tom added, "Same place where probably the same man took a shot at me. Same place where the rustling trucks loaded up." Like Marty, he saw the coincidence and wondered about it. He nodded toward the rifle Will had leaned against the wall. "That could have done it."

231

"Do you think it did? Is that it?"

"No." Flat statement. Tom left it there and sipped his whiskey. His eyes did not leave Will's face.

"And what does the Gestapo think?" Will said.

"If you're talking about Marty," Tom said, his voice cold now, "I don't know. He keeps his opinions to himself." Not entirely true, but close enough.

Will thought about it, nodded shortly, and turned away. He went slowly, thoughtfully up the stairs to his and Sue's rooms.

The two tiny pieces of Sue's bikini were on the floor of the dressing room. Sue herself was gone. Will picked up the bikini pieces, tossed them on a chair and stretched himself out on the daybed, hands behind his head, eyes staring incuriously at the ceiling. What was that sign he had seen once? DON'T THINK, DRINK.

So the unknown sniper had struck again, with success this time. It sounded like a bad headline. Kelly Garcia was innocuous. What was the point in shooting him? Just for kicks? A nut with a rifle? Some freaked-out kid? Or, as seemed more likely, had Kelly's sharp nose been on a scent that had turned out to be dangerous and in the end fatal? Will decided that if he had figured that out, both Tom and Marty would have seen it too. Which was probably why Tom was so sure that he, Will, had nothing to do with it. Well and good.

The rifle he had been firing had needed no sighting adjustment. It held fine, just the way he liked it, and although he had not touched a rifle in a couple of years, the old skills remained intact. It was good to see the shots go where he wanted them against the cut bank of the arroyo.

He told himself that he had nothing specific in mind, and knew that he lied. Looking through the sights of the rifle, he had tried to imagine what it would be like if instead of a small spot on the dirt bank he was looking at a man. Would his finger be as steady and gentle on the trigger, his breathing as controlled, his body as relaxed? When he squeezed off the shot and felt the recoil, heard the sharp crack, he watched fascinated as the dirt flew precisely where he had aimed, and he found himself wondering how the hypothetical man would react. Would he stagger, lurch, and fall? Or would he go down all at once, a doll unhinged, totally and forever ignorant of what had happened to him?

And then what? Obviously lay the blame on the unknown sniper. Or, better yet, let others draw that conclusion first. The less he knew about any part of the incident, the better. Or, new thought, should it be an accident, one of those hunting tragedies that happened all too often? It might be better, safer, because there were such things as ballistics tests and comparison microscopes, and Marty Romero would just love to demonstrate that the gun that had killed was the .30-06 from the downstairs gun cabinet. Had killed whom? Lying there, staring up at the ceiling, Will let the question echo and reecho in his mind without ever putting answer to it.

He roused himself at the sound of the door's opening. It was Sue. She wore the fine Chinese silk robe he had given her, and she was barefoot. The fine hair close to her neck was damp. She was smiling that secret smile that could infuriate. "Hi, darling. Did you have a good shoot?"

Will sat up slowly, the pleasurable reverie brutally ended. "What have you been doing?"

"Why, darling, what a nasty tone." The smile was unchanged. "Has big brother Tom been putting you down again?"

"I asked a question."

"I heard."

"Are you going to answer it?"

"Or what, darling? Will you go all virile male and beat it out of me?" Sue waited, smiling still, but there was no reply. "If you're interested," she said at last, still light, mocking, "I've been taking a bath. It was hot in the sun."

"Alone?" He should not have asked the question, he

told himself immediately. The word had just slipped out.

"Why, no, darling. You know I can't wash my back properly. All that suntan oil."

"Ethel?" Again his tongue betrayed him. Damn it, the way to play it was cool, cool, cool. But he was beyond that. Memories of that young maid in Cannes. Why should he suddenly feel now as if he had been cuckolded?

"Ethel was good enough to—help me, yes, darling. Would you rather it had been Tom? Or that fascinating policeman?" There was no answer. She had expected none. She took off the robe and tossed it on the chair with the bikini pieces and naked walked to her chest of drawers. "A nice long bath after the sun," she said. "I feel—refreshed."

Damn the woman anyway! She had not for a moment lost her light easy smile, the superior smile of the female. Will wanted to shout at her using words like whore and bitch and nympho and dyke, but he said nothing. Nor could he keep his eyes from her.

She was bending over an open drawer, side view to him. He could only admire the luscious curves of haunch and breast, the tiny waist, the clean carved legs. The two narrow stripes of white flesh across her breasts and around her loins somehow made her seem more naked than naked, totally revealed. Deliberately?

"Darling." Sue had straightened and turned, smiling still. Now she presented full front view. She was devoid of body hair, and that too had always intrigued him. "Darling," Sue said again. Her voice was slow, subtly mocking. "I was going to dress." She paused. "But if you have other ideas?"

Fresh from Ethel to him, he thought, and refused to speak. He was angrily aware that his face and his body betrayed him. Yet he accepted it.

"That's nice, darling," Sue said. "I enjoy being— wanted." Slowly she crossed the room to the daybed. She stood before him, unmoving, smiling, knowing exactly her power over him. He reached for her, and her triumph was complete.

Will lay on his back, naked and spent, defeated. The male might be the dominant sex, he thought, but at a time like this he was at the female's mercy until he had gathered his strength, regrouped his forces. Why, hell, Sue wasn't at all exhausted. She never was.

She lay on her side, propped on one elbow. With her free hand she traced light patterns on Will's chest. "Tired, darling? No wonder." She was smiling. "It was a stirring performance."

Mockery? He wasn't sure. "As good as with Ethel?" His tone was bitter.

Sue's smile spread. "Don't be like that. The word is different." She was without reticence. "With another woman it's not at all the same even if you do some of the same things. But never mind, darling. Ethel doesn't matter." She bent to kiss his shoulder. Her breast was warm against his chest. "Another shooting," she said. "The wild, wild West." She paused to kiss the shoulder again. "But not at Tom this time." Another pause, another kiss, and a gentle bite. "I wonder why."

Will said slowly, "Why not Tom?"

"Somebody shot at him once, darling. Doesn't it stand to reason that somebody might shoot at him again?"

Female logic, Will thought. And yet in a twisted way it did make a kind of sense. Hadn't he been thinking along exactly the same lines when Sue came in? He had the wild idea that his thoughts might be showing. It was what came from having your defenses down. Samson must have had the same feeling.

"You must have thought about it," Sue said.

"Thought about what?"

Sue moved to lie partially across him. Her body was warm. Her face was very close. "About Tom, darling. And what if there were another shot"—pause. A light kiss full on his mouth—"that didn't miss." And then, "Rub my back, darling. Mmmm. Lower. Yes, like that."

"That isn't your back." Her rounded buttock.

"Call it what you like. It feels good."

"Is there anything for you that doesn't feel good?" Her breath was warm, fragrant, her lips close to his ear. "It's the way you like it, isn't it, darling?"

It was, and she knew that it was, Will thought. The female was still in command.

"Haven't you thought about it?"

Denial would be futile and admission harmless. "Naturally. He's my brother."

"And you are your brother's keeper. Of course."

"That," Will said, "was what you had in mind, wasn't it? Good old brotherly concern."

Sue raised herself and moved closer. Her groin pressed warmly against his thigh. "Why, what else?" She moved again to lie flat on top of him at full length. Her lips touched his while she spoke. "And you'll keep thinking about it, won't you, darling?" Pause. "In just the same way." Her mouth on his prevented reply.

Ethel Wilding, relaxed now, still naked, lay on the big bed and smiled up at the ceiling. She wondered idly if Will had returned while she and Sue were in here together, if he had guessed what they were doing, and if he had, what his reaction had been. Never mind; Sue would cope.

Sue was incredible; there was no other word. You tended to think of her as empty-headed. It was not true; it was merely that you were blinded by her physical allure and the aura of sensuality she exuded, and you failed to see what lay beneath. As attractive as Sue was to her, a woman, Ethel wondered, what in the world would she be to a man? There was no way of knowing; you simply could not put yourself into a man's mind or his appetites. But she could see objectively that Will was totally immersed in his wife's spell.

Lying together in the sun she and Sue had talked of many things, Will among them. "I suppose we're useless," Sue had said, and smiled. "It's easier that way. Maybe if Will's grandfather had thrown him out, and made him stand on his feet if only for a little time—" She shook her head. "But he didn't. And I'm no help. I'm not like you. I always prefer the easy way. I admire you."

Was flattery the beginning of courtship? Probably. "I had to make my way," Ethel said. "It was that or nothing."

"You could have picked a man. With your looks and your body—" Sue smiled again. "But you did it your own way. Not many would." She sat up on the chaise. "Time to turn. Will you oil me?" She undid her halter and lay face down on the chaise, hands cushioned beneath her cheek.

The police lieutenant had been afraid to touch that lovely body, Ethel thought. She didn't blame him. As she smoothed in the suntan oil, she was affected too, and she had a shrewd idea that Sue knew it, but not for the world would she, Ethel, make advances. She was a guest here at the big house. She would behave with propriety. Unless. . . .

"You have a nice touch," Sue said. She was smiling again. "How are you on soaping backs in a bath?"

Ethel's hands paused, then resumed. "Not bad."

And that was all that was said. They lay on in the sun.

Ethel said at last, "I think I've had enough."

"Yes." Sue sat up and fastened her halter.

Together they walked into the house and up the broad stairs. At the door to Ethel's rooms, "I think a nice long bath—" Sue said. Her voice was conversational. Unsmiling now, her eyes steady on Ethel's face, "Care to join me?"

So there it was, as Ethel told herself, she had really known all along it would be. And Sue had known too; merely the words until now unspoken between them. "I think that would be pleasant," Ethel said.

Sue smiled then. "Your bath," she said. "I'll come back."

The huge ornate bathtub from the Denver bawdy-house, and the two naked bodies almost, but not quite, touching, the two faces smiling at one another. "I didn't think I was mistaken," Sue said. She held a cake of soap between her small hands, working it into a lather with slow sensuality. She handed it to Ethel. "In fact," she said, "I knew I wasn't." With the same slow, sensual movements she began to soap Ethel's breasts. . . .

26

Spring was ripening, and the air was warmer than it had been. Tom rode again the big gelding and sat old Matt's working saddle. Remembering Marty's warning, he had hesitated and then taken the 30-30 carbine. It was beneath his right leg now, resting in a worn leather scabbard. Time was, Tom thought, when a sheathed carbine was as standard as the coiled lariat lashed to the pommel, as the saddle itself. So we haven't come very far, he told himself, and disliked the cynicism the thought implied.

He had no particular destination, merely a desire for movement and solitude. As a boy he had often taken long aimless rides, something old Matt had understood, if Will had not. Come to think of it, there was a great deal that old Matt had understood. Maybe that was the problem between them: they were too much alike.

He came to the fenceline and followed it to the meadow where Borden's body had been found. There he reined in the gelding and sat motionless for a time, letting random thoughts flow through his mind.

Borden carried a backpack complete with sleeping bag and tent roll. Where had he spent the nights before his death? The specific night before his death?

And what on earth had brought that question to mind, anyway? It was something that probably could never be answered.

Borden was a geologist and he had talked with Pete Barkley about geothermal possibilities on the ranch. Well, right up there was the entrance to the mine that had been abandoned because of an excess of underground heat. A connection? Maybe, even probably, but what had that to do with his being shot?

Three shootings; one here, the other two in the tree area where the cattle had been held and loaded into the rustlers' trucks. The only link connecting them was the fact that shootings were not ordinary these days as they once had been, and when they did not occur you tended to try to pin them down to a single cause, which was probably ridiculous.

Or was it? Two rustlings. After the second, two shootings, and the odds were that both were connected with the rustling. Marty thought so, and Marty did not tend to jump to untenable conclusions. What, then, if the shooting of Borden had followed the first rustling? Possible? Think, damn it, think!

Tish had said that the first big snow of the fall had followed that first rustling and effectively wiped out whatever tracks there were. Had that same first big snow also buried Borden? Were the two events that close in time?

The gelding lowered his head and began to crop the meadow grass. Tom eased the reins automatically, and then turned in the saddle to look back at the trees from which the shot that killed Borden must have come. The fence led into those trees, and if followed far enough—not very far, actually—it reached the area where both rustlings had taken place. So?

So the possibility existed that Borden might have been close to the rustling scene, didn't it? Perhaps even in his sleeping bag in his tent when the trucks rolled up and the cattle were loaded? Had he seen the man on horseback who had rounded up the cattle and held them? Or, more to the point, had the man seen Borden? Was that why Borden was—eliminated?

Tom's own experience and Kelly Garcia's death seemed to argue that the man on horseback took no chances when there was even the slightest indication that someone might be getting close to him.

It was all conjecture, sure, but you had to start someplace and hypothesis to theory to proven law was the accepted route, wasn't it?

First, he told himself, the dates should be checked to verify Tish's memory that the first big snow had indeed followed hard on the first rustling. Then to talk with Marty Romero about the idea. Marty and Pepe Martinez could carry it from there. They were paid for such things and he, Tom, had other matters to think about.

He reined up the gelding's head and touched his barrel lightly with his heels. They rode on across the meadow.

After her last talk with Seth Porter, Tish had called. Kelly Garcia's death had pretty well put the call out of Tom's mind, but he went back to it now.

"Sam Waldo's bill is almost sure to pass," Tish had said. "That leaves it up to the governor, and Seth Porter won't even guess which way he will go." And she had added, "I'm sorry, Tom."

Unwelcome news, but no excuse for open lament. "How's your love affair going? Am I going to have to give a bride away?"

"I'm sticking my tongue out at you," Tish said. And then in a different voice, "Farley Wells has asked me to dinner."

"You're going?"

"I am."

"Keep your guard up."

Now, riding slowly across the meadow, Tom wondered if he had made a mistake in sending Tish to Santa Fe. Oh, if she got in over her depth, she always had Seth Porter to turn to. But would she? In many ways Tish was shy, even unworldly; witness that Denver period. But there was also in her an indomitable quality that emerged at unexpected times. There was that colt Matt had bought her years ago.

240

Tish had loved it and tended it, and when the time came, she had allowed no one but herself to train it to bridle and saddle. Tom had offered. Clyde Burley had offered. All offers declined. Tom had appealed to Matt.

"Leave her alone, boy," Matt had said. "She's going to be thrown on her ass, but that won't hurt half as bad as not being allowed to try."

"She's a girl."

"You've finally noticed? I thought you always thought she was your kid brother. All right, so she's a girl. This is something she has to do. Nobody's told her to do it; she's told herself, and that, goddamnit, is the kind of decision you don't back away from."

And so, Western-style, Tish climbed aboard the colt and was promptly bucked off. No one laughed, but Will wore his secret smile. Tish picked herself up, brushed some of the corral dirt from her jeans, wiped her mouth with the back of her hand, and climbed aboard again. This time she lasted a little longer, but the end result was the same.

Tom came down from the top rail of the corral fence and helped Tish to her feet. She shook his hand away. "Leave me alone, damn you!" There were tears in her eyes.

"You heard her, boy." This was Matt leaning against the fence.

Tish walked slowly to the colt. He watched her, but made no move. She collected the reins, tight on the near side, put her foot in the stirrup and swung again into the saddle.

The colt promptly buckjumped sideways, landed, and kicked out with both hind legs. He jumped again, and the rider stayed on his back. He went into a series of twisting jumps, and then all at once stopped and stood still, shivering. Capitulation.

Tish reached down and patted his neck. "It's all right," she said, "all right." Her voice was gentle. She touched his barrel with her heels and clucked to him. He hesitated and then moved off at a walk. Triumph.

"Good girl," Matt said. "I think maybe you've got

yourself a horse." He looked at Tom and said nothing. Then he looked at Will. "Wipe that silly smirk off your face," he said. "You wouldn't even have climbed on the first time."

Long ago, but well remembered. Tom was smiling as he rode now. Yes, he thought, indomitable was the word. And responsible. There were some you could count on; there were some, like Will, who were pure quicksilver when it came to being pinned down to any form of responsibility: they skittered out from beneath your thumb with the greatest of ease. But not Tish. Never Tish. Tish was one to ride with. Warm thought.

27

On this warm day, "I thought a ride up to the basin, if you'd like that?" Jimmy Thomas said.

"I'd like that very much," Tish said. It seemed as if they were already old friends, easy and comfortable with each other. She sat relaxed in the bucket seat of the little car and watched the country slide past.

Leaving Santa Fe and climbing, they were first in the piñon-juniper elevation zone; then came the ponderosas, tall and silent; at eight thousand feet the aspens began, mixed with the evergreens, their leaves perpetually shimmering even when no breeze was apparent. Tish breathed the high clear air and was content.

"The old gentleman," Jimmy said, "told me to ask you what the Wells character had in mind." He paused. "If it wasn't too onerous a chore for me to see you, that was." Smiling, he glanced at Tish's face.

Her answering smile was warm. "And," Jimmy said, "if you didn't mind talking about it, of course."

"I don't mind talking about it," Tish said, "except that I don't know what to say. Farley is very smooth."

They were entering the climbing turns now. Jimmy shifted down with unnecessary vigor. "Farley," he said.

Tish was smiling. " 'Call me Farley, please, ma'am.' " Her drawl was a good imitation. "We talked a lot about Tom, and about Will, and the ranch, how long I'd lived there, that kind of thing." Her smile returned, lighting her face, her eyes. "He didn't pinch me under the table, if that's what you're thinking."

Jimmy made himself relax. "The thought was in my mind." The road was steeper now and the curves sharper. He shifted down to second with less vehemence. "Did you get the impression that he was sizing up Tom, and Will, through your close knowledge?" He was the lawyer now, studying the case, his own feelings for the moment set aside. "It would figure," he added. He paused. "As a matter of fact, how do you see the two of them? I'd like to know too."

How did she see them? Did she really know? Well, certain things at least were plain. "Will is—sly. And weak. He has always tried to get out of anything that took work or responsibility." Her smile was without amusement. "And usually he's succeeded. There were times when I thought Matt was going to have apoplexy because of something Will had let slide or dodged, yes, or lied about."

"I take it," Jimmy said, "that you didn't like him all this time?"

"I didn't trust him. He—" She stopped and shook her head. "He made passes at me until I slapped his face and told him that if he didn't stop, I'd tell Tom."

Jimmy's voice was carefully expressionless. "Tom, not your stepfather?"

"Jimmy, please." Tish searched for words. "It was only that we tried to settle things without going to Matt, don't you see? Kids growing up, we tried to stay away from—olders, that was all."

The riposte was obvious. "But did you ever turn

to Will for help because of something Tom had done?"

The very concept was ridiculous. "No, of course not. But—" Her voice trailed off. "I can't explain, Jimmy, but you have the wrong idea about Tom—and me. I'm not sure I even like him. I've told him what a bastard he can be."

"And what did he say?"

"He laughed."

"He didn't think you meant it?"

Tish was silent, thoughtful. "No," she said at last, "I think he knew I meant it, but it didn't hurt him because he knows who he is and what he is, and that's all there is to it."

"He thinks pretty much of you, sending you down here."

"He thinks I'm more capable than I am." But he trusts me, she thought, and that is the important thing.

"Maybe," Jimmy said, "he's a better judge than you are."

They came out of the trees at the ten-thousand-foot level and there Jimmy pulled the car onto the turnout and switched off the engine.

Santa Fe was spread beneath them against its backdrop of mountains: the Cerrillos, Ortiz mountains, and Sandía to the southwest; the Jemez mountains to the west; and between, crouching clear and plain on the horizon a hundred miles away, the solitary mass of Mount Taylor.

Jimmy said gently, "Anything else you and friend Wells talked about that might have meaning?"

Tish smiled. "He likes his steaks rare."

"He would. Probably raw."

"He married once. It didn't work. No children. His wife wasn't interested." She half turned in her seat. "He isn't a bad man, Jimmy."

"That's what makes him dangerous."

"Is that what Seth thinks?"

"It's what I'm beginning to think. Do you know about the right of eminent domain?"

"Only vaguely."

Jimmy told her what Seth had pointed out to him.

"I had to have my nose rubbed in it before I saw it. Would Tom know?"

"I don't know." Tish hesitated. "That isn't fair, Jimmy. That they could force the ranch to be sold, I mean."

Jimmy's tone was dry. "As the old gentleman pointed out, fair doesn't figure in many situations." Like mine, he thought. How do I compete with Tom Granger?

"If he doesn't know," Tish said, "I'd better tell him. Or Seth had."

"Noted for further action," Jimmy said. "Now lets talk about us."

Tom reached the far edge of the meadow, crossed a small stream and began a slanting climb up the mountain's flank. There was sage here, occasional appache plume, and chamisa, all low growth. Tom let the gelding pick his circuitous way at an easy walking pace, ears forward, head slightly bent. A sound horse, ranch-bred, range-wise. But, then, would Matt have ridden anything else? Matt, Matt, Matt. Damn it, Tom thought, the old man is everywhere; his imprint is on everything.

They passed clumps of cattle, some with calves; good-looking stock, heavier, shorter-legged than run-of-the-mill range cattle; the result of interbreeding with those carefully bred animals Clyde Burley and his home ranch people produced. In the vastness of the country, because you saw only small scattered groups, you tended to think that there were not many cattle around, not like those huge herds you saw on TV. But cattle there were, thousands of head, grazing in meadows, in brush like this, on seemingly barren ground, in forests, on mesas, on mountain slopes; drinking at streams, stock tanks; lying in the shade of cottonwoods or willows; crossing arroyos, making their trails on hillsides; sometimes needing help in deep mud or snow, sometimes needing dropped feed in heavy winter, or herding to water when small streams dried up during drought. And, Tom thought, needing protection against marauders, animal or human.

POWER

They topped a small rise and movement caught Tom's eye, a flash of light color, another. Pronghorn antelopes sailing off through the brush as if on springs. He reined in and watched them, smiling. Beautiful little beasts. He hoped they would stay on ranch property and away from roads and highways. And hunters.

He nudged the gelding into movement and almost simultaneously something buzzed behind his back, and the crack of a rifle followed. He bent low over the gelding's neck and slammed both heels into the animal's flanks. They took off at a run, down the far side of the rise, circling, heading for a rocky outcrop, and there Tom grabbed the 30-30 and did a Pony Express dismount in a cloud of dust, dropping the reins and almost diving into the shelter of the outcropping.

Not again! was his first thought. His second was that Marty had known what he was about, and with this thought the anger came.

This time, goddamnit, he was not going to run. This time he had a rifle in his hands, and he was prepared to use it. This time two could hunt.

The gelding had stopped and, divided reins hanging, stood patiently, rooted as he had been trained.

Tom studied the rise where he had been so beautifully silhouetted. And what Marty would have said to him about exposing himself like that!

There was no one in sight, and Tom studied the angles and the possibilities offered by the terrain. The shot could have come from below that small rise. Or it could have come from higher commanding ground. Take your pick. Either way, high ground was the place for him, basic infantry strategy. Bending low, the rifle in his right hand, he began moving up the mountain's slope in short rushes, watching always to his right and above, the two directions from which the shot could have come.

He was quickly winded. A goddamn flatlander, he told himself, almost helpless above seven thousand feet. But he drove himself, one more rush of twenty yards, another, another, with pauses between for gasping breath.

Ahead was another outcropping, and from it he would have a commanding view of the far side of the ridge. Or maybe a face-to-face confrontation with the rifleman. So be it. He covered the last little distance to the outcropping at as fast a run as he could manage, rifle held now at the ready, hammer cocked, finger on the trigger.

He ducked above and behind the rocks. They were empty. He gave himself the luxury of half a dozen deep breaths, the deepest, before he moved forward for a look-down.

He saw a horse, like his gelding rooted to dropped reins. He saw no man at first, and he made himself study the entire area slowly piece by piece, clump of brush by clump. And then he saw the legs. And the body had to be just there, hidden by the chamisa bush, angled in the direction of the rise where Tom had sat his horse and smiled at the antelopes.

Kneeling, he took careful aim, allowed for distance and downhill trajectory, and squeezed off the shot. Dirt flew only a foot from where the man's head had to be. Automatically Tom levered another shell into the chamber as he raised his voice in a shout: "Drop it and stand up slowly! That was a warning shot! The next one won't be!" You son of a bitch, he thought. "Move it!"

The legs moved first, with infinite slowness. Then haunches rose above the chamisa, and torso, and the man stood up and turned uncertainly, not knowing exactly where to look. It was Will, the rifle still in his hand.

"Drop it," Tom said. His voice was cold. He stood up from the rocks, the 30-30 at his shoulder aiming at Will's belly, finger tense on the trigger. "I won't tell you again."

Will's hand opened as if of its own volition. The rifle dropped to the dirt.

"Now walk away from it."

Will's mouth was dry. He swallowed hard. "Look—"

"Walk away from it, you son of a bitch."

Will tried to shrug. The gesture failed. He walked a few slow paces, his eyes still on the rifle at Tom's shoulder.

"That's far enough. Now stay there." Tom came down the slope without haste, the rifle at the ready. He lowered the hammer as he drew close, and let the rifle swing at his side, held lightly by the balance. He said nothing.

"Look," Will said. "It—wasn't what you thought!" His voice had risen.

"And what did I think?" The tone was cold. What was in Tom's face and his eyes was frightening. "Just what did I think?" he said again.

Will's tongue came out, moistened his lips, and then like a small frightened animal fled back into his mouth. "Why, why, you seem to think I shot at you!"

"I don't think it. I know it." The words were slow, pitiless. "But you made a mistake. You missed."

"I wasn't shooting at you!"

Tom stood silent, implacable.

"There were—antelope! I was shooting at them!"

"There are antelope," Tom said. "But you can't see them from here. They're on the other side of that rise where I was." The anger was turning to contempt. "Among other things, you're a goddamn liar." He paused. "But, then, you always were, and always you expected to get off scot free. This time you're not going to."

Again the tongue appeared and again fled. "What are you going to do?"

"I ought to turn you over to Marty Romero." He saw the new fear in Will's face. "He threatened once to cut off your *cojones*. He just might do it. He doesn't like bushwhackers any more than I do."

"I tell you it was an accident!" Will took a deep breath. "And you can't prove it wasn't!"

Slowly Tom nodded. "You have a point there." He saw the sudden relief in Will's face. "So," he said, without change of expression, "we'll consider this an accident too."

He swung his left fist in a crashing hook driven by the full strength of his big body and the drive of his legs. The fist slammed into Will's face with a crunching sound, and Will took a quick step backward and then dropped to his knees, his head in his hands.

"Just something to remember this by," Tom said. He spaced the words for emphasis. "In case you get the idea of trying it again, you'd better not miss." He paused, looking down at the still kneeling, huddled man. "Because the first shot I fire won't be a warning." He paused again. "You'd better believe that."

He turned away then, walked over, and picked up Will's rifle. Carrying the two weapons, he walked back around the rise and down to the still rooted gelding. He slid the 30-30 into its scabbard. Holding the other rifle in one hand, he gathered the reins and mounted. He sat motionless for a few moments. All anger was gone now. He felt that he wanted to vomit in disgust.

Marty was at the ranchhouse when Tom rode back, turned the gelding over to a stableboy, and walked up the steps carrying the two rifles. He jerked his head toward the office and Marty followed him in and closed the door. He watched Tom unload both rifles and lean them against the wall. Then Tom crossed the room and poured two drinks from the bottle in the tantalus. "Sit down," he said, and walked around the desk to the now familiar chair.

Marty glanced at the rifles. "You carried the carbine," he said. "Who had the thirty-aught-six?"

"Will."

Nothing changed in Marty's face, the harsh lines unrelenting. "Go on," he said.

"He tried to bushwhack me." Tom described the scene, thought about it, and drank half the shot glass of whiskey in one swallow. He wiped his lips slowly with his cupped hand. "And," he said, "I came closer than I like to think to killing him."

"Maybe you should have."

Tom studied what was left of his drink. "Maybe you're right." He paused. "But I'm glad I didn't." He finished the drink.

Marty was smiling now, flashing those white teeth. "You think too much, amigo. A man like your brother—" He shook his head, smiling no longer. "I see a rattlesnake," he said, "and I walk around him. He is what he is, and if I leave him alone, he won't bother me. But a vicious man, a weak, vicious man—" Again he left the sentence unfinished. "He followed you?"

"I guess so. I wasn't paying much attention."

"I told you to look all ways at once." Marty paused, smiling again. "And stay off ridges. Because Will isn't the man we want."

The office door burst open and an angry Sue almost rushed in. "What happened? Damn you, what happened?"

Tom's face was bleak. "Ask Will."

"I did. You smashed his face and he isn't making sense."

Marty looked pleased.

Tom pointed silently at the two rifles leaning against the wall, and Sue turned to look. It was some little time before she turned to face the room again. "I see." Her voice was quiet. She looked at Marty and then again at Tom. "Are you going to—what is the way you say it?—press charges?"

"No. It's finished."

Marty said quietly, "Until maybe next time, amigo. Bear that in mind."

Tom was looking straight at Sue. "I am. I will." He paused. "If you want him alive, keep him under control. That's a warning."

Sue's eyes narrowed faintly. "Do you think I'm the one in charge?"

"Yes."

"You don't care what you say, do you?"

"Not after somebody has just tried to kill me."

Sue's face was angry again. "How do you know it wasn't an accident?"

"I know. So does Will."

"You're impossible!" Sue glared at both men. Then, to Tom, "I'm taking him to Santa Fe. His face has to be looked at. His nose is broken, I think." She waited, but there was no reply. "Well?"

"Suit yourself," Tom said. "He can always say he walked into a door in the dark."

"Or that his brother attacked him without warning." Marty hid his smile.

Tom said mildly, "Yes, he can always say that."

"He could press charges."

Tom nodded. "He could do that too."

Sue stamped her foot. "Doesn't anything—touch you?"

Nothing changed in Tom's face. "Attempted fratricide makes me unhappy. I imagine Abel would have had the same feeling—if he had lived. Will and I grew up together. We weren't all that close, but we are brothers, and that is supposed to mean something. Apparently it doesn't."

Sue was silent for a long time, her eyes steady and contemplative on Tom's face. "And you think I am responsible?"

"Partly, if not largely." Tom paused. The thought had been growing. It was fullblown now. "Lady Macbeth comes to mind."

"That's ridiculous."

"I won't press the point."

"Being here in charge of this place has gone to your head."

Had it? Tom thought about it. "It's possible. But that changes nothing."

"I suppose you want us to leave?"

"No. It's as much Will's home as it is mine." The two rifles caught his eye. "But from now on the gun cupboard will stay locked, and I'll have the only key."

When Sue was gone, flouncing out, head high, angry back straight, Marty got out of his chair and closed the door again. He remained standing. "As I said, it isn't finished, amigo. Will is not the man who shot at you in the trees. He isn't the man who killed Kelly Garcia."

Tom had forgotten his hypothesis. "Or maybe killed Borden as well," he said. "And for maybe the same reason."

Marty walked slowly to his chair and sat down. His face was thoughtful. "Explain that, amigo." And he listened quietly, immobile, a south-of-the-border statue carved in stone. When Tom was finished, he nodded. "It makes sense," he said. "It makes very good sense. I should have seen it. The pattern is there."

"With at least one piece missing," Tom said. "You've eliminated Clyde because the buckskin he usually rides—"

"Always rides, amigo. I checked that out. And the buckskin's tracks are not the horse tracks in the trees."

"All right," Tom said. "You've eliminated him. And you've eliminated Will, who wasn't even here last fall when Borden was killed."

"And when Kelly Garcia was killed, Farley Wells was in Santa Fe, presence verified."

"Who's left?"

Marty's face had altered. He stared for long moments at the far wall. He said at last, "I am reaching far out," he said. He smiled suddenly. "My mother was a *bruja,* a witch. Maybe some of it rubbed off on me." The smile disappeared. "What you thought you saw on the ground there in the trees. Describe it."

"I can't. I've told you. I had the idea that it was metallic and round and that's all."

"A coin?"

Tom closed his eyes and tried to picture the scene. He shook his head. "I doubt it. I think I would have recognized a coin."

"What about a metal washer?"

Again the strained attempt to recall. Tom said at last, "I guess that could be. It's closer than a coin, I think. But what does that do? I can't be sure."

Marty said casually, "How about a spur rowel? Could that have been it?"

"It wasn't a spur. That I would have recognized."

"I said a rowel, a loose rowel, not the whole spur."

Tom thought about it. Slowly he nodded. "It could be, I suppose. What about it?"

"Because," Marty said, "I saw a loose rowel recently and the spur it came from." He stood up. "As I said, very way far out. But worth thinking about."

To Tom, watching, the analogy of the hunting animal came again to mind.

The telephone on the desk rang with harsh insistence. Tom picked it up and spoke his name. Grace's voice said, "I'll come, if the offer still holds."

Tom's eyes went to the two rifles still leaning against the wall. "Look," he said, "this isn't the time." He was aware that it sounded false, evasive, but what else was there to say? That his brother had just tried to kill him and that there was at least one other potential assassin lurking in the area? "I'm afraid you wouldn't understand," he said. "What's been happening—"

"I think I understand very well what's been happening, Tommy." Grace's voice was cold, bearing undertones of anger, a woman spurned. "You've been shucking off your veneer of civilization." Pause. "As I was afraid you would." Another pause. "Well, I tried." The line went dead.

Damn the woman, anyway. Why wouldn't she take him on trust? The answer is unpleasant, he told himself: it is that I have done nothing to deserve her trust.

The message in Farley Wells's box was the same as the first one. He carried it upstairs to his rooms, and as before, shucked off his jacket and loosened his tie before he made the telephone call to Houston. "Farley here, J.R." Through the open windows he could see the cathedral towers. He kept his eyes on them as he listened.

The quiet voice said, "There will not be much publicity, Farley, so I wanted you to have the word. Environmental guidelines are being relaxed in Washington because of the energy problem. That is now official. Stack emission standards have been lowered. That means—" The voice paused. "I assume that you see what it means, Farley?"

"Yes, sir." It was obvious. "The high-sulphur-content coal comes into its own."

"Exactly." Another pause. "How is your project progressing, Farley?"

"Very well, I think."

"You *think,* Farley?" Only the faintest emphasis on the verb, but the message was clear.

"I was being cautious," Farley said. "The bill has already passed the House. It will come out of Senate committee within a day or two, and it looks very good for passage by the Senate itself. The governor—" Farley shook his head faintly. "I don't think he will be a problem."

"Can he be—persuaded, Farley? I told you that you had a free hand."

Which means free access to the purse, Farley thought, and suddenly found the concept distasteful. He temporized. "I haven't seen him yet, sir," he said, "but when the bill comes out of the Senate, I will."

There was a pause. Then, "Very well, Farley. I leave it to you."

Farley said quickly, "One thing."

Another brief pause. "Yes?"

"Joe Harlow, sir." Farley hesitated. "He was here last fall. He saw a man named Tito Abeyta, who is the sheriff of one of the local counties. He said he was here on a hunting trip." It was as close as he dared go to the actual question.

The pause this time was longer than before. The quiet voice said at last merely, "Perhaps he was hunting, Farley." The telephone clicked dead.

Farley hung up slowly. He walked to the windows to stand staring again at the cathedral towers. Strength, he thought, power; they were what was important, weren't they? Then why this sudden, sneaky feeling of distaste?

28

With Kelly Garcia gone, the *Las Grutas Bugle* was a day late that week. Consuelo brought Tom's copy to the office. On the front page a small box edged in black announced Kelly's death. Another small box, also edged in black but on an inside page announced the death of Carlita Vasquez, age eleven, after an illness of some duration.

Tom stared at the second item, thought about it, and then put in a call for Dr. Harry Walker at his small dispensary and makeshift hospital. He waited patiently, phone at ear. It was some time before the doctor came on the line.

"Unless it's an emergency I don't have much time," the doctor said. "Sorry."

"Only a minute," Tom said. "Carlita Vasquez. Was she—?"

"The child with leukemia. From the beginning hopeless. A blessing the end came quickly. Was that all?"

"Hold it, Doctor. Is it still thought that she died from radiation-induced leukemia?"

"Probably. That is out of my province. Now, if you will—"

"Goddamnit, Doctor, listen to me. There is not and there has not been any radioactive material on that reactor site. There won't be for months. Do you understand the implications of that?"

There was a short silence. The doctor said at last, "You sound like your grandfather. Never mind. You say there has not been any radioactive material there.

255

Very well. I will take your word for it. Will the people of Las Grutas?"

"That," Tom said, "is precisely the point. You and Father Enrique and one or two others, maybe Pepe Martinez, have to make them believe it."

"My business," the doctor said with slow distinctness, "is with their bodies, rarely with their minds. I have a compound fracture waiting on me right now, and I consider it more important than conversation—even with a Granger." The line went dead.

Tom hung up slowly and sat back in his chair. Wrong approach, he told himself; other people had short fuses too. It was something to remember. He sat up and called "Come in," to a knock on the door.

It was Ethel Wilding, tall, slimly rounded, self-possessed as always, wearing a skirt and blouse now, town clothes. Tom got out of his chair.

"I want to thank you for your hospitality," Ethel said.

"You're leaving?"

Her smile was gentle. "I think it best. There is a certain amount of—family friction, and the presence of an outsider doesn't help matters."

"I haven't been much of a host."

Again the gentle smile. "But I have enjoyed myself. I liked our walk. Sue has been very friendly. I've enjoyed seeing a feudal estate from the inside." She paused. "Even with the alarums and excursions. Maybe at least partly because of them."

"I'm afraid they aren't finished."

"Are they ever?"

And what was the answer to that? Face it, Tom told himself, the problems are never ended. Settle one thing and another takes its place. "They keep coming at you like a swarm of bees, boy," old Matt had said in one of their rare times of near intimacy. "There's two ways of running this place. One is to hire yourself a manager and sit back and let him cope—if you can keep your hands off, which I can't and I doubt if you'll ever be able to either. The other way is to take her on yourself, which means getting right down amongst it with both hands, and when trouble sticks its head up you slap it down just as fast as you can because more trouble is popping up right behind you and you can look only one way at a time."

Now, watching Ethel's smile, "Probably they are never over," Tom said. "You're right."

"And you like it just that way. Your brother doesn't, but you do." She held out her hand. It was firm and warm. "Thank you again."

"Maybe I'll see you in Santa Fe."

"I'd like that. I'd like to know more about—Granger the Third."

"I haven't settled in."

For the third time that slow, gentle smile. "Haven't you? I think you have. And I think you've just begun to fight. *Au 'voir.*" She was gone. The door closed gently. Almost immediately it opened again. "Any messages you would like me to deliver?" Ethel said. She paused. "To that nice Tish, for example?"

He was tempted to say that he would like Tish to return to the ranch, if only to keep him company. He stifled the temptation. It was childish. "Tell her to keep me posted," he said. Watching Ethel's face he had the feeling that she saw beneath the words and was amused.

"Will do," Ethel said, and that was all. The door closed again.

A strange female, Tom thought, perpetually under tight control. Or was she? She had been other than aloof on their one brief walk, hadn't she? And apparently she had relaxed in Sue's company. So maybe it was merely a matter of still, deep waters, the real Ethel not readily apparent. Why, hell, he thought, what makes me think I can analyze anyone? I'm not even sure of myself.

He started for the desk chair and all that paperwork that awaited him, and then changed his mind. The hell with it for now. He went instead to the gun cabinet, unlocked it with the key from his pocket, took out the 30-30 and loaded it. Then he locked the cabinet again and went out to the big hall. To Consuelo, "I'll be in Long Valley and maybe Las Grutas." He walked out to one of the ranch jeeps.

The guard at the reactor gate this time let him through without question. Tom smiled as he drove by. The guard's face was expressionless. Strange. Last time he had seemed friendly enough. No matter.

Work went on as before in and around the concrete building, but the sight now had taken on a new significance. One day, Tom thought, there *would* be radioactive material on the site, and then if anything went wrong, fact could replace rumor.

Radiation was invisible, and potentially lethal. Careful standards had been established for exposure, and even the terms used to describe those standards smacked of magic and mystery: RBE (relative biological effectiveness), QF (quality factor), DF (distribution factor), the basic unit called the rem, numerically equal to the dose in rads multiplied by the appropriate modifying factors. . . .

What it all boiled down to was that controlled radiation, as with X-ray, could be beneficial; but radiation out of control could kill, and all the fancy names and titles in the world could not alter the fact. One meltdown—the inhibiting and cooling mechanisms failing to act properly—and the genie was out of the bottle, the lethal radiation let loose, into the air, into underground water flowing no one knew exactly where, poisoning the ground itself.

From the doorway of the trailer Wayne Carter said, "Something wrong?" He stood aside. "Come in."

"Have you seen this?" Tom said and held out the *Bugle,* opened to the page carrying the notice of Carlita's death.

Wayne glanced at it without comprehension.

"The little girl with leukemia," Tom said. And then bluntly, "The one you are generally supposed to have poisoned with radiation."

"I told you—" Wayne began.

"I know you did. And I believe you. There has been no radioactive material here. But what the village thinks is something else again. And the girl is dead."

There was silence. Through the open trailer doorway came the sounds of two voices shouting a dialogue in mixed Spanish and English:

"Es corto!" (It is short!)

"¿Cuanto?" (How much?)

"About two and a half inches!"

"Shit!"

Wayne Carter said slowly in his pedantic way, "What are you suggesting that I do?" He paused. "Send flowers?"

First the doctor, now this one; it was hard to stifle the impatience he felt. "I'm not suggesting anything," Tom said. "I'm merely warning you. These people take death seriously when it happens to one of their own. First Kelly Garcia. Now this little girl."

"I take death seriously too," Wayne said, "even if I never knew the girl. But what can I do?"

"Keep looking over your shoulder. Tell your guard to keep his eyes open."

"Thank you." Wayne's voice was heavy with irony. "And what are you going to do?"

"I'm going into Las Grutas to talk to some people, try to stop trouble before it starts." Tom paused. "Maybe they'll believe me and maybe they won't."

Wayne thought about it. "Do you want me along for corroboration?"

Tom had already considered it and rejected it. He shook his head. "They know me," he said, "and they don't know you except as a stranger building something they're afraid of. You'd be a liability." He started for the doorway.

Wayne said, "You sent Tish to Santa Fe. I telephoned the ranch and they told me." There was vague accusation in his tone. "Because of me?"

Tom stopped, turned. He said as patiently as he could, "I sent her for several reasons, and you aren't one of them. You can reach her at La Fonda and verify that." He walked out to the jeep.

He drove slowly on the winding road that climbed to the village of Las Grutas. On his way he passed a small ornate cross set by the roadside, marking, as he knew, a *descanso,* a rest stop for the pallbearers carrying some heavy coffin by hand in the old manner from church to grave.

Here in these mountains established customs died hard, and for centuries strangers had been watched with suspicion. The mountains endured, the seasons came and went, one was born, lived, and died among friends, relations, familiar names that came easily to the tongue. What happened elsewhere had little meaning.

But change there was, inevitable as the winter snows and as relentless. If the change was not too violent or too mysterious, it could be accommodated. Electricity had come, and the telephone, indoor plumbing and radio, bottled gas to cook by, even the miracle of television, and these new things had taken their place in these northern counties and no longer met resistance.

But the mystery of the atom was beyond comprehension, and as the priest had said, the need for an atomic reactor defied explanation, outraged sensibility, and, worst of all, inspired fear. Now Carlita's death, and what the reaction to that would be, Tom told himself, you could only guess. And hope.

He drove straight to the church. The priest met him in the doorway of the little house and politely ushered him inside. The almost constant piñon fire burned in the corner fireplace and the room was pleasantly warm. No thermostat here, Tom thought; no fuel shortage edicts. He sat down at the priest's bidding.

"I hoped you would come," Father Enrique said. "You have heard, of course, of Carlita's death?"

"I am sorry about it, Padre. But the reactor had nothing to do with it. There has never been any radioactive material on the site. There will not be for months. You must believe that."

The priest thought about it. "The dead sheep? The dead fish?"

"From other causes."

"The rumors?"

"Where do they come from?"

The priest spread his hands. "The air."

"They start somewhere, Padre." And then, remembering the thought Farley Wells had planted, "The people of the commune in Jicarilla County?"

"They come to Las Grutas," the priest said slowly, thoughtfully. "They buy, usually at Wendall's. They, at least some of them, are educated people. They have traveled. In Tino's bar they talk of things they have seen, known, and sometimes people listen." He paused. "But to spread rumors deliberately?" The thought was painful.

"Listen to me, Padre," Tom said. "There are sincere, honest people who truly believe that atomic reactors are too dangerous to be allowed. To them any means of stopping the building of a reactor are justified. Rumors have been used before, and other methods. They will probably be used again. When people are afraid, there is no telling what they will do."

"Carlita will be buried tomorrow," the priest said. "I will say a Mass for her soul. The village will mourn for her." Again he spread his hands, work-hardened from the labor in his cactus garden, from the sawing and splitting of the piñon logs for his fireplace. "If as you say her illness was not caused by radiation—"

"Believe me, Padre, it was not."

"Then the village must be told."

"Yes."

The priest shook his head sadly. "I wonder if they will believe. Always it is easier to believe the—bad thing. It should not be, but it is." He heaved himself out of his chair. Tom rose with him. "But I will try," the priest said.

"Thank you, Padre."

Tom parked the jeep off the road near the commune. Joe, a second man, and two girls were working in the vegetable garden. Both men were bare to the waist. One of the girls wore her skin-tight cut-offs and no top. Her breasts were deeply tanned. Joe came to the gate of the vegetable garden fence.

"Slumming again, man?"

"This time," Tom said, "it's more than curiosity." He held out the paper and pointed to the notice of Carlita's death.

Joe read it quickly, his eyes hidden behind the dark glasses. He looked at Tom. "So? I didn't know the chick."

"The little girl with leukemia."

Nothing changed in Joe's face. "Too bad. But that's the chance you take."

"Chance?"

"When you let a lot of smart-ass physicists play their games with fissionable material. You know, like the toy at Hiroshima?"

"You're talking about the atomic reactor in Long Valley?"

"What else, man?"

"There is no fissionable material there. There hasn't been."

The dark glasses were impenetrable. "Tell that to the girl's people."

"I'm telling you," Tom said.

Joe hesitated. Then he shrugged. "Okay, so you've told me." He paused. "Why bother?" He gestured toward the vegetable garden. "Look, man, we grow our own food. Organic, you know? No fertilizers, no insecticides, none of the crap our lousy civilization has gotten itself used to. We don't need it. And we don't need an atomic reactor lousing up the ecology either, raising stream temperatures and killing the fish, leaking radiation underground, maybe even a meltdown, and then where the hell are you?"

"And you've made your feelings known?"

"A free country, man. Free speech. First Amendment."

"Which doesn't include the right to shout 'Fire!' in a crowded theater, as someone pointed out. And that is just about what you've done with your rumors."

"Man, man—" Joe was shaking his head slowly. "You are really uptight, aren't you? I mean really.

And dead wrong. All we've said is the truth. The AEC says reactors are safe. Fuck the AEC. They said those Central City mine trailings were safe too, didn't they? And what about those dead sheep in Nevada? Listen to the AEC and you'd think it was mass suicide. Byproducts of fission reaction are lethal, man! And some of them have half-lives of tens of thousands of years, and what you do with those?"

Tom was thinking of the dirty brown smoke flowing down the Rio Grande the day he had flown to the ranch. "How do you feel about coal-fired generators?"

"They fuck up the atmosphere, the air we have to breathe." Joe paused. "If you're going to ask what my solution is, it's this." His gesture took in the entire commune, adobe buildings, vegetable garden, parked trucks and buses, and open fields. "We have all we need, and all we want is to be left alone."

"Then leave other people alone," Tom said. "Stop scaring people who don't have your education and probably not your brains. If it's live and let live you want, then remember that it goes both ways." His voice was cold.

Joe hesitated. "Is that a warning, man?"

"We'll see. We'll see how much harm you've already done. And maybe you'll see it too."

"What does that mean?"

"You're a smart fellow," Tom said. "You make a point of making that clear. I shouldn't have to explain that when you scare people, you don't know what their reaction is going to be. The girl is dead. That brings it all home, all the things you've been saying could happen."

"Everybody knew she was sick with leukemia."

"Sick is one thing. And these people don't know what leukemia is. It's just a big name. But they know what death is, and that is something else again, and after they've buried her tomorrow and prayed for her soul then some at least will start looking around to see who's responsible."

"We're not." Joe paused, no longer quite so sure of himself. "All we've done—"

"Is tell them lies. Because there is no radioactive material in Long Valley or anywhere near it, which is what the priest is going to tell them, and the newspaper and radio will tell them, and they're going to remember your goddamn intellectual superiority and a lot of other things they don't like about you, including that kind of thing—" He pointed at Cindy, bare to the waist.

The girl stared at him boldly, and then she stuck out her tongue in a childish gesture of defiance. Tom was tempted to laugh.

Joe said slowly, "What do you think will happen?"

"For that," Tom said, "we wait and see." He turned away then and walked back to the jeep.

29

Sam Waldo sat at a table set for two in the cool dimness of the Palace bar. The man across the table from him, Harvey Scott, was the state senator whose constituency included both Grutas and Jicarilla Counties.

Sam sipped his whiskey, pinky elegantly extended. He set the glass down and regarded it thoughtfully. "I'll tell you how it is, Harv," he said with the air of a man about to turn his cards face up on the table. "We need your vote, we purely do. The bill has to come out of your committee with a loud do-pass recommendation, and it being your stamping ground that's affected, a lot of folks will follow your lead."

"I haven't made my mind up yet, Sam." Pause. "For

one thing, I want to see what the Grangers have to say about it."

Sam's face turned thoughtful, hesitancy plain. He pursed his lips and frowned down at his glass. He looked up at last. "Well, now, Harv, I'll tell you," he said. "I have it on very good authority, very good, that the Grangers won't cause any trouble. I have it straight from somebody who just spent a couple of days up on the big ranch with the Grangers."

"That right?" Harvey was impressed. "Old Matt didn't entertain much, at least not these last years. I can remember, when I was a kid, the big barbecues they used to have, but not recently. Why, I recollect one time there was maybe two hundred people from as far away as Denver. Party went on all night." He smiled in recollection.

"Ranch that size," Sam said, "ought to be enjoyed by a right sight more than two hundred people." He was beginning to believe his own propaganda. "That's the whole idea. Set aside all those mountains and woods and streams so everybody can enjoy them."

Harvey said, "Do you hunt or fish, Sam?"

"Well, not recently. Too busy these days, Harv."

"Because," Harvey said, "usually conservation bills get put up by somebody who cares about these things."

"I care, Harv. I just don't have the time right now." Sam paused. "And you care. I know that. So you ought to jump right in and help us."

"I don't know, Sam. I just don't know."

Well, Sam thought, there were more ways than one to skin a bobcat. "Let's have another drink," he said. "I had a hard morning."

They had their second drink and placed their lunch orders. They talked of the weather, the governor's message on the state of the State, recent news out of Washington, and the energy shortage. Sam said at last, "How's Pepe Martinez in Las Grutas these days, Harv?"

Harvey laid down his knife and fork. "I guess he's all right." His voice was carefully noncommittal. "Why, Sam?"

"Just wondering. Ambitious young fellow, isn't he?"

Harvey nodded. "Very." He picked up his knife and fork and then laid them down again. "Why were you wondering about Pepe, Sam?"

Sam's face was bland. "I had a letter from him, is all."

"About what?"

"Well, now," Sam said, "it was a—personal letter, you know? Pepe was kind of asking my advice. He knows Grutas County, and he just wanted to ask me a little about, you know, Santa Fe, state business, and like that." Sam's face was still bland. He cut a large piece of steak, stuffed it into his mouth, and chewed thoughtfully.

There was the usual lunchtime bustle in the bar and in the Red Room beyond the jalousies. Harvey Scott heard none of it. "Sam." His voice was quiet, solemn. "Level with me, Sam. What is Pepe thinking about?"

Sam finally swallowed. He had a large taste of coffee to wash down the steak. He wiped his mouth with his napkin. "Well, now, like I said, Harv, it was kind of personal." The letter was actually nonexistent.

"Pepe is ambitious," Harvey said, "that is for damn sure. He thinks he's too good to be just DA of Grutas County. So what does he have in mind, Sam?"

"He has a Spanish name," Sam said, "and that helps out in the country, doesn't it, Harv?"

Food was suddenly distasteful. Harvey pushed his plate away. "Just what are you saying, Sam?"

"Just if he's thinking of running for office, the Spanish name helps, doesn't it? That's all."

Harvey said slowly, "What office is he thinking of running for?"

"I didn't say he was thinking of running," Sam said. "He just—asked some questions about the legislature, is all."

"The House?"

Sam cut another large bite of steak. Fork poised, "No," he said, "he seemed more interested in the Senate." He popped the steak in his mouth and began to chew on it. His attention seemed turned inward on his taste buds.

Harvey said, "The goddamn little prick. When he was running for DA, I did everything I could to help him. Now he's too big for his britches and he wants my job? He wants to run against me?"

Sam finished his chewing, and went through the unhurried swallowing, coffee, and napkin routine. "Well, now," he said judiciously, "I wouldn't jump to conclusions, Harv. He didn't say that was what he had in mind, and if you asked him, I'd guess he'd sure as hell deny it."

"The tricky little bastard," Harvey said. "Of course he would." He beckoned a waitress. "Bring me another drink, honey."

The waitress looked at the almost untouched meal. "Something wrong with your steak, Senator?"

"It's fine. Just bring me that drink." And then to Sam, "You are so goddamn right about that Spanish-surname thing. If my last name was Gonzales or Romero or anything non-Anglo, I wouldn't have any trouble at all. As it is I've got an uphill fight every election. Goddamnit, my family has lived in northern New Mexico for five generations, five! And we're still Johnny-come-latelies!"

Sam said soothingly, "We'd sure miss you in the legislature, Harv. We purely would. We always know we can count on you."

The drink arrived. Harvey drank deep. "Sam. Have you answered his letter?"

"No." Perfectly true since there had been no letter to answer.

"What are you going to say when you do?"

"Why, I don't rightly know, Harv. I like to see a young fellow with get up and go, and I'd purely hate to discourage him. On the other hand—" Sam did not explain what was on the other hand. He cut more steak.

"I guess," Harvey said slowly, "he has a lot of respect for your judgment, Sam."

POWER

Sam chewed with thoughtful modesty. He said nothing.

"What I mean is," Harvey said, "if you told him maybe he'd better think about getting some seasoning in the House and then maybe even going the other route, toward the Governor's mansion, well, he just might listen, mightn't he?"

Sam's mouth was still full, but he judged an answer was called for. "He might. I just don't know, Harv." He resumed his chewing.

Harvey finished his drink in a thoughtful manner. He set the glass down with decisiveness. "About that bill of yours, Sam," he said.

"Mmmm?" Sam swallowed hastily. "It's a good bill, Harv. It will benefit a lot of people."

"You know, I'm beginning to think you're right."

"I wouldn't want to push you into something you don't agree with, Harv." Sam's tone was sincere. "But it is a good bill, and I'd purely like your help."

"You'll have it."

There was a short silence. Sam said at last, "I surely do appreciate that, Harv. And I won't forget it. I always know I can count on you."

"And I can count on you, Sam."

"You surely can, Harv. Always."

Farley Wells sat in Seth Porter's office. It was the kind of direct negotiation he enjoyed, *mano a mano,* as the Spanish said, hand to hand. "Tom Granger seems to have his hands full," he said for openers.

Seth smiled and nodded. "Holding that ranch together is a big lonely job. It always has been."

"You wonder why a man bothers."

"Do you wonder? I don't. He does it because he can't help himself. In a way it's the same reason I keep coming down here to the office after all these years and with all the bright young fellows we've got attending to matters just as well as I ever could. I could be out fishing."

"Will Granger," Farley said, "doesn't seem to have the same—compulsion."

Seth smiled and said nothing.

The old man obviously wasn't going to be led in that direction, Farley thought, and cheerfully changed the subject. "It's a pity that little girl died up in Las Grutas," he said. "Her death is going to start a lot of folks to wondering." His drawl was marked.

"About the reactor project?" Seth leaned back in his chair. "Maybe. But then a lot of folks have been doing a lot of wondering for a long time. Some folks just don't cotton to atomic energy. To them it means only one thing: the bomb."

Farley smiled easily. "Up to a point I plead guilty, or at least nolo contendere."

Seth took his time. He said at last, "One of the hardest things in the world is to tell what a man really thinks. Have you noticed that? All you have to go on usually is what he says he thinks, and maybe that's true, or maybe he only thinks it's true, or maybe it isn't true at all and he just wants you to think it is."

A shrewd old boy living up to his reputation, Farley thought. Seth didn't flimflam easily. "Well," he said, "I don't recall lying awake at night, worrying about atomic generators. On the other hand, I'd rather not see them proliferate. And as you know, I'm not alone in that feeling."

"I shouldn't wonder," Seth said, "if your numbers are legion." He was smiling and his voice was mild. "Particularly," he added, "among people in the coal, oil, and gas industries. Can't really blame them. They've been eating high on the hog for some time now, and they kind of remind me of a writer friend of mine here in Santa Fe who hit it right with one book —movie sale, book clubs, foreign sales, best-seller list, all of it. He raked in his loot with both hands and made no bones about it. 'I'm not greedy,' he said, 'I'm insatiable.'"

Farley was smiling too. "Well, now," he said, "we aren't quite that bad." He paused, and the smile spread. "Or maybe we are. Just like everyone else, we'd like to have things all our own way. But we recognize that we can't, so we go along with the system."

"Bending the rules a trifle every now and again?"

"Maybe an occasional—excess," Farley said, smiling still. "Most men like to see what they can get away with when there's profit involved."

"It's quite a system we have," Seth said. "It reminds me of what Churchill said about democracy, that it was the worst possible system of government—except all others. We don't have the absolute free enterprise folks keep talking about, but we don't have a controlled economy, either, and there is always room for skulduggery and maybe a little legal thimble-rigging here and there"—his smile spread—"which is what keeps us lawyers in business and eating regularly, so I have no real complaint."

"I imagine," Farley said, "that you have been known to twist an arm now and again. There are rumors to that effect." His tone was friendly. I like the old boy, he thought, and the one thing I'd better not do is underestimate him.

"I've had a few scratching matches," Seth said. He sat up in his chair. It was, he thought, time to get down to cases. "I ran into Sam Waldo yesterday," he said.

Nothing changed in Farley's face. He sat silently.

"Sam," Seth said, "is a funny fellow. Some folks think he's stupid. They're wrong. Sam is shrewd. Some folks, maybe most folks, think Sam is not above dealing from the bottom of the deck. They're probably right, but I have an idea that when it's to his benefit, Sam is just as honest as the next man. But I don't think anybody credits Sam with imagination and the kind of intelligence that sees beyond step one to maybe step four or five. That isn't Sam's style."

It was a shrewd assessment, Farley thought, identical to his own. But Sam was useful. Sam, in fact, was indispensable. Still he said nothing.

"Sam, for example," Seth said, "probably doesn't have the faintest idea how far the right of eminent domain can be carried." He used it as a throwaway line, but he thought he saw its effect in Farley's eyes. "Do you play chess, Mr. Wells?"

"Farley, please." Automatic response to gain time. So the old boy had thought it through, had he? Well, it was always a chance, and what did it change, anyway? "I know the moves," he said. "I gather that you do too."

"I dabble at it." Pause. "I'm sure Sam hasn't the faintest idea what the real purpose of his bill is." Another pause. A smile. "But I'm sure it wouldn't upset him or change his mind if he did know, so I saw no point in telling him."

Farley said, "What is the real purpose of this bill - everybody tells me about?"

Seth leaned back in his chair, smiling still. He shook his head gently. "No, Mr. Wells, total innocence is not credible. You've gone a long way around to reach your objective: neutralize the ranch, stop any proliferation of breeder reactors in the area. But you are far from home free, and it just may be that you'll have to find another way to try. On the other hand, the Grangers might decide to sell after all. Then you have accomplished your mission."

"That decision," Farley said, "depends on the Grangers themselves?"

"On Tom. His decision."

"That puts him right in the spotlight, doesn't it?"

"Where people are shooting at him, Mr. Wells. Have you any idea why?"

Farley made himself smile. "On that one," he said, "my plea is not guilty."

Ethel Wilding parked the Mercedes in the parking space she rented by the month from the Guarantee Store, and walked toward her office. Nothing of urgency awaited her, and she could just as well have gone straight home and called in for any messages, but in her present mood the office seemed an attractive sanctuary.

With what was obviously a blowup between Tom and Will, all social relationships at the ranch had come apart, and what had seemed like the start of a relaxed few days in pleasant company had ended abruptly with a feeling of unfulfillment.

The episode with Sue had been predictable, and pleasant enough, but neither more nor less than that: an episode. In Ethel's life, sexual relations with another woman were not something to be sought, they merely happened occasionally, were enjoyed, and then almost forgotten. Almost, but not quite, because inevitably these episodes left a legacy of heterosexual longing, and Ethel had already marked Tom down as the man to satisfy this one. At least for the present that was impossible, and there was no point in going home to an empty house to brood over it.

She was passing the building that housed Seth Porter's law firm when the door opened and Farley Wells walked out. He seemed preoccupied.

"Hi," Ethel said. And then, at a guess, "You've been tangling with his nibs?"

Farley smiled. "I have." He paused. "And I have an idea I came out second best."

Ethel hesitated. Farley was large, male, and attractive, not unlike Tom. She said slowly, "Do you want to tell me about it?"

"An attractive offer." Farley was smiling still. "From an attractive woman. I accept with pleasure. Where shall we go?"

Again the hesitation, and again the unanswerable question in Ethel's mind: Why not? "My house," she said. "You've bought me drinks. I'll buy you one."

Farley took her arm. "Better and better," he said. "Lead the way."

"My car is just down the street." Ethel felt the beginning of a sense of pleasurable anticipation. It wouldn't be long before the episode with Sue could be entirely forgotten.

Farley lay on his back, relaxed, arms behind his head. He stared thoughtfully at the ceiling. "A real fight?" he said. "Not just a squabble?" He turned his head to look at Ethel.

She was sitting with her legs tucked beneath her on

the edge of the bed, still savoring the sense of release that sometimes, but not always, was the aftermath of lovemaking. Another woman, Sue, for example, Ethel thought, would understand her delicious lassitude, and would not intrude upon it with serious talk. But men of course were different. "I don't think it was much of a fight," she said. "Will looks as if he had been kicked in the face by a horse. Tom doesn't seem to be affected."

"Do you know what it was about?"

"No." Merely the monosyllable.

Farley turned his head to look at her again. He was smiling, but the smile was meaningless. "Sorry, honey," he said. "This isn't pillow talk, I know. But it could be important. To me."

He was still somewhat astonished at the ease of the conquest, if that was what it was; and the possibility suddenly occurred to him that he might have been used. *As I use others,* he thought with some bitterness.

His talk with Seth Porter rankled. The old boy was smart, maybe too smart, but, worse, he was *free* too, his own master, able to play any situation strictly according to his own conscience, which was a luxury most men, like Farley himself, could not afford.

Ethel said, "I'm sorry. I don't know what it was about." *And I don't care, either,* she thought. The big ranch seemed very far away, and its problems unimportant. She started to get up from the bed, but Farley's hand caught her arm and held her.

"Don't go away, honey. Right now I'm enjoying the view." He made his smile seem real. "But in a little while, if you're interested, we might have a return match."

In this one respect at least, Ethel thought, women were dominant. There was pleasure in the concept. She made herself relax.

Farley released her arm and laid his hand on her thigh. *Information,* he told himself; *you get it any way you have to, because you have to have it. You even grovel for it.* He began to stroke the smooth skin. He said conversationally, "Sweet Sue will have had something to do with it."

Herself and Sue, naked together in that enormous bathtub. "Maybe," Ethel said. "I think what Sue wants, Sue gets." The hand on her thigh was spreading warmth into her loins, and suddenly there was perverse pleasure in idle talk as counterpoint to arousal. "Why is it important?"

"Only to me, honey." He moved his hand slowly farther up her thigh. "Seth Porter said people were shooting at Tom Granger. Now was that just a figure of speech?"

"Apparently not." Ethel's voice was not quite steady.

"And that newspaperman found dead up there," Farley said. "Things are churning."

Inside me things are churning, Ethel thought, and smiled.

Farley's hand maintained its steady gentle caress, spreading deep warmth that made concentration difficult. Still the perverse pleasure continued. "Just as Walter Borden was found dead," she said. She looked down at herself. Her breasts trembled when she breathed. She looked at Farley. He was watching her and smiling, and his hand moved on steadily. "It is men like you," Ethel said, "who make women resent all men." Her tone was without rancor.

"Why, I take that as a compliment, ma'am, I surely do." The drawl was very broad. "And it is women like you who make men admire all women." He paused and the smile spread. "Same thing, really." His hand left her thigh and moved upward, lightly brushing one breast before it caught her rounded shoulder. "I think enough talk," Farley said.

Ethel allowed herself to be pulled down on the bed. "For once we agree," she said.

30

Tito Abeyta shifted the holstered .357 magnum to a more comfortable position on his hip and leaned back in his chair, the telephone at his ear. For a long time he listened in silence. Then, "That's okay with me, Mr. Harlow," he said, "but not for a while yet. Things are a little tight around here." He listened again, and his face lost some of its customary expression of good nature. "You'll just have to take my word for it," he said. "Until things quiet down, I won't play."

Through the window he saw Marty Romero's pickup pull to the side of the road. "And I'll call you, Mr. Harlow," Tito said into the phone. "It's better if you don't call me." He hung up. When Marty walked through the doorway, Tito was smiling again.

Marty sat down. He stretched his legs and contemplated his dusty boots. "I don't know if I'm doing a damn bit of good," he said. He glanced at Tito. "How about you?"

Tito shrugged. "Things are the way I like them, nice and quiet. I don't go around looking for trouble." He smiled. "Like some," he said. The smile disappeared. "What's on your mind?"

"Kelly Garcia for one." Marty held up one hand, fingers spread. He touched the finger as he talked. "This year's rustling for another. The dead man in the meadow for a third. And last year's rustling for a fourth." He was silent.

"You're going to put them all in one package?" Tito's voice was amused.

"I might. And I might even throw in the shot somebody took at Tom Granger." Not Will's shot, he thought; we know about that.

Tito shrugged again. "Tall order," he said, "but what's it got to do with me?"

Marty took his time. He said at last, "Have you ever had any trouble with the ranch?"

"No more than you'd expect. Drunks in town, that kind of thing." Tito's voice was concerned. "Why?"

"Just a thought."

"The way I hear it, you get funny thoughts sometimes." Tito paused. "You thinking I might have some kind of grudge against the ranch, the Grangers?" He shook his head. "Forget it." He paused again, scowling now. "Besides, what would it mean even if I did have —which I don't?"

Marty said slowly, thoughtfully, "Old Matt threw his weight around."

"Sure he did. Among other things, he twisted a few arms to make damn good and sure I got that football scholarship I wanted."

"I didn't know that."

"Now you do," Tito said. "So why would I have a grudge against him or the ranch?"

Marty thought about it. "No reason I can see." Simple truth. He went off in a different direction. "How do you and Clyde Burley get along?"

Again Tito shook his head. "I see him maybe once every three, four months. He doesn't have much business here. I don't have any there." And then, "What is this, anyway?"

Nothing changed in Marty's face. His voice was noncommittal. "Just covering all tracks." He paused. "Kelly Garcia was here, wasn't he?"

"That goddamn Kelly Garcia covered these northern villages like a blanket. He was everywhere."

"Did he come see you?"

"Not recently. Not since the last trouble out at the commune. Look—"

"I'm almost through," Marty said. "Do you remember the date of the first big snow last fall?"

Tito shook his head. "I don't remember the date, but it was the day after the rustling. People weren't talking about anything else."

"And that fellow Borden," Marty said, "did you ever see him?"

"The fellow found in the meadow?" Again the headshake. "Far as I know, I never saw him at all. And nobody else knew who he was either when they dug him out this spring."

True enough. Marty got out of his chair. "Thanks."

"For what?"

Marty smiled. "For clearing away a little of the underbrush." He was gone then, down the steps to his pickup.

Goddamn secretive Indian, Tito thought; snuffling here, snuffling there. And again the similarity to a hunting beast came to mind, a bobcat, maybe, silent and relentless. Well, he, Tito, was no rabbit as far as that went.

Marty's face was thoughtful as he drove away from Tito's office. First a hunch out of nowhere, he thought; then a little sign here and a little sign there and the hunch began to grow like an *amanita,* that red and white toadstool, beautiful in its construction, deadly in its content.

He pulled suddenly over to the curb as he saw the parked State Police car. He could see Benny Baca perched on a stool in the diner, and he went inside to join him.

"Have some coffee," Benny said. "At least, that's what they call it."

"Screw you," said the counterman without rancor. He drew a heavy white mug of steaming coffee and set it in front of Marty. "Rape and rustling and murder," he said, "and some cops just sit on their asses."

Marty nodded pleasantly. "That's the way it goes." It was as he had hoped: obviously Benny Baca fitted into the community like a foot in an old boot. He would know many of its secrets. Marty sipped his coffee. It was strong and bitter. Like his thoughts, he told himself. "When we leave here, we'll ride around a little," he said.

They took the pickup. Marty drove. "Where does Tito Abeyta live?"

"He's got a place out of town," Benny said, "but if you want to see him, he's probably in his office."

"I want to see his place."

It was not much, an adobe house and an unpainted barn in a clearing in the trees. A four-strand barbed-wire fence on cedar posts marched off to a small meadow where three horses raised their heads and stared curiously. Near the house was a small corral. Marty headed straight for it, opened the gate and walked inside. Benny followed uncomprehendingly.

"Just stay where you are," Marty said, and stood quite still himself, his eyes on the ground.

Benny stared at the ground too and saw nothing but bare dirt and horse droppings. He opened his mouth to ask what they were looking for, and then closed it again in silence as he caught the look of concentration on Marty's face. He moved back and leaned against the corral fence to watch.

Marty hunkered down to study the dirt at a different angle. Then he stood again and walked a single pace to stand motionless once more. His head swung slowly, stopped, moved on. Again he squatted and this time remained motionless for long minutes.

Benny Baca said at last, "You want for me to bring in the horses?" His voice had a bilingual lilt.

"No need." Marty's voice held finality. He stood up and had one last look around. "Somebody told me once that in Portuguese you don't say you have ten head of horses, you count the number of feet. Maybe it sounds more important, I don't know. At any rate, there are twelve different hoofprints in here."

"Jesus!" Benny said. "You can tell that? All I see is dirt and horseshit."

"Only four of them are important," Marty said, "and I'll be willing to bet they belong to that big sorrel with the blaze." He walked through the gate. "Let's have a look at the barn."

A horse trailer was backed inside. Against one wall were stacked bales of hay; their odor filled the air. Three bridles hung from nails, and a stock saddle polished from sweat and wear rested on a wooden frame. A handwoven saddle blanket lay beside it. There was a rough workbench against one wall, tools stacked in a corner, a pile of scrap lumber. . . .

Marty led the way outside. There in the bright sun, looking idly at the horses in the meadow, "He lives alone?" he said.

"Always has."

They walked out to the pickup, got in, and just sat. Marty said, "What about friends? Girls?"

"He's the sheriff. He gets along with people, maybe drinks a few beers on Saturday night with whoever happens to be in the bar." Benny paused. "But girls? No. He wouldn't mess around with any local chicks. Everybody knows everybody else. What he does, he takes off for a few days maybe two, three times a year, usually up to Colorado, probably does his *borracho* drinking and his whoring up there."

Marty was silent, thoughtful.

"Look," Benny said, "what're you thinking, anyway? Everybody knows him here. Everybody likes him, as much as you can like the sheriff."

"People like you, don't they?" Marty's dark brown eyes watched Baca's face carefully.

"That's different. I'm just—*corriente,* run of the mill. He's been away to college, played ball, pro ball, why, hell, he's been all over, back East and everywhere."

"And now," Marty said, "he's back here." Food for thought.

"It was his knee. It happens to lots of them."

Marty merely nodded. He started up the engine, put the truck in gear, and drove slowly away. "Where does he go in Colorado? Denver?"

"I think Durango. It's closer." Benny hesitated. "I don't know what you're thinking, but—"

"Let's keep it that way," Marty said. "You don't

know." And, he thought, neither do I for sure. Yet. "I'll drop you back at your car."

Tom waited outside the church, sitting in the ranch station wagon, staring at the mountains, while inside the church the padre's voice rose and fell between raggedly chorused responses.

Alive, Tom thought, Carlita Vasquez had been merely one child out of many in the village. Now, dead, she was unique, a symbol—of what? Further intrusion by alien Anglo civilization? Proof that village life in its quiet isolation could not remain untouched? It was hard, no, it was impossible for him to know the villagers' thoughts.

He was not sure that he would be entirely welcome at the graveside; there might be those who would resent his presence. But it was something that you did, as Matt had done before him, and certainly Tully too in his day. Loyalty up, loyalty down. That was a funny way to put it, and yet it was apt. These were his people, and did it not follow that he belonged to them as well? He wished Tish were with him. She would understand.

And that brought a new train of thought. Was there point in Tish's staying longer in Santa Fe? Hadn't she already done all she could? Or was he merely rationalizing because he wanted her presence at the ranch? Because he *missed* her?

He had not missed her particularly during his time in the East. Or was that wholly true? Until he had seen the open vistas and the great mountains again, he had not realized how much he had missed them, either, and wasn't there a possible parallel? The mind played tricks, closing over memory as with scar tissue, and you forgot how good openness could be, and familiarity, deep sure knowledge of the local mores, the marvelous ease of companionship.

All it took was a phone call to bring Tish back. That he knew. Why, then, had he hesitated? Because she had said she thought she was falling in love? Poppycock. He didn't believe it. Didn't? Or didn't want to? And what might that mean?

Well, damn it, Tish needed someone to look after her, didn't she? As Matt always had? As in a way he himself had? Well? The reasoning had a false sound even in his own mind.

Face it, he told himself, he had not made a phone call to bring Tish back from Santa Fe because he wanted to see for himself the man she thought she was falling in love with, whoever the bastard was. Was he good enough for her. Could he support her and take care of her, make her laugh, make her love? Because if he couldn't—Okay, what then? Answer me that, you big smart fellow.

Do you put your foot down? What good would it do? Memory of that day in the corral, watching Tish pick herself up, dust herself off, and have another go at breaking her own horse. Tom had an idea that Tish's stubbornness that day would be nothing compared to what she would display if she even thought she was in love.

"You can be such a bastard sometimes," she had told him, and he supposed it was true. But how did you avoid being a bastard when you were trying to persuade someone you cared about that she was making a fool of herself with some clown who wasn't fit to shine her boots? There was the problem, and, by God, it wasn't something that could be settled on the telephone. He felt better that he had at least reached that decision.

The priest's voice was silent inside the church, and the sounds of foot-shuffling indicated that the service was over. Tom got out of the car as the pitifully small coffin appeared, carried by four men in worn, shiny dark suits. Their steps were awkward, out of time, as if grief had unbalanced them. One by one they looked at Tom as they walked past toward the cemetery. Their faces were closed, and they gave no signs of recognition.

Behind the coffin came the family, and the padre, and he alone nodded to Tom as if in approval of his presence. Tom fell in with the last of the mourners coming out of the little church. No one spoke.

The graveside ceremony was brief, and loud with opening mourning. It was not the Anglo way, Tom thought, but what of that? The grief was nonetheless genuine for open protestation.

When the coffin had been lowered into the grave and the first shovelful of dirt thrown down, the mother, herself only in her mid-twenties, had to be restrained from throwing herself into the grave.

She was led away. By twos and threes the other mourners left the graveside in silence. Tom, the priest, and a woman in her forties remained. "This," the priest said in Spanish, "is the grandmother."

The woman looked at Tom in silence. He spoke softly in Spanish. "I am sorry, *señora*. It is all there is to say."

The dark eyes searched Tom's face. Slowly the woman nodded. "Thank you, *patrón*." And that was all.

Father Enrique walked with Tom back to the station wagon. "I have explained," the priest said, "that Carlita's death could not have been caused by radiation, that it was simply God's will that she should contract her rare disease." He paused. "Whether my words will convince everyone, I do not know."

They had reached the car. Tom was looking at it. "Not everyone, Padre," he said. There was more of sadness than anger in his voice. "Look."

The antenna was broken. It lay across the hood of the car. The priest stared at it, and then looked up at Tom. "Evil," he said, "vicious. Who would do such a thing?" He paused. Sadly, "I am sorry."

Tom picked up the antenna and tossed it into the car. "It is all right, Padre. Maybe it made somebody feel better." Tom Granger turning the other cheek. It was, Tom thought, a ridiculous spectacle.

He drove slowly back to the ranch. Joe Valdes came out of the gatehouse to open the gate and swing it wide. Tom thanked him and drove through. Into another world: the thought was inescapable. Into a world where security was wrapped around him like a blanket. True? Not entirely, friend. You have been shot at twice. Isn't that enough?

31

State Representative Sam Waldo's piece of legislation, House Bill 435 came in for little debate on the floor of the Senate. State Senator Scott, in whose senatorial district the two affected counties lay, spoke eloquently of the benefits that would accrue to all the citizens of the state if the property in question were to become public land forever dedicated to recreational use.

"I remember as a boy," he said, "attending barbecues on El Rancho del Norte for as many as two hundred people. Two hundred! A hundred times two hundred ought to be enjoying a property that size!" Pause. "Can you deny it?"

At least in part the senator's fervor was due to a telephone conversation he had had with Pepe Martinez the afternoon of his lunch with Sam Waldo. The senator had been feeling outrage exacerbated by alcohol when he placed the call. "I hear," he had said without preamble, "that you're getting too goddamn big for your britches."

There had been a thoughtful pause on the line. Then, "Screw you," Pepe said politely, and hung up.

Now, on the floor of the Senate, "Selfish interests are at work trying to defeat this magnanimous piece of legislation!" the senator cried. "Let justice for all prevail!" He took his seat to scattered and largely un-interested applause.

Wayne Carter waited in the lobby of La Fonda for Tish's return. He was here on impulse, although he was not usually an impulsive man, and he would have been hard pressed to explain why, except that Tom Granger had something to do with it.

He did not pretend to understand a man like Tom Granger; he had never understood old Matt. They marched through life with a clear conviction that they knew what they were doing; and worse, were instantly willing to tell others what they ought to do as well. And some, like Tish, liked it just that way. There was the rub.

Just how far did Tom's dominance over Tish go? He could order her to Santa Fe. What else could he order her to do?

Unpleasant conjecture while he waited for Tish, and when at last she did walk into the lobby, smiling and alone, Wayne found himself almost prepared for accusation instead of greeting, which was ridiculous and he knew it. "I've been waiting for you," he said. "I should have called first. I am sorry."

"I'm sorry I wasn't here." Tish hesitated. "Was there something—in particular?"

Not only had he been impulsive, he had failed even to think of what he wanted to say or do once he was on the ground. Altogether a pretty poor show for an intelligent man. All at once he was at ease and able to smile at his own inadequacy. "I just wanted to see you. It is as simple as that." His smile was disarming.

"I'm flattered." Simple truth. Jimmy Thomas, Farley Wells, now this one—it had been a long time, if ever, since she had attracted this much male attention. And in just these several days her attitude had changed, eased, which was strange, but not unpleasant. It was perhaps the feeling of responsibility that had given her more confidence, and that of course was due entirely to Tom, who had trusted her to be his eyes and ears and judgment here in Santa Fe.

"I could buy you a drink," Wayne said, "or we could take a walk, or a drive, whatever." He paused. "If you're free, that is."

"I am free." Tish was smiling. "I would love a walk in the mountains. Give me time to change."

They drove up the road Tish and Jimmy had taken toward the ski basin, but well short of the scenic turnout they parked in a picnic area where a barricaded jeep road climbed at a steep angle back into the mountains. They began to walk at a steady pace.

For a time the road climbed sharply and talking was difficult. Then the gradient eased and, heart and lungs attuned, breathing was easier. "Tom came to see me," Wayne said. Was Tom this much in the forefront of his mind? Apparently he was. "The girl with leukemia died."

A red-tailed hawk swept into their view, flat wings spread, effortlessly riding the updraft around the flank of the mountain. Tish watched it, envying its freedom, while she thought about what Wayne had said. She said at last, "He wanted to warn you?"

It was precisely what Tom had intended, Wayne thought, and it came as a shock that Tish should have understood so readily. "How did you guess that?"

The hawk floated over a shoulder of the mountain and out of sight. "I know Tom," Tish said. "And I know the people in Las Grutas." She glanced at Wayne. "Children are precious to them. Death has meaning. They don't begin to understand what you are doing. Or why. All strange Anglos are suspect." She paused. "All those things together. I can't explain it, but don't you see?"

"Tom said they were afraid."

"They are. The whole world is afraid of you. Oh, not really, but in a way it's true."

"Are you?" His voice was gentle.

They walked steadily, long, easy strides. "Not as a person," Tish said. "But because of what you do, yes." She paused. "People who know far more than I do say atomic reactors are not safe. Other people who know just as much say they are. I don't know what to believe, so like most people I try to ignore it. But it's there. It won't really go away. You must see that."

A man and a girl, Wayne thought, walking companionably in bright sunlight—and talking about things like this. Ridiculous. "I'd rather talk about you and me," he said. It was as if he had not spoken.

"I'm not religious in any real sense," Tish said. She hesitated. "But are there things we aren't meant to know? Have we gone too far?"

"That's nonsense." His voice was sharper than he had intended. "Sorry," he said.

"No." Tish wore a faint, wry smile. "You meant it."

"Look," Wayne said, "what do I say? I'm not good at people problems. But I am people just like you. And Tom." Tactical mistake even to mention the man? Wayne had an idea that it was, but the words were already spoken. "A lot of people have the idea that scientists are the modern-day priests, like those of Egypt or Babylon who set themselves above the rest of the population because they could do things others didn't understand." He paused. "That's nonsense. We have no final answers. We do what we do a step at a time, hoping that each step is an improvement and will add a little more knowledge to the common store. That's all." He pointed suddenly. "Pygmy nuthatch."

Tish was smiling as she watched the little bird trudging headfirst down the trunk of a ponderosa. Her voice was gentle. "Go on."

"I feel silly talking about it," Wayne said. "I mean, here I am, walking with a pretty girl and talking about things that should have been settled freshman year over quantities of beer, the why-are-we-here-and-where-are-we-going questions."

"Are they ever really settled?"

"Probably not, but we learn to live with the partial answers. I don't have any guilt feelings because I work in the same field that produced the Hiroshima bomb. I wasn't old enough to be part of the Manhattan Project, but if I had been, I might have been part of it, and I still wouldn't have any guilt feeling. That too is nonsense. Knowledge is not evil even though some people think it is. My business is knowledge. How some may use what little new knowledge I produce is something else again. I hope it can be used beneficially, but if it isn't, I refuse the blame. Is that—ignoble?"

"No," Tish was smiling again. "I think just—human."

"Steller's jay," Wayne said pointing. "And a Clark's nutcracker. At least," he said, "I'm glad you put me in the human category."

"Please," Tish said. "I didn't mean to—hurt you. I think you—"

"Look." The words would not be stopped. "Are you in love with that stepbrother of yours?"

Tish stopped walking. Wayne stopped too, and looked at her. The world was still.

"It was the hell of a question," Wayne said. "I withdraw it." Futile words.

"I don't think I am," Tish said slowly. "I—like him. Sometimes, that is." Again that faint, wry smile. "Sometimes I could—kick him."

"You do what he says."

"I'm hired help." Clyde Burley's words.

"That's nonsense too."

Tish shook her head. "I like it that way. I earn my keep. I was raised as part of the family, but I'm really not. I have no claim on the ranch. It belongs to Tom and Will." Her smile was easier. "Let's go on."

"Are you sure?"

"You startled me, that was all." Tish pointed suddenly. "A downy, no, a hairy woodpecker."

Wayne could smile. "Good eye." On this level at least, he thought, they were in tune. It was small consolation.

It was a four-mile walk uphill to the last bend in the road. There at something over eleven thousand feet they could look down on the top of the chair lift and out over mesaland and mountains rising clear against the limitless sky. A brownish haze marked the course of the Rio Grande. Wayne followed it with his finger. "That's the competition," he said. "Fossil-fuel generators. Here it's only a minor annoyance. In cities it and other kinds of pollution can be lethal. One day there may be a temperature inversion in Los Angeles that will last long enough to turn their pollution into a killer smog, and if that happens people by the thousands will die." He smiled suddenly. "Do I sound like a salesman?" He paused, smiling still. "Or maybe more like a prophet of doom." The smile faded. "But I mean it. That one smog in London a few years back killed an estimated six thousand people. Los Angeles could be worse, much worse."

Basically a serious man, Tish thought. Unlike Jimmy. Unlike Tom too, as far as that went. That was not to say that Jimmy and Tom were merely frivolous; they were not. But their seriousness took a different form and was rarely as open. But all three men were to be believed.

She had heard forecasts of catastrophe before. Who had not? But now, looking at the brownish haze above the distant river, and thinking of Wayne's words, the concept of thousands of people choking to death was suddenly vivid and real. She turned away and looked back down the slope of the mountain where the evergreens and aspens stood cool and green, and the air above them was without pollution.

"Shall we go back?" Wayne said.

Tish nodded wordlessly.

"I've fouled it up, haven't I?" Wayne's voice was quiet, and suddenly bitter. "I have a knack for saying the wrong things."

"They have to be said. And believed."

"Not by you."

"Why not?" Tish was smiling. "Am I to be protected?" The smile spread. "That sounds suspiciously like male chauvinism." She caught his hand in hers. "Let's walk, and smell the trees, and look at birds. There's another hawk."

"That one," Wayne said, his voice light again, "is no hawk. It's an immature bald eagle."

They walked together into the lobby of La Fonda, and there they stopped. Tom was standing at the desk. He saw them and came toward them slowly. His face was grave. "We've been looking for you." He spoke only to Wayne. "You've got trouble at the reactor. An explosion—"

Tish said, "Oh, no!"

"One man dead," Tom said with no change of expression. "Quite a bit of damage."

Tish looked at Wayne. He said slowly, "You don't know how?"

Tom said, "Dynamite. That's just a guess."

"Dynamite doesn't go off by itself."

For the first time anger showed in Tom's face. "The thought," he said, "was in my mind too. Maybe you'd better go see for yourself."

Wayne hesitated. Then he nodded shortly. "Sorry," he said to Tish, turned, and walked away.

Tish watched him go. "You didn't give him much warning." Her voice was quiet, but the accusation was plain. She looked up at Tom.

"Explosions don't give much warning," Tom said. And then, "Is he the one you thought you were falling in love with?"

"No."

"Then who the hell is it?"

Suddenly her lips were twitching with suppressed laughter. "What gives you the right even to ask?"

Tom opened his mouth and closed it again carefully. "Somebody has to keep an eye on you."

Tish was smiling openly now. "Maybe I'm beginning to grow up," she said, "and my love life is my own. Had you thought of that?"

It was the best exit line she was likely to have. She turned away and headed for the stairs. In her mind was a wholly new sense of gaiety, the trouble at the reactor forgotten.

32

Tito Abeyta said, "Two men were here?"

"*Sí*. One was the State Policeman. The other I do not know."

"They came to the house?"

"No. They went to the corral and to the barn. Then they drove away. In a pickup truck."

Marty Romero, Tito thought; that goddamn Indian. But looking for what? "You were in the house?" he said.

"*Sí*."

"Did they see you?"

"No. I had brought in wood for the fireplace. I saw them and stayed in the house."

Tito thought about it. "Were they in the barn long?"

"No. They were longer in the corral. The other man would stand still. Like this. Then he would crouch. Like this." It was a fair imitation of Marty studying the ground.

So that was it, Tito thought. "Okay," he said. "Forget you saw them. Understood?"

No hesitation. "*Sí*."

Will's face was a mess. Both eyes were black and blue and swollen to slits. Sue found it hard not to laugh. "I can't think of anything to say," she said.

"Then just be quiet." It was the ranch, of course, the *goddamn* ranch that was responsible for everything. It devoured people, took them in, chewed them up, changed them beyond recognition, and then spat them out, mangled. Oh, the broken nose would mend, and the bruises would go away. In time. But the memory, the humiliating memory would never fade. There was the devastating fact.

"It was an accident, of course," Sue said. "You weren't really shooting at Tom, were you?" She knew both the answer she would get and the truth, but she could not stay away from the question. Out here in this mountain vastness, somehow, civilized niceties did not apply.

"I've told you and told you." Will's voice was rising. "It was an accident. But he doesn't believe it."

"And what are you going to do about that?"

"What do you think I can do?"

We used to be nice people, Sue thought. Maybe we weren't earth-shakers, but we went our own way, hurting no one, not even each other. Now. . . . "Lover," she said in a voice that was solemn, un-Suelike, "just between us, you swung and you missed. And there won't be another chance." There. It was out. She felt a sense almost of relief that it was so. "That cute lieutenant—"

"That cute lieutenant," Will said, "would cut out your gizzard and not even blink. Or mine. Especially mine."

"Exactly. So I think we'd better leave. If anybody takes another shot at Tom, you'd better be far away."

There were times, Will thought, when Sue's perception surprised you. The same idea had been in his mind. On the other hand. . . . "Looking like this," he said, "go where?"

"You aren't very pretty, darling," Sue said. "But it won't last." She smiled suddenly. "Painful, but not fatal."

"It isn't funny."

"Now, darling, don't be stuffy. If it had happened to somebody else, you'd break up." Sue paused. "Particularly if it had happened to Tom."

"Things like this don't happen to Tom. They always happen to the other fellow."

There was a pause. "Darling," again Sue's voice was

solemn, "you're trying to make me think I married the wrong brother. Every time you try to tear him down, you build him up. Just leave it."

But he could not leave it. The wound was too deep. "I can just see you spending the rest of your life on this Godforsaken ranch."

"I told you, lover; leave it."

"Nobody to talk to except the strong silent man and Spanish-speaking ranch people. It would drive you up the wall."

Sue's silence was eloquent.

"And can you see him in bed? Like a bull—or a buck rabbit—slam, bam, thank you, ma'am!"

"Lover—"

"You brought it up," Will said. In anger there was relief. "I didn't. Okay, he's John Wayne and Shaft rolled into one. You talked me into trying to kill him—"

"And all you got was a broken nose and two black eyes." There was scorn in her voice now. "You aren't half the man he is, and you never were. In fact I'm not sure"—

"Don't say it."

—"that you're any kind of man at all. A bundle of charm and a big smile, and that's about it."

"You never complained before."

"No," Sue said slowly, "I didn't. As long as we stayed in our own world, we got along fine. But out here you begin thinking you're a he-man, with ideas and everything, and every day you just get smaller and smaller—"

"Goddamnit, shut up!"

Sue's expression changed. She said quietly, "All right, lover, I'll be quiet. I'll listen. What do you want to say?"

There was the trouble: he couldn't think of anything to say. His nose throbbed, and it was difficult to keep the swollen eyes open, and somehow he had been maneuvered into this argument, which never should have begun but could not now with honor be ended.

Tom, of course, was at the bottom of it. No matter

where you turned, there was Tom, larger than life, as old Matt had been; ever invulnerable.

Silhouetted on that ridge, motionless, a sitting duck —how in the world could the shot have missed? But it had. And then that terrible bowel-watering moment after Tom had disappeared, when the shot had come from behind, and he, Will, had gotten, oh, so reluctantly to his feet and seen death in Tom's eyes as he came slowly down the hill, gun in hand.

"Well, lover? Has the cat got your tongue?" Scornful mockery.

There was only one thing to do: leave with what dignity he could muster. Will heaved himself out of his chair and stalked out of the room, down the broad stairs, and out of the big house. A ranch station wagon was parked nearby. Will got into it, started the engine with a roar, and sprayed gravel as he swung the car around and started off down the drive.

Marty Romero's pickup and the State Police car were parked by the construction trailer at the reactor site. A Grutas County sheriff's car stood off to one side. There was no sign of the ambulance. Wayne Carter parked his own truck and walked over to the reactor building.

From the outside it looked untouched, concrete walls intact. But when he walked through the doorway, he saw the results of the explosion: a great crater in the dirt floor, twisted beams, shattered scaffolding, blackened interior walls except in one large area, where there was a curious stain. It took him some little time to understand that the stain was blood. A faint odor of the explosion remained, hanging in the air like a threat.

Marty Romero walked over. "The dead man," he said, "is your guard, Pete Baca." He nodded toward the State Policeman standing motionless, staring at the stained wall. "Benny Baca's brother," he said. "Apparently work was finished for the day, and nobody else was here. A Forest Service man saw the column of smoke and came over to investigate." A column of smoke that reached into the sky and by a quirk of wind currents flattened at the top into a mushroom shape. Symbolic?

It was unreal, Wayne thought; totally, utterly, incomprehensibly unreal. He shook his head and said nothing.

"A couple of possibilities," Marty said. "Pete Baca did it. Or he came to see what was going on and walked into it." He paused. "You had explosives on the site?"

Wayne nodded. "There is solid rock here. We've had to blast in spots."

"Dynamite?"

"What else, Lieutenant? I'm tired of pointing out that there is not and has not been any radioactive material anywhere near here. Besides," Wayne added, "the fissionable material used in a reactor is not of explosive purity, anyway, so even if we did have some on the site, it could not have caused—this."

Benny Baca walked over. He had heard. He looked at Marty. "You want me any more?"

"I'm afraid so." There was no compromise in Marty's voice. To Wayne, "Let's go over to your office," he said. "We can talk there." He led the way to the construction trailer.

They sat on folding chairs. Marty said, "Pete did it, or he walked into it." His voice was without expression. Wayne, watching, listening, could find no trace of compassion, merely concentration on the facts. "If he did it," Marty said, "we want to know why. If he walked into it, we've got a murder investigation. I've already talked to Pepe Martinez, and he's happy to leave it in our laps. So is the Grutas County sheriff." Marty looked at Benny Baca. "He was your brother. What's your guess?"

Benny was sitting very straight. "What reason would Pete have to do it?" The bilingual lilt was accentuated. "He had a job. Jobs aren't that easy to find." He spread his hands. "Why?"

"I don't know," Marty said. He looked at Wayne. "Any thoughts?"

Wayne shook his head slowly. He was thinking of what Marty had said of the minor vandalism that was probably intended merely to annoy. This was a difference of kind, not degree.

"Will this set you back?" Marty said.

"Obviously."

Marty said mildly, "Come down off your high horse, Doctor. We're all on the same side. Will it set you back much?"

Rebuked, "I can't say," Wayne said in a different tone. "We'll have to check to see if there is structural damage to the walls. We'll have to reorder and replace some of that damaged steel. We'll have to reschedule the work."

"But," Marty said, "the work won't stop? You'll still go on?" He answered his own question. "So if somebody was trying to stop you, that wasn't the way to do it?"

Wayne said, "Only a madman would even think of it, Lieutenant. Later on when the units of the reactor are in place, all the piping and shielding, the control rod drive mechanism, the pumps, the steam generator, the controls—when all those things are present, then an explosion like this would be—" He spread his hands. "I want to say catastrophic, but that isn't what I mean. It would be terribly damaging. Now it is—"

"Just a nuisance?"

"You could put it that way. Only a madman would think of it."

Benny Baca had slid lower in his chair. He was staring, unseeing at the far wall.

"Madman," Marty said, and nodded. He spoke to Benny. "What was Pete like? I didn't really know him."

Benny roused himself with effort. "Pete wasn't—*loco*."

"What was he like?"

Implacable, Wayne thought; pitiless.

"He was like me," Benny said, "like anybody."

"He needed a job."

"Sure. Welfare isn't enough. Pete helped his *hija*, his daughter, her husband, and their poor kid." Again he spread his hands. "Why would he do this thing?"

Marty ignored the question. "He had other jobs before?"

"Sure. He drove truck. He pumped gas. He was in the Army." Benny shrugged. "Same like everybody."

Hardly everybody, Wayne thought. He had not realized before the vastness of the difference between the world he knew and the world of these villages.

Marty said, "Did he ever handle explosives?"

"In the Army in Viet Nam. But—" Benny began.

Marty raised his hand for silence. He took his time. He said at last, "You heard Doctor Carter say that there was no radioactive material here on the site? That there had never been?"

"Sure." Benny shrugged. "If he say so. But what about the fish? The sheep? Carlita?"

Nothing changed in Marty's face. "So you don't believe what Doctor Carter says?"

"Look," Benny said, "he's a smart fellow, educated, he knows about these thing. I don't. If he say so, okay." He paused. "But what about the fish? The sheep? What about Carlita?"

What about Heaven and Hell? Wayne thought. What about all the dogma that is taken on faith? What is faith?

Marty said quietly, "And Pete? What did he think?"

"I guess same as me. Like everybody. At the funeral the padre say no." He looked straight at Wayne. "Like you." He paused. "But when you ask about the fish, the sheep, he don't know."

Again Marty's quiet voice. "And Carlita? What about her, Benny?"

"The padre say it was God's will."

"But you didn't believe it?"

Benny hesitated, indecision plain. He said at last, "Easy enough to say God's will. The padre say that all

the time." He paused. "But this time, with Carlita—"
He was silent.

Marty's voice turned gentle. "Pete helped his daughter and her husband, you said."

Benny nodded.

"And their poor kid," Marty said. He paused. "Was their poor kid Carlita?" He paused again. "Was Pete the *abuelo*, the grandfather?"

Benny frowned. "I thought everybody knew." He paused. "I forget you come in from outside." He looked at Wayne. "And you. You come in. Fish die. Sheep die. We bury Carlita." He nodded. "Pete was the *abuelo*, the grandfather. Me, I'm, how you say, great-uncle." He paused again and studied Marty's face. "You think that's what happened? Carlita dead, Pete he come up here and try to blow this place up? Maybe so other little kids won't get sick and die?"

Marty said gently, "What do you think, Benny?"

The trailer was still. Benny drew a deep breath, let it out slowly. He said at last, "Maybe. I don't know. Pete—" He shook his head, and was silent.

"I don't think we need you any more, Benny," Marty said. "Better go back to your family. They've had enough." He watched Benny rise slowly from his chair. "Tell them," Marty said in a different, stronger voice, "that what Doctor Carter and the padre say is so, there has never been any radioactive material here. Tell them I said so. Tell them that fish can be dynamited and sheep can be poisoned—"

Benny's head came up. "Who would do this?"

"Who starts rumors?"

Benny was silent, thoughtful. He said at last, "Okay," and walked out.

Marty looked at Wayne. "We're intruders," Wayne said. "We don't know the people. We don't know the ground rules. We can't believe we're doing anything wrong because we aren't and we know it."

"But," Marty said, "what matters is what other people think." He nodded. "Too goddamn often it is." He walked to the trailer doorway. "See you, Doctor." He was gone.

POWER

Tom sat in Seth Porter's office. Jimmy Thomas was there too. "Jimmy," Seth said, "has been following Sam Waldo's bill pretty closely." He paused. "And keeping Tish up to date," he added.

Tom acknowledged Jimmy's effort with a small nod. "Thanks," he said. And then to Seth, "Where do we stand?"

So this was Tom Granger, Jimmy thought, big as the side of a barn and probably so sure of himself that practically nothing could touch him. For a fleeting moment Jimmy wished that Sam Waldo's bill would pass, would be signed by the governor, and would be rammed down Tom Granger's throat like a dose of salts. He roused himself and put the wishful thinking aside when Seth spoke his name in query. "Well, sir," Jimmy said, "it goes to a vote in the Senate today. It's close enough, but it ought to pass. Then it's up to the governor."

"And what is our position," Tom said, "if he signs it?" He spoke directly to Seth.

Seth leaned back in his chair. "If you want to sell," he said, "you can. We can get a fair price." He paused. "Even after taxes, you and Will will be wealthy men by any standards." Mere statement of fact, made without emphasis or recommendation.

"And if we don't want to sell?"

Here it came, Jimmy thought, and watched for Tom's reaction.

"There will be pressure," Seth said. "Not on you, but on the state to exercise its right of eminent domain, condemn the property and buy it whether you want to sell or not."

There was silence in the room. Tom nodded slowly. Nothing had changed in his face. "I thought there might be something like that," he said. Now his expression altered; his smile was bleak. "In that case we'll fight. What chance will we have?"

Jimmy's interest was caught now. So the man was real, he thought, and probably the legends he had heard about the Grangers were actually true, after all.

They would fight to hold what they had. He watched Tom closely.

"Well, now," Seth said, "it isn't hopeless. It might be expensive. Fighting city hall usually is."

"Damn the expense. We'll find the money."

Seth took his time. "You've made up your mind? You're staying?"

"For a while." Automatic response. But, he told himself almost angrily, it was no longer good enough: the time had come to fish or cut bait. "Correction," he said. "I'm staying, period. Nobody, Will included, is going to run me off."

Seth's eyebrows rose gently in question. "Will?"

"Never mind," Tom said. "We've settled it between us."

"Now, son," Seth said in his easy smiling way, "keeping everything to yourself may seem like the noble way, but frequently it isn't very smart. It's like not going to the doctor because you're afraid there might be something wrong with you." He paused. "What's Will done?"

Tom hesitated. The old man made sense, he told himself; secrecy accomplished nothing. "He tried to kill me and make it look like a hunting accident." He told how it was. He added: "Just the two of us. No proof." He shrugged. "He won't try it again."

"Sure of that, son?"

Marty Romero had said the same, and maybe their skepticism was justified. How much did he, Tom, know of Will, anyway? With Sue behind him, what was Will not capable of? The question was unanswerable. Tom shrugged. "I'll stay off ridges and keep looking over my shoulder." He paused. "Marty Romero knows what happened."

"That's a plus." Seth's voice was solemn.

Jimmy, watching, listening, found himself wondering if what he was hearing was real. He looked from one man to the other with wonderment.

Seth understood. "Two gentlemen named Cain and Abel," he said mildly, "if you're looking for a precedent, Counselor. And the word fratricide is still in the dictionary." Then, to Tom again, "All right. We do what arm-twisting we can do to get a veto of Sam's bill. Failing that, we try to prevent condemnation proceedings. If we still fail, then we fight in court. Is that what you want?"

"That's what I want," Tom said. He stood up. "But first I'm going to see a couple of people myself. Maybe I should have earlier." He nodded to Jimmy. "Nice to meet you." To Seth, "You'll hear from me." He walked to the door.

As the door opened, "Don't do anything rash, son," Seth said. And when the door had closed again, "Advice about as forceful as a fart in a whirlwind. Now that his dander's up, he'll do what he wants."

33

It all wanted thinking about, Marty Romero told himself. There were too many threads in the broad pattern, and some of them were connected and some were not, which made it difficult to see everything as a whole.

When he left Long Valley, he drove for a time on the Las Grutas road, turned off on a dirt Forest Service road, paused to put the pickup into four-wheel drive, and then began a steep swinging climb around the shoulder of the mountain.

At this latitude timberline lay at about eleven thousand feet. As he climbed, the ponderosa forest began to thin out and the aspens disappeared. He came into the area of alpine tundra, patches of grass and tiny hardy flowering plants defying wind and weather, clinging to what soil they could find. Still he climbed until he came at last to the abandoned lookout tower, and there he stopped the truck and got out.

It was an unobstructed view in all directions. To the north as far as he could see the mountains marched off in tumbled disarray. To the east the land fell away to the great plains. South lay Santa Fe and Albuquerque, the mesaland beyond sloping down to Texas and Mexico. West were more mountains, capped now with clouds; possible weather sweeping in all the way from the Pacific.

Looking down, he could see three roads, two of them dirt, following valley contours among brown piñon-and-juniper-dotted foothills. There was the crenellated ranchhouse; in the clear air Marty could see three of the Valdes kids romping by the gatehouse.

He saw Will Granger come out of the main house, get into the station wagon, and drive off as if the Devil himself were after him. He stopped for José Valdes to open the gate, and then he tore over the cattleguard and down the road in a plume of dust. Marty wondered idly where he was going, and why. Not, he told himself, that it mattered too much.

He squatted on one heel, picked a single blade of grass and began to nibble on it while he brought thoughts into focus.

Will Granger, of course, was part of the whole pattern. He and Sue, strangers out of a different world, their motives, but not necessarily their methods, plain as day. Avarice was their mainspring, and Will at least had been willing to kill for it. Weak, vicious, not to be ignored.

Will had known Kelly Garcia, but so had almost everybody in these two northern counties. Had Will known Walter Borden, the dead man in the meadow? What possible connection could there be between them? Marty doubted if there was any.

No, Will was part of the pattern merely because he was on the scene, and because, as Tom had explained, Will had brought both Farley Wells and Ethel Wilding to the ranch.

And those two, as far as Marty could see, fitted into nothing that had happened in this mountain area. They were cityfolk, not for that reason necessarily innocuous, but not geared to guns or dynamite or nighttime rustling trucks, either, and certainly not capable of spreading among the villages rumors of radioactivity that could cause leukemia and death. Scratch Farley Wells and Ethel Wilding, transients.

The commune, now, was a likely source of rumors. But anything else? Marty doubted it. The presence of the commune contributed to general unrest, true, and there had been those ugly incidents of rape, but in Marty's view the commune's part in the whole pattern was catalytic rather than basically active. Except for the rumormongering, scratch the commune and its little-dog-lost members.

Marty was keeping his thoughts under tight control, refusing to allow them to jump yet in the direction they wanted to go. Slow and easy, that was the trick, with a tracker's patience to examine every minute sign, because it was all too easy to settle early on a conclusion and then force the facts to fit the theory.

The reactor explosion he thought he understood. He doubted if it could ever be proved that Pete Baca, in a paroxysm of grief and rage, had tried to destroy the building. But the implication was there, strong enough to satisfy most doubts.

But where lay the real blame? Not with an unbalanced Pete Baca, Marty thought, but with those who had spread the rumors, and perhaps helped them along by poisoning a few sheep and maybe dynamiting fish in a stream. Enter the beautiful people of the commune again? Quite probably, Marty thought, and tucked that conclusion away for further consideration.

What was Pepe Martinez's place in the whole pattern? Pepe was abrasive, resentful, ambitious, and far from stupid. And all violent events had taken place in Grutas County, his bailiwick. So? Can you see Pepe with a rifle in his hands, venturing into a meadow and a forest of pines on his pointy-toed elevated-heeled city shoes to commit murder? Answer me that, Martín Romero. The answer was no.

Marty picked a fresh blade of grass and began to nibble on it. We come now, he thought, to Señor Grande, Mister Big, Tito Abeyta. And what do we have? Ideas, no more than that.

The horse tracks in the forest were those of the sorrel in Tito's pasture. Fact, but not the kind that would stand up in court. Marty could think of maybe two others, Indians both, who would agree with him that the tracks were identifiable, but neither of course would so testify. The white man wouldn't believe them anyway, so screw the white man. And Marty couldn't blame them.

But Tito had been there on his horse. No; strike that! Tito's *horse* had been there with a rider on his back. It was pure guesswork that Tito was the rider, no? Any guesswork at this stage we do not allow to be confused with fact. Slow down, Martín Romero.

What about the spur rowel then? It could have been what Tom saw, but Tom was not at all sure it was. *If* it was, then it's presence with the spur it had come from on Tito's desk that first day Marty had visited him would tend to indicate a very strong connection between the big man and the shot fired at Tom Granger the day after the rustling, no? Yes. But still mere conjecture.

The rifle that had killed Walter Borden—where was it? Was it the same weapon that had killed Kelly Garcia? No possible way of knowing since no bullet or cartridge case had ever been found, and without something concrete for identification and possible comparison, even the caliber of the rifle was in the realm of sheer guesswork. Borden had been shot from the trees, two hundred yards or so; at least that was a logical conclusion. But Kelly Garcia had been shot from fifteen feet, and—wait a minute, wait a minute!

Marty chose a third grass blade. Rifle, he thought; that is what comes of jumping to the obvious conclusion. If Borden was shot from the trees, then rifle it was, beyond a doubt. And there was that rifle that had turned up at the reactor site and was now in Pepe Martinez's hands. So that weapon could not have been used to kill Kelly Garcia. True? True.

Two rifles, then? Not necessarily, my blind friend. What about that cannon Tito wears on his hip, that .357 magnum? It will shoot through a man just as well as any rifle, and is a more likely weapon to be carrying in daylight when someone might happen to see, no? It fitted. He felt a sense of triumph, quickly stifled. Don't be so goddamn smug, friend. Conjecture is still all we have.

Horse tracks. A loose spur rowel. A handgun capable of shooting through a man. Small signs *maybe* pointing in a single direction: toward Tito Abeyta.

But why? Tito was sheriff of Jicarilla County, a big man among his people. Would he jeopardize that position merely to share in the rustling of a few head of cattle?

Once again, slow down, Martín!

Are you sure that the rustling is the basis for two murders and one attempt? Take a long hard look at that premise.

Well, for one thing, the dates apparently were right: Tito himself had said that the first big snow last fall came the day after the first rustling. Assume then, as Tom had guessed, that Borden had camped for the night somewhere near the forest area where the cattle had been gathered to be loaded into the trucks after dark. Might he not have seen what went on? Or if he had not, might his mere presence when discovered have persuaded somebody that he had indeed been a witness? More than mere conjecture this time: call it a working hypothesis.

In daylight, then, Borden, a potential if not a real danger, had been followed and gunned down in the meadow. And that day the snow came, covering Borden, tracks, and everything.

So the timing was right: a rustling, followed quickly by a shooting. And that was precisely what had happened again only a few days ago: Tom, investigating the scene of the rustling the day after, presenting a potential if not real danger to someone, and the shot was fired in a second murder attempt. But this time the shot had missed. Think about that, Martín.

Marty picked a fourth grass blade. At this rate, he told himself, he was going to denude the countryside. Martín Romero, worse than a flock of sheep.

The killer had not missed from two hundred yards, but from only seventy-five with a target as large as Tom Granger he had not even drawn blood. Of course, of course! The first time he was using a rifle. Suppose that the second time he had only his handgun? *Claro!* It was only in TV westerns that shots fired from a handgun at over fifty yards or so went precisely where they were intended. And Tom had not stayed around to give the shooter a second chance.

Entonces, the pattern emerged: one rustling followed by a murder; a second rustling followed by an attempted murder. Then what about Kelly Garcia?

The answer remained the same. Garcia was nosing around, asking questions, maybe too many of the right questions, from too many people who knew a few answers. Marty had no doubt at all that the people in these mountains were less ignorant of happenings than they chose to appear. And Kelly Garcia might have been just the man to pry out their knowledge. Then eliminate Kelly Garcia as another potential if not real danger, this time from a distance of fifteen feet, where not even a handgun could very well miss.

Very well then, the rustlings were the probable root cause of Borden's and Kelly Garcia's deaths and Tom's near miss. All by the same hand? It was likely, was it not? Only one man came to mind—Tito Abeyta.

What was it Benny Baca had said about his brother Pete? That he had pumped gas, driven truck, gone into the Army—*like everybody else?* Like *almost* everybody else. But not at all like Tito Abeyta.

Tito had gone off to see the world, to live it up in the cities of the league around the country, living in hotels and eating thick steaks and traveling by jet. There would have been girls, and successful, wealthy men interested in meeting and shaking the hand of a big pro footballer; newspaper and TV people to ask questions and hang on the answers. No gas-pumping or truck-driving for Tito Abeyta. He grew up in one world and moved into another that must at first have seemed unreal.

He had had how long? Six years of it, if Marty remembered correctly. Then the knee injury, the operation, and oblivion. Back to Dos Piedras.

Marty rose from his squatting position and stretched himself. Idly he glanced down into the nearest valley and saw the dust plume that marked the station wagon Will Granger was still driving like a bat out of hell. Working out a temper tantrum of some sort? In Marty's experience that kind of wild driving usually resulted from emotional upset. So okay; he, Marty, was not a speed cop. He hunkered down again and turned his thoughts back to Tito Abeyta, and, of course, to the ranch, because wherever you turned, it was there.

El Rancho del Norte, sprawling over the countryside, a feudal state unto itself, dominating villages like Dos Piedras and Las Grutas as thoroughly as those hilltop castles in the south of France had dominated their surrounding countrysides. To those who grew up in Dos Piedras and Las Grutas and stayed there, it was a normal and natural state of affairs.

Who grew up *and stayed there:* there was the operative phrase. Tito was the rare exception who had left, lived for a brief time in the Anglo world, and then come back. What would he feel?

Marty knew. The burning in your belly and the red rage in your mind. The futile attempts to cover yourself with your own culture, whatever the hell it was after all those centuries of foreign dominance and all those scores of years of Anglo putdown. The wild acts of machismo which proved nothing except that you never could really make your presence felt. Your *own* presence, not merely a presence as part of a group.

Were these frustrations and hostilities enough to drive a man like Tito to lash out at that symbol, El Rancho del Norte, by organizing rustling strikes? All by himself? Think about that.

Organizing, there was the word. Because the rustling strikes had gone off like clockwork, and that argued careful planning, and somehow Marty did not think that careful detailed planning was exactly Tito's style. He was more like a grizzly, inclined to charge his objective and overwhelm it.

So, who then? Or was it all tied together? Heckle the ranch by rustling? Threaten it with Sam Waldo's bill in Santa Fe? Spread rumors to discredit the reactor? All part of one plan? And Tito was merely part of the plan? As Sam Waldo was? It all added up, did it not? So now what do we do about it?

He stood up again and stretched. His thoughts slowed gradually. We go back down like Moses from the mountain-top, he told himself, and we sit down with Tom Granger, who may be an arrogant Anglo son of a bitch but who also has a long head *and* a large stake in all this because he is *el patrón* and these are his people as they were Matt's and Tully's before him and because, most importantly, he is not a man to walk away from his responsibilities. That is what we do.

As he walked to the pickup he looked down into the valley again. The dust plume still raced on recklessly into the curves.

Will was a good driver with a sense of speed and of balance, with sound reflexes on throttle and brake. The station wagon was no sports car. Its spring was too soft, its handling too imprecise, a typical piece of Detroit iron. But there was power under the hood and Will used it savagely.

He braked hard before each curve, took his foot off the pedal and bottomed the accelerator for a wide swinging turn that took up the entire width of the mountain road. Each curve frightened him a little, and by that much eased the angry torment in his mind.

That goddamn Sue, at last saying the things that were on her mind. That she could maneuver him, Will had already known, but as long as the maneuvering remained less than obvious it was small affront, and his male pride suffered little.

But now Sue had allowed her scorn to show in that vicious comparison of himself with Tom. Was she actually thinking that she had married the wrong brother? Was that really what was in her mind? And if it was, what then?

Was she thinking to use her considerable wiles to alter the situation? Will would not put it past her. As far as he knew in the few years of their marriage Sue had not been—to use that outmoded phrase—unfaithful to him. Except, of course, with other women like the little maid in Cannes and now Ethel Wilding. They did not really count. But what if he, Will, were to come in one fine day and find Sue and brother Tom romping together on the bed? That would be the ultimate putdown, would it not?

A new curve ahead. He stood on the brake, released it, and went into the turn accelerating. The rear wheels of the station wagon clawed for traction, lost it, went into a swinging skid, scattering dirt and gravel into the canyon below. And then they were into the straight again, and Will could even smile faintly in minor triumph, before the thoughts resumed.

Just what would he do if he were to walk in on that tableau? Well?

He could picture very well what Sue would do. Her reaction would be the same as it had been that warm day in Cannes. She would smile her slow smile, make no attempt to cover her nakedness, exhibit no shame, and probably say something like, "Hi, lover. Did I hear you knock?"

What would Tom do? Will had no idea. There was no deep puritanical streak in Tom to cause him immediate deep anguish; he certainly would not fall on his knees and ask forgiveness. But neither would he take refuge in cheap wit to say something like, "She's a good lay, this wife of yours." In other words his reaction would probably be normal: a certain amount of remorse, embarrassment, even contrition. But there would be no scarring of his psyche.

Another curve, another wide swinging skid, another

triumphant maneuver into the straight. And then the thoughts began again.

Sue and Tom then would take surprise in their stride. *But what would he do?* There was the question.

The wind howled through the open window of the station wagon, accompaniment to riotous thoughts. Suppose he were to rush downstairs to break open the gun cabinet, take one of the shotguns, load it and race back upstairs? Would he actually do that? Now, in the excitement of the drive, in the sense of adventure to the tune of the howling wind, he could almost believe that he would. Or might.

There was another curve ahead which, as he remembered it, was a long one, rounding the broad slope of the mountain, above the canyon and the turbulent stream forty yards below. He slowed only a little and the pitch of the wind's howl changed.

He could picture himself, gun in hand, blocking the bedroom doorway, dominating the two frightened naked people inside. Or would it be like that?

Sue would not believe that the threat was real; it would be beyond Sue's power to persuade herself that any harm at all could ever come to that lovely precious body of hers.

And Tom, goddamn him? How would he react? Certainly not cowering in the manner Will would want.

He braked hard now, released the brake and began to accelerate into the curve. The wind's howl rose with the increased speed and the engine roared. The rear of the station wagon began to swing.

Goddamn them both! Goddamn Sue for her open scorn! Goddamn Tom for being what he was and had always been: so sure of himself that nothing could touch him, nothing!

The rear of the wagon swung too far. Will eased up on the throttle, moved the wheel gently, maneuvered the car back into a controlled skid. His mind felt clear, even masterful, and his thoughts were a high fierce chant.

Maybe there would not be a denunciation scene with

himself in domination. Maybe there would never be even a scene of discovery. No matter. Sue had revealed herself at last, and by her scorn released him from all restraint. He would retaliate in his own time and in his own way against both of them. He felt strangely calm now, the decision made.

The curve ahead opened up and he was into the straight again. It was somehow symbolic. No longer feeling the compulsion for reckless speed, he began to slow. Movement on the hillside caught his eye, and he stared at it for a brief moment in helpless fascination before he began to brake.

Three deer were coming down the slope in great bounds, heading for the stream. They saw the station wagon, and one stopped, but the other two came on. They reached the road, began to cross, and then hesitated, ears up, nostrils flared as they faced the automobile that was hurtling toward them.

You pumped your brakes for a stop: that was the rule. But there was no time. Will stood on the brake. The wagon swerved, straightened, and then, wheels locked, swerved again. There was no room for maneuver as Will fought the wheel, let up on the brake, tried by sheer strength to come out of the skid.

The wagon struck the first deer broadside, and the force of the impact accentuated the skid. The wagon went over the side of the road, and as if in slow motion turned end over end as it dropped into the canyon. It landed on the rocks by the side of the stream, cartwheeled once, landed on more rocks and burst into flames. Will was already dead.

34

The word of Will's death reached Tom in Santa Fe via a blue police cruiser. "All I know, sir," the cop said who had pulled Tom's car over to the curb, "is that your brother is dead. An auto accident. The State Police alerted us with your license number."

Marty Romero, of course. Tom said an automatic, "Thank you." And when the cruiser had pulled away he sat quietly, both hands on the wheel.

Will was dead in an auto accident. Was anyone else hurt? That was his first thought, and he felt a sense of guilt that it should be so. Why should he automatically concern himself about others when his brother had just been killed? Had he looked at Will and himself in a mirror and seen their roles reversed? Was he, not Will, the counterpart of Cain? He was behaving like it.

He started up the engine again and pulled away from the curb. At a gas station there was a public phone, and he stopped to use it. His call was to Seth Porter. "The police tell me Will has been killed in an auto accident," he said.

"It's been on the radio, son." Seth paused. "I'm sorry."

"I'm driving up."

"Do you want company?"

"No." Always his instinct was to be alone to face his problems, make his decisions. "I'll call you in a

311

day or so," Tom said. "Then maybe you'll come up and we'll see where we stand."

"Whenever you say." Seth paused. "Give Sue my sympathy."

"One more thing," Tom said. "See that Tish gets the word." He hung up and walked to the car.

Afterward he did not remember the drive back to the ranch, only some of his thoughts.

He had been on his way to see Sam Waldo when the cruiser had intercepted him. Was there something strange about the timing of that? Because he had been prepared to deal less than gently, perhaps even violently, with fat Sam Waldo. And what good would it have done?

Violence begat violence—who had said that? No matter; it was true. And there had already been enough violence, too much. Was Will's death a sign of some kind making plain the fact?

I'm thinking like a school kid, he told himself, like Tom Sawyer in the graveyard. Will's death, the shootings, and Sam Waldo are unconnected, and nobody is sending signals to keep me from laying hands on anybody. And yet there it was: a sudden violent event that at least gave him pause for reflection, didn't it?

Will was dead, but where was grief? I didn't like him. I came very close to killing him myself. But he was my brother. And again the Cain concept would not be ignored.

Matt died. I knew he was dying, but it was some time before I actually believed it. Why? Did I think of him as immortal, indestructible? Perhaps. He was always there, larger than life, ready for anything that came along.

But what about Will? I knew him well, what there was of him. I won't miss him. Or will I? Will I sometimes wonder what might have been if I had behaved differently toward him? If, instead of giving him the back of my hand, I had—what? There was no answer. Will was Will was Will, and the only power to change him lay within himself and was never used.

Marty's pickup was parked in front of the big house, and Marty was waiting in the office. "I thought you'd like to know what happened, amigo." He had two shot glasses of bourbon poured. "And I finally figured out how to get into that thing." He pointed at the tantalus.

"Thanks." Tom dropped into the desk chair and picked up the whiskey, but did not taste it. "Was anybody else hurt?"

"A deer. He had to be shot. At the speed Will was traveling—" Marty shook his head. He told of seeing the station wagon from the top of the mountain. "I didn't see him crash, but when I heard about it, I wasn't too surprised." He sipped his whiskey and waited.

"Where did they take him?"

"Las Grutas." Marty paused. "It'll be a closed coffin funeral, amigo. The car caught fire." Another pause. "He was probably already dead with a broken neck."

"Does Sue know?"

Marty nodded.

"I'd better go see her." Tom set the untasted whiskey down and heaved himself out of his chair. "And make arrangements," he said.

"This," Marty said, "is the hell of a time, amigo, but there are things we have to talk about."

"They can wait."

"They cannot wait. Because if what I am thinking is right, you are still walking around with a gun pointed at your head. And that, amigo," Marty said, "would leave no Grangers at all."

Maybe it would be just as well, Tom thought; all we cause is trouble. He was never sure whether or not he had spoken the thought aloud.

"And that," Marty said, "is horseshit." Either he had heard or guessed what Tom was thinking. His gesture included the entire office, trophies, pictures, memorabilia, and all. "This," he said, "wasn't put together over all this time just to be thrown away."

True, of course. In Seth's office he, Tom, had made his decision to stay, but that decision was made in anger. This was something else again. I belong here, he told himself. They put it together and passed it along to me. It is my responsibility, whether I like it or not. "All right," he said. "We'll talk. After I've seen Sue."

"I'll wait here, amigo."

Up the broad stairs and down the hall to knock on the door of the dressing room of the suite Will and Sue had shared. Sue opened the door almost immediately. She was simply dressed in black pants, sandals, and a creamy-white blouse open at the throat. Against it her tanned flesh seemed almost lustrous. She held the door wide, and closed it after him.

They sat together on the small sofa. "I'm sorry," Tom said. "I don't know what else to say. Do you know what happened?"

"I know. Too well." She was calm, composed. "I won't try to fake it," she said. "No tears." She paused. "Maybe later, but not now." She paused again. "We had a quarrel, doesn't that sound like a soap opera? I put him down. He was probably driving too fast."

"He was. He hit a deer."

"I'm sorry for the deer. I'm sorry for Will, I really am." All at once there was a little girl wistfulness in the words, in the voice. "We shouldn't have come here. I told him that. He was—out of his league here. I told him that too. He was up against you, and there was no contest."

"Did you tell him that?"

"I did."

Tom got up from the sofa, walked to the window and stood for a little time with his back to the room. Over his shoulder, "That wasn't very—kind."

"It's the truth. But it doesn't matter. He's gone now. He tried to kill you. Now he's killed himself." The little-girl wistfulness returned as suddenly as it had disappeared. "What might have been," she said, and shook her head slowly. "Some people do things," she said. "Some don't. Some just serve their time working because they have to work. We didn't because of—all this." She paused and drew a deep, unsteady breath. Her voice rose quickly. "But we didn't do anybody any harm! Until we came here!"

"Easy," Tom said. "Easy." He had turned to face her again.

"Don't you see?" Sue said in a calmer, quieter voice. "It wasn't our fault. Nothing ever is, or was. Fault is only for people like you who make things happen." She paused and smiled faintly. "Go away now, please. I may cry, and I don't want you to see it. When I cry, I'm a mess." The smile spread a trifle. "And you don't want to see it. Men never do." She rose from the sofa, walked to the door, and held it wide. "Please."

Tom walked through with a sense of release. The door closed quietly behind him.

Back down the stairs and into the office to sit again behind the big desk. This time he tasted the whiskey. It burned briefly on his tongue, accompaniment to bitter thoughts. "All right," he said, "who's holding a loaded gun at my head?" It sounded unreal, but, then, much of what had happened recently was unreal. It became incredible.

"Tito Abeyta."

Tom set down the whiskey glass. "You're putting me on."

"No." Marty's voice was grave. "I have parlayed some hoofprints, a spur rowel, and a handgun into a theory. Hear me out and tell me what you think."

Tom listened in silence, interrupting only once when Marty mentioned "arrogant Anglo sons of bitches."

"We are," Tom said. "I won't deny it." He sipped his whiskey and listened some more.

"So there it is, amigo," Marty said at last. "Do you find a flaw?"

Will's death was for the moment forgotten. Tom concentrated on what Marty had said. There was no flaw. The pattern was right, cunningly arranged, sketched with care. Hoofprints, a spur rowel, and a .357 magnum, as Marty had said, and each was a signpost

315

pointing the way. Still. "You're sure of the hoofprints?" he said.

"Amigo." Mild protest.

Tom nodded. He had seen the man at work. He knew his reputation. "Okay," he said. "Then everything else follows, doesn't it?"

"If you mean is it all wrapped up?" Marty said. "Then the answer is no. You have heard of proof?"

"Colorado. The trucks. The men who drove them, men Tito has to know."

"We are talking about two murders and one attempted murder, not just cattle rustling."

Tom sat silently for a long time. He said at last, "We are talking about a great deal more than that. We are talking about the people behind Tito and Sam Waldo—"

"That Houston dude," Marty said.

"He isn't the beginning. He's only the one they send to take charge on the spot." The anger Tom felt now was like nothing he had felt before, deep, solid, caring nothing for consequences. He had the eerie feeling that both Tully and Matt were watching, listening, waiting to see how he would meet this new challenge to the sovereignty of the holding they had put together and held against all comers. What had been old Tully's response to the Army colonel who had complained about his handling of the rustlers? "I held this ranch against Apaches. Do you think I'm going to take punishment from a flock of raggedy-assed cattle thieves?"

"Tito," Tom said in a new, colder tone, "is your business. Mine is with the ones behind him, the pissants who pull the strings and cause people to be shot, and poor damn fools to mess around with dynamite and blow themselves up, accomplishing nothing, and whole villages to go out of their skulls in fear of things they hear and can't understand." He paused. "Those are the sons of bitches I want to settle with."

Marty sat quiet, expressionless. "Only one question. amigo. How?"

"I don't know"—pause—"yet."

There was a message at the hotel desk to call Seth Porter. Tish placed the call from her room phone, and listened quietly while Seth told her of Will's death.

"I'm sorry, honey," Seth finished. "Tom wanted you to have the word before you read it in the paper."

She sat silent for a few moments. Then, in a quiet voice, "You don't really believe these things, do you?"

"It takes some doing."

"Did Tom say what he wanted me to do?"

"No, honey."

So she was on her own, without orders. "I am going back to the ranch," she said. "I don't know what good I can do, but I'll feel better just being there."

"I kind of thought you would, honey."

"Any message for Tom?"

There was none. Tish hung up, redialed the same number, and this time asked for Jimmy Thomas. "I'm sorry," she said when he came on the line, "but I have to go back to the ranch."

Jimmy's voice was careful. "He sent for you? The emperor?"

"Jimmy, please." And then, "Will Granger's been killed in an auto accident."

"I see." There was a pause. "I had big ideas for tonight."

"So did I." At least I think I did, Tish told herself. I wouldn't really have known until the time came.

"My wild roommates are clearing out for the evening."

"And you were planning to show me your etchings?"

"Something like that."

"Jimmy, I'm sorry."

There was silence. Then, "I met your leader, did you know that?"

Tish had not known. "And?" she said.

"Quite a fellow." Jimmy's voice was noncommittal. "Yes."

"Well," Jimmy said, "tonight probably wouldn't have worked anyway." He paused. "Would it?"

"I don't know, Jimmy. I honestly don't know. I—like you enormously—"

"But can't we be friends?" There was a trace of bitterness now.

Tish said slowly, "I have to go now." She paused. "I'm sorry, Jimmy." She paused again. Then, quietly, "Maybe it's better this way." She hung up, and began to pack. Now what in the world did I mean by that last remark? she asked herself; and heard no answer.

North, with the great mountains to her right and the Española Valley opening its vista as she topped the rise at Tano Road. It was an ever astonishing truism, Tish thought, that the same journey was so different going and coming; the same scenery, but you looked at it from different sides. And maybe, new sudden thought, you looked at it with different eyes too. Could that be, and if so, why?

Because driving one way, you were leaving familiarity and heading for you knew not what? And now, settled comfortably in the seat, her hands easy on the wheel, her mind almost at rest, she was heading home, and even the colors of the wind-carved rocks were somehow different, warmer? Idle speculation.

She thought again of Jimmy, and found that she regretted that last remark. It was ungenerous and unkind, and why on earth had she said it? Jimmy was sweet and he had been good to her, probably even good for her. In just this little time in Santa Fe she had felt shyness melting away, and certainly Jimmy had been at least part of that process, maybe a large part.

His roommates were clearing out for the evening? So the stage would have been set. And what would she have done? Probably I would have—cooperated, she told herself. And why not? Moral scruples concerning sex were pretty much a thing of the past, and, Heaven knew, there was no longer need for fear of pregnancy. And so she might very well have welcomed a brief pleasant interlude with Jimmy. Or, would she?

Would her enjoyment have been less than complete because her thoughts would have been elsewhere? Where? On the ranch? On Wayne Carter's trouble at the reactor? On her responsibilities toward Tom? Just her responsibilities? Or was it more than that?

I told Tom I was falling in love, she thought, and at the time I meant with Jimmy. But when Tom asked me only today who it was, I refused to tell him. Why was that? Mere female perversity? Or was it something else?

The scenery fled past. She saw it without looking, her eyes in automatic attention fixed on the road, from time to time in flicking glances checking the instruments. As somebody had taught her. Matt? No. It was Tom. To Matt, automobiles were mechanical horses, supposed to look out for themselves. If they stumbled or faltered, then they had his full attention; not otherwise.

So Tom had taught her some of the finer points of driving. And riding. And shooting. And walking free in the meadows and mesas and forests and mountains of the ranch. They had fished together and skied, and even, but only once, spent a night together miles from the ranchhouse, sitting against a low overhanging cliff with a small fire throwing heat against them, watching the slow progress of the full moon across the sky, her idea, and just talking, about what Tish could not now remember.

Old Matt had been furious. "Goddamnit, boy, she's a girl, and you don't take her out on your raggedy-ass treks and freeze her to death or drown her in some stream. You hear me?"

And Tom had said merely, "Yes, sir. My fault."

"It wasn't," Tish said. "It was mine. I wanted to sit up all night and watch the moon. I never had."

"Your fault, boy," Matt said. "I'll agree with that. Females get ideas, but, goddamnit, it's up to you to be responsible for them. Is that clear?"

"Yes, sir."

Responsible: there was the word. Everyone ought to be responsible for his own actions, although many were not, but some there were, like Tom, like Seth Porter, like Matt, who felt themselves responsible also for those around them, who willingly accepted the burden, yes, of command, and they were the ones you could lean on in need, they were the ones who could be trusted with power.

Why had that word *power* come to mind? Was it because of Wayne Carter's trouble at the atomic power plant? Or because of Farley Wells and the power of money he obviously wielded over Sam Waldo? Or the power of persuasion canny old Seth Porter could exert on the governor of a state and probably on some of its legislators and congressmen as well? Or was she thinking of the ranch, and the power that was both active and latent within its enormous confines? And Tom now in control?

35

There were voices inside the office when Tish came into the big house. She put down her bag and knocked on the office door. At Tom's command, she walked in. Marty Romero was in one of the leather visitor's chairs, his Indian face as inscrutable as ever. In many ways an unpleasant little man, Tish thought, utterly without compassion; but Tom likes him and trusts him, and that is that.

"Seth Porter told me about Will," she said. "I'm sorry."

"Thanks." Tom's voice was distant.

"Am I interrupting?"

Marty's smile was bleak. "Not really. We were just discussing ways of trapping a bear. Maybe putting salt on his tail is best." Humor from Marty Romero?

Tom said, "You didn't have to come." He paused,

and produced a faint smile. "But I'm glad you did."

Warm words, warm thought. "What can I do?"

"You might see Sue. She might like to talk to another woman."

Tish nodded. "What about—arrangements?"

Tom said slowly, "You made them for Matt, didn't you? I keep forgetting how much you do for this place."

Like a good first sergeant, Tish thought, helpful, but not indispensable. Maybe. "Did they take him to Las Grutas?" She watched Tom's nod. "I'll go down if you'd like me to. And I'll see Father Enrique." She saw the doubt in Tom's face. "He will conduct the service," Tish said. "He is a good man, and he and Matt were friends. If the request comes from you, he'll listen."

Again that faint smile. "Carry on," Tom said.

As she walked out and closed the door gently after her, Tish heard Marty's voice say, "Now, about that bear." It was funny, she thought, but he didn't sound at all facetious.

Consuelo, smiling her sweet smile, said, "Welcome, señorita. The house has missed you." She had Tish's bag in one hand. "I will attend to this. You will speak with the señora?"

"Yes," Tish said. If she will speak to me, she thought, and put the concept aside as ungenerous. "Has the señora eaten?"

"Nothing."

"Perhaps some tea?"

Consuelo nodded, content. "Immediately."

Tish climbed the stairs and walked down the hall to knock on the carved door. Sue's voice said distantly, "Come in."

She was standing at the windows, staring out at the great mountains. She turned slowly, and for a moment was silent. "Did Tom send for you?"

"No. I heard the news and I came. I am sorry, Sue."

"Are you?" And then, "I suppose you are. You grew up with him, didn't you? Sister—"

321

"Technically stepsister. Actually nothing." Still compelled to probe that sore place. "Consuelo tells me you haven't eaten. I've ordered tea."

"Will that help?"

"I don't know," Tish said. "It depends on what you are feeling." She doesn't like me, she thought, and I don't think she ever will. There is no—communication. Sue surprised her.

"I have been trying to find out just what I do feel," Sue said. She came away from the windows with only a backward gesture toward them. "I know that I hate those mountains. Do you ever feel that?" She paused. "No, you wouldn't. Neither would Tom." She walked to the small sofa and sat down. "Are we going to have tea together?"

"If you like." Tish made herself smile.

Sue patted the sofa beside herself. "Then sit here. Humor me." She waited until Tish was seated. "Do you know why I hate those mountains? It's because they make me feel small and exposed, and I have the feeling that maybe God himself is watching me and probably not liking much what he sees. Don't say anything. There isn't anything to say." Her smile was bitter. "What do I feel about Will now that he's gone? The answer is nothing, absolutely nothing."

"Emptiness—" Tish began.

"No. Nothingness. I can't even remember what he looked like before Tom broke his nose and blacked his eyes." She saw the surprise in Tish's face. "You didn't know?"

Tish shook her head slowly.

"Will tried to kill him, and Tom didn't much like the idea."

Tish closed her eyes. She was silent.

"When you were a little girl," Sue said, "and something scary happened in a movie, did you ever tell yourself that it was only a movie and everything was going to be all right?"

"We didn't see many movies up here, but I know what you mean."

"Well," Sue said, "it's like that now. We came to

this never-never land to bury Grandpa, that's all it was, collect the loot, and go back to the real world." She smiled suddenly. *"Our* real world." She paused. "But the movie goes on and on."

"I am sorry," Tish said, and meant it.

Sue's face brightened suddenly. "Never mind. Here's our tea. What shall we talk about now?"

The voices were still murmuring indistinctly in the office when Tish, changed into normal clothes, came down the stairs and walked out to her car. She did not pretend to understand a Sue Granger, she thought, and there was no use even trying. How could anyone hate those mountains that loomed so large and protective? How could anyone forget what the man she had lived with looked like? Even allowing for hyperbole, the meaning there was clear: Will was already scrubbed from Sue's slate as if he had never been.

I didn't like him, Tish told herself, but I will remember him. He could be bright and witty and in his teasing way full of fun. I'll try to think of him that way. Never mind the other sides of him. Am I being what Matt would have called a goddamn Pollyanna? Or Tom? So be it. Good luck, Will, wherever you are. I'll take care of your remains.

Father Enrique said, "If it is Tom's wish, and yours." He nodded. "I shall come to the ranch."

"Thank you, Padre."

"Sad, sad, sad," the priest said suddenly. His voice was almost angry. "Crime, violence, death. Where did it begin? Where does it stop?"

Tish shook her head in silence.

"The explosion in Long Valley," the priest said. "Pete Baca, uselessly dead." He shook his head sadly.

Tish had almost forgotten the word of the reactor explosion. How was Wayne taking it?

"And now," the priest said, "more—trouble in the commune in Jicarilla County."

"Oh, no!"

"They are foolish people," the priest said. "I think that some of them at least are honest, sincere people, but foolish to come here, foolish to behave as they do, dress as they do, live as they do." He paused. "But they have done no harm." He paused again. "Except that they have spread rumors, and that can be harmful."

"What has happened, Padre?"

"The same as before, beatings, rape." He saw the shock on Tish's face. "You must understand, *hija mía*," the priest said gently, "that although anger is evil, it is also human and sometimes cannot be controlled. And the worst anger of all is that which comes from helplessness. Then there is a rage against all humanity, and particularly against those who are —different."

Tish thought of the boy Luis, sitting sullen and angry in the jeep holding the 30-30 pointed at Tom's head. "I understand, Padre." She shook her head. "But that is not excuse."

"Understanding can show the path to forgiveness."

Tish was thinking of the young girl she had seen that one time at the commune in her tight cutoffs and inadequate bandana halter. Was she the one who had been raped? Would she find the path to forgiveness. Tish doubted it. "Perhaps, Padre." She paused. "I would find it hard to forgive."

The priest nodded. "It is not easy."

"What will happen now?"

"Very little. As before." The priest paused. "You have heard of the *penitentes* who scourge themselves with whips?"

Tish nodded slowly.

"I think the people of the commune choose to scourge themselves too. For what reason, or to what purpose, I do not know." He paused and studied Tish. "You are Anglo. And educated. Do you know?"

I don't dig the commune either, Tish thought. I am too square. "I am sorry, Padre. I am no help."

The priest nodded sadly. "And so they suffer, and we suffer for them without knowing why." He made a small gesture of dismissal. "Enough. Send for me, and I shall come to the ranch."

"Thank you, Padre." Tish turned away to her car.

She did not drive off immediately. Instead she sat quietly and went over the mental list she had prepared. The service would be identical to that held for old Matt, plain coffin, a few simple wreaths, no music, the padre, only the family and the ranch people present. Yes, and Seth Porter; he should be on hand as before; he represented the family's ties to—what? Call it civilization, which was a funny way to put it, but somehow apt.

Old Matt had made the point often. "We live out here," he had said, "sometimes like a bunch of raggedy-assed hillbillies. I say, 'frog!' and, by God, everybody jumps. Times I find myself forgetting that there are rules and laws and they apply to us just as much as to all those piss-ants who scurry around in cities. That's when it's time for me to go down to Santa Fe or up to Denver or out to San Francisco and see if I remember how to behave. Or get somebody out here to remind us. Give Seth Porter a call. Tell him the fishing is good and there's plenty of whiskey." Power.

She found that she was smiling now, remembering the old man and his violent manner. He had exaggerated, of course, speaking of the way they lived at the ranch. As long as Tish could remember, so she did not think her mother was responsible, they had dined, but not breakfasted or lunched, on damask carefully laundered and ironed by the ranch laundress. They had eaten with the heavy, worn silver that had come out by freight wagon from the East, on bone china, and drunk their wine, watered down for the children, from cut crystal. There had been music in the big house, recorded music of symphony orchestras, chamber groups, piano, violin, classical and flamenco guitars. The library was filled with books, and there were standing orders at the Villagrá Book Store in Sena Plaza for Southwesterniana, good biography, new history, mysteries. There were magazines: *Newsweek, Foreign Affairs, Natural History, Harper's;* and newspapers, late, but better late than never: *The New York Times, The Christian Science Monitor, The Wall*

Street Journal. . . . Raggedy-assed hillbillies? Hardly, and yet old Matt's point was cogent. They could too easily lose touch. So she would call Seth Porter, and he would drop everything and come.

She had, she thought, covered everything. She started the engine, put the car in gear, and drove off. Those poor people at the commune, she thought. And Wayne Carter, what of him with an explosion and a death on his hands? How would he react? And Jimmy down in Santa Fe: he was back in her thoughts again. Should she ask him with Seth? The answer was no. Not now. Maybe not ever. She drove the familiar road without conscious thought.

Joe Valdes held the gate for her with his dignified bow. Marty Romero's pickup was gone from the front of the big house, Tish noticed, and so was the ranch car Tom had apparently been driving. Idly she wondered where they had gone. She parked and went inside to telephone.

The office door was open. It rarely was. She went inside without hesitation, closed the door, and sat down at the desk that was now Tom's to make her call. Mr. Porter was busy on another line. Would she care to hold? She would. She sat quietly, the phone at her ear.

All the trophies and pictures collected over the long years, carefully tended by Consuelo's housemaids. The tantalus Tom had mastered and made himself sick drinking from. The gun cabinet with its arsenal. That magnificent Navajo rug—

"Hello, honey." Seth Porter's voice in her ear. "Sorry to keep you waiting."

Tish could almost see his placid smiling face. It was his father, no, his grandfather who had first handled the Granger legal problems. And again the sense of the past was strong. "Will's funeral," she said. "Will you come up for it?"

"Of course."

Explanation was needed. "Tom has put me in charge," Tish said.

"Naturally."

She felt a warm glow of pleasure at his quick and obvious acceptance. "He isn't here right now—" she began.

"No, honey. He's on his way back down here." Seth paused. "I called him." Another pause. "Sam Waldo's bill passed the Senate an hour ago."

Tish closed her eyes. She opened them again and concentrated on the far wall where the grizzly head snarled defiance. "What does that mean?" she said.

"It means, for a start," Seth said, "that we go to the governor."

Remembering what Jimmy Thomas had told her of the right of eminent domain, "And then?"

"It is possible," Seth said slowly, "even probable that we are in for a fight, honey."

Tom's reaction would be defiance. Tish knew that as surely as she knew her own name. Her eyes were still on the grizzly head. The great bear had been defiant too, and strong, in his own world invincible. But he was dead. "Have Tom call me, please," she said, and hung up.

How long she sat at the big desk, she never knew. She roused herself at a knock on the door.

It was Sue, still in the black trousers and the creamy blouse, strangely quiet, almost subdued. "May I come in, please? I'm—afraid to be alone."

I don't like the woman, Tish thought, but I am sorry for her. And then, new thought: and we all feel fear; it is in the air. "Of course," she said. Her voice was gentle. "Tom is on his way to Santa Fe."

"I saw him drive off." Sue dropped into one of the leather chairs, and tucked her legs beneath her in a little-girl posture. "He and that police lieutenant both left." She paused. "That was when I felt—alone."

In the silence the phone rang. Tish picked it up as if it were a live thing.

"You wanted me to call," Tom's voice said.

He was angry, that was plain, and again the concept of defiance came to mind. Tish kept her eyes from the mounted grizzly head. "Seth told me about the bill."

327

She paused. "I am sorry." Another pause. "Do you want me to come to Santa Fe? Is there anything I can do?"

"No." His voice was suddenly softer, easier, some of the tension gone. "But thanks anyway." He paused. "Take care of Sue."

"Yes."

"And take care of everything else as you always do." There was even a hint of one of Tom's rare smiles in the voice now. "Do you remember Matt turning over that ring of keys to you in front of Will and me, saying that you were the lady of the house now and you were to call the tune and, by God, if somebody didn't dance, you were to come tell him about it?"

"I remember." She was close to tears. She had been twelve years old then, her mother only recently buried. "I'll look after things," she said. She hesitated. "And you look after yourself, do you hear?" It was a tone of command.

The rare smile became a chuckle. "I hear."

Tish hung up. Sue was watching her. "You've been in love with him for a long time, haven't you?" Sue said. Her voice was not unfriendly. "I don't blame you." There was a wistful quality in the words. Then, in a different voice, "You will look after things," she said. "That means you are in charge." She paused. "What do we do now?"

Simple enough; and like many simple things, difficult, Tish thought. "We wait," she said.

36

Violence begets violence, Tom was thinking, and the aphorism was undoubtedly true. But there were times too when only violence could counteract violence, and turning the other cheek might be all very well as a Biblical injunction, but it sure as hell wasn't the way you protected your own against those to whom the rules did not mean a thing. From Apaches to squatters to cattle thieves and now power interests, there was only one answer when you were attacked, and that was to fight. "I'll meet you at the governor's mansion," he told Seth Porter. "You set up the time."

"It might be better, son, if we went together." Seth studied Tom's face and sighed. "Suit yourself." He punched the button on his desk and picked up the phone. To the switchboard girl, "I want to speak with the governor, honey. I imagine you'll catch him at the Roundhouse." He hung up the phone and leaned back in his chair. "Tito Abeyta," he said. His voice was sad.

"Marty doesn't think he organized the rustling," Tom said. "Neither do I. And I don't see him pushing rumors about the reactor, either. That isn't his style." The anger now was banked, solid, deep and warm, a steady force under control. "Just as Farley Wells is behind Sam Waldo, somebody is behind Tito, and he's the one we want."

"It seems to me," Seth said mildly, "that Tito has quite a bit to answer for himself, son."

True, of course. Borden the dead man in the meadow, Kelly Garcia, the shot fired at Tom himself;

329

for all of these Tito was answerable. And yet somehow the men behind the manipulators, bore the deeper guilt. "Marty will take care of Tito," Tom said. In his mind there was no question about that. Tito was big and tough and fast on his feet. But Marty was Marty, the hunter, the tracker, and now that he had his quarry in plain sight, the end was no longer in doubt.

Seth said, still in that mild, easy voice, "Do you know who's behind Farley Wells, son, because Farley is just house counsel?" He paused. "Fellow named Benson, J.R. Benson. That mean anything to you?"

It did, of course, but nothing showed in Tom's face. "It just means that he's a bigger son of a bitch than most. Because he has a few hundred million dollars, does that mean he can reach into a mountain valley and turn the lives of everybody in it upside down with impunity? Does it mean that he can buy a state legislature just to get what he wants? Does it mean, by God, that he thinks he can run me off my own land?"

"Shouldn't wonder," Seth said, "if that isn't exactly what he does think. I've never met the man."

"One way or another," Tom said, "we will."

The phone rang and Seth picked it up. His eyes were still on Tom's face, and his look was appraising. Into the phone he said, "Thank you, honey." And then, "Hello, George. I know you're a busy fellow, but this is a matter of some importance. Tom Granger and I would like to come see you this evening. Maybe a little before suppertime?" He listened, and smiled. "Now, George, when was the last time you heard me cry 'Wolf!'?" He nodded then. "Six-thirty. We'll be there." He hung up. "You were saying, son, that one way or another we were going to meet J.R. Benson?"

Tom stood up. "Six-thirty at the mansion. I'll be there." He walked out.

When you hunted a grizzly bear, Marty thought, you came upwind to him, and if possible on his blind side. Unfair, maybe, but also a tribute to the beast's strength, vitality, and cunning. For grizzly bear, read Tito Abeyta.

To Benny Baca back on duty, in familiar routine trying to bury his bewilderment and grief, Marty said, "Tell Tito Abeyta I want to see him at the Jicarilla DA's office. Tell him it's important, very important. Got it?"

"Sure." Benny hesitated. Then, in rapid Spanish, exposing his thoughts and deep concern, "Pete killed himself. That is a sin. The priest—"

"I will talk to the priest," Marty said. "Pete did what he thought was right. The priest will understand." He caught Benny's arm and gave him a gentle shove. In English now, "Go tell Tito what I said. I want him pronto." He walked out to his pickup.

Tito Abeyta, large and solid in his chair, scowled up at Benny Baca. "He wants me at the DA's office, why?"

"He di'n't say." Benny had always gotten along with Tito, and that was the way he liked it. The big man was frightening when his temper was up. Well, as far as that went, so was Marty Romero, if anything a little bit more so. "He just tell me to come tell you," Benny said.

"You were out at my place the other day," Tito said. His tone was not particularly friendly. "What did you want?"

Benny shrugged and hoped he looked unconcerned. "Marty, he just want to look around."

"And what did you find?"

Benny shrugged again. "Me, I di'n't see nothing. Just hoofprints an' horseshit. Marty, he say some of the hoofprints belong to that big sorrel in the pasture." It still meant nothing to him.

Nothing changed in Tito's face, but his voice altered almost to a growl. "I don't like people poking around without my permission." He pushed back his chair and stood up, eased the pistol holster into a more comfortable position. "Okay," he said. "Go tell Romero I'm coming. Soon as I shut up here. Goddamn kids will steal me blind even if I am sheriff." He watched Benny walk out to the cruiser, get in, and drive off. "In a pig's ass I'll meet the son of a bitch at the DA's office," Tito said softly. He walked out to his own car without even closing the office door.

Driving without haste out of the village, away from the courthouse where the DA held forth, Tito told himself that he was a damn fool and got no argument. He was a defensive lineman, wasn't he? And wasn't it axiomatic that a lineman was nothing more than a running back with his brains kicked out? No match at all for that smooth-talking Joe Harlow son of a bitch. Sure, Harlow had the old man, the boss man, old J.R. Benson himself behind him, and when you took on little chores for him, you tended to think you were walking around under the protection of a security blanket, so that made taking the bait a lot easier.

But where was he now? Where was Harlow now? And Tito was willing to bet that J.R. Benson had never heard of Tito Abeyta except as a name on the football program, and that was long finished. Goddamn.

Tito had no way of knowing how much Marty Romero knew or had figured out. Nor could he be sure whether or not Tom Granger had actually seen and recognized that spur rowel on the ground. But Marty Romero had tied hoofprints to Tito's sorrel, and that was all Tito needed to know to decide that Marty knew entirely too goddamn much, and this particular ballgame was over.

Get lost in Colorado, he told himself; although for a man his size getting lost wasn't all that easy. Still, what else was there? Stay in this state and he would have that goddamn Indian tracking him down, wouldn't he, and was that what he wanted? Physically Tito was afraid of no man, but that Romero was at least half *brujo*, witch, and that was what tightened your puckering string. Colorado it was, just as fast as he could haul his ass up there. Collect a few clothes, also hard to come by for a man his size, pick up his stash of ready money, and get the hell out.

He turned into the drive of his house, and got out

of the car. There was that goddamn sorrel which had apparently left hoofprints all over the place for the *brujo* to see. He was a good horse, but Tito wished he would drop dead. He started for the house, and there he stopped and stood for a brief moment uncertain, his hand hovering near the holstered .357 magnum.

"I wouldn't try it, Tito," Marty said. He was standing fifty yards away, beside the house, his rifle at his shoulder. "Classic form of Western suicide, a handgun against a rifle. Just take it out slow and easy and drop it."

Tito lifted the handgun out gingerly. Still he was tempted. It showed.

"You're too big a target," Marty said. "I couldn't miss if I tried." He watched Tito drop the handgun; and he lowered the rifle and gestured with its barrel for the big man to step aside.

"Sneaky bastard, aren't you?" Tito said.

"I just put myself in your place." Marty's voice was casual. "I wanted to see if you'd run. I was pretty sure you wouldn't want to see the DA and me together."

Tom did not particularly enjoy what he was doing, but, he told himself, he had not established the ground rules in the first place, and since the opposition wanted to play rough, why, so be it. "We're going to have a heart-to-heart talk," he told Sam Waldo, and watched the fat man's face lose some of its color. They were sitting in the shabby hotel room Sam always took when the legislature was in session.

"Your bill passed the Senate today," Tom said. "Now we're going to talk about it, who thought it up, who paid you to sponsor it and push it along—"

"Now you look here." Sam sat up straight and tall, his chest as far out as his belly would allow. "You come in here, by God, and start throwing your weight around, and I'm not going to stand for it! I've got friends—"

"They aren't going to do you a bit of good, Sam." Tom's voice was quiet, even. "Piss-ants down here in Santa Fe have been trying to mess with Granger property for a hundred years. Do you know what's happened to some of them? Shall I show you what's going to happen to you?" He started to rise from his chair.

"Don't!" Sam's voice was a loud hoarse whisper. "Don't you lay a hand on me!" He was sweating.

Tom looked at his watch. "We have about an hour," he said. "I'm going to ask questions, and you're going to answer them. No witnesses, no tape recorder, just the two of us, Sam. Did you know my grandfather?"

Sam swallowed hard. "I heard about him."

"And his father?"

Sam nodded violently.

"They did what they had to do," Tom said. "And that was the way I was raised, too. That is my property you are trying to screw around with. It belonged to my granddaddy and to his daddy before him, and if you think I'm not prepared to do whatever I have to do to protect it—" Tom paused for long emphasis. "Then you'd better think again, Sam. Long and hard." He stood up and started forward.

At precisely six-thirty Seth Porter rang the bell at the white-columned adobe-colored Territorial-style governor's mansion on the ridge, smiled at the maid, and followed her through into the governor's study. "Evening, George."

"Seth." The governor looked around. "Where's Granger?"

"He said he'd be here. I think he will."

They heard the doorbell ring again, and Tom's voice said, "My name is Granger. I believe I am expected." He came into the study, urging a reluctant Sam Waldo ahead of him. "I thought I would bring *this* along," he said. His large hand closed gently on the back of Waldo's fat neck. "Sit down, Sam. And listen."

The governor looked at Seth Porter. Seth smiled. "My grandfather and my father had their problems dealing with the Grangers as clients too. It's his play. I knew nothing about it."

The governor hesitated. Then he walked to a chair and sat down. "I'll listen for a while."

So here it was, Tom thought, right up to him. He had still that eerie feeling that both Tully and Matt were watching, listening, measuring his performance. All right. "We're easy to get along with," he said. "Most times that is." He paused. "I think that's been said before to somebody else who sat in your chair, Governor."

The governor acknowledged the comment with a tight little smile. The tale was well known.

"But," Tom said, "when they start coming at us from all sides, we tend to get a little riled." He paused. "This is a tale, Governor, of fake rumors that have produced beatings, rapes, a senseless explosion, and a death; of planned and organized rustling out of which came two murders and one attempted murder—the State police are on that now." He paused again. "And all of it to soften us up and create a climate of hate in Grutas and Jicarilla Counties in order to give support to the bill this little piss-ant was hired to sponsor. And that bill has only one purpose: to stop the development of nuclear power in Long Valley so a selfish old son of a bitch in Houston can sell his low-grade coal in the Four Corners area."

The governor was frowning.

Tom said, "Does that sound incredible?"

Slowly the governor nodded. "In a word, yes."

"Well, now," Seth Porter said, "I do believe we can hang it all together, George." He looked at Tom. "You brought Sam Waldo along for a purpose, son?"

Tom nodded. His face was cold. "We've been having a long talk, haven't we, Sam?"

Sam squirmed in his chair, looked around the room as if he thought to run, and then sighed deeply and nodded. "You got no right—"

"In this game, Sam," Tom said, "might is right, and I've got the might wherever you try to hide. That isn't a threat. That is a promise." He paused. "You were paid to sponsor the bill, weren't you?"

Sam licked his lips. "A campaign contribution. There's no law against that."

Tom nodded. "As far as I know, none. But you also spread some money around, didn't you, Sam? You see, when the lid blows off and your bill is tied to two murders, a death by dynamiting, and a few other assorted felonies, I don't think a lot of your friends are going to know you any longer." He raised his head as the doorbell sounded yet a third time. "Here is one of them now." He looked at the governor. "I took the liberty of leaving a message for Farley Wells, saying you wanted to see him. He is Sam's—benefactor—"

Farley Wells followed the maid, and at the doorway paused to look around the room. "Come in," Tom said. "We were just speaking of you."

Farley's aplomb was intact. "I am flattered." He nodded to the governor. "I don't believe I have had the pleasure, Governor. But I got your message and hurried right over."

The man was good, Tom thought, and it would take some doing to shake him. "My message," he said, and watched the first real reaction in Farley's face. One step, he told himself. From here on we go faster. "Tito Abeyta," he said. "He is either already under arrest for rustling and murder or he soon will be. You went to see him? Any connection?"

For a moment surprise showed. It was quickly gone. "We talked of several things," Farley said, "but murder was not among them."

"But," Seth Porter said in his mild voice, "you don't seem too surprised, Counselor."

Farley sat down. He looked at the governor. It was that damned fool Joe Harlow, he thought, and he hasn't even appeared. "I dislike being cross-examined," he said, "about matters I know nothing about."

"Then," Tom said, "let's take a matter you know a great deal about, Sam Waldo's bill." He paused and looked at the governor again. "As a matter of principle," he said, "I would assume that the sovereign state resents carpetbaggers coming in and pushing local people into sponsoring and pushing their legislation?"

The governor thought about it. He nodded. "As a matter of principle, yes, we resent interference in our affairs."

Tom's voice turned gentle. "Who thought up your bill, Sam?"

Sam squirmed. He looked at Farley. He looked at the governor. He looked at the floor. He found no comfort.

"Farley Wells will go back to Houston, Sam," Tom said. "You'll still be here. So will I."

"That," Farley said, "is an obvious threat. With all due respect, Governor, this has gone far enough."

"Offhand," Seth said, "I would say that it's just begun." He paused. "Three men are dead, Mr. Wells. A valuable installation has been damaged. Cattle have been stolen and an entire village has been terrorized into brutalities they would ordinarily never dream of."

That thrice-damned Joe Harlow, Farley thought, and the old man sitting in Houston never letting the right hand know what the left hand was doing. "And what does all that have to do with me?"

"Now, Mr. Wells," This was Seth Porter again, his voice gentle, his expression placidity itself. "It was all intended to help along your bill, now, wasn't it? Pressure here, pressure there, on the reactor, on the village, on the ranch?" His smile disappeared. "And all of it, I quote, 'so a selfish old son of a bitch in Houston can sell his low-grade coal in the Four Corners area'?"

In the silence Farley said, "In the first place, it is not my bill."

Tom said, "Over to you, Sam." His voice was soft. He paused. "We're waiting."

Sam looked at the governor. The governor's face was expressionless. No support there. Sam swallowed hard. "It—seemed like a good idea at the time."

"Go on, Sam." Tom's voice, still soft.

Farley started to rise.

"Sit down, Mr. Wells," the governor said. "We wouldn't want you Texans to think we were inhospitable."

Farley hesitated, and sat down.

"Sam?" Tom again. His eyes had not left the fat man's face. "It seemed like a good idea—when?"

The governor was watching Sam again, and Sam had said it himself: the governor could be meaner than a bobcat when he chose. And old Seth Porter had been skinning witnesses alive for more years than Sam could remember, like his daddy and his granddaddy before him. And that Tom Granger: if Sam had known how he would react, he would never have touched that bill in the first place, never. Those goddamn Grangers didn't care what they did when they got their backs up. Sam took a deep breath. He pointed at Farley. "He come here and told me about the idea. It—sounded good to me. I mean if the Grangers wanted to sell, all that land for people to fish and hunt in—"

The governor said, "We've heard the propaganda, Sam. Now let's hear about the—campaign contribution."

Sam swallowed again. "Well," he said, "when a man goes to a lot of trouble and spends a lot of time—"

"And," Seth said, "maybe has to bribe a lot of people?"

Farley said, "If I were a defense attorney, Mr. Porter, I would object to your putting words in the witness's mouth."

Seth was smiling again. "But this is not a court of law. It is an informal talk." He looked at Tom. "Go on, son. You're doing fine so far."

Tom said, "I'm not a lawyer, but I doubt if there is anything actually illegal in what either Sam or Farley Wells did. I think I've heard of money changing hands in the legislature before."

The governor said without a smile, "It's been said so."

"Then may I ask," Farley said, "what is the purpose of all of this melodrama?" There was scorn in his voice.

Tom nodded. "You may." He paused. "The purpose is to put your ass in a sling, and to do the same to whoever was behind Tito's shenanigans. You're going to be taught to leave our part of the world alone.

And so is that old son of a bitch sitting in Houston."

The governor's eyebrows were raised. Farley said, "I have to assume that you are speaking of my principal? That is twice he has been—maligned."

"There'll be a third time at least," Tom said. "When I talk to him, I'm going to tell him what I think of him." He saw the beginning of a smile on Farley's face. "Oh, yes," Tom said, "I'll talk to him. You put through two calls to Houston through La Fonda's switchboard to the same number. I'm guessing that is a private line." He looked at the governor, "If I may use the phone?"

The governor hesitated and then nodded. "Help yourself."

Seth Porter said, "You're sure you know what you're doing, son?"

"We'll see." Tom walked to the phone, picked it up, and began to dial.

The room was still. Eleven numbers. Seth, watching, listening, tried idly to guess what each was. He had read somewhere that it could be done from the sound, but he had never been able to do it. He watched Tom's face, which wore that Granger let's-step-right-up-and-see expression he had seen Matt wear so often, and even as a boy old Tully. They were all alike, he thought. Oh, Bill Granger hadn't amounted to much, and Will was a bad lemon, but from Tully to Matt to Tom the strain bred true, and he had a hunch that if Tom ever married and had kids the line would continue. It was somehow a comforting thought.

Tom said into the phone, "J.R. Benson? My name is Granger, Tom Granger, and I'm standing here, looking at one of your flunkies named Wells and the pissant he hired in the legislature who goes by the name of Sam Waldo. Does any of that interest you?"

There was a pause. The quiet, uninflected voice said, "Go on, Mr. Granger."

"Your boys have blown it," Tom said. "All around. I've heard tell that you don't like publicity. This time you're going to get it. In spades. You're going to be tied into two murders, a dynamiting death, cattle rus-

POWER

tling, and a fake legislative bill that is against the public interest."

"I doubt it, Mr. Granger, I doubt it very much. There are libel laws."

"I own a newspaper. It prints what I tell it. It will print this and I will see that copies go across the country."

"Then I will sue, Mr. Granger."

"Will you? Because that is exactly what I want, everything out in the open, under oath, in a court of law where everybody can see what a son of a bitch you are and how easy it is for you to turn an entire mountain village into a madhouse just by sending out lesser sons of bitches with orders to see that no atomic reactor gets in the way of your low-grade coal. Sue, and be damned. We've held our land and our country against Apaches. Do you think I'm going to roll over and play dead for a raggedy-assed old billionaire like you?"

Seth Porter was listening carefully, and nodding, but his eyes were on Farley Wells. Farley's color was gone and his eyes stared at Tom in, yes, it was, actual fright. Seth thought of the reputation of the powerful old man on the other end of the line. He would not take it lightly that his people had bungled and the cat was now out of the bag.

The voice on the phone, still quiet, still uninflected, said, "You are bluffing, of course. A profane bluff, but a bluff nonetheless."

Tom smiled. "Then call me. Because when I leave here, I'm going home, and the next edition of the paper will carry the entire story. It isn't a big paper and it has a funny name, *The Las Grutas Bugle,* but neither is it a paper you can buy, or intimidate, because that would mean buying or intimidating me, and I won't scare."

There was a long pause. Then, "You say Farley Wells is there?"

"He is."

"Let me speak to him."

Tom held out the phone. Farley took it with a hand

340

that was not quite steady. "Farley here, J.R." He listened. He glanced at Tom. He took a deep breath and let it out slowly. "I'm afraid he means what he says, J.R.," he said. "That is the Granger reputation around here. I'm—sorry." He listened again and swallowed hard. He opened his mouth and closed it again in silence. Then he held out the phone to Tom, sat down, and closed his eyes.

Tom said, "Yes?"

"What is it you want, young man? I assume you have something in mind? Money?"

"Screw your money. I told you I wasn't for sale."

"Then?"

"I want the name of a man, the man who ruined a perfectly decent ex-football player who had come back to his mountains, the man who caused the rumors that drove mountain people out of their minds, the man behind the cattle rustling on my ranch. He's the other lesser son of a bitch you sent out here." Tom paused. "That's the first thing I want."

"And the second?"

"Is for you to stay out of this part of the world. For good. Come in once again, and if it is the last thing I do, I'll spread the whole story across this country no matter what it costs."

"And what do I get in return?"

Tom's smile was grim. "The satisfaction of knowing that you killed three men, caused a few rapes and beatings, tormented some ignorant people beyond their endurance—and got away with it. For a son of a bitch like you that ought to be quite a bit."

"Over the telephone you are quite free with your epithets, Mr. Granger."

"I'll be happy to repeat them any time, any place, with as many witnesses as you like."

There was another long pause. Then, slowly, reluctantly, "You have a deal, Mr. Granger. Farley will give you the name you want. Tell him I said to. And tell him to come back to Houston." The telephone went dead.

Tom hung up slowly. He felt no sense of triumph,

merely a deep loathing for the avarice that could produce such actions and reactions. To Farley he said, "You're to give me the man's name."

Farley opened his eyes. "You know what you've done, don't you?"

"What I said I was going to do, put your ass in a sling."

Farley's smile was wan and weary. "Understatement." He stood up. "The man's name is Joe Harlow. Tito knows him."

"And you're to go back to Houston."

Again the wan, weary smile. "Obviously." In silence he walked out of the room.

The governor said slowly, "I knew your grandfather." He spoke to Tom. "I think he would approve." He paused. "I will veto the bill." He looked at Sam. "And I don't believe you will try to rally votes to override the veto, Sam. I surely wouldn't advise it." He stood up. To Seth he said, "Thanks for an interesting evening. You were right, you weren't just hollering 'Wolf!' "

The road back to the ranch seemed longer than usual and, remembering Will, Tom forced himself to drive carefully when what he really wanted was speed.

It was done; that was the basic thought. Thanks to Marty, the puzzle had been put together, the pieces fitting neatly, and then the solution was clear. He had obviously wounded the pride of the old man in Houston, and from what he had heard the old man did not take that kind of thing lightly, so some kind of retaliation was possible, but Tom was not going to lose any sleep over the possibility. You took your problems one at a time, solved them, and forgot them; there was no other way. If after one Apache raid you immediately started worrying about the next, you were headed for insanity. Forget J.R. Benson.

The moon was up now, and he could see the loom of the great mountains. This was his country, he thought; he could never be content anywhere else. Content? That was a strange word, because he doubted if contentment would ever come. Contentment implied satisfaction with things just as they were, static, unchanging; and in his world, his life—he saw this now with sudden clarity—there was always going to be change, new problems to face, decisions to make, struggles that could be avoided—until at last they put him in a box and lowered him into the ground as they had old Matt. Only then would change be ended.

But the overriding fact was that from here on there would be no more vacillation, no more wondering where his duty lay. It lay right here. He would have to call Grace, he thought, and break off that part of his life, if it wasn't already broken by that last telephone call. And he would have to call Tim Jonas. Perhaps Grace had been right after all when she said that she understood already. And it was likely that Tim Jonas did too. All of which made it no easier in his mind. But the decision was made, and in that fact was a measure of relief. Not much, but some. He could live with it.

He stopped the car and blinked the lights and Joe Valdes came out of the small house to open the gate and hold it wide. He smiled his greeting and bobbed his head. *El patrón* was back, his attitude seemed to say; it was well. Tom drove through in a thoughtful mood.

Tish and Sue were in the office, empty coffee cups at their sides. Tom wondered what they had been talking about. He sat down in the big desk chair and stretched out his legs to relax.

"Two phone calls," Tish said. Her voice was expressionless. "Marty Romero called to say that the bear was in a cage."

I am sorry about that, Tom thought, but there was no other way. And tomorrow would be soon enough to tell Marty about Joe Harlow.

"The other call," Tish said, "was Seth Porter. He told me what happened at the mansion." There was pride in her voice.

Tom shook his head. "No big thing," he said. "I just bullied an old man over the telephone." He looked

343

at Sue. "What now for you?" His voice was gentle. "Do you want to stay here?" He paused. "It is your home for as long as you want it to be."

Sue could smile faintly as she shook her head. "It is not for me. As it was not for Will." She paused. "But I thank you, anyway." She stood up from her chair. "You two belong here." She smiled again at them both and walked out, closed the door behind her.

"She is right," Tish said. "This is where you belong."

"Yes." No hesitation this time. One day he would have to go East, tidy up loose ends. But how important were they really?

"You will stay and carry on where Matt left off."

Tom thought of Sam Waldo and Farley Wells; of Wayne Carter and his troubles and his dreams; of the villages and the commune; of Will now dead, and of Sue for whom in a way he, Tom, was now responsible; he thought of Tito; and of an angry old man in Houston.

Some things finished, he told himself, some continuing, others yet to come as of now unseen. You did as old Matt had said: took each problem as it raised its head and slapped it down because others were already coming up behind your back. There was no other way. "I'm staying," he said. "I won't do as well as he did, but I'll try."

Tish smiled. "I am glad." She started to rise.

"Sit down," Tom said, and he waited until she was again in her chair. "I'll try," he said, "but I can't do it alone."

"You'll have help."

"Not the kind of help I need." It was clear to him now, at last, and he wondered that he had not seen it long before. Maybe I wasn't ready to see it, he thought, or to admit it. But he could say it now without either pain or shame. "I need someone to hold my hand. Someone to help me up when I fall on my face. Somebody to laugh with me, and cry for me when I can't, to listen to me and talk to me and tell me when I'm wrong." He smiled suddenly and spread his hands. "All of those things, and more. Somebody to share—everything."

Tish sat quiet, unbelieving.

"A large order," Tom said. He was smiling still. "Do you know anybody who might fill it?"

Still she was silent, and unbelieving still, but there was a warmth growing in her mind, spreading ease and gathering conviction that came from she knew not what source.

"It has to be somebody I've come to know well," Tom said. "Somebody I can trust."

"What about love?" Her voice surprised her.

"That too." He shook his head. "No. That first of all." He paused. "I learn slowly." He paused again. "Would you be available for the—position?"

The room was still. Tish took her time. Not full capitulation, she thought; not yet, maybe not ever. "You ride high," she said. "You always have." She paused. "So did Matt." Another pause. "I will stay," she said. "I will help you." A third pause, longer than before. "And we shall see," she said.

37

They stood again in the family burial ground, Father Enrique, Seth Porter, Sue, Tish, Tom, and the ranch people while the words were said and the coffin was lowered into the grave.

Tom stood beside a silent subdued Sue, and his eyes strayed around the fenced plot. There was Tully's tombstone and his wife's; there was Matt's and those of his two wives; there the single stone to remember Bill and

POWER

Liz, Tom's own parents. Will's would join them, and one day his own, and Tish's. Who would carry on then? Another question yet to be answered, but the solution would come. He caught Tish's eye, smiled faintly, and watched her answering nod.

Sue by her own choice walked alone to the big house. Together Tish and Tom walked with Father Enrique to his pickup truck. "It is done," the priest said.

Tom shook his head. "Wrong, Padre." He looked around, at the gravesite, at the mountains, at the limitless sky. Then he looked down at Tish. She was watching him. "It is just begun," Tom said.

THE BEST OF
BB
BALLANTINE BOOKS

▼ Available at your local bookstore or mail the coupon below ▼